DID
YOU HEAR
ABOUT
KITTY KARR?

DID
YOU HEAR
ABOUT
KITTY KARR?

A Novel

CRYSTAL SMITH PAUL

HENRY HOLT AND COMPANY
NEW YORK

Henry Holt and Company
Publishers since 1866
120 Broadway
New York, New York 10271
www.henryholt.com

Henry Holt® and Ⓗ® are registered trademarks of Macmillan Publishing Group,
LLC.

Library of Congress Cataloging-in-Publication Data is available.

ISBN: 9781250815309

Our books may be purchased in bulk for promotional, educational, or business use.
Please contact your local bookseller or the Macmillan Corporate and Premium Sales
Department at (800) 221-7945, extension 5442, or by e-mail at
MacmillanSpecialMarkets@macmillan.com.

First Edition 2023

Designed by Omar Chapa

Printed in the United States of America

1   3   5   7   9   10   8   6   4   2

This is a work of fiction. All of the characters, organizations, and events portrayed in
this novel either are products of the author's imagination or are used fictitiously.

For

Mamie Helen, Nellie Gray, and Mary Magdalene

Half of the work that is done in the world
Is to make things appear what they are not.

—E. R. BEADLE

DID
YOU HEAR
ABOUT
KITTY KARR?

CHAPTER 1

Elise

Saturday morning, October 28, 2017

Elise never went to sleep, and she wasn't the only one. Her father was tucked away in his musical bunker. Her mother was pacing, hidden deep in the labyrinth, but every so often Elise could hear her feet kicking up gravel. Situated steps from the back porch of the St. John estate, the labyrinth was constructed of leafy green hedges and rose bushes that increased in height and girth further into the maze.

It was cloudy, and the only light was from the spokes of the Ferris wheel. It sat low on the fourth tier of their property, so only half of it was visible from the house. It was a gift, given to her mother more than two decades ago by a French director courting her for a film she ultimately declined. Her mother thought it was an eyesore but kept it for the sake of good conversation. Visitors likened it to a giant dream catcher, fitting considering that what and who lay behind its presence mirrored the collected, albeit programmed, wants of many. It was a symbol of celebrity, a club into which everyone wanted entry—a partition between gods and mortals. From the Perch, Elise did feel somewhat godly.

Not meant for sitting, the six-by-six wooden landing was situated below the apex of Elise's childhood home. Suspended amid the canopy of the thick sycamore branches, it was hidden from those on the ground but had an enchanted bird's-eye view of the four-tiered grounds and the entirety of Los Angeles below the hill upon which the St. John estate sat. That week it was Elise's refuge.

Sequestered for a week already, Elise found her stress now was compounded by her sisters' pending arrival. Physical proximity would force the closeness that only a shared childhood could bring. Everything had changed overnight, and she didn't know how to pretend with them that it hadn't. Elise could mimic emotions she didn't feel on command but had no ability to express the ones that were true.

She stayed on the Perch until her 6:00 am alarm for her workout, mandatory for her anxiety management. That morning she finished the entire hour and still felt unsettled.

She was sitting outside on the front door's single step, waiting, when Andy Davis, her driver and bodyguard of the last five years, arrived with her publicist and best friend by proximity since preschool, Rebecca Owens.

"Morning!" Rebecca handed her a Starbucks cup.

Elise frowned and placed it in the cup holder between them. "You know I hate Starbucks."

"Sorry, we didn't have time to get you the lavender latte you would have preferred."

"Bet you had time to FaceTime Gabe." Rebecca's longtime beau was on tour in Europe with one of the biggest rock bands in the world.

"So my relationship's going to be the theme of our last few months."

"Just stating facts." Elise caught Andy's eye in the rearview as they sailed through the twenty-foot-tall black iron gates of the estate. Fit for a castle, they had intricate designs of birds and trees etched in.

On the main street, the paparazzi, who usually waited in the enclave outside the Bel Air gates, spotted Andy and jumped into a van to follow.

Rebecca gestured toward them, raking her silver-painted nails through her thick mop of red hair. People stopped her every day to compliment its vibrancy. "The cameras are going to be aggressive. First photos will go for upwards of two hundred thousand dollars. Someone else should get Giovanni and Noele from the airport."

"Andy doesn't provide car service for the entire family," Elise said.

"Even picking you up—for a while, it may make sense to change drivers."

"I don't plan on leaving the gates. We don't want to feed the flame."

Rebecca's phone began to buzz. "No . . . we don't." Her voice trailed off as she read its screen.

"Is it *Vogue*?"

"My mom. I'll call her after the meeting." Rebecca and her mother, Alison, ran one of the most respected celebrity publicity firms in the industry. They represented the entire St. John family.

"Have you heard from them?"

Rebecca gave her a look. "Of course, they want you to talk about Kitty."

"I wouldn't know what to say."

"First things first," Rebecca said, as they drove through the security gates of Looking Glass Studios.

Elise sucked her teeth. "I feel like I've been summoned to the principal's office."

Elise and Rebecca walked into the studio conference room with their feet and arms in sync. Startled to find the sixteen-seat conference table full, they didn't break stride as they took the two remaining seats. All the executives behind *Drag On* were seated with their coffee mugs and ballpoint pens, ready to get their film's petite star, Elise St. John, in line. Elise sat in the empty end seat opposite the studio head, Tom. Rebecca sat on her right.

"Elise, good to see you, darling." Tom edged his pencil eraser across the glass as if there were a list written there. "How's February for the wedding?"

"That's in three months."

"We could have a wedding tomorrow if you wanted to." Susie, Elise's agent, sat in the middle of the table to Elise's right.

"But we don't," Rebecca quipped. It was clear it was the first time she was hearing this.

Susie ignored her, eyeing Tom. "The when is not so important as the effect on headlines." She was two decades older than both Elise and Rebecca and had never been impressed with Rebecca, whose childhood playmate had been her first and only client for the last ten years.

Tom used his hands to gesture. *"Elise and Aaron set to marry on the heels of their Oscar-nominated*—hopefully, *winning—film.* Good news won't hurt ticket sales."

Elise wanted to say how stupid it was but instead said, "Fine." It pained her to acquiesce, but with ten years of acting and five hundred million dollars in box office sales under her belt, Elise's life hadn't belonged to her in years. Sometimes the emotional restraint it took to conceal her unhappiness was just a hair away from masochism.

"We think it'll help." Tom stumbled over his words, surprised by her immediate agreement. "No one's talking about you two at all. You used to be the hottest couple in town." When they first met, Aaron Oliver had yet to have his breakout moment. Dating Elise got him *that* role, and their relationship became famous. In the three years since then, they'd starred opposite each other twice. Elise and Aaron owned a modest (aka four-bedroom) house behind a sliding gate in West Hollywood and had been engaged for a year.

"Couldn't go a day without seeing you two lip-locked." Tom's mouth moved as if he was about to say *caliente*, but instead, he merely extended his hands to open dialogue.

"There's plenty of skin in the film; people can go see it as many times as they'd like," Elise said.

Rebecca reminded everyone about Elise's February *Vogue* cover. "It'll be out early January, and we gave them exclusivity. The interview is Friday."

"That's only days before the Oscar nomination announcement," Susie said.

"Softening things now is crucial," Tom said.

"Fine." Rebecca sighed. "We're happy to try. Being nominated, and winning, is our primary goal." Elise had Golden Popcorn trophies and Viewer's Choice awards, but an Oscar win would be pivotal to her career.

"We welcome that, but Elise and Aaron, together, as a unit, were listed as an asset in the marketing of this thing. We need to ensure those benefits." Tom pushed his chair away from the table to cross his legs. His toes, visible in his worn Birkenstocks, looked as if they had never seen lotion—ever. "We're getting ready to do European press, so set a date and share it next week."

Elise pumped her fists in the air. "Five days till takeoff!"

A few execs clapped, which was enough for Tom. He kicked his feet in the air. "Good work, everybody!" He was gone before anyone could say thank you.

"Now the Internet's going to be flooded with hypothetical stories about my wedding, when it's supposed to be flooded with news about my movie," Elise complained in the car.

"Better than the Kitty talk," Rebecca said.

"Which they tap-danced around, even though that's really why they called the meeting."

"Right." Rebecca went back to her phone.

"It was disrespectful of them to pretend to ignore it. They could have at least extended their condolences."

"No one knows how to handle it," Rebecca said.

The death of eighty-one-year-old Kitty Karr Tate had dominated that week's news. It was no easy feat competing with politics, and the pause in presidential tweet reports spoke to the breadth of Kitty's legacy. She was an American icon, an Academy Award–winner, a writer, television star, and philanthropist. The tributes were numerous, and her films and decade-long-running television show shot to the top of digital sales.

With the praise came theories about her mysterious life and the circumstances of her demise. Kitty had become an urban legend postmortem, a Sunset Boulevard caricature who, rumor said, had committed suicide after years of seclusion. Kitty quit acting in her early fifties and, aside from a few rare public appearances, hadn't been photographed in more than twenty years.

Public conspiracy theories had exploded after news leaked that Kitty bequeathed her entire fortune—about six hundred million dollars—to Elise and her sisters, Giovanni and Noele. Really, it was closer to a billion; the reports got it wrong because the leaked documents only listed Kitty's personal assets. Her estate also included the inheritance from her late husband's parents *and* her husband's studio stock and royalties *and* real estate.

The St. Johns had issued a statement asking for privacy, but interest in the notoriously private family only quadrupled.

The world danced around the one question burning holes of curiosity in everyone's minds: Why had the White Hollywood icon given her fortune to the Black ("Black" being the key word) daughters of her costar in a sitcom that first aired almost fifty years ago? Some came right out and asked it, and social media was a cauldron of racist epithets; it was Meghan Markle hysteria times three. None of the sisters had been on the Internet in days because of it.

They didn't know what they were going to do with the money and, yes—thank you, Internet!—they all knew they didn't need it. Each daughter had been a multimillionaire from birth.

"So, did you know my grandmother is coming to Kitty's memorial?" Rebecca asked. At Kitty's request, the St. Johns were hosting a memorial and private auction the next evening at her home.

Elise shook her head. "I told you, Sarah took over the guest list." Her use of her mother's first name spoke to Elise's frustration.

"Kitty invited her. She got one of the cards. Isn't that funny?"

Kitty had written out twenty-five invitations to her own memorial service for her lawyer to mail after her death.

Elise looked at her now. "Why funny? Your grandma had to have been running in the same circles as Kitty."

"Funny she's never mentioned it to any of us before now. She told my mom they met back when Kitty was acting."

"See, there you go." Elise pushed open the car door as they stopped in front of the house. "Tell *Vogue* I'm sticking to the wedding and the film."

Elise paused at the kitchen door, surprised to see her sisters had already arrived. Their luggage littered the space as they munched from the charcuterie tray on the island. Giovanni, happy to flee cold Canada, had donned Bermuda jean shorts and a cropped, open-backed fuzzy violet sweater that displayed her ebony skin. Noele was in a royal-blue sweatsuit, more appropriate for the fickle October weather in LA.

Sarah was talking, accentuating every word with her hands. She'd been awake almost twenty-four hours, and Elise could see the rhythm of her mania, although to her sisters it probably looked like excitement.

It had been four years since the entire St. John family had been together. Days after Noele's NYU graduation, Giovanni, the middle daughter, had moved to Toronto to film what became a hit AMC show. Their parents, working through a battle in their marriage, took up residence in Paris by that December, granting Elise family separation and consequent career growth. Three or four out of the five gathered every few months or so during holidays, events, or times when their work obligations converged, but Noele's college graduation had rendered the St. John estate a true empty nest, and everyone but Elise had scattered.

A year ago, the sisters had all promised to come home to celebrate the thirtieth anniversary of their parents' legendary Halloween costume party.

It was the occasion they all loved most and, for that reason, it almost felt as though Kitty had planned her passing now, knowing her neighbors, the St. Johns, would all be together.

Feeling a rush of tears, Elise turned from the kitchen entry and walked farther down the driveway to the backyard. The fog was low and thick, so she removed her heels before descending to the third tier of yard and through the vegetable garden that hid her father's studio.

Though the studio was made to look like a garden shed, the steel door was actually bulletproof. She punched in the keypad code and entered to find her father fingering a drum machine.

"Your daughters have arrived."

James didn't look up. "My daughters, huh?"

His bald head was brown like a walnut and shiny-smooth underneath the bright light above his workstation. He gestured to the drum machine. "I'm working." James was a producer who played fourteen instruments, wrote and arranged music, and had a vocal range from Maxwell to Barry White. His love for blues, jazz, and classical made his music complex and varied but somehow timeless.

Elise collapsed on the couch, staring at her father's self-portrait on the wall. Painted from a photograph of him at Zuma Beach back when he wore a beard, it commemorated his first days in Los Angeles as a paid musician. He would continue sleeping on the floor of a friend's apartment for another year, but it was the first time he realized he could—even as a Black man—make money doing what he loved.

He came to join her, scratching his gray beard shadow. "How was your meeting?"

"They didn't even mention her."

"I'm not sure why you expected them to."

"Even to Mom, it's like Kitty's death is a footnote. All she cares about is us being here."

"That's happiness for her. And for me."

"It's just—Mom would rather talk about anything else."

"Kitty wouldn't want us moping. There will be plenty of time for that tomorrow night."

Elise rolled her eyes. "Mom changed everything."

"It'll all be fine, honey, I promise."

"Do you think I should talk to *Vogue* about Kitty?"

"If Kitty didn't want a spectacle, she wouldn't have left you the money."

"It seems so unlike her."

"I know you idolized her, but she was human, I assure you."

"I know that," Elise pouted, resenting the truth that she clearly hadn't known Kitty as well as she thought.

"There are as many sides to the truth as people telling the story."

"How many sides do you think there are?"

"Baby, I don't know. Kitty lived a long life. She knew a lot of people."

She squinted her eyes at him, feeling as though he knew something more than he was admitting.

He laughed and used the arm rest of his chair to stand. "Let's go see my other babies. I also believe it's time for a cocktail."

Elise let him off the hook for siding with her mother, knowing he would never betray his allegiance to his wife for anyone.

"Welcome home, girls." James walked into the dining room with his arms open for hugs. Giovanni and Noele crashed into him. James was six foot three, and they both fit well beneath his chin.

"You look pretty," Giovanni said, hugging Elise. "I mean, with everything going on, you still look rested." Giovanni was the spitting image of their mother, her clone in beauty and talent. General consensus named her the prettiest of the three sisters, with a curvy body wanted for the cover of every men's magazine in America. Giovanni knew it, too; she was ever ready for a paparazzi shot. Even now, she wore full makeup.

The studio had been lucky to see Elise in some tinted moisturizer. Elise was, however, the most unusual-looking of the trio, with eyes that changed from dark blue to gray with her moods. They'd been steel gray for weeks now, unenthused by life.

"I don't *feel* rested."

Noele embraced her next. "Missed you." She smelled sweet, like the amber-honey hue of her complexion. Despite their span in skin tone, among the three, Elise and Noele looked most alike. Perfect mixes of their parents' best features, they had their father's big, wide-set eyes, their mother's signature Cupid's-bow lips, and her thick, dark-brown hair that reddened in parts in the sun. Elise kissed her sister's cheek and tousled her hair. Elise flat-ironed her own hair, but Noele liked hers natural and wild.

"How's Aaron?" Sarah asked Elise while holding out her empty glass for another mimosa. "I'm sorry he couldn't join us."

She wasn't; it was an inquiry about when she would see him. "He's filming, Mom."

"Is everything all right?" Sarah asked, noticing her tone.

Elise compiled a bagel, lox, and veggies to make a sandwich. "It is." Elise stole an I-told-you-so look at James. Her mother always assumed that anything wrong with her had to do with Aaron. Under the circumstances, it was both annoying and offensive. She handed her mother her replenished flute. "Can I get you anything else?"

Sarah shook her head hard. "I had a full breakfast this morning." The family waited, knowing she would list the details. "Half a cup of oatmeal with a drizzle of maple syrup and three strawberries."

"Three, huh?" Noele said. "Save some for someone else."

"Mom, it's almost noon."

Sarah went back to her agenda. "What did the studio want to discuss?"

Elise sighed, hoping her mother would get the hint that she didn't want to talk. "The European press tour." She fisted some brownie bites, then poured herself an inch of whiskey before opting for the chair on the other side of her father.

"Are they asking about Kitty?" Giovanni tried to sound casual, but Elise could tell she was asking for the benefit of their mother.

"Not yet."

Sarah gestured around the room, able to accommodate a hundred standing people. "Isn't it beautiful in here this time of day?" It was. The crystals on the three-tiered chandelier, hanging fourteen feet high, reflected rainbows onto the white walls, surrounding them as though they were at a disco party. Their mother was an ethereal beauty, like the rainbows decorating the space. She was the stereotype of what one would expect of one of the most famous, beautiful, and celebrated actresses in the world. She'd starred in more than thirty films, graced the covers of most magazines, and was in the double digits for award nominations. She exuded excellence from her pores.

Elise's sisters smiled, as if it was only the fourth or fifth time she'd said this.

"I wish we were enjoying it under different circumstances," Elise said.

James, taking over, peeked around a vase at Noele. "We can have a lot more family time if Noele decides to move back home." He winked to liven the mood.

"Dad, I'm going to law school."

As the fighter of the trio, eight years in New York had molded Noele into someone confident enough to think she knew who she was. Being older, Elise knew she didn't but saved her lectures. If the smiles and shared meals posted on her private Instagram account were any indication, Noele was satisfied with her life.

"Baby, I'm happy you want to help people, but—"

"What could you possibly have to say to that, Dad?" Noele said.

"You're fortunate enough to be able to buy your own law firm and have them all work pro bono."

"So, then I'd have time to take singing lessons again, right?"

James looked at Elise. "Who said anything about her singing?"

Elise, not in the mood to translate, kept eating. However happy Noele appeared, she was sensitive about this subject. Her voice was indeed a gift, and Elise, like everyone (though only their father voiced his opinion), thought it was going to waste. Still, Elise admired Noele's resolute commitment to building a life outside of her family—though she wondered how the next few days might change that.

"I know what you were thinking," Noele said.

James laughed at his youngest, who thought she was the smartest person in every room. "You're wrong." He pointed his fork at Noele. "You want to be a lawyer? Be a lawyer. As long as you get some good security."

"I could barely get to the airport." Noele passed her phone around the table for the visual. Noele had chosen New York University for the sake of anonymity, which came relatively easily because she had never been in show business. Her last name had stoked interest in her for the first couple of months, but she had moved somewhat anonymously for years—up until that week, of course.

"Where were you?" Sarah asked, frowning. "This view isn't from your place."

"Rebecca said first photos will go for upwards of two hundred thousand," Elise said.

"Everybody has to eat," James said.

"Stay at the apartment," Elise said. The St. Johns had an unknown residence on the Upper West Side.

"It's too far from my job," Noele said. "But I may have lost that already." She worked with domestic violence victims, and her being followed risked the victims' safety.

"Probably, with all the media attention," Giovanni agreed.

Elise sat back as the whiskey took effect, and Giovanni moved to business, as always. "So, my executive producer credit comes with a new arc."

Now in its third season, the AMC period piece suspended boundaries of race and gender and had become very popular. Giovanni, who played a teacher at a boarding school in early-nineteenth-century New York City, would become a series regular that season.

"Not that you didn't deserve it ages ago, but good for you," Noele said. Their father tipped his head to second the sentiment.

"It feels good to have a say."

Giovanni was an Oscar-winning actress by the time she was thirteen but, at twenty-eight, still didn't have nearly the visibility of others without the same accolades nor time in the industry. Publicly, she chalked it up to resentment over her pedigree and simply worked harder; she had taken acting lessons every week for years. But the slight had nothing to do with her talent. Finally, "ethnic" was in, and while Giovanni should have been included in what felt like a trend, casting directors often still said she was too "exotic," *not like a* real *Black girl.*

"Will there be a love interest?" Noele said.

"Yes, finally!"

"I thought she already had something with one of the other teachers?" Giovanni gave Elise a look; it delighted Elise to see her blush. "What's his name?" Elise teased again. Her sister was, as few besides Elise knew, sleeping with said actor in real life.

"So it's a new story line?" Sarah exclaimed.

"We had our first kiss two episodes ago."

"I can't keep up," Sarah said, laughing.

Giovanni looked hurt, but only Noele watched Giovanni's show religiously.

"No one watches everything I do either," Elise said.

"It *is* a soap opera," Giovanni reasoned.

Moments later, Sarah's roaring laugh at Noele's impression of Giovanni in the show began to compete with Elise's stress as the cause of a deep, sense-dulling headache. Her joy got louder, and it was infectious. Their glee made Elise mad, and she started nibbling on her right middle finger, a long-standing nervous habit that prompted Sarah to scold her to stop.

Elise listened, but only because at that same moment, Sarah, reminded of something, left the room.

She returned with what had to be her favorite dessert: a lemon cake, punctured with lighted candles and bearing the words WELCOME HOME etched in white icing. Sarah awaited praise for her thoughtfulness. The table obliged as expected, and for Elise, the sentiment was genuine. Lemon cake had been Kitty's favorite too.

"To Kitty," she said, raising her glass.

James threw her a warning look, but she continued. "Remember she made all those cakes and pastries for our production of *Alice in Wonderland*?"

Her sisters' eyes lit up with the memory, only to be extinguished by their mother's fury.

"Yeah, and all of my cake platters got broken." Sarah's resentment bounced off the rainbowed walls. "Kitty had you all marching through that damned thicket with all my good china, like little servants."

CHAPTER 2

Elise

Saturday afternoon, October 28, 2017

Built over the kitchen and accessible only by a door that most mistook as belonging to a hallway closet, the south wing was the four-bedroom apartment where the sisters had spent their childhood.

After naps and showers, Giovanni and Noele found Elise in the apartment's den. The site of numerous slumber parties and fights, the living room in its varied shades of pink was an expression of innocence, from a time before the sisters discovered boys.

Noele settled in the armchair in front of the room's only window, an octagonal stained glass pane of a red rose. Giovanni followed, with a mint julep mask smeared on her face. "Plane air makes me break out." She sat on the floor and leaned against the couch next to Elise.

"Why did you wear makeup, then?"

Giovanni folded her hands in her lap in the same way she collapsed her legs underneath her on the carpet. "I don't go anywhere naked."

Elise rolled her eyes. "You're prettier without it."

"We can't all be as naturally gorgeous as you, sister."

They both knew it wasn't true, but playing along, Elise imitated Dolly

Parton from her favorite eighties film, *Steel Magnolias*. "It takes effort to look like this."

"Shut up."

Noele's eyes widened. "Can we talk about Kitty now?"

"I got worried after your toast," Giovanni said.

"Mom was forcing cake down our throats!"

Noele and Giovanni picked fun at the memory of how Sarah had cut them huge chunks of cake, portion sizes wholly uncharacteristic of her usual food philosophy. "Five minutes into me being here," Noele continued, "she's railing at me about my weight, and then she gets mad when I refuse a giant piece of cake."

"It wasn't about your weight; you look fine," Elise said. "She was probing to see how serious things are with you and whatever his name is." Noele had been photographed with a long-haired White guy a few times, and the entire family was curious.

"Makes sense. She asked if I was pregnant! Inspected me." Noele demonstrated how Sarah had lifted her shirt above her bra to examine her belly, then shrugged. "I'm not used to her being so . . . nosey." She was a talented evader.

"Mom's secretly jealous." Elise knew because *she* was too. Noele had a freedom that none of the other St. John women had.

"Is she eating?" Stress had always taken their mother's appetite, but in someone who treated food discipline like a military exercise, any decrease in intake was always cause for concern.

"Seems so."

"Are she and Dad okay?" Noele asked.

"I guess, but I don't live here."

For decades, their parents' union had been protected from the normal celebrity pitfalls by nearly parallel career positioning; they had steadily grown together to build an empire. But when James, now almost sixty, hit a creative slump five years ago, he pushed for Sarah to retire. She refused at first, but after almost a year of dissension, she quit a major film in the middle of production to save her marriage, and they went to Paris—where James's creativity soared.

He began working on his first album in decades, flying other producers and musicians out to work with him. When they returned home, James went on tour, leaving Sarah alone to face being blackballed from the industry, ignoring the fact that his ultimatums had caused irreparable damage to her career. Planning the upcoming Halloween party was the only thing that had consistently gotten her out of bed over the past year.

Giovanni and Noele exchanged a glance that seemed to reference a prior conversation between them.

"Sorry we couldn't get here sooner," Noele said.

"We know how hard this has been for you. How close you were to Kitty." They had been too young to bond with Kitty when they were kids, as Elise had.

"Honestly, there's not much you could have done. Kitty left the work to me. One of her many dying wishes." Elise made the little joke so as to avoid other details.

"Can you think of any reason she would leave her estate to us?" Giovanni asked.

Elise shrugged. "We're the closest thing she had to family."

"You don't just give that kind of money to people who aren't blood," Noele said.

"She said she was going to give it to charity . . ."

"We should still," Noele surmised. "That would get people off our backs."

"Or, if we keep it, we could buy Noele a law firm!" Giovanni joked.

"Are you going to stop acting to run said law firm?" Elise asked.

"I would run it!" Noele said.

"You don't even have a law degree yet."

Giovanni spoke over them. "Kitty never said anything to you about it? In all this time?"

"No." Despite the months spent at her bedside, Elise had sat in Kitty's lawyer's office with her parents, her sisters on speakerphone, and heard Kitty's last wishes for the first time. Sarah was so upset by it, she left.

"The studio hopes announcing wedding plans can overshadow interest in her, and us," Elise confessed.

"That's ridiculous," Noele said.

"I understand the need to lighten the air around you. You reminded people that you're a real person, not an avatar. You obliterated the fantasy."

After Colin Kaepernick was blackballed from the NFL for taking a knee during the national anthem to protest police brutality against Blacks, Elise had posted to her Instagram in solidarity. People were having trouble understanding why he was taking a knee, and Elise wanted to show them. She'd edited together footage of police brutality against Blacks across a span of fifty years, using newsreels, documentaries, and American films, and set it to music by Black artists from each decade whose lyrics also referenced the problem.

The well-worn American social fabric was hanging by a thread, ripping at the seams, and it had felt inappropriate to Elise to ignore it and continue posting self-gratifying content for likes. The video's run time was less than a minute, but it went viral. The incident had doubled her follower count, split evenly between supporters and hateful trolls.

"Now people from Montana to Rhode Island know you're Black." Giovanni winked at her.

Elise was grateful for Giovanni's rare but continued display of kinship. Forever the devil's advocate, Giovanni's comments about Elise's appearance danced on the edge of appropriateness which sometimes sounded like jealousy. Elise had expected her to be the first one to admonish her post and statements, but she'd been the first to reach out when Elise went viral with a simple DM: FUCK 'EM.

"Much to Aaron's dismay."

Noele gasped. "He said that?"

"No, but that's when he told me he 'needed space.'" The backlash had hurt her feelings, but she didn't need to act. Aaron did—for his ego and his bank account. To continue to be seen in the right crowds, with the right people, he needed to remain neutral. Elise had since wondered if this need impacted his attraction to his current costar, Maya Langston, who was mixed with a little bit of everything. She had five flags in her Instagram bio.

"Also, everyone in his family is light-skinned. It's like passing the paper bag test was a marriage requirement."

Her sisters thought it was funny, but it bothered Elise, who had been harmed by this perception. Though both were classified as light-skinned, fair, high yellow, or redbone by other Black people, and assumed to be mixed by White people, neither Elise nor Aaron had a non-Black parent. Elise was lighter than her parents, sisters, and most of her extended family due to the common sprinkles of Whiteness on the family trees of many Black Americans, resulting in unexpected characteristics that sometimes just cropped up. These reminders appeared in every generation, causing tremors, triggering the spaces of the blended race.

Often people seemed disappointed or puzzled to discover Elise was just Black and not biracial. Her explanation always began with "somewhere down the line," and every time she veered down that path, the inquirer's eyes would glaze over. They wanted her to validate the banana-pudding hue of her skin, her light eyes, and her hair that grew like a weed down her back, as if these qualities weren't possible within the Black race. Slavery and its attendant sexual violence wasn't what they wanted to be reminded of.

The industry wasn't even polite about it. They wanted Elise's hair straight and her body stick thin. Publicly, they praised her Blackness, to show their commitment to diversity. Still, they pushed her into roles in which her race was never established, where it didn't exist, hoping no one would notice. And she had let them, for years. But the joke would maybe be on them now. After #oscarssowhite, her winning an Academy Award could be perceived as a handout—and worse, one that might not even be celebrated by the Black community. She wasn't exactly qualified to be a "win" against the system; money and skin tone aside, her nepotistic ties to the industry screamed extreme privilege.

"Start choosing different roles," Giovanni said. "Or diversify, like me."

"I don't know what I'd rather do." Elise felt stuck in acting. People relied on her to feed their families, and the obligation was suffocating. "Maybe nothing for a while after the Oscars—I need a break."

"Talking about Kitty could help things now."

"I agree with Gio. We should make a joint statement."

"We're not going to say anything about Kitty. We can't even talk about it as a family," Elise reminded them.

Discretion functioned like a religion in the St. John home. The spawn of a billionaire entertainment couple, the sisters were famous before they knew the meaning of the word, and their inherited celebrity came with rules. They were never to make personal admissions on a public stage—not ever, even when their art did it for them. They weren't to answer questions about lifestyle, politics, or their personal lives. It was safer that way. Celebrity was an image, an ideal model. It was a title that wore you, heavy like a crown, except your skin became the costume; your face, the mask. Any distraction from the fantasy detracted from the art—and, if they weren't careful, the legacy.

Elise feared the damage had already been done. All *Vogue* wanted to talk about were rumors. Funny enough, they explicitly did *not* want to address those Instagram posts.

"So, what then? We're just going to continue to let them hypothesize and harass us?"

"It will pass."

"It's barely November," Giovanni reminded her. "Kitty will come up at every awards show, every interview."

"We aren't to speak about Kitty." Her sisters grumbled audibly in protest but deferred to Elise's authority. "Besides, all anyone wants to know is why she gave us the money."

"So do we!" Giovanni exclaimed.

"Have you asked Mom?"

"I haven't."

"That's 'cause you know she never has a worthwhile thing to say about Kitty."

"That's not true." Giovanni was defensive, as if she'd been waiting for this. Elise wondered what their mother had said behind her back to prompt her sisters' stance. "Imagine how she feels—the guilt."

"She was right next door the whole time. That's on her. Everything is on her," Elise shot back.

"She's dealing with Kitty's death in her own way." As her physical twin, Giovanni idolized their mother and romanticized her narcissism. She was the only one convinced her long disappearances for work were rooted in her need to provide, as if another film would make the difference between their lifestyle and homelessness.

"And how's that?"

Giovanni crossed her arms. "I talk to her twice a day," she protested. "She's been staying busy. I support that."

"I hear her lying to you from the bed," Elise said. Sarah slept so much, Elise had usually felt compelled to check on her, after leaving Kitty's, before going home. "She's running from something."

"People deal with grief in different ways," Giovanni tried again. "We should show her some sensitivity."

"Trust me, I have." Unexpected tears began to flow. Giovanni put her arm around Elise's shoulder, and Noele joined them.

Sarah claimed to be busy handling Kitty's affairs, but Elise hadn't believed her then.

Kitty had scolded her for saying it. *She'll come when she's ready.* But Elise didn't say this aloud to her sisters. Instead Elise lamented how, for a woman who was once so beautiful, death had pulled on Kitty from the inside. Her eye sockets darkened; her cheekbones hollowed. The fat drained from her face, and her nose collapsed inward. "Still, she requested her lipstick every day." This garnered a sad chuckle from Giovanni.

Trying to distract Kitty from her pain, Elise had bribed her with foot rubs in exchange for a story. "She pretended like she didn't want to, but once she started talking, she didn't stop."

Elise had asked to record her—it had been years since Kitty had told her a story. Kitty talked for two hours that first day, her eyes closed the whole time, as if she was watching herself and her friends run all over Los Angeles. The next day, she was ready with another tale. Not long after, Kitty started hearing knocks late at night on her walls and front door, as if someone was trying to get in. "She told me it was death, and that she wasn't afraid to die."

Elise had wondered if she would hear the knocking when it was Kitty's time. But she didn't. Death took Kitty in the middle of the night, so silent, so quick that Elise slept through it, cocooned in the covers on the floor. With Kitty went Elise's ability to rest.

Elise climbed out onto the Perch after her sisters went to bed. Over the hedges on her right, Kitty's house looked dilapidated, as if it knew she wasn't coming back. The floodlights highlighted the peeling flamingo-pink paint on its exterior and the weeds that had overtaken the grass. There were a few cracked, although not broken, windows on the second floor.

Insomnia had brought Elise there in the wee hours of every morning since Kitty died. It sent her mother to roam the labyrinth in a silk nightgown, despite the forty-degree night weather. No one had seen Sarah shed a tear for Kitty, and the stroll was the only evidence of her suffering. Elise watched her chain-smoke in the dark middle of the maze.

Kitty was the only person Sarah smoked with. Kitty went through packs a day, but for a woman who had been eating organic since long before it was popular, tobacco was by far the dirtiest habit Sarah had. The two women had been photographed *together* at an Oscars party years ago, side by side, lit Lakes cigarettes in hand in front of an ashtray full of butts. The photograph was published everywhere and earned Sarah the wrath of her daughters, who had just lost their grandma Nellie, their mother's mother, to cancer.

Upon Sarah's second waking each day, she was cheery and accommodating, so far outside her basic nature that she seemed manic. It was as if she thought efficiency and speed would convince everyone she was all right.

It seemed to be working. Her sisters noticed nothing new. Elise wasn't going to out her, because she didn't want to draw attention to herself. She was only a witness to the solitary manifestation of her mother's pain because she also couldn't sleep and was up smoking a joint and talking to Kitty in her head about the burden of all she had to do, coupled with the memories left on her shoulders.

Nothing was the same, but Sarah was intent on making everything seem so—a task that didn't appear to be sitting well with her either. A few nights, Elise had thought about leaving the Perch to comfort her, but rooted by anger and blame, she couldn't move.

CHAPTER 3

Hazel

July 1934

When Hazel met the preacher, he was living in Wadesboro, North Carolina, in a one-room house by the creek. He had deep wrinkles around his eyes and mouth like the grooves in a tree trunk.

He was half-blind, so his niece escorted him every day to the bread shop where he worked as a baker. He needed no assistance on Sundays, when he caught the spirit. He hopped around on one leg, waving his arms, turning his head this way and that as if he was playing two parts in a play, and never ran into the chairs or stumbled down the pulpit step.

Hazel accompanied her mother to choir practice an hour before church to ensure a good seat. The seventh child of eleven, she was thirteen and, despite having the highest marks in her eighth-grade class, her schooling was over. Her parents were sharecroppers, and as the landowner continuously increased the prices of seed and other supplies, all their children, except the four little ones, were now needed to break even each year.

The pain that you've been feeling can't compare to the joy that's coming. Hazel recited the preacher's words as she tilled the earth under the hot sun, trying to distract herself from the wet heat and the mosquito bites that swelled and itched just minutes after an attack.

Trees lined the fields, but their shade was reserved for the Whites. Everyone hated field work, but only Hazel was allergic to the sun; though she was deep hued, her siblings teased her about having skin like the Whites. Hazel's mother would shoo them out of the house to give Hazel privacy when Hazel had to take oatmeal baths to calm the constant heat rash.

Though she was a middle child, Hazel was the runt. And as she grew, she remained daintier than her siblings, preferring to read rather than play outside. Dirtying her clothes meant extra laundry and less reading time. Her mother kept her old school books hidden in the back of the kitchen cabinet, though school was a sore subject. Hazel had the highest education of anyone in her family; neither of her parents could read.

Her mother didn't work the fields. Instead, she cleaned fish and shrimp for the distributor who supplied most of the county. Anything that didn't sell by Friday would be offered for sale to the employees. Hazel's mother, after setting aside enough for her family, sold the rest to their neighbors. So, every Friday, everyone made fish—and cornbread and greens.

Hazel liked to listen to her mother sing while she cooked. Like the Sunday sermon, her voice—alone, or accompanied by the choir—caused a flutter in Hazel's stomach.

One morning she was sitting in the lone rocking chair on the church's porch when the preacher arrived with his niece.

"Your purpose is beyond here." He told Hazel she was a vessel of the Lord, like Jesus Christ's greatest disciple, Mary Magdalene, who received the Father's teachings purely, unburdened by the need to compete and compare like the men. She was a witness to the evil and godliness of men. She witnessed Jesus's murder and was the first to witness his Resurrection. The preacher said jealous-hearted people would downplay Mary Magdalene's role in history with accusations of moral corruption, mistaking her identity or ignoring her significance to Jesus altogether. The joke, though, the preacher said, was on them. With one's attention turned outward, one forgets one's own ability to harness understanding of the truth.

Hazel believed him. Born into slavery, the preacher had the gift of inner sight. He had grown up in a one-room cabin in Tennessee with a man everyone called Grandfather, who traveled among plantations to calm unruly slaves with the word of Jesus. One night, the preacher, then a young boy, warned their massa that Grandfather was in trouble. Massa shooed him away, but sure enough, Grandfather's corpse arrived home days later. Slave catchers had mistaken him for a runaway and, after being beaten, forced to walk tied to a horse, and denied water, he had died.

Massa, having heard the boy recite Bible passages at will, put him in charge of church for the slaves. See, Grandfather had made the boy memorize the verses first, before he taught him to read them. These verses were the ones the boy taught Belle, a house slave from birth as he was, to read. Belle taught the horse trainer, who taught his wife, who taught her sister. Pretty soon all the plantation's thirty slaves could read. They ran one Saturday night, giving them an additional five hours before they'd be discovered absent from church. Miraculously, all thirty stayed free. That's what the preacher told Hazel, anyway.

As he spoke, the preacher had pointed at her as if he could see her, as if he could see something good promised. Hazel was convinced this was true until her entire family drowned on the distributor's fishing boat, and not only did Hazel lose faith in the preacher's words, she stopped believing in God.

Hazel's scaly skin had prevented her from helping her family serve the fish buffet at the distributor's end-of-summer fete. Two boats were needed to transport the equipment and workers, but due to a miscalculation or corner cutting, everything and everyone went on one.

The waterfront event ended early due to a summer monsoon. The captain waited until the rain stopped to undock, but the rain and wind started again, heavier, halfway through the ride. The force made it hard to steer, and they hit a cluster of rocks. Eventually, the boat began to go under and Hazel's family, including her baby niece, drowned.

She worked for another year in the fields, after being taken in by her neighbors, who loved to remind her of how much of a sacrifice it was. When she got tired of hearing it, she left for New York. Her mother had traveled there once with a White family and liked it. She felt a lightness in the air, despite the muggy, sticky August heat. Negroes there were, for the most part, left to themselves.

———————

A couple of years after losing her family, Hazel was sitting just hours from her hometown of Wadesboro, North Carolina, in a new church, amongst Negro women who could afford hats decorated with lace and beads and netting. Everyone could speak in tongues but needed the hymnals to sing along with the choir. They all felt the spirit the same way—head back, eyes closed, rocking on the wooden pews; *Hallelujah, thank you, Jesus*, with a faint to finish. They weren't godly, or else they wouldn't have been so cruel. Grown women sneered at her pregnant belly, and the preacher, a married man in his thirties, announced a departure from his planned sermon. *The Lord called upon me to speak on sins of the flesh this morning.*

Hazel was the one they'd heard about: the new girl from the country with the captivating eyes, who'd gotten herself in trouble with that White boy. And not just any ole White boy—one of them Lakes boys.

She almost left when the preacher spoke of a prostitute named Mary Magdalene who fell at Jesus's feet, begging for absolution. Hazel's hands went to her stomach as the old preacher from home came to mind for the first time in a long while. She could see an outline of his face in her mind's eye, smiling at her as though he were there, listening. A warmth came over her, and even though the sermon was meant to shame her, she smiled for the first time in a while. *She done gone crazy*, she heard them say.

What happened to Hazel was added to the lengthy list of warnings remitted to every Negro girl in Winston-Salem, North Carolina, upon the first budding of a tit. White men were as much of a threat to Negro women and girls as they were to Negro men and boys. Instead of lynching, the Negro female body could be snatched to satisfy some White men or boys' curiosity, frustration, or lust. This fact, being central to the early education of a Negro girl, caused blame for her predicament to rest on sixteen-year-old Hazel. Many said she had invited the attention of the twenty-three-year-old tobacco heir upon herself.

The Lakes name was a brand, and the unborn child a marker of Hazel's past. Hating where and whose she'd been, Negro men thereafter would want nothing to do with her. An orphan and new in town, Hazel would raise her half-breed alone.

Some might have hated the baby growing inside them, but Hazel fiercely loved her child from the moment she felt the spark of life below her belly button. She began to pray again, this time for her child's deliverance, and when a baby girl was born, looking as White as any White child, Hazel decided that maybe there was a God. Her daughter might escape the life that Jim Crow said Hazel's dark skin consigned her to.

Hazel named her baby Mary Magdalene, believing in the preacher's words that her daughter was more than a witness—she was the spawn, the magnificent physical manifestation of the worst in the world, one who would one day, Hazel believed, absolve the sin of her creation. Hazel was in fact a vessel, the incubator of a tiny miracle.

Others pointed to the child's ears. "See that tawny brown? She's gonna darken." It was an old wives' tale that a baby's skin color would settle to the color of the tips of its ears, but when Hazel looked, she couldn't tell if Mary Magdalene's were brown or just a little red.

With each passing month, and then year one and two, Mary Magdalene remained lily white, with straight, reddish-brown hair. Her hazy blue-gray eyes were the only physical marker of her maternity. Peering into her baby's eyes, Hazel was reminded of the family she'd lost and how hard it would be to keep her daughter safe.

Hazel, two of her siblings, her mother, an aunt, her grandmother, and her great-grandmother had had those same eyes. A striking juxtaposition to their shades of brown skin, the blue-gray irises were a recessive gene and proof of forced miscegenation generations before.

Hazel had left her family home with two valuables wrapped in her waistband: her parents' five dollars in life savings, and her great-great-grandmother Elizabeth's gold ball earrings. Family lore said Elizabeth had been a senator's house slave in Washington and the mother of two of his eight children, one gray-eyed girl and a blue-eyed male. Their births increased the senator's slave stock to forty-one.

Hazel had kept her arm close to her side during her journey. The earrings were her only physical connection to her lineage, her only inheritance—her only offering of wealth to any offspring.

CHAPTER 4

Hazel

July 1936

Lakes Tobacco, grown and cured for hundreds of years by Negro hands, was the foundation of Winston-Salem, North Carolina's economy. It cornered the national market and, whether smoked or chewed, it was consumed by everyone in town: poor and rich, Negro and White, young and old, male and female.

The Lakes factory provided paths to management positions for White men and office work for White women. Negro men and women were offered steady hourly and seasonal work.

A half mile's walk out in any direction, the neighborhood of Cottonwood bordered the wealthiest White neighborhood to the north and the poorest to the south. The Lakes factory was east, next to the railroad tracks, and to the west was downtown. Though Cottonwood was centrally located, allowing Negroes to walk to work, the thick woods that surrounded it made it necessary for them to travel in groups. At night, the tree limbs felt like death threats, pillars upon which they could be staked.

Hazel got there by accident. She'd gotten off her bus to use the bathroom, but because there wasn't a Colored one in the station, she'd had to walk up the road to find a shady spot under a tree. From a squat, she saw the bus leave. The station was already closed, so she crossed the street toward the sheriff's station, and steps from the door, an older Negro woman blocked her path.

"What you doing?"

"I'm lost. My bus left."

The woman gripped Hazel's wrist. "They won't help you in there. Lock you up and have their way with you until your kin comes." Most of the woman's teeth were missing, and the few she had were black, rotted. Oddly, there was a corn kernel stuck on the side of her mouth.

"I don't have any kin."

The woman smacked her gums. "Come on, child."

She slapped Hazel's hand, meaning for her to mimic the downward posture of her head, shoulders, and back that allowed her to torpedo past the Whites-only shops and restaurants. They had to walk in the street, and Hazel, nervous so close to the cars, struggled with her canvas bag to keep up, careful to step in the woman's dirt footprints. Hazel's family hardly ever went to the city because of these rules.

Not until they were among their own kind did the woman's pace slow and her back straighten. "Don't tell none of them White folks you don't have no kin." She demanded Hazel's eye contact. "You hear me?"

"Yes, ma'am."

"Too pretty, you are." She said it like a warning before knocking on the door of Adelaide and Lefred Bends.

The Bendses had one of the biggest homes in Cottonwood—three bedrooms and one bath—and welcomed overnight guests expecting nothing in return, or perhaps only a barter for food and shelter. Jim Crow prohibited Negroes from lodging establishments, but there wasn't a Negro community in America where you couldn't find temporary shelter.

After learning she was an orphan, headed to New York alone, the Bendses wanted Hazel to stay. The decision became easy when their neighbor, Bessie, offered Hazel a job as second cook at the Lakes manor. Bessie had been the Lakeses' cook for twenty-five years.

"They treat Bessie so good, sometimes she forgets she ain't really family," Adelaide joked, setting a plate of turkey necks, rice, and collard greens in front of Lefred. He was in his usual spot at the head of the table, still in his factory coveralls.

"Say what you want, but they're as loyal as White folks can be." Bessie kicked off her house shoes then and, after shifting her thick stomach rolls, bent over to touch her feet. Her toes were gray from a lack of circulation. "I get pain in my soles from standing too long and I need to train someone to do things right."

Bessie's cooking was loved far and wide—"*Nationally*," Adelaide later fumed to Hazel. It was Bessie's recipes that Mrs. Nora Lakes used to open the famous BabyCakes bakery chain, a fact that bothered Adelaide more than Bessie.

"I couldn't open my own shop with this face." Bessie was matter-of-fact about the world. "Besides, more people, whether they'd admit it or care, know."

Bessie was responsible for the recipes, but it was Mrs. Lakes who made the cakes sell. Her dreamy, girly decorations and odd icing colors were a significant part of what made a BabyCakes cake a *cake*. In the early days, Mrs. Lakes's decorations had made it possible to charge double for the confections. "I made sure they were good, but you had to buy one first to taste it."

"More of that money coming in would be nice," Adelaide said.

"Oh, Addy. The Lord has blessed me with everything I need. Can't take any of it with you."

Adelaide sucked her teeth. "You deserve better. We all do." Adelaide cleaned house for a family two blocks over from the Lakeses and always came home cursing.

"Now, now, Adelaide. Enough with all that tonight." Lefred pointed his fork at her. Normally, he would pat her hand, and she would quiet, realizing she too had had enough. "I just want to eat."

"Piss-ass world, if you ask me."

"We didn't ask." He went to bed first that night, leaving the women and Hazel to their gossip. Usually he stayed up on the porch smoking until Bessie was back inside her home.

Bessie scolded Adelaide as soon as the bedroom door closed. "Stop reminding him about all your wishing for a life you don't have."

Adelaide waved her off. "He knows what I mean."

"You think that makes him feel any better, you bringing it up all the time?"

Hazel understood Adelaide's anger. She remembered how hard her parents had worked, how tired and short-tempered they were at night. Bessie was still cooking three full meals a day, six days a week, despite having to hobble around the Lakeses' kitchen. Adelaide, in her fifties, suffered from back pain. Still, she was always up first, making breakfast, and she cooked dinner every night, despite the scrubbing and washing she did all day. Though he never had much to say, Lefred was a good man, a faithful man, and he did deserve better than what he got—he deserved a fair chance at happiness.

Bessie, it seemed to Hazel, had found some semblance of it at the Lakes manor. She was famous there, an institution, having fed the town's wealthiest residents. Her food—and her desserts especially—were part of what made a Lakes party a Lakes party. Every one of her bready, sweet, gooey, custardy, chocolatey, buttery treats disappeared within minutes of being served. This seemed to be enough of a compliment for Bessie.

Life seemed to be just as sweet for Hazel at the Lakes manor—until it turned sour.

In August the family's second-eldest son, Theodore "Teddy" Lakes, came home for a visit before his first year at Harvard Law School. The oldest son was married and living in South Carolina, and the youngest was in college out West.

"They keep him away in hopes he'll turn out good," Adelaide hypothesized.

Days after Teddy's arrival, while passing Hazel in the narrow hallway near the kitchen's second entrance, he reached out and pinched her right breast through her uniform. He smiled when she clutched her chest in pain. "I thought y'all liked that sort of thing."

Back in the kitchen, Bessie looked up from the pot of beans she was stirring as if she knew what had happened. "They all gon' take after their daddy."

Gossip about the Whites in Winston-Salem circulated through Cottonwood by way of the Negro maids, nannies, butlers, and drivers who overheard and observed the town's deepest secrets. Teddy, like his father, and *his* father, even three generations before him, enjoyed every pleasure he fancied; Mrs. Nora, it was said, had her front door painted bright red so her husband would know which home was his. Mr. Lakes had three sons, but Bessie claimed there were at least two other redheads from other women. The three Lakes boys were blond now but had been true gingers, like their father, until puberty.

"He'll be gone to school in a few weeks. Stay around the kitchen till then," Bessie warned. "I'll have Mr. Ford serve."

"Are you going to keep working until then?"

"Lord willing."

Teddy had been forced to attend college in Virginia after groping the daughter of one of his father's employees. Legal justice didn't exist for such circumstances, but Mr. Lakes agreed that his son would leave town; the White foreman had a degree of power, even against the uber-wealthy Lakes family, that was denied the fathers of the two Negro girls Teddy and his brother had forced to strip in the woods that surrounded Cottonwood back in high school. Murmurs about Teddy's behavior with White girls in Virginia had required a hefty donation to ensure his acceptance into Harvard Law.

Teddy returned that Christmas with his new wife, the former Miss Lanie Crew. They'd married late in the fall at her family's Virginia estate. She was an unremarkable blonde, and Teddy, who despite his reputation always had his choice of women, was a catch for her—and they both knew it. Still, she was wealthy, educated, and had been matched to Teddy by their fathers years before.

On the morning of Christmas Eve, the Lakes family drove, per tradition, an hour away to cut down the tree. They'd spend the rest of the day trimming it and wrapping gifts before their annual Christmas Eve party that evening. Being that he and his wife didn't have children yet, Teddy's presence at the tree lot wasn't mandatory, and he offered to stay home and fetch the decorations from the attic.

He appeared in the kitchen not two minutes after everyone had left, pushing the service door so hard it swung and hit the wall behind it. "Are the biscuits ready?" He came to Bessie's side where she stood in the middle of the room at the table, making a list. He kissed her cheek with an exaggerated, wet pucker.

"Not yet," she said.

He went to kiss her again, but she turned her head, still writing. "Stop with all that kissing now."

He chuckled, and Hazel looked up from picking the ends off the green beans, watching as he reached for Bessie's face. "I love your cheeks, Bessie."

She raised her arm, blocking his proximity to her face. "Get now."

"Can I—"

"*May* I," Bessie scolded. As the person who had fed them chicken soup when they were sick and bathed them, Bessie turned maternal with the Lakes boys.

Like a child, Teddy bowed his head. "May I have a turkey and dressing sandwich?"

"You can't wait for dinner?"

"I'm starved."

"I have to get to the store, but I'll make it when I get back." Bessie walked him to the service door. "You go on now. Stay outta here. We have work to do." Bessie threaded her arm through the strap of her dark-blue leather purse. "I'll be right back." She insisted on running all the food errands herself, despite the strain on her seventy-year-old legs and feet, and always returned with two of something—bananas, canned meat, toilet tissue—and sometimes a third for Hazel. She said the Lakeses didn't mind, and Hazel didn't think otherwise considering the silver Cadillac they had bought her a few years ago.

She pointed to the icebox. "Start cutting that butter, will you?" The butter had to be at the perfect temperature and consistency to use; otherwise, it would ruin her famous Christmas biscuits. Served at midnight during their Christmas Eve party, with jam, Bessie's biscuits were half the reason guests came. She served the Lakeses another small helping on Christmas morning with eggs and bacon, but the rest were Bessie's Christmas present to the house staff.

Hazel pulled the churn from the icebox, hearing Bessie's tires crunch down the gravel driveway as she did. The butter was the palest yellow, indicative of the milk's freshness from the fattest cows on the Lakeses' farm. Hazel thought about how delicious the biscuits would be that night, fresh from the oven with the peach-pear-blackberry jam Bessie had gone to buy. It was a specialty brand from Charleston that Mrs. Nora gave her as a gift from a trip there once.

Dare I say, that jam is better than mine. Bessie had been as excited as a child is for a new toy. She usually made the jam for the biscuits from scratch (Bessie would have cultivated her own sugar cane if she could), but squirrels had wiped out the Lakeses' fruit-tree groves in August.

By the time Hazel was aware of Teddy's presence, his knees were pushing her legs apart; knowing every give in the kitchen's hardwood floors, he'd crept up behind her. The shock of his body against hers sent the churn to the ground, where it split. She struggled against him as his feet forced hers wider. She lost her balance and fell against the table, sliding into and blackening the butter with her soles. Her eyes locked on a piece of wood from the churn. Her fingers inched toward it, itching to bash Teddy's head in, and she would have, had he not slammed her palms against the table. Part of her resigned itself to being restrained. Had she fought back and really injured him, the Whites would have used it as an excuse to burn Cottonwood to the ground.

Worse than that moment would be being the reason everyone she knew lost everything they had.

Her cheek hit the wooden table and, having been warned about the unnatural thing he would do if she resisted, she stared out of the back door, wishing the shiny nose of Bessie's silver Cadillac would slide into view.

It was Teddy's wife, Lanie, who first found Hazel on the floor amid the butter and flour. When she couldn't stop humming one of the hymns her momma used to sing, to explain how the churn busted, Lanie took it upon herself to fire Hazel without severance pay.

Bessie came over after her Christmas Day shift at the Lakes home with a basket of biscuits for Hazel and the Bendses.

"No butter and no jam."

"Don't matter." Adelaide went to pour Bessie some cider.

Bessie looked surprised to see Hazel at the table but didn't say anything.

"We were just about to eat. You want a plate?" Adelaide kept moving, making only two plates for herself and Hazel, expecting Bessie to refuse as always.

"Yes, thank you. I'll have some."

Adelaide reached for another plate.

Hazel looked at Bessie as she sat down next to her.

"She gave away all my jam to the guests," Bessie said. "Even the three jars I'd set aside in my spot. Called herself apologizing to them for the break in biscuit tradition."

"Sticky fingers is always taking something," Adelaide said.

"What did she tell them happened?" Hazel asked. Adelaide sat plates of yams, mustard greens, and butter beans in front of her and Bessie.

"That the butter spoiled."

Hazel heard "soiled," and with it came the downward vision of her black, round-toed work shoes sliding and stomping into the pale butter mounds. She felt sick.

Bessie lowered her voice to speak to Adelaide as Hazel left the room. "Is she all right?"

Though Hazel closed her bedroom door, their voices carried. She wondered if Lefred could hear from the porch.

"You know she doesn't say much."

"You gon' take her to see Dr. Cardwell?"

"Did today."

"I came back from the store and they were cleaning. The butter was packed into the floor cracks."

"Who was cleaning?"

"They made Teddy do it. That dummy wife he's got was in there helping. They boiled pots of water to get it to liquify."

Teddy and his wife had left in the middle of the night after a terrible fight. Mrs. Nora was unsure of when he'd return. She came in the kitchen shortly after Bessie arrived with a Christmas surprise: a solitary jar of jam she'd stashed away. They had some together on toast. Bessie laughed while narrating the moment. "If I told you my life story, I swear you wouldn't believe it."

Hazel never did find out what had been so funny but didn't want to ask. Bessie's absence of yesterdays was what made Hazel feel so comfortable around her. They had an understanding, and Hazel had learned, after her family died, not to ask people questions she didn't want to be asked herself.

A few weeks later, morning sickness and a hardness beneath her belly button sent Hazel back to the Lakes manor. She needed a job, and her firing had made her unemployable. Aside from ruining the town's favorite Christmas Eve fete, she was "pretty for a Negro girl," and no woman wanted to hire help for whom her husband might form an affinity.

Mrs. Nora grasped Hazel's hands, pleading for her silence. There were political plans for Teddy, and while his having his way with a Negro girl wasn't a threat to that future, a child could be.

"How will I feed her?" Hazel glared at Mrs. Nora. Fully aware of the illegality of direct eye contact, she was bolstered by the need to protect the life inside her.

Mrs. Nora looked at Bessie as if she needed her permission to speak. "A job here as long as you want it," she finally said. "Bessie will be retiring soon, and I'd like you to stay."

"He'll be settling in Virginia after law school," Bessie said, reading Hazel's mind.

"Dear Lord, give me strength." Mrs. Nora bent over and took in a long breath. Bessie started patting her back like a tambourine. "It's gon' be all right. It ain't your fault."

Days later, Hazel found an envelope in the pocket of her apron. Folded inside was a notecard, with FROM THE DESK OF NORA ALLISON LAKES inscribed in gold at the top:

Employment and living expenses to be paid for the entire life of Hazel Ledbetter and one child who shall be the eldest and firstborn at time of birth, whether male or female. Giver humbly suggests that this money be kept in a savings account in a bank until the child is eighteen years of age and wishes to embark on his or her own life.

Hazel signed the card and returned the envelope to her pocket. Days later, she found a deposit receipt in its place. Bessie pretended she didn't know anything about it, but only she would have known which white apron on the hook was Hazel's.

Nightmares about Teddy came when she slept. She felt his breath steaming up her ear and heard the staccato tempo thumping her eardrum. She smelled the cigarette he'd smoked and the bacon he'd had for breakfast. She felt the edge of the kitchen table cutting into her pelvis, which left a permanent scar, with every jab into her body. Then she saw his face, a view she had not had in real life. His features were twisted with the pleasure of his power, eyes slit and tongue licking, snakelike, with every thrust. She woke up after her daddy appeared and blew Teddy's head off with a shotgun.

Bessie busied her mind by day. Acting as sous-chef from her seat at the kitchen table, she remitted recipes to Hazel in between stories about her son in Chicago who just had his third baby.

Hazel entertained it because doing so was kind: after asking Adelaide if she planned to accompany Bessie to Chicago to see the baby, Hazel learned that Bessie's son had been dead for more than ten years. He'd been found hung after organizing a boycott at the lumberyard where he worked, demanding other work for Negroes besides the backbreaking job of hauling timber.

"She sat in the tub for days, wailing as if a body part had been cut off," Adelaide said. "She was too close to death after losing that boy." When the water ran cold, Adelaide boiled more and fed Bessie broth. "Then one morning she got out the tub, got dressed, and went back to work as if it had never happened. Forgetting is the only reason she's still breathing."

Bessie wasn't the only one in the Lakes house who was haunted. Mrs. Nora never spoke Mary's name but proffered a cake to Hazel on her first birthday.

"She didn't ask for my help," Bessie said, hearing of it later.

Mrs. Nora didn't pretend to be interested in baking anymore; she sold BabyCakes, and Hazel overheard her laugh with guests, hating how easily she lied. *The last thing I ever want to do again is sift flour and cut butter.*

The exception didn't soften Hazel. It was a weak acknowledgment of Mary's existence, but Hazel, believing the world needed more spoiled little Negro girls, carried the pink box home, punctured the three-tiered confection with the exorbitant number of candles provided, lit them, and sang her daughter "Happy Birthday." Mary's eyes shone with wonder at the candlelight as she clapped her hands.

After the third September of this, Hazel began to dread the day when Mary would ask where the tiered cakes in the petal-pink boxes came from.

The truth was hard to voice. She could have left the Lakeses but would have had to move to another city, alone, to find another job. Besides, having ties, however complicated, was comforting.

When Bessie died, Hazel started having nightmares again, dreading Teddy's return for her funeral.

"He won't come," Adelaide said.

Hazel, knowing how much the Lakes boys adored Bessie, skipped the funeral, unsure. It was a decision she soon regretted, as it all happened without Teddy, just as Adelaide said.

That night, Adelaide took Hazel to Bessie's grave, dug into the edge of the Lakeses' land underneath one of the peach trees in the orchard. Staring down at the mound, Hazel couldn't help but think about how Bessie's decaying flesh would dissolve into the roots of the tree and help nourish the juicy fruit they'd eat all year. Now she would be the one to make the preserves and Christmas jam. Instead of tears, gruesome thoughts about the other bodies that may have been buried beneath these trees rose up and turned her stomach, until Hazel felt her dinner coming up her esophagus. Adelaide started patting her back, and Hazel sank to rest her hands on her knees.

"You was a daughter to her."

Hazel wanted to say what she felt but couldn't, feeling a sense of betrayal against her own mother. Adelaide took her hand as they wound through the grove, in and out of the web-like shadows created by the branches under the moonlight. Hazel turned back before the main street and thought she saw someone duck back behind a tree.

Hazel's heart was a slow-to-scab wound that continued to ooze, desperate to seal any exposure, but losing Bessie scraped what little scab was there clean off. In her will, left in Nora Lakes's possession, Bessie left Hazel her house. Hazel refused to move in, instead offering it to Adelaide and Lefred, who could use a larger yard for their vegetable garden.

"We don't need to live there to do that," Lefred said. He liked the view from his porch, which allowed him to see an entire 180 degrees around

Cottonwood. "Girl, what's wrong with you? Why you actin' funny about the house?"

Hazel began to cry. "I never even told her I loved her."

"Doll baby." He reached for her hand. "She knew."

Months later, after Hazel and Mary moved in, Hazel found a drop floor in their one closet. Inside a tin box was a family Bible, Bessie's BabyCakes recipes, and her will, bequeathing everything to her son, William. Hazel knew then it was Mrs. Lakes who had intervened and made sure Hazel got the house that would have otherwise been left empty. Hazel softened on Mrs. Lakes a bit after that. She couldn't put her finger on it, but there was something different about Mrs. Lakes, a speck of *something* to like.

The summer before Mary's fourth birthday, Teddy and Lanie returned to the Lakes manor. Their daughter, Shirley Claire, was almost three and old enough to spend summers with her grandparents while her parents vacationed.

Mary fell ill with a chest cold days before they were due to arrive. Adelaide and Lefred were visiting family, and her backup couldn't take a sick child, so Hazel snuck Mary into the maid's quarters. To ensure the child stayed asleep, Hazel rubbed Vicks on her chest and gave her a taste of brandy, molasses, and lemon. Hazel panicked later that afternoon when she returned to find Mary had disappeared. She found her in Shirley Claire's room, on the third floor of the four-story house.

Hazel peered through the doorway crack as the sisters played on the rug among stuffed animals, books, and wooden blocks. They looked nothing alike, save for their father's widow's peak and the red tones of their hair. Shirley Claire was a bright redhead with orange wisps flickering at her edges; the inherited trait on Mary was hidden, like her parentage, and only showed up in sunlight. Hazel wouldn't have known what other qualities Mary had inherited from her father. Teddy, Hazel assumed, had been told to stay largely out of sight that trip; Hazel only caught a glimpse of him arriving. He and Lanie had eaten all their meals out.

Still sick, Mary curled up atop a stuffed giraffe and closed her eyes. Shirley Claire, still eager to play, snatched the toy. Mary pulled at it, causing Shirley Claire to fall back. A thudding smack sounded against Mary's arm, and her murderous scream sent Hazel running in to scoop her into her arms. A hardback book lay open on the floor where Mary had been, launched, Hazel now realized with a jolt, by Lanie Lakes seated in a rocking chair in the left corner of the room. Mary nestled her face, wet with tears and mucus, into Hazel's neck, worming her tiny arm between their bodies. Shirley Claire, equally startled, started crying and pulling on the bottom of Hazel's dress, reaching for her playmate.

Lanie was even colder than when Hazel had first met her, having settled into the grim reality of her arranged marriage. For a split second, she looked ashamed of her cruelty, but then her mouth snarled as she realized Hazel was her only witness. "She shouldn't even be here."

"She's sick, ma'am. I had no one to keep her."

"And so you brought her here to infect us?" Lanie brushed past her own child to shake a finger at Hazel. "You know we're going away. You were trying to ruin our trip."

Hazel began to back out of the room. "No, ma'am," she said, patting Mary's back faster. The girl's sobs showed no sign of ceasing. Lanie followed them and watched from the top of the staircase, ignoring her own daughter wriggling in a fit across the floor, until Hazel disappeared with Mary around the bend.

———————————

The doctor said Mary's arm wasn't broken, but it was so swollen she couldn't raise it for two weeks after Lanie's assault. Fantasies of harming Lanie dominated Hazel's thoughts: a fall down the eighteen-step wooden staircase, a slip on a newly waxed floor, the slamming of her fingers in a door.

Unsure of how much longer she could resist after a ten-minute contemplation about grinding glass into Lanie's soup, Hazel praised God upon arriving, one morning, to learn that Teddy and Lanie were gone. Mrs. Nora met Hazel at the kitchen door with their traumatized daughter, who was screaming and throwing her body against her grandmother's restraint. "She screams louder when I put her down. Won't let Mr. Lakes even look at her." She gave Hazel a pleading look as she handed the child over.

Shirley Claire stopped crying and clutched the shoulders of Hazel's uniform with her wet hands. She looked back at her grandmother with an expression of relief.

Mrs. Nora chuckled. "Babies know where they're safest." A hand went to her forehead. "I'll need your help this summer. I haven't had a baby in almost thirty years."

Mrs. Nora didn't consider Hazel's feelings about caring for the second child of the monstrous man who had violently fathered her daughter. Hazel decided that Mrs. Nora either wholeheartedly trusted or completely underestimated her. But Hazel didn't have the capacity for cruelty to a child. The overwhelming emotion she felt for the little girl was sympathy.

Shirley Claire attached to Hazel as if she'd never had a mother, and because the Lakeses couldn't stand to hear her cry, Hazel's schedule changed to revolve around Shirley Claire, requiring Adelaide to take up the slack to avoid neglect to Mary.

Sometimes it took hours to soothe Shirley Claire. Hazel assumed these were the rare times when she missed her parents. In an unexpected gesture, Mr. Lakes took the child from Hazel one afternoon. "Let me try." They disappeared into his study, and within minutes, Shirley Claire quieted. Astonished, Hazel crept to the door to hear him reading to her:

What is this life if, full of care,
We have no time to stand and stare?—
No time to stand beneath the boughs,

And stare as long as sheep or cows:
No time to see, when woods we pass,
Where squirrels hide their nuts in grass:
No time to see, in broad daylight,
Streams full of stars, like skies at night:
No time to turn at Beauty's glance,
And watch her feet, how they can dance:
No time to wait till her mouth can
Enrich that smile her eyes began?
A poor life this if, full of care,
We have no time to stand and stare.

Shirley Claire was asleep by the end, curled like a puppy in her grandfather's lap. Seeing her in the doorway, Mr. Lakes beckoned Hazel into his library. She rocked back and forth on her heels, hesitant. "Did you want me to take Shirley Claire to her bed?"

Hazel could see a droplet of sweat running down from the top of his head. Mr. Lakes was always sweating, even in the winter months. She imagined he smelled like a towel that never quite dried out.

"I'll do it. Little thing is heavy." Mr. Lakes jostled the tot to readjust her head in the bend of his arm. "She's dreaming now." He pointed to the book of poetry on the small table. Hazel saw the name on the spine: W. H. DAVIES. "I used to read that poem to my boys when they were little," he said. "I suppose it was soothing. The description of what a life should be."

"What's that?"

"Time spent doing nothing in particular."

Hazel thought about the way Mr. Lakes spent his time and began to understand. She listened as he began to recite the poem by memory.

The words were melodic and shifted her attention outside, to the streams of sunlight piercing through the trees, and onto the wooden floor at her feet. She put her hand out, wanting the sun to drench her skin. Hearing the creaking of the wooden floor, she was pulled from the warmth. Mr. Lakes was at the door with Shirley Claire. "Take the book; it seemed to work with her too."

Having read the poem to Shirley Claire at every slumber thereafter, Hazel quickly memorized it and started reciting it to Mary on the rare nights she was home to tuck her in. Sometimes Mary was forgiving and reached for Hazel immediately, others she clung to Adelaide, refusing Hazel's touch.

Then one day in July, nothing worked, and Shirley Claire's cries became unbearable to the older couple.

"She's bored, and it's hot. She can't stay in this house all day anymore," Mrs. Nora said, handing Hazel a wad of cash. "Go to the park, get her some ice cream, take her to a movie—anything."

"But Mrs. Nora, I'm not allowed."

"You are while in charge of her." Negro women were tolerated in Whites-only spaces when attending to White children. "If any of those bums even look at you wrong, tell them to call me."

Required by law to keep her eyes to the ground, move aside to make way, and speak little, Hazel felt like a ghost among the White residents of Winston-Salem. They passed her, smiling at Shirley Claire, never once looking her in the face. She didn't mind. Being seen by White folks led to situations you couldn't get out of. Being seen meant they wanted something to kick, much like a dog. That lesson Hazel had learned for good. Besides, being ignored allowed Hazel continuous observation of the world to which her child should belong.

Given enough money every day to indulge Shirley Claire's every whim many times over, Hazel began squirreling some away for Mary, deciding that one day, everything Shirley Claire got and did, Mary would too. It wasn't until August that Hazel got up the courage. When Shirley Claire's August birthday passed without the three-tiered cake and candles from Mrs. Nora that Mary always received, Hazel decided Mrs. Nora would want Mary to have the extras money afforded.

CHAPTER 5

Hazel

Summer 1942

The next Sunday, and every Sunday thereafter, Hazel took Mary to Charlotte. Only two hours by bus, it was the closest big town to Winston-Salem. No one knew them there, making it the perfect place to pass Mary off as her young mistress.

"Don't you ever call me 'momma' around White folks. Call me 'Hazel,' hear?"

"Yes, ma'am."

"Let me do the talking, no matter what happens—you understand? Don't answer anyone's questions but mine."

Mary's skin was a cloak of acceptability, and Hazel used it to open the front doors of every space where Negro children weren't allowed. They went to the library, and Mary learned to swim in the public pool. They enjoyed picnics in Royale Park. Hazel borrowed one of the Lakeses' garden blankets from the downstairs closet, one with a big "H" on it, to sit on. Hazel listened to Mary read aloud while she rebraided her ponytails; every so often, she checked to make sure the strands were still growing straight from her daughter's scalp. Every week, Mary came home with new ribbons, a pair of gloves, a book or, in some special cases, a doll from Ivey's department store. The store only sold White dolls, but they all had Mary's eyes.

Their favorite place was the movie theater. Hazel had to stand—Negroes were only permitted to sit in the balcony—but wore her comfortable shoes, more concerned with exposing her daughter to the serene lives lived on the screen than with her own comfort. Mary sat like a little lady, alone, in the White section of the theater, pin straight and still for the entire picture, except for the occasional smile and scrunching of her shoulders in delight. Shirley Temple was her favorite.

Mary skipped up the theater aisle afterward as if there was no one else around, swinging her arms wide and lifting her agile knees up to her chest. People moved or were hit with an arm; regardless, they smiled at the beautiful, happy little girl. Hazel trailed Mary as she cleared their path through the lobby, and out of the exit. Hazel didn't stop her even then. It felt good to be able to walk a straight, unobstructed path through the White world.

They went to the diner for grilled cheese, hamburgers, and pickles. Hazel couldn't eat but enjoyed watching Mary. During their third visit, Mary handed half her grilled cheese to Hazel.

Hazel pushed her hand back to her plate. "Eat your food. It's a special treat for you."

"But you like cheese sandwiches too."

"Yes, but eating it here is what makes it a treat."

Mary looked around the diner. "All these people are special?"

Hazel smiled. "Everyone is. Each in their own way."

"So why are treats just for White people?"

"You're not White," Hazel whispered.

Mary had another question but continued eating as the you-better-do-as-I-say look she knew well crossed Hazel's face. "Eat."

"I'm bright," Mary announced later on the bus home. She touched her arm to Hazel's. The difference was stark. "You're Negro."

There were snickers from other Negroes on the bus, all of whom likely had had similar conversations with a Negro child. The Negro race spanned hues from snow white to ink black. Children didn't understand how they were all called "Negro" or "Colored."

Hazel nestled her to her side, whispering that they'd talk at home. "You're the same as me, but we don't need to talk about it. White folks don't think about being White every second, so why should we?" A chameleonic character would have to become second nature to the child to achieve what Hazel had in mind for Mary's future. "Let people think whatever they want to think about you. It's none of their business anyway. You learn to fit in, wherever you happen to be."

Hazel never told her daughter not to tell anyone about their trips to Charlotte, but somehow Mary knew better than to mention the White ladies who sat her on their laps, fed her candy, and played with her hair when she visited Ivey's salon or restaurants to anyone in Cottonwood. Hazel watched, swelling with smug knowledge, as the White salesladies fawned over her daughter. They'd spit on her if they knew the truth.

Born fair, Mary would remain that way until the day she died. She had a petite, thin frame with shapely legs, big doe eyes, a slender jawline, and a tiny nose. Each feature was smooth, like an ivory bust with perfect lines. Her eyes changed from a brownish blue to a gray blue, as if they knew the pain of her origin and the murky future it had sowed. Hazel, knowing the troubles beauty could bring, tempered others' praise. "Pretty is as pretty does."

White ladies' compliments did nothing to overshadow the way Mary was treated at home. Any degree of conceit was impossible in Cottonwood, where those who knew the girl rejected her and offered only insults. Her beauty made her a target of male desire and, thus, female envy. Her mother's stain ostracized her, rendering her unsympathetic to her teachers, who watched the cruelty happen every day without intervention. People hated her, but still she drew all the attention in the room, a power she didn't yet know she possessed.

While everyone was seated in church on Sunday morning, Hazel and Mary were seen marching out of Cottonwood in their Sunday best. The women, who were the hardest on Hazel, assumed she was taking the child to see her father; according to rumor, Hazel had never stopped seeing the Lakes boy. No one knew the truth, but all agreed that whatever happened between Hazel and Teddy Lakes couldn't have been that bad if she was still working in the Lakes home after all these years. And from their view, it looked like she was getting a lot out of it. Getting paid pretty good, too, they'd heard.

At school, the kids repeated the things they had heard their parents say. Mary came home from school one day gasping for air and inconsolable with questions about who her father was. The kids had called her a "mutt," a "golden retriever mix," circling her with the slur during recess as the teachers looked on.

"Don't they know I have to sit in the back of the bus too?"

Mary was barely six years old, too young for this conversation. Hazel would have preferred to sprinkle in the delicate bits over the years, like the trail of breadcrumbs in the fable Shirley Claire liked. The moment reminded Hazel that no matter how fair Mary was, she wasn't White. Her innocence couldn't be protected. The world forced Negro girls to mature faster than anyone else; the ugliness in the world was inflicted upon them first.

"His name is Theodore T. Lakes the Third," Hazel said, tapping the family name on the label of the tin can of snuff tobacco sitting on their kitchen table. "Named after his daddy and his daddy before him." She enjoyed a pinch of the tobacco in her bottom lip every night while Mary read aloud to her from the books she took from Mr. Lakes's study.

"Does everything belong to me too?" Mary asked. The red-and-white Lakes Tobacco label was plastered everywhere—on buses, buildings, and billboards. The family rode through town on a street-wide float in the state-famous Fourth of July parade every year.

Hazel flung her arm around their two-room house. "Does it look like it?"

"But why do the other kids say I'm rich?"

"'Cause they don't know any better."

"But my daddy is."

"Your father is, yes."

"But why—"

"That's just the way things are, you being a Negro girl. But we'll never go hungry or be out in the cold."

"Why hasn't he come to see me?"

"He doesn't live here anymore."

"Well, where is he?"

"Last I heard, Virginia."

"Won't he visit?"

"Maybe, but not to see you." Hazel pulled Mary onto her lap to deliver the most important sentence. "And should you ever see him on the street, you can't speak to him."

Mary's face crumpled, and Hazel hushed her before a tear spilled. "There are some truths in life you better come around to accepting sooner than later. This is one." With that, she slid her daughter to the floor and walked into the bedroom to retrieve her prized gold ball earrings from the drop board in the dresser.

Still seated on the floor, Mary looked up at her when she returned. "I hate this ugly place."

Hazel knew she was more embarrassed than hurt; the Cottonwood kids knew more about her than she knew about herself. "You know, people like you—all mixed up with a little this and that—have been born since even before America was called America. They were the sons and daughters of important men in this country."

Mary perked up a little.

"And trust me," Hazel said, "they couldn't call their daddies 'Daddy' either."

"How do you know?"

Hazel opened her left hand to show Mary the shiny gold spheres in her palm. "These earrings have been in our family since slavery times. Your grandfather four times over gave them to his slave, Elizabeth. They had two children. He gave us our eyes."

"Why?"

"Why what?"

"Why did he give them to her?"

"I suppose he loved her, and he was a rich man."

"Well, did he give her her freedom too?"

"No."

"Then what did she need earrings for?"

Hazel chuckled at her daughter's logic. "They can serve as a reminder."

"Of slavery?"

"No, of who you going to be. There are two types of people in this world, Mary: people with time to sit under the trees, looking up at the sky and pondering life"—she jostled the gold balls in her hand—"and those who end up hanging from those same trees, looking down on the life they might have had, had they been born different. You were born different, by the grace of God, so you get to choose. Choose the gold-earring life."

Mary looked at her with big eyes, unable to process what she was saying. But Hazel knew she eventually would—she'd be sure of that, if it was the last thing she did.

Mary took one of the earrings. "Your momma gave these to you?"

"Something like that."

"What was she like?"

Hazel smiled, realizing it was the first time Mary had asked. "She sang a lot." Looking back, Hazel realized her mother had been happy, despite her days spent cleaning fish and caring for a household of thirteen. Even if it all hadn't been her choice, she acted like it was. "She had a beautiful voice. She had our eyes, too, you know."

Mary sighed. "You told me. But I still want dark brown eyes like everyone else's."

Hazel sucked her teeth. "Take it up with God. You look how you look, and it ain't ever gon' change."

The next day, Hazel went up to the school to confront Mary's teacher, Mabel Wish. Most of Mary's troubles at school were attributable to things she couldn't control, and Mabel's hatred of Hazel was one of them. Mabel had been one of the self-appointed leaders of the teen group at church who had wanted nothing to do with the pregnant Hazel. Ostracizing her became an obsession when Mabel's boyfriend carried Hazel's groceries home one evening after seeing her struggling to calm an infant Mary. Mabel shared her speculations about Hazel and Teddy Lakes with anyone who would listen. Now, here was Hazel's child in her class, smart as a whip, pretty as a doll, and as unfortunate as one could be in terms of circumstance. Hazel suspected that it had felt good to Mabel to put the child in her place.

When she arrived in the school building, Hazel looked so angry Mabel thought she might hit her. The woman blamed all of Mary's problems on her high intelligence. Mary was writing stories during class and ignoring the lessons, all while the others were still struggling to read.

"You're the teacher. It's your problem if she's doing other things in class."

Hazel had taught Mary to read when she was four. She first made Mary memorize their bedtime poem, then taught her to read the words. Since then, they'd spent many afternoons at the park in Charlotte—and even more evenings, Mary with warm milk and Hazel with her spitting cup—immersed in a tale. As a result, Mary was emotionally and academically eons ahead of her age.

"I was going to suggest that Mary take her writing and reading lessons with the second graders."

"And when she writes and reads better than the second graders, then what?"

"We'll handle it then."

"Just like you handled the little ones?" Hazel gestured in the direction of the woods. "Mary ran home alone, in tears. No one cared about her safety. You all watched her go."

Mabel sighed. "It's your fault she's so different from everyone else."

"Everyone's different from everyone else, Mabel. My daughter can't help how she was born."

"She stands out like a sore thumb, like a spotlight—blinding to all of us."

"Is that why you're so mean? She's a little girl. Knows nothing of the way she came into this world."

"I didn't do anything to your precious daughter."

"You're right; you did nothing—when it was your job to protect her. My child was scared and confused. Kids asking her about a White man she'd never met, calling her names. I didn't want to have to tell her anything about him, but thanks to you, I did."

Mabel didn't look remorseful enough. Hazel heard herself hiss, "If you don't make the assaults on my daughter stop, I'll go door to door and tell *everyone* about you and the preacher." Mabel's back door could be seen from the slit in Hazel's outhouse, and on more than one occasion, Hazel had seen the preacher—the same man who had once publicly scolded her morality—hitching up his pants and creeping out her door.

"No one would believe you."

"The Bendses have seen it too." It was a lie, but Adelaide and Lefred were elders in Cottonwood, and Mabel knew no one would refute their testimony.

"You and that daughter of yours just think you're better than everyone else."

Hazel stomped back across the room, one second from physical contact, but instead pointed a finger half an inch from Mabel Wish's face. "Mary has to sit in the back of the bus, too, you know. She's a pupil at this school, instead of the shiny White one, cause I'm her momma. She can't help that. Shame on you."

———

Hazel was washing potatoes later when Mary came skipping through the door. Two girls in her class had broken from the group to walk home with her. Typically, Mary trailed the others, who didn't want to be seen with a "White girl" in the woods.

Hazel didn't look up from the sink. "Don't forget how they treated you before they had to be nice."

"But they said sorry."

Hazel picked up a knife and began peeling a potato as she felt the urge to tell her daughter the truth. "I went and talked to your teacher." Hazel had seen Mary picking flowers during recess that afternoon, at the edge of the school grounds where the wild roses grew. She waited until her back was turned to cross the field to the building.

"Today?" Mary's eyes sparkled and turned the Atlantic blue they did when she was happy. She wrapped her thin arms around Hazel's waist. "I knew it! I didn't see you but I could feel you!"

Hazel, whose hands were still occupied, bent to kiss the top of her head. "I hope you'll always be able to feel me, baby."

CHAPTER 6

Elise

Sunday morning, October 29, 2017

The rain started around 3:00 am. Still on the Perch, Elise watched her mother abandon her teacup on the tiny table in the labyrinth's center in favor of her flat-ironed hair, which she covered with both hands to sprint through the path, up the porch steps, and inside the sliding glass kitchen doors. Elise climbed in then too.

When the rain began to beat and splatter against the windows, Elise changed into her workout clothes, expecting to be able to go to the gym that morning with some privacy. Moisture gave Los Angeles residents, even the celebrity stalkers, pause about commuting outside of necessity. A single accident—likely in a town where perpetual sunshine caused drivers to respond to any degree of rain as if it were hail—could deadlock the entire city. The loss of precious weekend hours to traffic could cause even the meekest Angeleno to lose it.

Beyond that, Elise had worked out at 6:00 am most mornings for years, so the market was oversaturated with pictures of her sweaty style exiting the Tracy Anderson Method studio. Scandal or not, no paparazzi would venture out so early, in the rain, for a photo they couldn't sell.

And if they did, Elise didn't care. For the past week, her bedroom had been her gym, and it was an inadequate substitute.

When her sisters woke up to join her, she reminded them about the photographers' aggression, but they insisted. Relieved they weren't followed when Andy turned onto the freeway, Elise suggested breakfast on Melrose afterward. "We'll get there at seven-thirty—hours before the brunch rush." They'd be fed and gone before the devoted foodies willing to brave the downpour arrived. It was a gamble, but it would make for a good memory, important in a time that felt so wistfully orchestrated.

Breakfast anywhere but at home was impossible after their workout; the paparazzi now crowding the alley behind the gym would follow them and obliterate everyone's peace. Fame begot privilege, but you traded it for freedom. The St. John sisters preferred not to subject others to their inconveniences.

Elise stayed behind Andy. Always her first line of defense, the six-foot-six, 320-pound former pro football player was a fortress. He elbowed his way through, using his arms as a barricade against the photographers, but they slung their cameras into the sisters' faces despite his girth and arm span. Cold air hit Elise's sweaty back as Noele gripped the back of her T-shirt. Lens shutters snapped like the sound of an annoying toy as they began the twenty-five-foot walk to Andy's nondescript black Range Rover, parked in the middle of the street. They maintained their composure: heads and eyes down, sunglasses on, unresponsive to the prying chorus desperate for answers:

What happened to Kitty?

How does it feel to be six hundred million dollars richer?

Why did Kitty Karr leave her money to you?

How did she die?

They crowded the car for shots through the windshield and side windows.

"Holy shit." Noele covered her face with a towel and slid down into the second-row seat behind Elise.

"I told you."

Giovanni waved to the cameras between the front seats, showcasing her D-cup breasts stuffed into Elise's B-cup-sized sports bra.

Elise pulled the waistband of her sister's stretch pants. "Can you not?"

"Dad's right—everyone has to eat." Giovanni climbed over the seats into the third row as Andy stuck his middle finger out of the driver's window. He revved the gas. "Have some respect, assholes! They're in mourning. All of Hollywood is." The photographers scattered like ants to follow in their cars.

"You shouldn't have said that." Elise met Andy's brown eyes.

"I'm sick of them," he said, making a fast left. "Damned parasites. Profiting off others' pain—it's not right."

"They didn't conceptualize the industry, Andy."

"It's fine." Giovanni spoke up from the back row. "He said 'all of Hollywood.'"

Elise didn't bother to turn around. "'All of Hollywood' hasn't become a part of the narrative."

Rebecca's call to Elise's phone sounded through the car's Bluetooth speakers. Knowing she was calling to bitch about them being photographed, Elise silenced it and texted her: BUSY WITH THE FAM. CALL WHEN OTW.

"Is she coming tonight?" Noele asked.

"Of course."

Her sisters whispered about this behind her back. Giovanni spoke for them both. "What does she think we should do about Kitty?"

"I don't know," Elise said. "I haven't asked, and she hasn't said."

"She would know how to handle it," Noele said.

"I doubt that. She hasn't once mentioned the inheritance." Elise knew Rebecca was avoiding talking about the racist invective that had erupted online—which, shamefully, she let her get away with.

"Are you guys still fighting?" Giovanni asked.

"We're not fighting; we fundamentally disagreed."

"I'm sure that for her, learning you had opinions about Black Lives Matter was shocking."

"Sadly."

Aaron's call came through the speakers next; she silenced it too. A text illuminated her screen in the same second: WYD?

"Who said we're not to comment on Kitty?" Giovanni said.

"Mom decided. Okay? *Mom.*" Elise tapped Andy to ask him to turn up the radio.

Giovanni's voice rose above it. "I thought you didn't talk to her about it?"

Elise hit Andy on the arm. "Louder, please."

"Take it easy," he mumbled, before passing a small joint and lighter over his shoulder to her. Elise tapped him twice to say thank you as he sped onto the freeway on-ramp.

She rolled down the window and lit the joint as they picked up speed for a few minutes before slowing again in traffic. Her exhalation matched the gray morning. Paparazzi were still trailing them, but driving slower than normal in the rain. She didn't care if they got a picture. Aaron, of course, very much did; she scanned the paragraph he'd written about her selfishness in leaving her parents' house. Elise hid his alerts and scanned her playlists.

Cloudy days made Elise imagine they were all caricatures in a snow globe, being overturned and peered at as the elements of their world settled. The thought of something bigger, of a greater plan, comforted her, and with it, some of her grief lifted. The whisking of tires down the slick freeway, the smacking of sheeted rain on car windows, and Tupac—"How Long Will They Mourn Me?" started the week's playlist—created a symphony that put her into a meditative state.

The past year had made this practice—workouts, playlists, and weed—routine. Sanctioned by the two people she spent the most time with, Andy and Rebecca, it kept her sane despite fame's accomplice, the paparazzi, on nearly twenty-four-hour surveillance that simultaneously isolated and exploited her.

Music was both a distraction and mood boost, and when she combined it with a workout, she was able to zone out. It was in that state, all sweaty and strong, that she had found the courage to share a real opinion on her public platform. She needed some of that courage now. Hearing her sisters' whispers again, she turned. "What?"

"I didn't know you smoked." Noele was always ready for an interrogation.

"Why? You don't?" Elise asked.

"I do. I just didn't know you did." Noele had to be the authority on everything.

"It's too early to be high." Giovanni's voice peaked on the end of the sentence, and her freckled nose scrunched with disapproval.

"Why? I'm off until Friday." Elise knew Giovanni hadn't forgotten about her shoot. A *Vogue* cover was one of her dreams too.

"Nothing prior to?"

"No, I gave them exclusivity."

"Before or after Kitty?" Giovanni sounded drier.

"Before," Elise said. Not expecting congratulations, Elise relit the joint and put her feet up in the seat, leaning her body against the door. Her hair flew out of the open window, drying and growing in volume with each second. Andy hit the car's door locks.

She passed the joint to Noele, who held it, ripping open a bag of trail mix with her teeth. "So you're not going to talk about her?"

"No."

"Have they asked?" Giovanni rubbed a wipe over her face before tossing the plastic package over the seat to Elise.

Elise lied. "I don't know."

Andy accelerated up the driveway to the estate. Midway to the house was a row of catering and party rental vans parked in the grass.

"How many people are coming to Kitty's memorial?" Noele fought against a cough as she handed the joint back to Elise.

"Was supposed to be twenty-five," Elise said.

"Mom said seventy-three. I'm surprised Kitty had twenty-five people to invite," Giovanni said, in defense of their mother's logic. She reached over Noele for the joint from Elise, who passed it, declining to remind her sister of how "early" it still was.

"Kitty knew half the world," Elise said. "She just didn't see them a lot."

"So, old people."

"It's not a party," Elise reasoned, suddenly worried that the vans weren't for Kitty's memorial.

"Isn't the memorial at Kitty's house? Why are the vans here?" Noele asked.

"Bet Mom didn't cancel her birthday party," Giovanni said. She finished the joint and tossed it through the window onto the pavement.

Elise threw her a look of annoyance as they climbed out of the car. "Halloween isn't even her real birthday." Sarah had been born in September, like Kitty, but she claimed Halloween after moving into the Bel Air house because it was her favorite holiday and the new house was a "dream" to decorate.

Elise had long suspected that her mother's affinity for celebrations had little to do with sentimentalities and was, rather, an urgent need for distraction. When they were younger, she'd sometimes throw a party simply because it was a Tuesday.

CHAPTER 7

Mary

August 1946

The COLOREDS ONLY signs were always smaller than the WHITES ONLY signs. They were always older, dirtier, as if they'd been hanging for centuries, as opposed to the WHITES ONLY signs that always looked new, despite being printed or handwritten.

Mary stood pin straight in the bus aisle, looking up at the COLOREDS ONLY sign that swung by a rusty, bent wire above her head. She planted her feet, bracing herself, as the driver took yet another turn too fast. Her momma's hand was heavy and hot on her right shoulder, pulling her in close to ensure that not even her head crossed the line marked in the air. She eyed the WHITES ONLY sign neatly bolted in all four corners at the front of the bus.

The White section was empty except for a young woman, her fussy baby, and her husband, who had moved to the first row to talk to the bus driver. His legs were stretched across the aisle, feet up in the empty seat.

Besides their conversation and the baby, the bus was silent, despite the crowding in the back. That's how Negroes behaved in public spaces, even when their bodies often dominated it. More Negroes rode the bus than Whites, because many Whites had at least one car. The bus was unusually crowded that Sunday—besides the bumpy two-hour ride to Charlotte, most Negroes didn't want to spend their only day off around White folks who rode public transportation for leisure on the weekends—but it was late August, and the start of school made the trip imperative for some.

Mary was half-Negro and half-White—like the bus, like the world. She used to look for the delineating line, imagining one hidden somewhere, drawn with chalk. For whenever she left Cottonwood, she encountered Jim Crow.

"He's their superhero. Gives them power over us, lets them get their way. If they didn't have him, they'd have to do their own work—really try."

"So worried about making sure we don't step an inch over the line. A lot of 'em near as poor as us."

"And lazy."

Behind closed doors, Hazel and Adelaide talked about White folks like dogs. Everyone did.

Without Bessie as a buffer between her and Mrs. Lakes, Hazel was bothered by her idle time.

"I pray every day for the blindness to be removed from their eyes. I get so mad sometimes, I want to stab it out!" Except for work, Adelaide never left Cottonwood anymore, to avoid interaction with Whites.

The women howled, ignoring Lefred's warnings that they'd wake Mary, who always fell asleep after dinner on the Bendses' living-room couch.

"Aw, she ain't sleep," Hazel said. "She over there listening to every word we say." Feeling her momma staring, Mary giggled.

Hazel pointed at her. "We have to make our own luck. Be twice as smart, three times as good—but don't you let them know it."

To Mary, Jim Crow was a trickster: sometimes friend, sometimes foe. In Charlotte, he was her superhero, too, and gave her freedom to skip on the sidewalks and play in the clothing racks. At home, Jim Crow was foe to her and everyone she knew. He kept her classmates, who couldn't cross the line like she could, on a short leash. Mary felt guilty for being able to escape, for the spurts of freedom, the luck she could never share. Not even Adelaide knew the game she and her momma played in Charlotte.

In Cottonwood, adults were dictators. You spoke only when you were spoken to, and your preferences were immaterial. There was love, and lots of food, but lists of rules:

- *Use lotion.*
- *Go to church every Sunday.*
- *Keep your legs closed.*
- *Don't take wooden nickels.*
- *Keep your hair neat.*
- *Don't look White folks in the eye.*
- *Mind your manners.*
- *Don't call adults by their first names.*

There were rules about the bus, and the schools, and the sidewalks, and where they could live, and where they could work. Eventually Mary stopped asking why, because no one ever gave an answer that made sense. She did what she was told with the utmost compliance, having learned very early in life that breaking Jim Crow's rules often meant death. Days before third grade started, Joshua Hunt, one of the high schoolers in Cottonwood, was found with a cracked skull and broken ribs in the woods, just off the path they all took to school. He'd been beaten with a baseball bat and died at home a few days later.

Additions to the warning lists were always made after an atrocity, further shrinking the width and breadth of their world.

Don't go in that store no more.

Follow the rest of the class home down Johnson Street.

Stay from around that field.

With Joshua, there was only anger—no explanations, no takeaways to be had. An agile athlete who, at only fifteen, was invited to practice by the head coach of the White college baseball team (there was no Negro college team), his death had devastated Cottonwood, but the guilty parties boasted without fear. Mr. Atkins, who lived across the street from Hazel and Mary, was a cook at the Collins Street diner and overheard some White men admitting to have burnt a cross on the coach's lawn for even asking the boy to attend practice. They had intended to just scare the boy, but *that stupid nigger raised his bat, and we had no choice.*

The woods became haunted, and Mary, like the rest of her schoolmates, started filing out in a line and around their perimeter to school. Mary hated the extreme dead of winter and the swelter of summer but found that North Carolina's beauty prevailed all year long in the thicket of the trees surrounding Cottonwood. Icicles glistened on barren limbs in January, green fuzz sprouted in late April, and vibrant pink, yellow, and purple blooms came in early June. By the middle of September, yellow, orange, and red leaves blanketed the ground almost two inches thick, creating a perfect palette for her birthday that always seemed to match the icing on her birthday cake. That year, the autumn colors resembled the various stages of drying blood.

It wasn't until they left the bus station on arrival in Charlotte that Jim Crow became a friend. Mary welcomed him because only then did the light change, the air lift.

It grew heavier, stickier again at the bus stop at the corner of Ardsley and Kings Drive. The last stop before the expressway, it was where her momma got off for work.

The Lakes mansion sat on the corner diagonal to the bus stop. Situated on a hill, the white brick, four-story house was in the wealthiest part of Winston-Salem, where all the houses were set back from the street, lined with thick-trunked oak and maple trees that had been growing for hundreds of years. Their boughs and that late summer's lush green leaves canopied the road, revealing patches of sky through their entanglement.

In that afternoon's light, the red front door of the Lakes mansion shone like a beacon. Mary had not been there in years but used her imagination about what lay behind that tomato-red door to put herself to sleep.

Mary used to believe it was Jim Crow who forbade her parents' love, that her father had left Winston finding it unbearable to live minutes away and not see them. Hazel shattered her delusions. "He doesn't think about, let alone love, either one of us."

"What about my grandma? Does she love me?"

"*So* much, but she's in heaven."

"No, the one who makes me cakes. Does she love me?"

"People can tell you they love you three times a day and still treat you any kind of way when it really comes down to it."

Knowing it was the Lakeses who made sure they had food on the table, Mary assumed that meant yes. Now entering the fourth grade, she rarely thought about the Lakeses, until her birthday, of course. The cake was always pretty, but messy after the humidity of the Indian summer melted the icing. Most of it ended up in the trash.

The bus lurched forward after the White family debarked. Mary stumbled backward against her mother, whose body caused a domino effect behind them. Mary steadied herself just in time to see the driver, with a neck the width of his head, chuckle before taking the very next turn too hard and too fast. In the rearview mirror, his face turned pink-red with laughter, and a Cheshire grin disfigured him. She'd heard about the evil that made people mean for sport. It was that day she'd see it twice: Jim Crow had the power to possess.

———

Hazel bought Mary a vanilla ice cream cone as soon as they arrived in Charlotte; usually a part of their end-of-the-day routine, it was a reward for her composure on the bus. Happy and high on sugar, Mary followed her mother through Ivey's to the children's section but became distracted by the colors in the makeup displays and ran headfirst into one of the White ladies spraying perfume.

Mary gasped as ice cream dribbled down the woman's black suit skirt. "I'm sorry!" She took a jerky step back, and the entire scoop toppled and splattered on the marbled floor between them. Knowing she'd done a horrible thing, Mary began to cry as the woman looked around. "Who are you here with?" Her long blond braid squiggled on her back like a snake.

Mary pointed to Hazel, whose eyes hit the floor as they always did around White folks. Mary flinched when the woman barked at her mother.

"Are you just going to stand there? Clean this!"

Hazel's head dropped chin to chest. "I'll need a mop, ma'am."

Mary went for the tissues on the counter—"I can do it"—but the woman grabbed her arm. "You know better than that," she hissed. "That's what your mammy is for." She pointed to Hazel and then, a second later, because Hazel hadn't yet moved, yelled. "Get them."

"A mop would be better, ma'am," Hazel repeated.

"You think you know better than me?" Spit flew out of the woman's mouth.

Frozen in front of the stranger who asserted herself as a greater authority than her mother, Mary shifted her eyes as Hazel walked the ten feet to retrieve the tissues sitting only inches from the woman's shoulder. She sank down on all fours in her best Sunday dress—the light-blue one with the lace collar that she'd gotten on sale before Easter—and wiped the floor at their feet. Mary watched the smear grow, as the footsteps of other patrons navigating around the scene became louder and continuous in her ear. They never broke their stride, immune to the sight of a Negro woman down on all fours. Mary didn't want to look, either, and her eyes drifted to the second floor, where a White girl about her age was peering down over the rail.

The sweet smells of milk and vanilla invaded Mary's nose, making her feel claustrophobic and then sick. It was the day she lost her appetite for ice cream.

"You're making it worse." The woman smirked to a coworker behind a counter.

Hazel didn't look up nor change her tone. "I need a mop." Only Mary could hear her cursing the woman.

The woman scoffed. "Just leave it. I'll call the janitor."

Hazel rose, adjusting her suit jacket.

"What are you doing in here anyhow?"

Hazel nodded at Mary. "School clothes."

"Perhaps ice cream *after* shopping next time."

"Yes, ma'am."

The woman studied Mary. "Her eyes are striking. Is she Spanish?" She reached to touch Mary's cheek and, instead of recoiling like she wanted to, Mary froze like a mannequin, understanding the woman's dominion over her.

"No, ma'am," Hazel said. Had the woman had the courage to look Hazel in the eye, she might have realized the answer to her own question. Instead, having lost interest, she flicked her wrist. "Well, go on now."

Mary watched the woman as the escalator ascended to the second floor, hating everything about her, including the way she punched and held the phone buttons down longer than necessary to call the janitor.

Her mother pulled her against her side. "Don't pay that woman no mind."

"Why did she ask if I'm Spanish?" Mary didn't know what someone "Spanish" looked like.

"Because she didn't believe you could be mine."

Mary fell silent. For in that moment, if only for a second, Mary had wished that she wasn't her mother's daughter. She wanted to be that girl on the second floor, looking over the rail. Had she not been her mother's daughter, it wouldn't have hurt so much to see her crawl.

Hazel would remain the king and queen of Mary's world, but the encounter lodged an insecurity in her that became the undercurrent of her soul. She was now acutely aware that there was someone else, someone bigger, meaner, in charge over them all. She kept this realization to herself, sensing it would embarrass her momma to know Mary had just discovered how little control she had over Mary's life and her own.

In the children's department, Hazel handed her three blouses. "Take these and go sit with that girl."

Cross-legged on the bench was the girl Mary had seen. She shook her head.

Hazel bent over to make eye contact, which made Mary feel like she was looking in the mirror. It calmed and scared her all at the same time. "You're going to have to talk to people when we're out."

Mary didn't know what to talk to that White girl about. The older she got, the more nervous around White people she became. Mary may have looked White, but she spent every moment of her life, except the four to six hours every Sunday when they were in Charlotte, being Negro.

"Now, take these blouses, go over there, and say hello. I'll get you when I'm done."

Mary dragged her feet across the white marble floor, scuffing the toes of her black dress shoes.

Before Mary could speak, the girl wiggled her tongue at her through the gap between her front teeth. "I'm Lillian." She slid over to make room for Mary to sit.

Mary didn't move but introduced herself using her full first name.

"Mary Magdalene? That's a funny name," Lillian said. Her face was round and rosy like the pair of ruby studs in her ears. They sparkled in the overhead light. Mary's hands went to her own unpierced earlobes.

"It's in the Bible."

"My momma says religion was given to make us feel that suffering is noble. It's not." Lillian nodded to the left, where a short Negro woman was looking through swimsuits. "That's my mother." The woman had hair straight enough, like Mary and Lillian's, to be brushed smooth into a bun without grease, but her skin was the color of bread crust, too brown for her to pass.

Mary had never seen a pair like herself and her mother. Mary pointed at Hazel, still at the blouses rack. "That's mine."

Lillian didn't seem surprised. "How old are you?"

"Almost nine."

"You're small for your age."

"How old are you?" Reference to her height made Mary feel like she was being challenged or sized up, assumed to be the weakest.

"I'll be twelve in three days and I'm already taller than my mother." Lillian slumped over. "I wish I was small like you. I'm growing out of all my favorite clothes. I'll probably be tall like my father." Lillian stuck her tongue out.

"I like your dress." Mary touched the pale-yellow fabric. The white lace sash and trim matched Lillian's ruffled socks and white patent-leather shoes. Mary scrunched her toes in her black ones and tucked them under the bench, regretting ruining them. They were hand-me-downs from church, but Mary had loved them before seeing Lillian's new ones. The girl's dress was new, too; Mary could tell by the smoothness of the fabric it had never been washed.

"Thank you; it's my favorite. We're here to take my birthday picture."

If she were Lillian, it would have been her favorite too. Their skin was the same color, that of cream atop fresh churned butter—so Mary knew it would look good on her. Mary wondered how many dresses the girl had. Mary only had two good ones, a light-pink one and the tan one she wore at that moment. Hazel only took her shopping when the season turned or when she'd outgrown something, so most trips to Charlotte were spent looking.

Lillian touched her arm. "Maybe you can get your picture taken too."

Mary turned to see her mother talking to Lillian's at the coat rack on the back wall. Hazel's ease told Mary that they knew each other.

"I'll go next month, for my birthday," Mary said. It was a lie; Hazel thought portraits were a waste of money. *People see themselves every day in the mirror, why they need a reminder is beyond me.* Hazel, everyone said, was a beauty—*prettier if she ever did something with herself*—but Hazel only dressed on Sundays. The rest of the week, she barely brushed her teeth, let alone put on lipstick. *What do I need to look pretty for those people for? Pretty is as pretty does, and most of these folks ugly inside and out.*

Both mothers came over, and Hazel motioned Mary to her. "Come meet Mrs. Catherine." She said her name in three syllables: Cath-er-ine.

Mrs. Catherine bent to Mary's eye level and then looked back up at Hazel. "What a beautiful child."

Dressed fancy, like a White lady, Mrs. Catherine wore heavy face powder and was the color of cinnamon up close. Mary wondered if the powder was meant to cover her freckles or lighten her complexion, because it didn't work for either aim. Lightening one's complexion, only to still be too dark to pass, seemed as pointless as a Negro playing paleface. But Mary decided that if Mrs. Catherine was one of those Negroes who worshipped White traits, Hazel wouldn't be so friendly to her. She talked about Mr. Ford, the Lakeses' butler, who was enamored by the way Mrs. Lakes's gray-streaked hair blew in the wind. He came in the kitchen every morning to watch her from the window.

"What happened down there today wasn't your fault," Mrs. Catherine said.

Mary hated that there had been two witnesses. "I should have been looking where I was going."

Mrs. Catherine squeezed her hand. "It was an accident." She led Mary to the railing, where the woman with the braid was scowling at a salesgirl who was being flirted with. "She's sad-looking. She saw your momma with those eyes and cheekbones and wanted to spit. When people don't like themselves, it makes them mean. You understand?"

When Mary smiled, Mrs. Catherine beamed at Hazel, as if she had the magic touch.

Mary left Charlotte that day with two dresses instead of her school clothes.

"You'll be fine in your summer things for another few weeks. These dresses will serve you better than anything you have."

CHAPTER 8

Elise

Sunday morning, October 29, 2017

"Have a good workout?" Sarah wiggled her fingers at her daughters from the gray marble island. Even first thing in the morning, with her hair bushy from the early-morning rain, she looked perfect.

"I enjoyed it," Giovanni said.

"It was way too hot in there. I thought I was going to faint." Noele opened the refrigerator.

"The more you do it, the stronger you'll get," Sarah said. Her hands went to her own taut waist. She had maintained a lithe figure into her midfifties through daily exercise, a habit only Elise adopted. They sometimes worked out together. Elise hoped to look as good as her mother did when she reached her age. At thirty-one, people said Elise looked twenty-two and glowed like she was made from fairy dust. She went for a glass of water and took her vitamins, watching Noele remove the cake stand topper.

"Cake after your workout?" Sarah exclaimed.

"My body's already in calorie-burning mode; seems like the best time to me." Noele chopped a thick slice and palmed the icing side.

Sarah's eyes stretched, watching as Noele pranced to the counter.

"Why are all those vans outside? I thought Kitty's memorial was at her house," Elise said.

"It is," Sarah said.

"How much food did you order?"

"Sushi can be light, so we'll have teriyaki stations too." Sarah winced at the screech of the barstool legs across the floor as Giovanni pulled herself in toward the counter and reached over Noele for a banana in the fruit bowl. Noele's first bite of cake sent a waterfall of crumbles onto the gray marble countertop.

"People will never leave," Noele said, wiping her mouth with the back of her hand. Sarah handed her a paper towel.

"How many people confirmed?" Elise asked. "I didn't sign up to make a videotaped speech."

Sarah put her hands in the air, cracking at last under her daughters' pressure. "They're setting up for my party, okay?" She pointed to Noele. "I'll make you some eggs with that. Anybody else?" She didn't wait for answers before extracting the egg carton from the refrigerator.

Her daughters negotiated behind her back about who was going to confront her. They decided it was Elise. "With the news about the inheritance out, the party is going to be a circus."

"How fitting! The theme is 'Mystic Circus.'" Sarah started juggling three eggs.

Elise had little patience for her mother's joking. Sarah was a masterful illusionist: she understood how it would look to have the party under the circumstances but didn't care. She didn't want anything to ruin her fun. "It'll look like we're celebrating Kitty's death, or worse, the inheritance. Not to mention at the memorial tonight—all the tents going up on the other side of the hedges? Mom, come on."

"I told her to cancel it." Their father came from the hallway, rubbing his eyes. He was always the last to rise, having spent part of most nights in his studio. He shuffled barefoot to the stove, tightening the belt of the dark-blue bathrobe Sarah had made for one of their early anniversaries. He wore it for a few hours every morning, despite the holes in the chest area that put his sparse, graying sprout of chest hair and the thin gold chain he never removed on display. He stooped to rest his chin on his wife's shoulder. "Can I have my eggs fried hard?"

"Celebrating my birthday looks bad?" Sarah kissed him before pointing at Elise. "You're both still working. Everyone else took off."

"I've been off for a week, but you know I can't change my promotional obligations."

"And somebody has to keep these bills paid," James said. Everyone groaned. No matter how rich he'd become, James still had alerts set on his financial accounts for transactions over a hundred dollars and wore his gold Rolex every day, even with his sweats. Elise looked at his wrist then to see it there, knowing he'd slept in it.

Elise raised her voice to compete with her mother's clanking an eggshell against the aluminum bowl. "And no one else took off. Giovanni's show is on hiatus, and Noele doesn't have a job."

"I do too!"

"Maybe," Elise said, referencing their conversation from the previous day.

"Noele should be in the studio with me." James flicked her in the head. He was coming to his wife's rescue, Elise knew, trying to change the subject.

"Dad, for real. Stop." Noele jabbed their father's side. "You and Mom are wearing me out."

"How many people have RSVP'd?" Elise walked past her mother at the stove for another glass of water from the filtered spout.

"Everyone. The party is on, and that's just that."

"Well, I'm not going." Elise leaned over the sink to open the window, gagging on the smell of her mother's overcooked eggs. Sarah only cooked three things well: lasagna, spaghetti, and tacos. Being the busy working actress, Sarah had relied on first her mother and then Julia, their cook, to feed her family. "It's just another opportunity for us to be questioned and gossiped about."

Sarah shoveled the eggs onto Noele's plate and, in another swoop, removed the last of the cake. "You know how to not answer."

"Perhaps, but it's hypocritical, don't you think?" Feeling her mother's glare on her back, Elise walked out of the kitchen and up twenty stairs to the south wing. Elise and her sisters had learned of the contents of their mother's semirecent book in its *New York Times* review, which hailed it as "an honest testament to the perils of motherhood and marriage despite the celebrity slant." Sarah had spent two years writing about her ambivalence toward marriage and motherhood—a feeling, she wrote, that never went away, even after three children. It had been a year since its release, but her words were impossible to forget.

———————————

Elise hurried past the family photographs lining the wall and into the den, collapsing at the arm of the couch, where the floor vent allowed for the best eavesdropping on the kitchen.

"I have a right to celebrate my birthday," Sarah was saying. She sounded unsure.

"A less elaborate night would be more appropriate," James replied. "Or a postponement."

"I can't cancel now; I'll lose the money."

"I'd like to see them try to keep my money." Her father sounded like he had food in his mouth—probably also cake. "Just scale back."

Her mother sighed. "I'd hoped it would do your sister some good."

"*Your* birthday party is to cheer up Elise?" Noele asked with obvious uncertainty.

"She needs some fun. She's taken Kitty's death so hard, and she's been so busy, I fear she's going to exhaust herself."

"She's not eating," Noele said. "You should see that class she does—I'm worried she's developing some kind of eating disorder."

"It's nervous energy, and there are worse habits," Sarah said. "I need you girls to help your sister. She never left Kitty's side these last few weeks."

"She slept there," James said, cosigning his wife's concern.

"You told us," Giovanni said.

"Why do you think we went with her this morning?" Noele said.

It was nice to hear everyone rallying in solidarity on her behalf, but Elise resented her mother deflecting the attention onto her.

Sarah sucked her teeth. "I can't believe Kitty would put all of this on her. Selfish to the core, until the end." She began to detail Kitty's cataloging system. "Dozens of audio recordings: instruction for how her belts should be folded, how to preserve clothes, her old letters and photographs, how to clean certain pieces of her jewelry—it's insane."

Giovanni laughed, so Sarah elaborated, happy someone else thought it was as ridiculous as she did. "And this auction, my God . . ." The coffee grinder came on, drowning out everything but her mother's contempt for Kitty.

Elise pushed the rose window open and climbed onto the Perch. She'd expected her mother to display a greater degree of respect, considering all Kitty had done for their family.

Only some of the rumors about Kitty were true. She was an eccentric, recluse Virgo writer who hoarded her memories and accomplishments inside her home, but she didn't lock herself inside, nor had she committed suicide. Kitty simply didn't have much admiration for the human race, and with the exception of a handful of people, she wanted to be left alone to create the characters that continued to add to her assets. The St. Johns were among the lucky because the person closest to Kitty had been Sarah's mother, Nellie.

Kitty, the White screen siren, and Nellie Shore, a Black single mother, had met at the peach bin in a grocery store in 1968, when Kitty invited a then-five-year-old Sarah to audition at Telescope Film Studios. After Sarah's casting in *The Daisy Lawson Show*, Kitty and Nellie became close, with Nellie always on set with her young daughter.

Their friendship was kept a secret outside the studio walls. Even after years of the show's success as television's first interracial sitcom, Telescope worried fans and advertisers wouldn't approve of interracial friendship behind the scenes. That was why, even today, people didn't know Kitty and the St. Johns were neighbors, let alone how close the families were. Life before social media had made that possible.

Kitty was the reason Sarah became the little Black darling America loved. Eventually, Sarah had a dressing room to rival Kitty's. Kitty had mentored her after the show ended, helping Sarah land roles not originally written for Black actresses. Kitty even introduced her to James, a union which sent Sarah skyrocketing emotionally, mentally, and professionally. After her husband died, Kitty moved next door to the St. Johns, where Nellie already lived as primary caregiver to Elise, Giovanni, and Noele.

When Nellie died, Elise was twelve, Giovanni was nine, and Noele was seven. Her care was replaced by a college-aged nanny, and Elise had started hiding out after school until dinner at Kitty's house, where she could talk about her grandma. Kitty missed Nellie, maybe even more than Elise, who felt as though her death had taken her family's heartbeat.

Hours would pass when Kitty started talking about the "golden years," a ten-year period she cited as the happiest of her life. Kitty had been an It girl in the late fifties and early sixties and found joy reminiscing about the parties and the legends she'd rubbed elbows with. Elise never got tired of hearing about her adventures, but the things Kitty never talked about were what mattered now.

Her mother was right about one thing: Elise did need comfort and insulation. Everyone was trying to manage her. Even Kitty had managed her mourning, managed her pain, giving her the truth in small doses, like a slow medicinal drip.

Kitty's Virgo efficiency was appreciated, but leaving the management of her afterlife in Elise's hands had been thoughtless. Kitty knew how hard Elise would take her death and that the aftermath would affect her in ways she couldn't have been prepared for.

She pulled half a joint from the old tin can Kitty had used as an outdoor ashtray and flicked the lighter: no flame. After four attempts and no light, she swore and hurled it off the Perch.

CHAPTER 9

Mary

August 1946

Lillian and Mrs. Catherine were waiting at the bus stop in Charlotte the next Sunday when Hazel and Mary arrived, and for years thereafter.

On that first Sunday, Catherine handed money to Lillian, with instructions to get their picture taken and have lunch. Mary pulled aside her mother, who had uncharacteristically deferred to Mrs. Catherine. "Where are you going?" They had never been apart in town for more than the few minutes it took Mary to change in the Whites-only dressing room of Ivey's.

"Around here somewhere. Stay with Lillian, hear?"

Lillian pulled Mary's arm. "We'll be fine," she called over her shoulder as they made their way down the street. "*À tout à l'heure, Catherine et Hazel.*"

"What did you say?" Mary asked.

"That I'd see them later, in French."

"You speak French?"

"French, Italian, and German." Lillian pulled her again, this time through the front doors of Ivey's, where the first floor was bustling with customers. She parked Mary in the shoe section. "If anyone asks, your mother went to the bathroom."

"Where are you going?"

Lillian sashayed away to the cosmetics counter and, while one of the salesladies was helping someone, took a perfume from among the testers. Mary froze as she watched Lillian then disappear behind the counter. She reemerged empty-handed.

"What did you do?"

"You'll see. Come on, let's go get our picture taken."

There was a line, but Lillian wormed her way past the White children with their parents and maids to the front. "Hi, Jack!" she said to the photographer.

He stopped clearing the small set to look for the speaker. "Hiya, Lilly!"

Lillian walked up to him. "Our father dropped us off between meetings. He can't be late to his next one."

Somehow, they were seated next. They posed on a bench with white umbrellas in front of a park background. They left with two free copies of the picture and two lollipops. Lillian put her arm around Mary's shoulder for them to look together. "Sisters," she said, before taking off into a run.

Mary, loving the adventure, entered Ivey's again breathless. Lillian left her to catch her breath and marched up to one of the salesladies. "I want to report a thief."

The woman trotted off and returned with a White man wearing glasses. He took them off to talk to Lillian. Mary watched as Lillian pointed at that lady with the blond braid. She hadn't seen her earlier.

"I saw her put a bottle of perfume in her purse," Lillian was saying as she walked with the man over to the counter. The blond lady stood erect, seeing the man. Mary couldn't hear the rest of the conversation, but watched the lady retrieve her purse with a puzzled look. The manager opened it and produced the perfume that Lillian had taken earlier from the counter. The woman's mouth dropped open as she began to make her case.

Lillian pointed back at Mary, as if to say, *We both saw her.*

The man motioned for the woman to come with him. They ascended the escalator, and this time, the woman watched Mary as she went.

A sly look crossed Lillian's face after they were outside. "Don't be mad."

"Thank you." Mary hugged Lillian, who grasped her back as if she was starved for touch. They started toward the diner near the bus station. "I get scared a lot."

Lillian nodded knowingly. "Because of mean people like her."

"Mean people at home too."

"White people?"

"And Colored."

"No one like us there, huh?"

Mary shook her head as they sat down at a table. There were other sunny-colored girls in Cottonwood, but no one as fair as Mary. And no one as smart; she could have skipped grades but opted not to. Mary had started pretending she didn't know something about whatever, to avoid becoming a target again.

"I get lonely too," Lillian said. "I don't have any friends."

Mary was startled by Lillian's honesty. "Me neither."

Lillian reached across the table for Mary's hand. "Now we have each other."

For the first time in almost a decade of living, Mary experienced what friendship felt like. It was nice to meet someone who didn't know her origins, and even rarer to meet someone White-but-not, like herself, who didn't judge her for breathing.

Mary rode home giddy, fueled by Lillian's revenge.

"What you giggling about?" Hazel asked. She looked pleased to see it.

"Nothing."

She wanted to tell Hazel but didn't, knowing she wouldn't approve.

Hazel raised her brows. "Did you two have fun?"

"It was the best day."

Charlotte was the only place Mary and Lillian's friendship existed, and they bonded, each being the only other person either knew whose mother encouraged such a game of make-believe. But that was where their similarities stopped.

Lillian moved in the White world as if she belonged in it. Sometimes it felt as though she went out of her way to forget her manners. She interrupted adults, bumped into them, didn't say please or thank you. She even called the waiters in the café by the first names on their uniforms. At first, Mary rebuked Lillian's behavior, until she realized no one else admonished her. Maybe manners were just Colored rules.

"You only follow rules because someone told you to," Lillian said as they walked into the park a few Sundays later. "So, pretend no one told you."

Lillian never seemed to consider reality. "I don't want to get in trouble," Mary protested.

"You can't. No one will know if they don't find out."

"What?" Mary rubbed her forehead. Lillian was always reasoning in circles around her. Even though she was three years older, she was the only friend close to being Mary's intellectual match. Mary thought Lillian was smarter because she could read, write, and speak in three languages. But on this count, Lillian was wrong. She acted like it was her right not to be what the world said she was. "No, I mean *trouble* trouble."

"Oh, like with White people?"

Mary rolled her eyes. "Yes."

"They're easy, because they don't want to see." Lillian tried to coach her. "Let's play a game." Lillian covered Mary's eyes. "As ever fine and good and lovely as you can imagine a world, hold on to that dream, open your eyes, and pretend that's what you see." Mary's eyes opened, and Lillian lightly pushed her in the direction of a group of four older girls smoking cigarettes. "Go get me a cigarette." The group were on a blanket, shuffling through magazines. Their laughter sliced through the breeze, and Mary's hair whipped across her face as she shook her head to say no.

"Stop being a scaredy-cat." Lillian gestured around the grassy field. "There aren't any Negroes anywhere, so we're free."

"What if they're mean?" Mary wasn't just timid because they were White;

she wouldn't have asked a group of Negro teenagers either. Teenagers were mean. "And you're not supposed to be smoking anyway."

"It's not about the cigarette; I'm trying to help you!"

"Help me with what?"

"You have to feel like you *belong* somewhere, Mary."

Mary felt like she belonged with her mother. "I don't want to."

"Fine." Lillian's head cocked to one side as she constructed a new plan. "You're going to do all the talking when we're in town."

"Fine!"

Lillian laughed at her stubbornness. "I love you, little friend."

Mary, relieved Lillian still liked her after her refusal, smiled as she rarely did, with teeth.

From then on, Mary was required to order for them, ask for directions, and get assistance. To Lillian's chagrin, Mary's manners stayed fully intact, but she occasionally attempted to please Lillian by interrupting the conversation of adults with an "Excuse me."

Lillian was indifferent to Mary's bold attempt.

———————————

Lillian had the best of everything, and Mary never saw her wear the same thing twice. Her clothes and hair ribbons were from France, and she and her mother spoke French between themselves. Hazel griped about how rude it was and mocked them with Adelaide.

Assuming Catherine was also a maid (Mary didn't know any Negro women who weren't in service), she wondered how they afforded the things they did.

"My mother is a governess for a family in Asheville," Lillian explained when Mary finally asked.

Mary was impressed. Governesses had a higher level of skill in the languages, ancient history, and cultural customs than teachers, and education received at institutions from which Negroes were prohibited.

"My grandmother was too. She was born free and passed—"

"Died?"

"She's dead now, but no—I mean she just up and left one day, went to go live as a White person."

Mary's eyes got big. "Forever?"

"Yes, many people in my family have." Lillian shrugged. "Guess learning to fit in is in my bones."

But Mrs. Catherine couldn't "pass," Mary thought. "My grandparents on my Negro side were sharecroppers, and their parents were slaves."

Lillian didn't comment. She prided herself on her family's upper-class history and was embarrassed by Mary's mention of her Blacker roots and the grim histories they unearthed.

Having only ever been aware of the differences between the way White and Negro people lived, Mary had never considered how her and her mother's lives may have differed from those of other Negroes. Mary had the necessities, but extras, despite Hazel's long hours, were always out of the question. Some Negro children lived in houses with two parents, like the ones in the movies, and *they* were the girls who took dance and music classes. And learned French. Maybe Lillian was one of those girls.

As curious as she was, Mary didn't ask any questions about that. It was rude to inquire about the things people didn't volunteer, so Lillian never mentioned her father, and Mary never mentioned hers.

Their conversation, like their Sundays, was rooted in fantastical tradition. They spent most afternoons in the movie theater. It was the coolest place in the summer and the warmest in winter. Hazel and Catherine joined them sometimes, watching from the back of the orchestra, both preferring it to the balcony.

The girls idolized the movie stars, with their blushed cheeks and silky hair. The films inspired chronicles about their futures as housewives, living next door to each other with maids of their own and six kids between them who were Boy Scouts and took ballet and swimming classes together. Their banker husbands would drive into the city together every day and watch football on Sundays. They volleyed stories back and forth each week, one picking up where the other left off.

When Mary was twelve, Hazel started doing two overnight shifts a week at the Lakeses'.

To busy herself while home alone, Mary acted out her stories. They helped to distract her from the violence that often trampled her fairy tales: someone's uncle, husband, or son was lynched; a cousin left town in the trunk of a car; someone's windows were smashed in; someone's daughter or wife was raped.

Lillian refused to talk about these things. She either changed the subject or ignored Mary altogether, leaving her to process the brutality internally, fear etched into her psyche. Mary began to understand that Lillian's lightness came from her ability to ignore things; that's how she knew White people could do it too.

When Lillian started menstruating two years ago, Catherine let her start wearing perfume and lipstick and curling her hair. "I told Catherine she might as well dangle her from a string," Hazel said.

All of Lillian's conversation started to center around marriage and babies instead of music and school. She had names chosen already for her future children—Jillian and Jackson—and the family dog, Max. Mary got a little bored with these stories and started writing out her own and reading them to Lillian.

When Mary started her cycle only months into her twelfth year, Hazel forbade anything to change, even to let Mary wear her long hair down.

"You want me to be ugly!"

"I don't want you saddled too young with babies." Knowing where this conversation could lead, Mary went back to her homework. Adelaide was best suited to endure her mother's burgeoning rants, especially after Hazel drank too much whiskey. Hazel didn't drink often, but when she did, she said things one's child should never have to hear. Mary was pretending to be asleep on the couch one night like always when Hazel's emotions got the best of her, and she was forced to listen past wanting to.

Hazel got low sometimes, and only Adelaide knew the depths. Sometimes, Hazel said she was "teetering."

It was a word Adelaide didn't like to hear. "You stop that talk. No one's ever going to hurt you again."

"Or love me, either, huh?"

Mary started high school with a class divided by who was going north after graduation and who was staying. Like almost everyone, Mary wanted to go. She dreamed about the West, moving to Los Angeles and becoming an actress. She'd write her own movies and live at the beach in a big white house with black shutters and a gravel driveway, like her favorite house on the White folks' side of town. She didn't share this fantasy with anyone, knowing it was an impractical goal for a White woman, let alone a Negro one. Even Lillian, as cultured as she was, would laugh. Besides, Mary couldn't imagine leaving her mother. Los Angeles was too far, and she doubted she'd ever convince Hazel to come.

"I'll get a job and take care of you," Mary promised her mother when the subject came up one fried-fish Friday. They were on the porch with lemonade and coleslaw, dipping the croaker in Hazel's perfect mix of tartar and hot sauce. Kids were jumping rope and chasing one another in the street. Puffs of red dirt swallowed their shoes and legs, dusting their skin with a thin, ashy film.

"I don't need taking care of," Hazel said with her mouth full. Pieces of cornbread shot out onto their porch railing, as if to illustrate how she couldn't renounce help fast enough. Somehow Mary believed her. Their house only had two rooms—it wasn't the best in Cottonwood, but it wasn't the worst—and they didn't have money for meat every week, but Hazel didn't seem to mind the frugality that governed their lives.

Lillian didn't care where she went. West or north, she just wanted to leave Asheville. She was debuting in a cotillion, and Catherine pressed Hazel to let Mary join. "She's bound to meet a nice boy."

Hazel refused, blaming money, as always, but Mary felt certain it was because Lillian was debuting in a White cotillion. Mary had for years suspected that Lillian, and maybe Catherine for that matter, passed beyond their Sundays in Charlotte. They had a level of comfort around White people Mary couldn't seem to catch up to, even with the weekly practice. Mary assumed that was why Lillian didn't say much about her life in Asheville.

Lillian and Catherine missed a few weeks of Sundays in Charlotte before the cotillion; Mary figured they were busy with preparations. Lillian had dance practice and had to memorize the collection of poems she'd written in French.

When the date of the cotillion came and went, and then another month passed, Mary inquired.

"They moved." Hazel was puzzled. "Lillian didn't tell you?"

"No. Where?"

"I don't know."

"Aren't they going to visit?"

"What makes you think we're that important?" Hazel chuckled. "People have lives, Mary, and everyone moves on."

CHAPTER 10

Elise

Early Sunday afternoon, October 29, 2017

The long, thick border of bushes and trees that separated the St. John property from Kitty's was dense to the naked eye. Invisible to anyone who didn't already know were three points of entry through the foliage. The one most often used was across the driveway from the St. Johns' kitchen door; it opened onto the dirt walking path encircling Kitty's enormous lot.

Already ahead of her sisters, Elise kicked up dust in her old black Converses, eyeing the Green Jungle—the wild thicket of trees, bushes, and flowers that surrounded Kitty's house and hid it from view on all sides. Built to resemble the park near her childhood home in Boston, Kitty preferred her replica because it stayed green all year. Every year, the homeowners' association pressured her to cut it down, citing it as a haven for wild animals, but they could never muster any proof.

"The site of some of our best plays," Giovanni said.

"I barely remember anything besides the tea party."

"I was only in it for the costumes," Noele said. Kitty had always offered her gowns and jewels equally for dress-up and, later, for special occasions.

"We thought we were being so mysterious." The girls preferred to playact among themselves rather than perform, so no one, not even Kitty, witnessed their productions. Elise pointed up. "Of course, Kitty could hear everything we said from the window in her writing room."

"I'm surprised Kitty didn't want her ashes spread out here." Noele pushed ahead of Elise, entering first through one of the four iron archways that led to the house.

"Spread?" Elise rubbed her arms, in the shade. She frowned at Noele, who expected an answer. "Kitty wouldn't risk her ashes being peed on by animals. Her final resting place is a solid-gold box."

Elise heard Noele snap a picture of their initials carved into the willow by the front door as she unlocked it.

All of the doors were glass, so that Kitty could enjoy her garden from inside. The house got ample light during the day, but at night, the perpetual shade of the jungle made it darker than dark and eerie, its interior illuminated only by table lamps and candles. Kitty had uninstalled all the overhead lights because they reminded her of being onstage. The result was a tomblike environment Kitty found comforting.

Giovanni and Noele lingered behind Elise, respecting her dominion over the mausoleum-like space. It appeared both cluttered and empty, due to the twenty-foot-tall ceilings and long hallways jumbled with furniture, mannequins, and rugs stacked like Fruit Roll-Ups.

It had taken a crew two days to sort things before Elise could even begin to tag, photograph, and log everything for liquidation, auction, display, and storage. Kitty had always insisted on doing her own cleaning, which she never did well or often enough. The dust was always inches thick, and the air heavy with cigarette smoke. Elise pointed to the neon Post-its on various items. "Yellow stays, green goes for appraisal, pink is for storage, and orange is for repair, then it's staying." Elise touched the edge of the dining-room table. "If there's no sticker, it's up for auction tonight."

"Mom said you needed our help, but it looks like you have everything covered."

"Still need to sort all her photos."

"I bet Kitty was the cutest baby."

"I haven't found a picture of her younger than nineteen," Elise said.

Giovanni shrugged. "Doesn't seem unusual for that time period."

"It's sad not to have at least one baby picture of yourself." Noele walked ahead of Elise again. "I'll take the elevator."

"It's off." The staircase was fifty deep steps and winded even Elise. They took their time as they ascended, admiring Kitty's wedding photos lining the wall. The romance between the studio's newest, youngest star and the new, inexperienced studio head had once been a scandal. She was the gorgeous ingénue and Nathan Tate was the dashing heir to the studio.

He and Kitty were grinning in every picture, the epitome of the perfect couple. It reminded Elise of the photographs of her and Aaron: the strained, wide-eyed, frozen joy.

"He was so handsome," Noele said of Nathan.

"Charlie Hunnam could play him for sure," Elise said.

"Were they happy?" Giovanni wanted to know.

Elise shrugged. "Happy enough, I guess." Kitty and Nathan's relationship, like her own, had had public rules and private ones. Along with the rest of the world, Nathan had been obsessed with his wife and never embraced her professional life outside of acting. "She said in death he rewarded her patience with him by leaving her everything."

———————

Oversized white pillar candles sat in the mouth of Kitty's bedroom fireplace and on the six windowsills. Kitty liked candles lit all the time, even during the day. Elise did so then, waiting for the quick but strong whiff of Kitty's perfume she was relieved to discover could be conjured by the flicker. When she'd first returned to pack, the first thing she did was light candles. Kitty's scent had swirled about her body, reminding her of its permanence. Elise closed her eyes then, hoping for the smell.

"Everything's gone," Giovanni interrupted, emerging from Kitty's closet. She was into fashion, made mood boards for her stylist, and attended every show during fashion week. She would have pursued modeling full-time if there had been any hope she was going to be of height. "I assume you claimed everything good already?" Giovanni quipped. Kitty had been petite, too, and her clothes would fit all of them.

"It's all photographed and cataloged. Rebecca has the book. Make requests before it's shipped to storage."

"There's some jewelry I'd like," Noele said.

"That's all of us," Giovanni retorted.

"I just want this." Elise ran her palm over the top of the oversized Louis Vuitton trunk at the foot of Kitty's bed. She'd perched there for the past few months as if it were an extension of the bed. Kitty never minded.

Noele fumbled with the trunk's brass lock. "Why? What's in it?"

"It was stale linen."

"Where are the pictures?" Noele yanked open a drawer in Kitty's six-drawer dresser. "Oh." It was stuffed to the brim. Every drawer in the room was the same. The prints were piled atop each other in haphazard fashion, their drugstore print jackets and negatives long gone. Elise had been perplexed as to why Kitty had used her bedroom dresser drawers for photo storage when there was room on the walls among the others displayed.

Noele pointed to the Louis Vuitton trunk. "Would have made sense to keep all of them in there."

"Kitty did a lot of things I don't understand." Elise grabbed a pile of photos. "Help me. Sorting first will make digitization easier."

Her sisters took her lead and began hauling armfuls from the drawers onto Kitty's bare mattress.

"Make a pile for pictures of Kitty with us, pictures on set, pictures of her with Nellie." Elise pointed to spots on the bed. "Be specific."

Noele's hand dived into the cluster, producing a photo of Kitty and her only sibling, a sister, Emma. "It must have been hard to be Kitty's sister." Kitty had been striking in her youth, prettier than most humans.

"Or friend," Giovanni said.

"Or the woman behind her at the grocery store," Elise said.

They exchanged smiles of nostalgia, remembering the one-up game they used to play as children.

"Eventually people find their path—look at you," Giovanni said, snatching the photo out of Elise's hands.

Elise nudged Giovanni with her hip, and her sister cried out in pain. "You're very bony. Are you on one of Mom's diets?"

"No . . ." She wasn't dieting on purpose, but her appetite had waned over the last few weeks.

"The stress. That makes sense." Giovanni returned to the photo, comparing it to another Noele handed her. "Did Emma have kids?"

"I don't think so. When she died, it was a week before her body was found."

Noele mimicked being sick at the thought.

"Their parents died when they were young, right?" Giovanni asked.

"Yes." It was one of the few things Elise remembered Kitty saying about her childhood.

"How old were they?"

"I'm not sure."

"Wasn't their mother a teacher?"

"I'm not sure."

"For all the time you spent over here, it seems like you'd know more." Giovanni crossed her arms.

"Gio, she taught her to read when she was barely four, but I don't know if she was a teacher."

"These are just the basic life questions no one can answer." Giovanni was referring to Kitty's obituary, which read like a résumé. Elise had emailed her draft around, but no one could piece together common facts to pen the usual phrases. Kitty had shared so much about her triumphs and mistakes in life, Elise had never considered what she didn't know.

"Are you trying to make me feel worse?"

"She's not, but you seem like you're lying about something." Noele entered the conversation, going straight for the punch.

Giovanni tried to smooth things over with the mothering tone she usually reserved for Noele. "Are you all right? Mom and Dad are worried about you."

"I'm worried about Mom."

"*We're* worried about *you*. There's this cryptic undertone in everything you say."

"I mean, I'm sad," Elise said.

Noele wore a pensive look, as though she wasn't sure if she should say what she was thinking.

"Say it."

"Are you lonely?"

Their mother must have expressed her concerns to them about her and Aaron. "No. Aaron's been working."

"He should be here," Giovanni said. She was the only one in their family who genuinely liked him.

"You'll see him tonight."

"Would you tell us if you were lonely?" Giovanni asked.

"Probably not. The last thing I need is more family time." Pretending to be offended, Giovanni hit her, and Elise pushed back. They play-fought for a second, like children.

"Think of it as a long weekend."

"A long nightmare, depending on the dreamer," Elise said. Giovanni's expression changed as if she was really offended. "We *are* here for a memorial, is what I meant."

After an hour, the room was littered with Kitty's documentation. Elise watched her sisters gorging themselves on the never-before-seen photographs of their mother as a child on set, of themselves during the holidays or on family vacations.

"Aww, look." Giovanni held up a picture of their mother with their grandma Nellie and Kitty at her high school graduation. Sarah was in the middle, beaming and gripping each woman at their sides.

"I wonder when things changed between them."

"Probably when Kitty left the life." Giovanni was horrified by Kitty's relinquishing of her social position to the same degree Noele resisted her own. "They no longer had things in common."

"Kitty was still writing and consulting on projects."

"I know, but how do you give up being one of the most famous women in the world?"

"She said it didn't mean as much after Nathan died." Only in his midfifties at the time, he had passed away three decades before Kitty, and since he was gone, she had only dated one man, a doctor who had no Hollywood profile. Elise wouldn't ever say it aloud, but she hoped to find one man to love her the way two men had loved Kitty. A little knot formed in her stomach, knowing the state her life was in today.

Done reminiscing for the moment, Elise picked up her cell phone to see a dozen missed calls from Rebecca. "Rebecca's here for the pictures. We're having some life-sizes made that'll be set up around the house."

"That's creepy," Noele said.

"I thought it would be cool."

"It's creepy," Giovanni said, following them downstairs.

"And overly sentimental," Noele said.

CHAPTER 11

Elise

Sunday afternoon, October 29, 2017

Rebecca was calling Elise from the St. Johns' driveway. She shouted out of her car window upon seeing the sisters emerging from the hedges. "Welcome home!" She flung herself out of her Jeep for a three-way hug before Giovanni and Noele went inside.

"Are you ignoring me?" Rebecca waved her phone at Elise. "I've called you so many times."

"I'm sorry—we were at Kitty's; my phone was on silent." Answering Rebecca's call, no matter the time of day or night, had always been her duty as a best friend and a client. She hadn't been sending a message by not answering—rather, she was weaning herself from a relationship at its end.

"Did you tell them I'm leaving?" Her boyfriend's tour was being extended, and Rebecca wanted to join him and take time to "clarify my next career steps." It was a good cover story, Elise thought.

"Not yet. It'll only make them panic. They seem to think you can help with all of this."

"Imagine that," Rebecca said. She was, Elise knew, refusing to be guilted or roped into a fight. Her need for some separation or change would have been plausible had the lifelong struggle between them not come to a head that March, after Rebecca deleted several of Elise's controversial Instagram posts. Rebecca had said she deleted them because similar content was reposted everywhere; she didn't think it mattered. But then she admitted being uncomfortable with some of the recent comments on Elise's page. Then, she said she thought all of Elise's content as of late had been "off brand."

Rebecca reminded her about the real racists in the world, waiting for the right moment to reclaim their country. She had always spoken about the "embarrassing" paraphernalia her family collected—her great-great-grandfather and uncles had fought for the Confederacy—in a whisper. "They're a bunch of sore losers with those sad flags. You know people still dress up and act it all out for entertainment?" Rebecca had had a lot to say after the events in Charlottesville that August.

But back in March, Rebecca had told Elise to focus on acting. She didn't understand the responsibility Elise felt, as a Black American woman, to speak out. "You donate, a *lot*. Isn't that enough?"

Finally, they had stumbled upon the real issue, which was that Rebecca thought Elise's posts about the #blacklivesmatter movement were "racist."

Elise was instantly annoyed. "Black people, being the minority, *can't* be racist."

"I understand the philosophical argument, but everyone suffers."

Elise was speechless. Rebecca had attended one of the best private schools in the country since nursery school and apparently still didn't know American history. Once, when they were kids, they'd been headed off to Girl Scout camp, and Elise had been nervous she'd be the only Black girl there. Rebecca, trying to help, had suggested, *Just pretend like you're White. No one will notice.*

Stunned, Elise had worked to deconstruct Rebecca's solution. *How does someone pretend to be White? What is being White as opposed to being Black?*

Elise had given her a pass all those years ago because, well, they were eight. The two had never talked about it again, and Elise sighed, deciding it was childish to bring it up now. Race was never not an issue for Elise, but for Rebecca, there was always a simple solution.

"That's not even the point." Elise decided it was time to politely kick Rebecca out her house. "There's nothing else we need to discuss before tomorrow, right?"

After the blowup that spring, Rebecca had gone to her mother, worried about Elise's safety and her own. Demands for an apology had come from all sides, but Elise refused. She didn't have a "sorry" left in her. That week's inheritance news leak had unleashed a second wave of racist hostility that her team, so far, had ignored—in order, Elise knew, to avoid apologizing for trying to force her apology in March.

Rebecca followed her into the house. "The studio called back. They want you to talk about Kitty, explain your relationship with her."

"What happened to the wedding angle?"

"They don't think it'll stick."

Elise began shaking her head. "No shit." She handed the stack of photos to Rebecca. "I love how they say what they want to say after the meeting."

"This is a difficult position for everyone." Rebecca sat down. "They're worried about people boycotting *Drag On.*"

"So, Kitty's death explains my anger about racism and police brutality?"

Rebecca squirmed, which let Elise know she had helped craft the spin. "You have a job to do, Elise. They can sue you for breach of contract."

Elise gave her another look. "I thought you agreed. I can't talk about Kitty."

"I don't know how we get around it now. The studio said—"

"Well, I have *not* agreed. It's no one's business."

"First, you complain when they say nothing, now, you complain—"

Sarah appeared in the kitchen, having heard Rebecca's voice. "My gingersnap! You're here early." Sarah looked Rebecca over from head to toe. "No jeans tonight."

"I'm coming back. I just came to pick up the photos."

Sarah looked between Elise and Rebecca. "What photos?"

"For the life-sizes of Kitty for tonight."

"Oh, yes, that's going to look nice." Sarah produced a bottle of Riesling from the double refrigerator. "Where's your momma today?" Sarah said, asking about Alison. After working together for thirty years, the two normally talked a couple of times a day.

"Over at my grandmother's."

"How's she doing?" Rebecca's grandmother was newly widowed and having a hard time being alone. She called Alison and Rebecca constantly.

Rebecca motioned her hand as if to say, *So-so.* "Flustered about tonight."

Sarah reached for a glass in the cabinet. "What's tonight?"

Rebecca and Elise exchanged a look.

"Kitty's memorial, Mom."

"I know, but Rebecca's talking about her grandmother." Sarah still looked puzzled.

"Kitty invited her," Rebecca said. "Apparently, they knew each other back in the day."

"I look forward to hearing that story." Sarah put more glasses on the table. "You girls want some?" Sarah started a pour for Rebecca before she could answer.

"How are you all doing?" Rebecca asked, touching Sarah's arm.

"I think we're all in and out," Sarah said.

"But mostly out," Elise said, pouring her own splash of wine. "*Vogue* and the studio want me to talk about Kitty." She waited to take some pleasure in her mother's discomfort.

Sarah took a sip of wine. "So, talk about Kitty, Elise. Someone has to dispel the rumors about her being deranged."

"How about *you*?" Elise asked.

"I'm not the one she left money to. Obviously, she wanted you and your sisters to go to bat for her, defend her honor."

Despite the sarcastic undertone in Sarah's take, Elise sensed that something about what her mother said was right, but she didn't think it was about honor. That seemed too egotistical, too shallow for Kitty, who had been so antisocial.

"What did Alison say?" Elise asked.

"We haven't discussed it," Sarah said. Rebecca shook her head to cosign Sarah.

Elise started for the door. "I'm going to get dressed."

"And I need to get to the printer," Rebecca said, collecting the photographs on the table.

Elise waved and ascended through the gateway of her little slice of heaven. The only thing on her mind, for a change, was a bath and another joint before the night began. Feeling nothing was her aim.

CHAPTER 12

Mary

May 1955

Years flew once Mary fell in love with Richard Collins. They had first met in the third grade, when Richard's family moved to Cottonwood. He quickly became popular because his father owned a janitorial services company and made enough money for his momma not to have to work.

Mary became fond of him after he announced to the class that he wanted to be a doctor. His confidence had received some snickers.

Mary cornered him later, at recess. "What kind of doctor do you want to be?"

Startled she was speaking to him, he stammered. "I—I don't know yet."

"Is your father a doctor?"

"No. He wants me to be. He's been saving since I was born to send me to medical school."

Noticing their one-on-one, some of the kids surrounded them, making kissing noises. Richard ran, and thereafter said maybe three words to her until freshman year, when they both ended up in geometry. Richard had spent the summer in Chicago and was taller, darker, and more handsome. They became friends over their shared distaste for their teacher. Sophomore year, she asked him to be her chemistry partner, and midway through the year he finally got the courage to ask to walk her home. They became a couple after a few fish Fridays at her house, at which point Richard admitted he'd been smitten with her since the third grade.

Hazel wasn't thrilled but, knowing she couldn't stop Mary's social activities given her work schedule, continued to impress upon Mary just how much a baby would impede her life. "And he'll be gone, with another girl just as pretty as you." Her warnings over the years resulted in Mary being a virgin valedictorian. Richard came in third. All they did, besides some kissing and rubbing, was study.

Hazel filled her Sundays with double doses of church, but Mary had been allowed to come home after morning service to "do homework" with Richard, cook for the week, and write. Her storytelling was the only thing that had lingered post-Lillian.

She thought about Lillian sometimes when they went to Charlotte, but those trips were few and far between. Whenever they did go, it was to run errands for Mrs. Nora, who liked a dress shop and the butcher there. Jim Crow said White patrons had to be helped first, so even if it was Hazel's turn and another White person walked in, she would have to wait. Hours could be wasted, and on Hazel's one day off, it was the last way she wanted to spend it. Mary's skin circumvented such inconveniences.

Late one Saturday afternoon, they were on the bus headed to Charlotte because Hazel had forgotten to pick up Mrs. Nora's dress for her husband's eightieth birthday party the next day. Mary squashed herself against the window, as far away from her mother as she could get.

"I know you better stop with that attitude," Hazel said. "I forgot, and I'm sorry."

"She could have worn another dress." Mary could feel her mother's eyes on her. They had been steel gray for days; completely devoid of blue and the lightest Mary had ever seen them. Mary, knowing they darkened when she was angry, worried this lighter gray indicated a posture devoid of emotion altogether.

It was Senior Week, and Radley's, the drive-in movie theater, was show-ing *Frankenstein* that night in celebration of the Negro class of 1955. The drive-in only permitted Negroes once a month, and for the two weeks since they had gotten the Senior Week schedule, it was all Mary talked about. She hadn't been to the movies since Lillian stopped coming to Charlotte. It was too risky for her to pass in Winston, and she wouldn't have sat in the balcony if someone paid her.

Beyond that, she'd been expecting Richard to propose that evening. He was going to borrow his Dad's Cadillac and had made a reservation for din-ner. The weather was supposed to be balmy and romantic—88 degrees, with a breeze. Graduation was in a week, and Mary imagined that the dinner his mother had already planned might be their engagement party.

"You hear me talking to you?"

"Yes, ma'am," Mary mumbled, even angrier at being pulled from her fantasy.

"We'll be back in time."

They arrived in Charlotte minutes before the dress shop closed. Hazel hustled, giving Mary a sly dagger stare every two steps to hurry. Mary, still seething about how Mrs. Nora could have driven to get her own dress if it was so important, stopped to admire a mustard-yellow dress in a store win-dow with a plunging neckline and a slim, structured bodice. It was perfect for graduation.

Hazel commanded her to "come on" through tight, motionless lips. Mary ignored her and stepped inside the store, knowing Hazel couldn't. "May I try that dress on?"

"Miss. Mary—"

Mary waved a hand at her mother. "A minute, Hazel." All this time spent pretending to be White: Mary figured she might as well go all the way and do what she wanted for once.

"Yes, of course, Miss." The clerk disappeared into the back of the store.

Hazel's body swelled with anger, consuming the width of the doorframe and blocking the afternoon light. Her eyes narrowed at Mary until they appeared to be closed. Mary heard the clerk's heels coming behind her and watched Hazel's anger melt into feigned happiness. "I'll let the dress shop know you'll be right along."

Mary snatched the dress from the woman. "What took you so long? I'm in a hurry." She shut the dressing room door, breathing fast, too fast, unable to face herself in the mirror. Panicked about the wrath awaiting her, she pushed the door open. It slammed against the opposite wall, alarming the clerk. She ran out without an apology.

Hazel was standing in the street in front of the shop, smoking. She nodded at the CLOSED sign. Her face was straight, her voice was flat. "He's there but won't open the door for me."

Mary knocked, and the white-haired, older White man behind the counter scurried over, smiling and smoothing what little hair he had as he turned the lock. "I'm sorry; we're closed, Miss."

"Please? I sent our maid to tell you I'd be right over."

He eyed Hazel over her shoulder. Mary tried again. "It's for my grandmother, Mrs. Nora Lakes. I forgot to pick it up earlier. She needs it for a party."

"Ah, you must be Shirley. I'll be there tomorrow."

Mary didn't know who Shirley was but smiled.

He dipped his head in apology. "You know they'll say anything. I thought she was lying. Wait here."

Hazel didn't speak or look at Mary during the two-hour bus ride home. As soon as they were alone, Mary started to apologize but couldn't form her lips to speak before Hazel's hand came across her face so hard that she tasted blood.

———

Richard's big hands tilted her face toward the hanging light in her kitchen. "She hit you like you cursed her."

Mary just said she'd mouthed off. Had he known the extent of her disrespect, he would have agreed she deserved it. And she did. "It'll bruise." She touched her lip which had started to swell.

"And on graduation." He kissed her, pulled away, and then kissed her again. "But you're still the prettiest girl I've ever seen."

Mary pushed his hands. She felt bad about herself right then, and he was always fawning over her looks, as if it were her only virtue in the world.

He went for his pants pocket. "I have something to cheer you up."

She involuntarily held her breath as he produced a map. "We just got that new building on Fifty-Fourth Street." He opened it across the kitchen table to show her the downtown location of his father's newest contract.

Disappointed his news wasn't a proposal, she clapped. "That should help with costs next year." Richard's father had promised to pay for their schooling so they didn't have to work and could finish on time. After they were married, they would live in his parents' attic until they graduated and moved up north, maybe to D.C. or Chicago, for Richard to go to medical school.

"It's more than that, baby! He wants to show me the ropes and retire."

"How will you work and keep up your classes?"

"I'm not going to school."

"Did you not get in?" Mary hadn't wanted to ask, but his admittance letter from Central was late. Hers had come weeks prior.

"That's not why. This is my decision. My father needs me."

"But you want to be a doctor. He wants you to be a doctor." Richard had been so committed, he had endured taking AP physics and calculus at Reynolds, the White high school, that year.

"I'll be almost thirty years old by then."

"The time's going to pass anyway! Do you want to spend it managing janitors?"

"It's not about what I want. We'll be better off with me owning my own business."

"Better off than a doctor?"

"Better off than a *Negro* doctor, yes." His hand smoothed her hair and felt heavy, like the pressure to support his new plan. "We can get our own house sooner, have a baby."

She wiggled out from underneath the weight of his arm. "But I don't want to have a baby and live here." They had talked about her passing up north, in order to get a teaching job that would support them through his medical school. She'd make twice as much money as a White teacher than as a Negro one. Teaching wasn't her dream, but it was better than the service jobs most of their classmates would begin by summer's end.

Richard was upset at first by her mention of passing, until he learned she'd never considered crossing over. Passing for convenience in Charlotte or for financial reasons was one thing, but integrating oneself into the White world meant isolation. Among other losses, she'd never be able to see her mother again.

Even when she and Lillian used to tell their stories, Mary always saw herself marrying a Colored man and having Colored children one day. That's why she never told Richard about Lillian and those Sundays in Charlotte, or that she passed now occasionally—and with Hazel, no less.

"Why not?" He crossed his arms. He was daring her to admit that staying wasn't good enough. "Get your degree and teach here. Negro children right down here in the South need good teachers too."

"We planned to move north!"

He lurched off the steps. "Opportunity beyond the South is a farce. That's what's wrong with Negroes now, always discounting what we do have. They don't want us here but they don't want us up there either. They aren't going to run me away from my home."

"But you're letting them run you away from your dreams."

"How is owning a business not a dream worth having?"

"Because it's never been *yours*."

"My father wants to give me his business. I can't say no." He walked to the door. "I'm going to meet everyone at the football field. I don't imagine you'd want to come with your face looking like that."

The screen door shut before she could answer.

Mary vomited in the grass of their chicken-wire-fenced backyard before she could make it to the outhouse. The root of truth in the pit of her stomach said she wasn't sure she still wanted Richard to propose; his overnight abandonment of his dreams made her unsure about hitching her wagon to his. She'd dismissed her aspirations of acting for reasons of practicality but feared that Richard's relinquishing his own would make him bitter. More than one woman in Cottonwood warned, *A man without a dream isn't one worth having*. Even Adelaide complained about the mood swings of the gentle Lefred, whose aspirations of fighting in World War I had ended with an assignment as a cook for its entirety.

Mary couldn't sleep thinking about Richard, even with the luxury of having the bed to herself. He knew Hazel was working an overnight and should have come to apologize after he cooled off.

When the frogs and owls started their symphony, she went to the kitchen to make coffee. She'd been sitting in the dark for an hour, waiting for her mother, when she heard the bus roll down the street.

Her mother was carrying the pink BabyCakes bakery box Mary knew all too well. Seeing Mary through the screen door, Hazel spoke. "What are you doing up?"

Mary pushed the door open for her. The air felt cool and wet, customary for early summer mornings before the humidity absorbed the dew. "I couldn't sleep." She didn't want to tell her why.

Mary's decision to stay in Winston for another four years had disappointed her mother. Hazel blamed Richard, but really, it was Hazel's loss of weight and hair that had made Mary rethink even applying for colleges outside of Winston. She'd gained a considerable amount of weight over the last few years and then lost it suddenly. Now she complained about her aching bones.

The doctor couldn't find anything wrong beyond her nerves. When Hazel's hair got too patchy to cover with pressed hair, Mary went to Charlotte to buy two wigs: one for work and one for church.

Hazel set the cake box on the wooden butcher block they used as a counter. "For your graduation, I assume."

"That's nice of her."

Hazel grunted. She had a moiling relationship with Mrs. Lakes, grateful and resentful all at the same time. Mary knew better than to incite her further with a reply.

"Remember, we have dinner at the Collinses' tonight," Mary reminded her mother.

"Have to work." Hazel pulled at the bodice of her gray uniform; her back was wet with sweat.

"Couldn't someone else watch them breathe?" Mr. and Mrs. Lakes had been in poor health for years, with little to no contact with any of their children. The Lakeses had nurses but trusted Hazel more; she slept there most nights now.

"Stop that." As much as Hazel griped about her employers, she tried to temper her daughter's feelings. *They're your kin, and hating them means you'll end up hating a little of yourself too.*

Mary used to wonder if she'd be named in their will. Her grandmother's cakes were proof of her sentimentalities toward her, but considering how the Lakeses refused to support Mary beyond her mother's pay, which afforded them hardly anything, she had lost optimism for their goodwill.

"You're going to have to spend some time with them before the wedding," Mary said.

Hazel scoffed. "Not if I can help it." She didn't care for Richard's mother, who wore her Sunday best even to the grocery store. *Always trying to remind people of how much money she has.* She was the only able-bodied woman in Cottonwood who didn't work; her claim to fame was the book club she hosted every month. Not once had she invited Hazel. Though she couldn't have gone anyway, on a Thursday night, Hazel thought it was rude not to extend the offer to the woman who was feeding her son every week.

"You like Richard, don't you?"

"I like him fine."

Mary sighed. "Momma, we've been going steady for two years."

Hazel pulled at her girdle. "So he deserves your whole life?"

"He's a good man, Momma."

"I don't doubt it." She limped into the bedroom, leaving Mary contemplating whether to tell her about Richard's plans to take over the janitorial business. She decided against it, though it was bound to come out soon. Telling Hazel would make it feel permanent.

Hazel returned in her long teal housecoat that zipped up the front, and handed Mary an envelope. "Your graduation gift."

It was a train ticket to Los Angeles. Mary was suspicious—she had never shared her dream of going West with anyone. "Why Los Angeles?"

"Catherine wrote me. Lillian's living there now."

Mary was surprised to hear their names. It had been four years, and Lillian had never written or called. "Doing what?"

"Working at a film studio."

Mary felt several things she couldn't name. "Doing what?"

"See for yourself. She wants you to come visit."

Hazel pulled a picture from an envelope. In it, Lillian wore a white, wide-brimmed hat and a tailored mid-length blue dress that made her body blend into the sky. Her dark hair looked thick and bouncy and blew in the wind as she pretended to bite into an airy glob of cotton candy. Behind her was a Ferris wheel, and beyond it, the ocean seemed to go on forever.

Mary had never seen the ocean in person before. The closest beach to Winston was four hours away, but they wouldn't have gone anyway. The coastal cities didn't permit Negroes on the beach, even while in service.

"She's gotten real cute, hasn't she?" Hazel said.

Mary couldn't see Lillian's face well underneath her hat. She'd never considered whether Lillian was attractive or unattractive until Hazel made the comparison between them one year after showing Adelaide their Christmas picture. *She has a lot of face, huh?*

Adelaide had hollered. *What does that even mean?* Hazel had a wickedly dry sense of humor, the type of wit likely to incite a laughing fit at a funeral.

You must know, Hazel had replied as she pounded a chicken breast with a wooden block against Adelaide's kitchen table. *You the one laughing.*

"You might be able to leave tomorrow if you can exchange it for a first-class ticket." Hazel's suggestion brought Mary back to the moment. Negroes couldn't purchase first-class train tickets, even if it was for a White patron. Established only to further humiliate the Negro class, it was one of the sillier rules that also inconvenienced Whites who discovered the first-class car was sold out when they went to exchange the holding ticket. Jim Crow became dumber and blinder the older he got, outsmarting the interests of the people he was supposed to help.

"I can't leave. Richard's going to propose."

"Postpone the wedding for a few months. He'll be here when you get back," Hazel said. "Do this one thing for yourself."

"A few *months?*"

"School doesn't start until September. Enjoy yourself. I'll send money with you."

Mary noticed the ticket was one-way.

"Buy the return when you're ready." Hazel adjusted the silk scarf, patterned in a whirl of hunter green, burgundy, and gray, now tied around her head in place of her wig. The bow at the peak of her head highlighted her angular face. She looked younger with her scarf on but refused to wear it outside the house for fear people could tell she was bald. Mary didn't know how to tell her, but her wig, even though it was of high quality, did nothing to hide the truth.

"How can you afford this?"

Her mother watched every penny, mumbling, whenever Mary asked for something, about how little they had. It didn't matter what Mary wanted; outside of the basics, her mother didn't have it.

"I've been saving," Hazel said, setting her snuff can on the table. Its contents—thick, sticky, black saliva from the wad of tobacco always marinating in her bottom lip—reminded Mary of prune juice. She had knocked it over one time and had to boil pot after pot of water to get the floor clean. "You may never leave this town again after you marry."

"I told you, I'm moving north after college. You're coming too."

"Girl, I ain't going nowhere." Walking to the stove, Hazel pulled her scarf down at the nape of her neck to cover the few short hairs that lingered. "You hungry?" Hazel reached for a knife.

Mary nodded, watching as the cake sprang back before parting. The palest beige yellow, the inside of the cake matched her skin. It had taken Mrs. Nora years to discover her favorite: Her first cakes were chocolate, which Mary hated, then vanilla, too bland. Strawberry was a favorite for years, until she tasted carrot with pineapple bits and walnuts. Her favorite, though, was the lemon, received the year Lillian stopped coming to Charlotte. Perfectly round and three cake pans high, her graduation cake had been iced by hand. Mary could see the turns in her grandmother's wrist in the peaks of the icing, the ends of her stroke. Each speck was moist and maybe even slightly underdone, the bite as a whole, dense. Her relationship with her White family was the same, an unfinished and complicated matter glazed over with a decadent birthday cake.

Thoughts of her father—Theodore Tucker Lakes the Third, Esq., now the senator from Virginia—and his family evoked the taste of the sourest lemon: bittersweet.

Hazel set two cups of coffee and plates of cake on the table. "I'll get my money back if you don't want to go." She went through the back door to the porch to air out her uniform.

Mary took a bite of cake. Outside, her mother started to hum, a habit for joy and worry; Mary wondered which Hazel was feeling then. Beyond her, the first peak of sunlight hovered in the sky. Blackbirds made an arrow formation as they flew over the roof across the street and over the trees, west. She looked down at Lillian's picture again.

Would she have ever heard from her again had Catherine not contacted Hazel? Mary felt a way about her friend's silence, but her reemergence felt like a sign she couldn't ignore.

It seemed Lillian was living the life Mary had dreamed about—wishes she tried to forget after falling in love with Richard. But his new plan changed things.

"I'll go for a week . . . maybe two."

Hearing her, Hazel came inside and patted her back. "Good, baby. Good." Mary closed her eyes, indulging in her mother's touch.

Hazel pulled her grandma Elizabeth's gold ball earrings from her robe pocket. "You keep these. Wear them for graduation."

CHAPTER 13

Mary

June 1955

Mary walked to the first-class train car with the wicker basket of food Hazel had packed for the trip.

"That was smart." The attendant, a chatty White teen younger than her and intent on making conversation, trailed her with her luggage. "Food's not very good on this route. Where are you from?" Mercifully, another, older attendant hurried him along.

"Everyone likes a pretty girl," he said, apologizing for the younger one's interest. Grateful, Mary reached for his hand onto the car, crossing the threshold of Whiteness. His touch was her ticket.

Mary had been nervous about passing alone all the way to Los Angeles. She'd never been on a train and had only traveled as far as Charlotte. She found the courage knowing she'd be hot and cramped in the Colored cars. Inferior cushioning meant her bottom would be throbbing for days on the wooden bench. And there was likely to be only one bathroom for the entire Colored section.

Seated in the first row on the right was a lady wearing a long-sleeved, high-necked black lace dress and a black feathered hat. Her wiry black hair was nestled into a bun, but little spirals decorated the nape of her neck. Only mourning explained her oppressive clothing in the humidity, but Mary noticed she looked more uneasy than sad.

She caught Mary's eye the moment the royal-purple velvet car curtain opened and then turned to the window, a deliberate gesture which told Mary that she was also passing. It brought to mind what Hazel had told her to do.

Smile if they're White but make as little conversation as possible. If they ask, say you're going to see family in Los Angeles. If they're Negro, avoid eye contact. They'll leave you alone.

Mary sat on the left, three rows back, at the recommendation of the attendant, who said the view would be better. Despite having the row to herself and the comfort of the thick seat cushion, it was hard to get comfortable with the small leather pouch her mother had insisted she wear around her waist underneath her dress. *Don't take it off until you get there*, Hazel had warned. Inside was some money, Lillian's picture, and her address. *Never tell anyone how much money you have—not even Lillian.*

Mary rested her head against the window as the train caught its rhythm. Her stomach grumbled in the middle of the night; she nibbled like a kitchen mouse on biscuits and pear preserves. Outside, the stars illuminated the flat fields, and to her, the landscape didn't look any different from home. She wondered what time it was in Winston and if her momma, Richard, Adelaide, and Lefred were sleeping. She hoped they all already missed her, because she already missed them.

She thought about Richard's proposal after graduation. He had knelt before her after the exit procession with a single pink rose, sweating in his cap and gown. She was nervous to tell him, but he was happy about her trip to Los Angeles. He even gave her some money to buy herself something nice.

The night sky was vast and pitch-black, nothingness save for a belt of glittering starlight that seemed to follow the train. She became transfixed by it, sucked in, as if she was a part of its light. She awoke sometime later when a small voice interrupted her sleep. "You've been taught well to keep to yourself."

It was the lady in black. The brim of her hat nearly hit Mary's eye as she leaned in closer to whisper. "You can never be too careful."

Mary stood to see her exiting the car. The five other passengers in the car were asleep. The woman returned just before daylight and gave Mary a quick nod of acknowledgment before sinking into her seat, exhausted from her excursions beyond first class.

Mary became her de facto lookout every night. She wanted to ask where she went, but they never spoke again, knowing better. Someone else could have been awake.

Mary saw Lillian the moment the train rolled into the station, waving wildly from the platform as if she knew everyone on it. She was dressed in the same outfit from the picture Hazel had showed her and she ran down the platform steps, blocking the exit to embrace Mary. "It's so good to see you again." She smelled like a strawberry hard candy.

"You too." Mary pulled from her embrace, feeling the patience of those behind them waning. A few pushed past. "Excuse me," they said, shaking their heads at the inconsideration.

Lillian didn't seem to notice or care, but Mary, mindful of her Southern manners, tried to steer Lillian to the left. Her feet didn't budge, but she did release her grip around Mary's waist.

"I have missed you." She wore a center part, as she had as a child. In line with her tooth gap, it brought some symmetry to her round face. Seeing her now after almost five years, Mary understood what her mother had meant by "a lot of face." Her chubby cheeks made her features look like chocolate chips nestled in a cookie.

"Me too." Mary looked down, uncomfortable with Lillian's gaze on her brown shift dress. She fumbled with an earlobe, realizing she still had on her mother's earrings. She felt out of place in front of Lillian, whose curled hair, red-painted lips, and nails matched the magazine styles. She dropped

Lillian's hand and picked up her suitcase, squeezing the handle to settle herself.

Lillian took it as a cue and started up the stairs. "Isn't the train ride majestic?"

"I slept most of the way."

"That's a shame." Lillian pivoted on the stairs, slowing the line again. "Who knows when you'll make that trip again?" She walked on her toes, bouncing like a child unburdened by the world. Her deep brown hair swung from side to side, shining in the sun. "Seeing the land and the trees—oh, I just loved it."

Mary struggled to keep up. "I'll try not to sleep as much on the way back."

Lillian navigated through the crowd, expecting people to move for her; most did. If they didn't do so fast enough, she turned her shoulders to slide through. Mary stayed at her heels, excusing them both, careful not to bump into any of the Whites.

In the parking lot, Lillian tossed Mary's suitcase in the back seat of a silver Buick convertible.

"This is your car?"

Lillian beamed as if it was the first time someone had noticed. She slapped the hood with a flat palm. "I've been saving for a year. Early birthday present." She'd be twenty-one in August.

Mary slid into the passenger's seat, running her palm over the white leather. "It's beautiful."

Lillian started the engine. "We'll go home first to change, and then we're going out."

"I don't have anything to wear." The wrinkles in Mary's dress were so deep they looked like stains.

"Don't worry. I have clothes for you at the house. None of my old things worked here either."

Mary found that hard to believe.

Lillian rolled down the windows, turned up the radio, and began singing along with Ray Charles. "*I got a woman, way over town, that's good to me.*" She was off-key and too loud, which garnered the attention of others in the lot.

Mary was embarrassed until she saw them smiling. Lillian's unburdened nature was a rarity at home, where women—both White and Negro—were reared to be reserved. She realized she'd missed it a little.

Among the stream of pedestrians leaving the train station was the woman in the black dress. Mary watched her cross to the bus stop, where a Negro man handed her a baby.

Mary touched Lillian's forearm and motioned her to look. "She was passing on the train."

"Weren't you?"

"Yes, but I'm alone."

Lillian stared, summing up the situation. "I bet it was hot in the Colored car. Or maybe she's White."

"No, she was passing. She told me."

"No use in everyone being uncomfortable, especially if she's still feeding."

Mary wondered what her and Richard's baby might look like. Would they have to travel separately? Would she have to sneak to the Colored train car at night to feed her baby?

"What would have happened had she been caught?" Mary asked. It wasn't illegal after the Mason-Dixon Line, but it would have angered passengers and train personnel, who had jurisdiction out in the middle of nowhere.

"I don't even want to think about it," Lillian said. She turned up the radio and cruised onto the street.

Los Angeles was a maze of roads lined with buildings, bigger than any in Charlotte. The palm trees were as tall as she'd heard, but ugly, with rail-thin trunks and sparse tops of green, beige, and brown leaves. She preferred the substantial oaks and maples at home.

Mary wiggled her fingers through the wind as Lillian picked up speed. It was sunny and hot, but not sticky like at home. White people walking down the street wore sharp suits and long dresses. The few Negroes in the flow of foot traffic were dressed as nicely, if not better, in hats and heels. Mary couldn't wait to tell Richard about it. She had started a letter on the train, but the forward motion of the train combined with the left-to-right motion of her eyes and hand had made her queasy.

Lillian announced their arrival to her home on Orange Drive, a wide, paved street with single-story houses and green manicured lawns. If this was how Negroes lived in Los Angeles, Mary might never leave.

"I'm only a ten-minute walk to work."

"My momma said you work at a film studio?"

"Telescope. Smaller studio, but very well respected."

"And they hire us?"

"I'm a phone operator."

Mary tried not to show her disappointment. She had hoped for something more glamorous—if not an actress, a secretary at least. Lillian noticed and defended herself. "Anything pays better than a service job."

Mary couldn't argue. "I'm going to be a teacher." Thinking of Catherine then, she turned down the radio. "How's your momma?"

Lillian swatted her hand and turned it back up. "Fine."

"You really came out here all alone?"

"She didn't want to come."

They parked in front of a quad of pale-pink houses. Four stairs led up to the property, enclosed by a rectangular partition of bushes. Lillian pointed to the right. "I'm the first one. Eighty-Eight Orange Drive."

The porch was shaded by ivy vines sprouting from the iron awning mounted into the cement. The vines hung long and thick, obstructing the view of most of the porch and the entire front door from the street.

The living room was dominated by books. Thick novels, magazines, and crinkled, yellowing newspapers adorned every surface: the shiny hardwood floor, the green couch, the two matching chairs, the fireplace mantel, and the coffee table. Most amazing was that the room didn't look cluttered. It was twice the size of Mary's entire house in Winston. "Wow."

"I love to read," Lillian explained.

"Me too," Mary said, pretending to have been reacting to her collection. "Borrow anything you'd like."

Old questions about Lillian's life outside of their Sundays in Charlotte swirled in Mary's head as Lillian led her through the three-bedroom, one-bathroom house, with its custom cabinetry and intricate wall and floor tiling in the kitchen and bathroom. How did she have all this?

Lillian opened one of three doors accessible from the hallway. "This is your room." Everything was white, and the window had a view of the court-yard, where a black iron table and four chairs sat in the grass. Lillian tied back the curtains. "I sit out there sometimes. It's peaceful."

"Are your neighbors nice?" Mary asked. At least one window of each bungalow faced the courtyard.

"Nice enough. I don't associate too much. Being the landlord, I don't want to make friends."

"You *own* all of this?"

Lillian nodded.

"How?"

"It was a well-deserved gift."

Mary's mind exploded; she'd never heard of such a thing. "From who?"

"No time to go into all that now." Lillian went to the door. "You must be dying for a bath. I'll go draw one for you."

Lillian was still full of secrets, but Mary planned on getting all the answers while she was there.

Bubbles expanded in the water, from a bottle labeled Roseland Body Bath. Mary had never bathed in a ceramic tub before but wasn't going to tell Lillian that. At home, the bath was a pail and strictly a splash, wash, and go situation. *Get in there and hit the hot spots*, Hazel would say. It took forever to boil enough water to fill the pail, and so they didn't.

The water rose quickly to fill the depth of the basin, and the bathroom began to smell syrupy, like Lillian.

"I like my bath on the hot side," she said. "Turn this knob to adjust. Make yourself at home."

The door closed, leaving Mary to investigate the contents of the little glass bottles and containers on the sink. Her face tingled after slathering a scoop of Lillian's cold cream on her face. It began to burn, and as she bent over the sink to wash it off, the constraints of the leather belted pouch dug into her waist. Undressing, she saw it had chafed and bruised her skin. The pouch was damp with sweat, and she had to struggle to remove a thick stack of bills from it.

She counted a thousand dollars. It was more money than she'd ever seen, and more than she'd need if she planned to stay in Los Angeles for only a few months.

In the middle of her third count, Lillian knocked on the door. "The washrags are in the cabinet."

Worried she might try to come in if she didn't receive a reply, Mary shouted, "Thank you!"

It had to be a mistake, she thought of the money as she sank into the tub, letting the water wash over her chin and mouth. She closed her eyes, comforted by the warmth, until dread washed over her as she realized what some part of her already knew: her mother didn't have a thousand dollars to give—mistakenly or otherwise.

She leaped out of the tub, barely covering herself with her towel before entering the hallway.

"I was just coming for you." Lillian had an armful of dresses. "My friends are waiting." As their proximity narrowed, she frowned. "Is everything all right?"

"I need to call my momma."

Lillian walked into Mary's bedroom as if she expected her to follow. "It's late there. We really need to get going." Mary silently agreed. She needed privacy, and Lillian only had one phone.

"I brought you a few things to wear until we go shopping." Lillian pointed to a white lace dress on top of her stack. "This would look pretty on you."

"I don't have any clothes as fancy."

"I had to buy all new clothes when I came. Didn't want to look country."

"You always dressed so nice."

"Thanks. I used to get all my clothes for free." Mary wondered why Lillian never gave her any of her old clothes.

Lillian nudged a pair of white heels near the bed with her toe. "Sorry, they're a little scuffed." The heel was only two inches high, like her church shoes, but Lillian's, as always, were better.

Lillian crossed to the vanity at the window, giving Mary the opportunity to tuck the leather pouch inside her suitcase lining. "Let me go finish washing up."

When Mary returned, Lillian was fluffing her hair at the vanity, "Tonight we're going to Mitch's. Everyone from the studios goes there after work. It's just up the street." Lillian spun around in the chair to look at her. "I hope you don't mind, but we need to dress you up some. You look like such a little girl."

Mary wasn't offended; she wanted to be taught to do all the things women were supposed to do. But when Lillian painted Mary's lips in her signature red, she blotted it, reminded of one of those clowns who dressed in blackface. Mary chose a petal-pink color instead.

"I can't even see it now." Lillian dabbed some red on top. She pawed through Mary's hair, which had formed ripples from the bath steam. "Have you ever ironed it?"

"You mean hot comb?"

"No, an iron. White people *iron* their hair if it's curly."

"No." Mary never used a hot comb either. "Give me the brush." All she did to ensure her hair stayed pin straight was brush it back and let it dry. She demonstrated, using the bristle brush to wrangle her hair into a low bun.

Lillian looked relieved. She secured a rose-adorned hairpin in the back and touched her cheek to Mary's, admiring their reflection. "Sisters."

Mary beamed from the inside out. But as quickly as the joy came, it was replaced by a nagging question. "Why didn't you ever write me?"

"There was nowhere for you to write back to." Lillian pouted her lips in the mirror and pulled Mary from the chair. "We're so late."

———————

Mary had assumed Mitch's was a fancy place with candles, tablecloths, and napkins. In reality, it was half bar and half restaurant, a step above diner décor, made worse with dim lighting, dark-red carpet, and a fog of cigarette smoke. A few couples swayed to whatever was playing from the jukebox lodged in the back right corner. Mary couldn't hear the music over the clank of glasses and buzz of conversation between sips and puffs.

Lillian led her through the crowd. Everyone in the room was White; there wasn't even a Negro waiter. Being the only one, or even among a handful of Negroes in a room full of White people was never ideal. She pulled the back of Lillian's dress. "Should we be in here?" Jim Crow wasn't law in the West, but that didn't mean the Whites who lived there weren't in support of the rhetoric.

"Don't be silly."

Three White women in a booth in the back waved in their direction. "Emma!" they called.

When Lillian waved back and hustled over, Mary realized that Lillian was passing.

They stood in front of a table of eager eyes. "Everyone," Lillian said, wrapping her arm around Mary's waist, "this is my sister, Kitty. Kitty Karr." She pointed around the table to introduce Judy, with brown hair, then the blond twins: Daphne, with the shorter hair, and Meredith, chubbier, on the end. All three women slid around the booth to make room.

Mary sat, knowing she had no choice but to pass too. That meant saying little and listening a lot, so she didn't contradict anything anyone said. Was it "Emma" Lillian called herself? She didn't remember what Lillian had called her either.

Meredith pushed the Bundt cake with white icing, sitting in the middle of the table, toward Mary. "I had to go all the way to my maid's apartment on Central, but it's the best coconut cake you'll ever have. I hope you like it." Her eyes pleaded for acceptance. "Emma said you love cake."

"I would love a slice; thank you."

"We can order ice cream if you want."

"No ice cream," Lillian answered before Mary had to.

Judy started cutting slices and passing plates. Daphne poured champagne. "The bubbly is nearly flat."

Lillian apologized. "Kitty's train was late."

"It's fine. I'll order another bottle." Daphne looked for a waiter, tapping her blood-red nails on the table.

Mary finished half her piece of cake before anyone else had taken a bite. She had never had coconut before and liked the unexpected complexity of it. It was fitting for the moment.

"How do you like LA so far?" Daphne turned the table's attention to "Kitty."

"She just got here," Lillian said. "She can't have an opinion yet."

Mary could tell Lillian wanted to protect her from idle conversation, but Daphne waved her off. "Every city has its own mood, an energy." She raised her brows at "Kitty." "So? What does it feel like?"

"Free."

Daphne looked impressed by her answer and raised her glass. "To being free."

They all looked as though her words meant something to them too. Mary wondered what they needed freedom from. She knew they weren't passing, otherwise Lillian wouldn't be calling herself Emma.

"Where are you all from?" Mary was careful to hide her Southern accent. It didn't occur to her until that moment, but Lillian had never had one, despite her growing up in North Carolina, because of her mother's perfect use of the King's English.

"Philadelphia." Meredith gestured between herself and Daphne.

"Here," Judy answered proudly. "My father is a retired film director."

"I bet you're happy to be reunited with your sister," Daphne said.

It was a question Mary could answer truthfully. "Yes. I missed her."

Lillian laid her head on Mary's shoulder. "I missed you too." She sounded genuine, like the person Mary knew, but sitting with her and the strangers at the table, Mary questioned whether she had ever really known Lillian at all. She wasn't angry—Mary had her own secrets—but she wished she'd known about this particular circumstance before they arrived. Lillian would probably argue that passing wasn't dangerous in Los Angeles. But in Mary's mind, no one liked to be made a fool of, especially White folks. The precariousness of the present moment now entitled Mary, she felt, to answers about a whole lot of things.

"Emma hated leaving you to care for your aunt," Judy said. "All that responsibility on your shoulders."

"Emma" scolded Judy for mentioning it. "This is supposed to be a cele-bration!"

Judy perked up. "Sam told me he loved me last night. It won't be long before he proposes."

"Who is Sam?" Mary asked.

"My boyfriend, the head of production." It took Judy twenty minutes to relay the details of her date—daisies; a dinner of champagne, oysters, and crab; and kisses on her porch.

"So romantic," Meredith gushed. "Imagine when he proposes."

Mary thought of her own proposal again.

"It's only been a few months. Don't get your hopes up, Judy," Emma said. The twins gave her a look, but she defended herself. "I'm just trying to protect her."

As the night progressed, Mary noticed that "Emma" nitpicked a lot: the cake had too much icing, Daphne's lipstick wasn't her "best look," and Judy talked too loudly. On first introduction, Mary wasn't sure she liked Emma as much as she remembered liking Lillian.

She cut herself another slice of cake. Eating was a good excuse to stay quiet. When she went for thirds, Lillian moved her plate and slid her third drink to her instead.

"I'm starving," Mary said, reaching for the cake back.

"Nothing like a weight problem to complicate your life," Lillian snapped.

Judy leaned over Lillian to explain. "The studio has us on weigh-ins. To make it fair for the actresses."

"How often?"

"Monthly."

"Really?"

"Yes, this is the movie business," Daphne said. "We're selling fantasy."

Seconds later, a gold cigarette case cascaded across the table and hit Mary's fingernails. Mary curled her fingers, embarrassed by how nubby hers looked compared to everyone's long, painted ones.

"Settle in," Daphne said. "We'll eat soon."

Lakes cigarettes weren't just a muddied yellow anymore, Mary saw. They were white with green stripes, brown with red dots, all red, and all white. The product line had expanded years ago to appeal to women and college-aged city dwellers.

Daphne favored the white ones. Mary took an original and leaned into the flame Lillian sparked. She had never smoked a Lakes cigarette before, fearful of the inevitable jokes or questions that might ensue. She wondered what Lillian and her friends would say if they knew who she really was. She felt superior having this secret. Her confidence swelled with every inhalation; combined with a few sips of Lillian's drink, it soon served to dissipate her discomfort.

"Do you all work at Telescope?" she asked.

"Phone operators," Judy said. Mary understood now that there were no Negro phone operators.

"Do you like it?"

The table threw her varying looks of displeasure.

"Nonetheless, we're like a little family," Judy said.

"And it's a good place to meet men," Lillian said.

"How, if you're answering phones all day?"

"Proximity is half the battle."

"It's how my parents met," Judy said. "My mother was working as an assistant and met my father in the cafeteria. I met Sam walking to my car."

"One of the casting agents sent me flowers," Meredith said.

"I've been seeing a producer—met him in the lobby. He brought me roses last week," Daphne said. "Red ones."

Mary wondered why that mattered more than any other color.

"Red screams passion," Lillian said.

"Are you seeing anyone, Emma?" Mary pressed.

Judy answered for her. "She has a crush on Nathan Tate, the soon to be president of Telescope."

Nathan's father, Abner Tate, was retiring after forty years and turning operations over to his only heir. The real reason, the women whispered—which had remained a secret from the public—was that Abner had Alzheimer's disease.

"He's really good-looking," Meredith said.

"But inexperienced," Judy chimed in.

"You're just repeating what Sam says," Lillian accused. "How much experience does he need to keep things going?" She seemed tired of this conversation.

The early succession, originally planned for ten or fifteen years down the road, made Telescope executives and creatives nervous, Mary was informed. On one hand, the studio needed a new voice and direction. Respected as a smaller competitor to the Big Three studios, Telescope had lost its edge, and everyone's opinion on the solution differed. On the other hand, everyone agreed about Nathan's limited experience and worried that his need to prove his genius in the shadow of his brilliant father could be more devastating to business than Abner's illness.

"We're going to see." Judy looked at Kitty. "Have you ever had a boyfriend, Kitty?"

"I'm engaged." Realizing the truth had slipped out, Mary covered. "Well, was engaged."

"Oh, honey, I'm so sorry." Judy reached for her hand, giving Lillian a scolding look. "We had no idea."

Lillian had an explanation. "They've known each other since grade school. His father owns pharmacies in Boston, so he never planned to move."

Daphne looked at Kitty. "Did you try to convince him?" Her eyes said she knew what it was like to leave someone behind.

Mary regretted saying anything. She was grateful when Lillian spoke for her again.

"No. He wouldn't be happy here. It would be too hard for him to make his own way." Lillian's ability to improvise was impressive, but hearing how close her words veered to the truth, Mary wondered if Lillian knew more about her life than she acknowledged. Underneath the excuse of having to, Richard's reasons to take over his father's business were exactly what Lillian said. He feared his ability to compete not because of a lack of intelligence and skill, but because these qualities were just two more things that could get him killed. His two years at the White high school had taught him that the road to being a doctor could lead him off a cliff.

Judy leaned across Lillian. "Well, you'll have no trouble meeting someone here."

"True. You're gorgeous," Meredith said. "And so tiny! My God—your waist."

Mary blushed, unaccustomed to compliments. "Thank you."

"Let's see if she can keep it with that appetite," Lillian said. Evidently, the women didn't believe in eating at all. Dinner had still not been served.

"You were a little girl in all the pictures we've seen," Daphne said.

"I showed them the portraits we took every year," Lillian said. She began a story about the private photography sessions "their" father insisted on having in their living room. Her ease and animation made Mary wonder whether it was an experience Lillian had really had.

To help mend "Kitty's" broken heart, the girls began tossing around the names of men to set her up with. She politely listened, knowing she'd never consider dating a White man. Beyond the horror stories she'd heard, her very life was evidence of the trauma they caused. She was relieved when one of the names finally turned the conversation away from her personal life. When Chuck Berry came on, the table left to dance, and Mary ate another slice of cake, watching.

They finished their last Lakes well past one in the morning, leaving the ashtray full of lipstick-stained butts.

When they got home, Lillian fell asleep in her clothes on the living-room couch. Mary was wide awake, fueled by the thrill of the night. She wanted to call her mother but didn't, realizing she wasn't home yet from her night shift. Her momma couldn't have known about Lillian, Mary reasoned, or she never would have sent her there. Willingly abandoning one's family was something Hazel would never support, having tragically lost her own. Lillian's social integration into the White world meant she intended to disappear. Pretty soon, Lillian would have only White friends and date only White men, hoping those in her past forgot her—or, perhaps, understood.

Mary wasn't going to tell on Lillian, because truthfully, it had been fun to play on the other side with her again. It was a welcome break from the mounting stress she'd felt since her graduation. She finally fell asleep, reasoning that once she was home, whatever Lillian was in Los Angeles would no longer matter. As long as she got to ride that Ferris wheel in the picture and go to the beach, she'd return south, to Richard, a happy girl.

She wrote this information to him in the letter she had started on the train. She described the pole-like trunks of the palm trees and the well-dressed Negroes leisurely strolling the streets. Looking at them made her imagine the two of them living in Los Angeles together, she wrote. She closed the letter with all her love and no mention of her return.

CHAPTER 14

Mary

June 1955

"Want eggs?" Lillian's head popped out of the refrigerator as Mary entered the kitchen. Without makeup, she had red splotches on her cheeks, as if someone had pinched them. Remnants of red lipstick settled in the dry cracks of her lips like food stuck between teeth.

"No, thank you; I don't like eggs."

"There's oatmeal or grits." She opened a cabinet, still in her green dress from the night before. "And some canned peaches."

"Just coffee, thanks."

Lillian looked relieved. "I have a headache." She opened a bottle of aspirin and offered one to Mary, who refused.

"Why didn't you tell me you were passing before we got there?"

Lillian poured coffee beans into a grinder. "I thought you'd sound more natural if you were surprised. And I was right; you did. They loved you."

"I've never done that before. Been around White people, ate a meal with them."

"It's like riding a bike."

"I don't know how to ride a bike."

"It means you'll never forget how."

"I know, but"—Mary stopped herself growing impatient with the diversion—"who are Kitty and Emma?"

Lillian reached for the butcher knife on the drying rack. "You don't like your name? I guess we can call you Lane. That's your middle name. Or Lanie." She opened the refrigerator again and offered a green apple to Mary. When she took it, Lillian handed her another one. "Wash them, please."

"It's not about the name." Mary turned on the sink, cradling the apples in her hands. Though they were alone, she lowered her voice. "Why did you lie about us being sisters?"

"I couldn't have you show up out of the blue."

"Why not? I'm visiting."

Lillian pivoted with two coffee cups in her hand. "My God—you don't know."

"Know what?"

Lillian handed Mary a towel. "Dry your hands." She pointed for them to sit. "Your momma sent you here to live with me. She wants you to pass."

"Can't be."

"I have a job for you here. I've been waiting for you."

"I'm starting school. I'm getting married."

Lillian smacked her teeth. "A Negro boy, right?"

Mary crossed her arms in defense against Lillian's disapproval. "His name is Richard."

"Don't you want more for yourself?"

Mary felt a flash of anger—Lillian didn't even have a boyfriend. "He's going to be a doctor."

Lillian held out her hand. "Let me see your ring."

"I said I'm getting married."

"Where's your engagement ring?"

Mary didn't know what that was. The ladies she knew wore the band they received at the ceremony.

Lillian read her thoughts. "An engagement ring is what a man gives you when he asks you to marry him."

Her tone prompted more defense from Mary. "We don't have much now, but he's going to be a doctor. We're moving north when he goes to medical school." Hearing the claim aloud, even Mary doubted its validity.

Lillian slid her chair out to stand. "It doesn't matter to me what you do, but it does matter to your momma. She sacrificed everything to send you here."

"I don't believe you. She would have told me."

Lillian pointed to the phone sitting in an alcove in the hallway. "Don't take my word for it."

———————

Hazel answered on the first ring, as if she'd been expecting Mary's call.

"Is it true?" Mary blurted.

The line sounded dead; Mary couldn't even hear her mother breathe. "Is this because of what I did? Momma, I'm sorry. I didn't mean it."

"It's what's best." Hazel's voice sounded strained. "You have your own life to live."

"Is that why you gave me all that money?"

"I've been saving for this your whole life," Hazel said.

"Momma, I'll never be able to see you again." Mary started crying, feeling the weight of her words.

"Hush now. It's done. Being a White woman won't be all roses, but it's better than any life you'd have here or anywhere else being a Colored one."

"What? You should have told me."

"You wouldn't have left."

"Come to LA. We don't have to pretend."

Hazel stayed silent, her way of saying no.

"We'll talk on the phone every day, then."

"Hearing your voice and never being able to see you makes it too hard for the both of us."

"Write?"

"Go on with your life now. Don't worry about me."

Mary yelled into the phone. "Momma! I don't want to do this!"

Hazel's voice held a level of desperation Mary had never heard before. "*I don't want you back here.* You hear me? If you don't have enough sense to take advantage of the gift God has given you, then I don't want your fool self back in my house."

In response to Mary's tears, Hazel only sucked her teeth. "You stop that, you hear? Lillian's been waiting for you. You two take care of each other."

"You should have told me." The line went dead. "Momma?"

Mary called back several times, to no answer. The gravity of her loss evoked physical pain, nausea, and sent her fleeing to her room. She slammed the door behind her wanting to break it. She didn't even have a picture of her mother. She collapsed on the bed and closed her eyes, remembering their goodbye and how she'd hurried Hazel's hug; Richard was coming to see her off, and she hadn't yet finished her hair. *I'll be back in a week, momma.*

Within her grief was a degree of relief. In the pit of her stomach, she knew it was true: being Negro was akin to being a jack-in-the-box. Sometimes the lid opened, and you were able to shine, but eventually, you ended up back inside the darkness of limitation until someone got the notion to open the box again.

No one talked about these things. Dwelling caused crippling anger that was sure to get you or a loved one killed; the hum of it below the surface was the undercurrent pulling thousands of Negroes away from the South, away from their homes. Whether she was conscious of it or not, it was what had made Mary dream of going to Los Angeles in the first place.

Lillian woke Mary sometime later.

"I didn't get to say goodbye," Mary said, raising her head from her pillow.

"You can write letters. We have a post office box down on Third Street. My momma writes me a few times a year."

Mary buried her face in the covers. It hurt too much to admit that her mother didn't want to hear from her. "I want to talk to her, see her."

"We can't have everything we want in life, Kitty. The sooner you accept that, the better."

Mary's entire life had been a series of nonnegotiables. "Don't call me that. My name is Mary."

Lillian sat on the edge of the bed. "They planned for this. Your mother saved almost everything she made to send us out here. She sent me money until I got a job."

Mary understood now: every Sunday in Charlotte, while the girls visited, their mothers had plotted their futures.

Like her answered prayers for her daughter's White appearance, meeting Catherine and Lillian had been a godsend to Hazel. From the day Mary was born, Hazel had been grooming her to pass for White, but she was apprehensive about sending her to the other side alone. Hazel had seen Catherine and Lillian before and jumped at the chance for the girls to meet that day in Ivey's.

Mary's entire life had been lived in preparation for this, a dress rehearsal. Their trips to Charlotte were meant for Mary to gain comfort in the White world and, once Hazel met Catherine, for the girls to bond as closely as sisters. The mothers had made a pact to send their daughters out into the world together, and they would be each other's support as they dealt with the pain of losing their only children.

"My mother lives in Winston with yours now." The day Mary left for Los Angeles, Catherine had arrived from Asheville.

"When did you move here?" Mary asked.

"Three years ago."

"But why Los Angeles? Do you know anyone here?"

"No, but it's the farthest I could get from my family. The weather is a bonus."

Mary questioned the necessity of crossing over—different from passing, which allowed a person to slide back and forth over the color line when able and necessary. "There's no Jim Crow here. We can be ourselves and have a good life, a better life."

"Not that much better. As women, the only protection we have is marriage. And a Negro man, whether he works as a janitor, bus boy"—Mary started to interject, but Lillian kept talking as if she knew what Mary was going to say—"*doctor*, lawyer, or Indian chief—here, up north or down south—can't offer me or you much." Lillian, Mary saw now, shared Richard's cynicism. "But you're free to go if you want to. I won't tell."

Mary understood now that a return south would break her momma's heart. "I don't have anywhere to go."

Lillian turned her head to one side, as if she was analyzing her sincerity. "You can't come here and ruin things for me."

"Never."

"Come on, then."

In the living room, Lillian removed a stack of books from the seat of one of her green-velvet-upholstered chairs and dragged it over to the couch. After lighting a cigarette, she began a lecture on what she called the Seven Rules:

1. *Discretion is paramount.* "Don't share unnecessary information about your life now, or your past. The more you volunteer, the more comfortable people are asking."

2. *Never comment on or engage in conversation about race or politics.* "It's unladylike to have too many opinions. Some of what people say will be difficult to digest; it's best to condition yourself not to have a feeling either way."

3. *Ignore Negroes.* "The city is so segregated you can go months without ever even seeing a Negro." She said "Negro" with a sliver of distaste on her tongue, as if she wasn't Colored, as if she had never been Colored. It was obvious she preferred the

separation of races for reasons outside of safety. In case Mary was unsure, Lillian made it crystal clear: she was not to go to the Negro part of town for any reason, or engage with Negroes in service or whom she encountered on the street.

4. *Never get pregnant.* "Traits skip generations—who knows what the baby will come out looking like. Even the slightest bit of brown or hair kink won't be able to be explained."

"How does one perform wifely duties and avoid pregnancy?"

Lillian laughed. "Wifely duties? You're so old-fashioned." She explained what a diaphragm was. "There's no guarantee every time, but it helps."

"And if?"

"There are things that can be done."

Mary cringed. She'd heard of the things midwives did, things other than deliver babies. She never had the stomach for pain or bodily secretions—even her own. She'd fainted when she started her period.

"You used to talk about having children all the time. You really want to give that up?" Mary asked.

Lillian picked at her thumbnail. "Who's to say my children would be wonderful? If they were awful, I'd regret staying Negro just to have had them." She went back to her rules.

5. *Marry well. Money is the best protection.* "I could have stayed Negro to be poor." Clearly, Lillian's preoccupation with marriage hadn't changed. But when they were children, her stories always either began or ended with her being swept off her feet. Her shift from romanticism to security struck Mary as sad.

6. *Die White.* "You telling someone about you, tells about me. I intend to die White, which means you have to too."

7. *Stay away from others who are passing.* "There's a whole group of them that run around together. It isn't safe."

"What about us?"

Lillian went to her bar, a shelf built into the wall near the door. She poured herself a generous splash of gin. "That's different. Having family makes people less suspicious of you, less apt to pry. Those other girls, they invite attention, and if one of them is found out, they're all under suspicion."

Mary found that idea ridiculous; it gave White folks far too much credit. "They'd never suspect we'd be so cunning. Besides, without evidence, no one could prove it."

Lillian pointed a finger. "Evidence doesn't matter. Stay away from them. If something happens to you, it happens to me. We're stuck together now. Oh, and most important: from now on, never call me Lillian," Lillian—*Emma*—said. "Not even when we're alone. Otherwise, you'll slip up in public. And your name is Kitty, Kitty Lane Karr." She tapped her chin with her pointer finger. "Seriously, do you prefer Lane? Lanie? Lana, even?"

"I like Kitty." Mary thought it sounded like a movie star's name.

"Kitty it is. Mary is dead from this moment on. Forget she ever existed. Cut off your memory from everything that Mary experienced, or else it'll come back to bite you—I promise. Speaking of which, you have to write to your fella. Make sure he doesn't come looking for you."

Dread washed over her again. No matter the reason she gave, Richard would only hear that he wasn't good enough. With the world constantly saying it, Mary didn't want to be another reinforcement of that message.

Emma pulled a photo album from the bookshelf built between the fireplace and the front door. She dropped it on Kitty's lap. Its edges were frayed, and it smelled stale, as if it had been locked in a dank basement. The pages were overstuffed with yellowed, curling photographs. "You'll have to study this. It's filled with pictures of people we can call kin."

She opened it on Kitty's lap and pointed to a portrait of a young couple.

"Our parents, Jack and Grace Karr, died in a car crash in Boston. That's where we're from. I was eight, and you were five. It happened in the summer. Don't ever be too specific."

On the next page was an older woman in a wheelchair. "Our father's rich aunt Carrie took us in. She got sick two years ago, your junior year in high school. I had already moved to Los Angeles at that point—and you stayed to take care of her."

"That's who Judy was talking about," Kitty remembered.

"Yes, and when she died last month, you joined me here. You have to be able to recite that story in your sleep. If you don't believe it, no one else will."

"You made all that up?"

"Everything but the names. Karr is my last name."

"And our first names?"

"I suppose you wouldn't believe me if I said I made them up?"

"No."

"They're my sisters."

"Do you have a picture of them?"

"No." Emma flicked her cigarette into the brass horse-head ashtray atop a pile of books she was using as a table. "Don't volunteer the album, but if you have to, it's here."

"Have you had to do it?"

"Once."

"Who are these people really?"

"Relatives of the White folks our mommas worked for."

"They stole them?"

"Over time, here and there."

Kitty flipped the pages, curious if any of the Lakeses were in the book. She wouldn't have recognized them, but if the pictures were stolen as Emma said, all of Hazel's contributions would have been from the Lakeses.

In the back were the portraits of the two of them taken at Ivey's. Emma fingered a Christmas photo. "I remember that day." Emma had been sixteen and Kitty thirteen, and it was the last time they agreed to match. Now Kitty understood that their mothers had insisted on matching outfits so they would look more like sisters.

"Why did you stop coming to Charlotte?" Kitty asked.

"We had to move. I was going through a lot back then. I'm sorry I wasn't a better friend to you."

"I missed you, is all."

"I missed you too. And after everything, terribly."

"Why did you have to move?"

"It was a long time coming. I grew up living in a house with my momma, my father, his wife, and their eight kids. Nine, with me. It was a big house, and my momma and I lived in the attic," Emma said, "because it wasn't always appropriate for me to be around."

Emma spoke about her past with ease, something Kitty never would have expected from Lillian. It was as if her new identity had erased some of the shame she used to carry. "I got new clothes and toys when my siblings did but I wasn't allowed to go to their school, sleep in a bedroom downstairs, or eat at their dinner table. I called him Father but never in front of company."

Emma took a long drag from her cigarette and watched the billow of smoke escape from her lips, thinking. "I understood there were rules we had to abide by to keep our family arrangement intact. Then I became a threat to my sisters' marriage prospects, and we had to leave."

"The cotillion."

"Yes. It was one thing to let me be in it, but when my sister's beau became interested in me, rumors passed that I was Negro. That gave my father's wife the excuse she needed to get rid of us. She'd been waiting for that day my whole life."

"What did your father say?"

"Truth was, he couldn't afford to take care of all of us anymore and was too ashamed to say it. His clothing store was losing money. Had been for a while. With four girls left to marry off, he got scared. My momma and I moved to the Negro side of town. No one would talk to us. We moved a few times, until I just couldn't take it anymore and came here."

"I'm sorry." Kitty had felt unwanted and lonely sometimes growing up, but home had been a safe place.

Emma finished her drink and got up to pour another. "Don't be. It prepared me for all of this."

Kitty worried her own education wouldn't be enough. She'd been tricked into leaving; she hadn't wanted to. Emma had always had an edge she didn't.

"What about your father?" Emma asked.

"I don't know who he is." The lie came out before Kitty considered whether Emma already knew the truth. "My momma never talked about it."

"Why should we carry the bad things with us?"

When Emma didn't let on that she knew different, Kitty realized that Hazel must have felt the same shame she did. After all those years, it seemed she would have shared her past and Mary's parentage with Catherine, especially since they were planning to tether one daughter to another. "Why did you take your family's names? You said to leave everything in the past."

"I picked names I'd always answer to." She took a broom from the coat closet by the front door. "I told Ida, my supervisor, you'd start at the studio Monday."

Maids answered phones, Kitty thought. She wanted none of it. "Thanks, but I'm going to look into colleges here."

Emma stopped sweeping to stretch her eyes at Kitty. "You can't—your high school transcripts are in your real name. I arranged this job for you. You have to take it, or it'll be rude. You can quit if you want after you get settled."

"Well, what other jobs do they have?"

"A few girls do hair and makeup. Some work in costumes, one of the restaurants on the lot hires waitresses, and there are also secretaries who—"

"I'm interested in a secretary position."

Emma put her hands to her hips. "Jobs at Telescope don't open up often. Judy and Daphne both have college degrees and have been there a lot longer than you. You going after one of those jobs would anger everyone, and it's best we don't make ourselves too noticeable. Besides, we're not trying to advance at work. The goal is to marry well so you don't have to work at all." She sang the last part as if it was a line in a musical and returned to sweeping.

"Don't you have to make yourself noticeable to find a husband?"

Emma let the broom handle hit the wall. "Men will seek you out whether you want them to or not. You need to work on making yourself likable."

Kitty balked. "What's unlikable about me?"

"Nothing yet, as long as you follow the rules."

CHAPTER 15

Elise

Sunday evening, October 29, 2017

"Kitty was my best friend since I was twelve."

Elise stood inside the mouth of Kitty's wall-to-wall living-room fireplace, avoiding eye contact with her audience. She found it hard to continue. Elise was a natural public speaker, but trying to deliver Kitty's eulogy in front of people who didn't know her personally, with a spotlight and camera in her face, made her palms and underarms sweat. She regretted her recent switch to natural deodorant.

The strangers on Kitty's guest list occupied the front, arranged in rows like schoolchildren. They were heads of the charities Kitty supported, who introduced themselves with stories about how Kitty had changed their lives and sent Christmas cards every year.

Elise got caught in a corner with Lyndsey Mack, who had just formally taken over operations of the women's and children's shelters Kitty funded. She was up front now, with her parents. Her mother, Laurie, had been the operator and figurehead leader of the shelters for decades. Recently diagnosed with Alzheimer's, she was in a wheelchair that evening, but only for containment. Her disease had turned her into a social butterfly who continuously met everyone for the first time.

Her parents' famous peers lined the wall like spectators, accessorizing the somber mood with chic black suits and netted face coverings. None of them had been on Kitty's list. Sarah said she needed them for insulation from the strangers, but Elise knew her mother preferred to simulate mourning in front of an audience, to avoid real emotion. Giovanni had confessed that some of their parents' closest confidants were, like the masses, surprised that Kitty lived next door.

Kitty's friends were gathered with their families on Elise's right, as if they were waiting in the wing of a stage to speak. It didn't seem likely. Grief had turned the Golden Girls stoic.

They used to visit Kitty on special occasions—more when Grandma Nellie was alive. Elise had tried to eavesdrop, but their voices were so low behind the door, it sounded as if the room was empty.

Maude Taft was clutching her daughter, Millicent, by the green silk shoulder of her blouse. Having lost her husband a year ago, and now Kitty, she was too aware of her own mortality and upon arrival had told Elise she wouldn't be speaking.

Maude had been the well-respected gossip columnist for the *Los Angeles Times* for forty years until her granddaughter, also named Millicent, converted the brand into a Web entity. She now stood arm in arm with Giovanni, glaring at Elise. The two had met in middle school and bonded over a bottle of Wildroot; the creamy hair lotion Giovanni used to smooth her hair into a ponytail was a miracle for Millicent's frizzy-curly blond hair. Millicent, to this day, credited Giovanni with helping to restore her confidence.

Elise's arrival came with inquiries from Millicent about where Aaron was *and* a bid for an interview.

Can you find out how the news of our inheritance got leaked? Elise had pressed. *That's the story, isn't it? How our private business got put out into the news? And how we're forced to then comment about something that wasn't anyone's business to begin with?*

Giovanni had appeared from nowhere to pull Elise away.

Behind them stood Lucy Schmitt, wearing a pink, beaded floor-length gown akin to a packet of sprinkles. Her husband, white-haired and bearded, was in a black tux. They were always the overdressed but fly White couple; they were into "soul" music and had had Lakers season tickets ever since you could. Lucy had done the character makeup and costuming for almost every Telescope production anyone cared about. She and her husband, a retired senator, were each ninety years old and still in good health; she'd visited Kitty every so often in recent years, by way of a car service.

Lucy gave Elise a thumbs-up now to encourage her to continue speaking.

She had arrived first, leading Elise down the hall to where Kitty's pictures sat on small easels.

"Put a sold sticker or something on this one." Lucy pointed to a framed photo of her, Kitty, and the rest of the Golden Girls in evening gowns of the fifties.

"This is the first time your Kitty came out with us. I haven't seen this photo in years."

In her younger days, Lucy could have been a doppelganger for Ashley Olsen, but Kitty, always the prettiest, stood out on the end of the photo. One of her slender thighs jutted out of the slit of her long dress. Even in black and white, Elise could tell it sparkled.

"Do you remember where you guys were going?"

Lucy gave her a little wink and nudge with her arm. "Oh, out somewhere; you know." Neither Kitty nor her friends ever missed a chance to remind someone just how *it* they had been.

Elise indulged her. "You guys were cute!" She pointed to the woman in the middle, whose long hair was draped over each shoulder like a shawl. "She reminds me of Cher." Her hair in the photo was ink black, darker even than the car they stood in front of.

Lucy looked surprised that Elise asked. "Cora Rivers? She was once the biggest thing at Telescope—before your Kitty came along, of course."

Now that Lucy said it, Elise remembered Kitty talking about Cora in the past tense. She and Lucy had been among the first people Kitty met at Telescope. "She died, right?"

"Cora is not dead."

"I don't think I've ever met her."

"I don't know if you have or not." Lucy got a far-off look on her face as she touched the face of the woman next to Kitty, short-haired and flinging her arm in the air. "This is Nina. It's probably the only picture we have of her." Lucy looked down the line at the next couple of photographs. "She drowned. She was only twenty-four."

Elise put her hand up. "Spare me the details."

"Acknowledging death helps us celebrate life, child. Kitty led an exemplary one, and it ended because her work was done."

Elise could only settle with half of that notion.

"I know you miss her, honey, but she'll always be with you."

Billie Long came in next, ahead of her family, having coordinated her arrival time with Lucy to secure first dibs at the auction. The songwriter had four children and three times as many number one hits. She and her husband, a retired judge, lived at the top of a cliff in Malibu. They had three daughters and a son, all lawyers now, who sat steps from her in the window seat.

The Golden Girls mostly hadn't seen Kitty in years, but that didn't lessen their loss. "Kitty used to have us over every quarter without fail," Billie said. She always held her eyes wide, as if she'd seen a ghost.

"Why'd she stop?"

"You know how life goes."

Lucy had quickly claimed another ten photographs to sticker as sold before she and Billie left her to greet others Elise didn't recognize. Elise found Rebecca pawing Kitty's trinkets on a table in the hallway.

"Remember this?" She pointed to a small brass compact mirror with a wistful smile. They exchanged a smirk, remembering how Rebecca had stolen the mirror from Kitty's bathroom in the fifth grade and then gotten it confiscated for whipping it out every ten minutes to apply her Dr Pepper Lip Smacker.

"She'd want you to have it." Elise touched what used to be a rose adorning its top. The lacquer was chipped now, and only the metal imprint remained intact.

Rebecca took a picture of its bid number.

Had things gone Kitty's way, Elise wouldn't have had to speak; the memorial would have been over already. There would have been thirty people (including the St. Johns) from 11:00 am to 2:00 pm for lox, bagels, cake, and a champagne toast to the "good life." But Sarah had switched the time to 6:00 pm and the menu to sushi, which meant no one was leaving before midnight. Kitty had planned every detail of her desired memorial, yet Sarah had still felt the need to make alterations.

Elise had pushed back: evening would make it difficult to see the auction items. Sarah hired a lighting crew and a videographer—and a deejay. Elise was working hard to give her mother the benefit of the doubt, but her ignoring Kitty's last wishes felt spiteful. Worse, Elise didn't appreciate her own forced complicity, having to now share her private memories about a private person in front of people who didn't know Kitty personally.

But this wasn't why she kept the trigger line in her speech. Mostly, it felt disloyal to Kitty to exclude it.

"Kitty was a friend to me, and now that she's gone, I realize I've lost the closest thing that I had to a mother."

Elise saw the flinch of her mother's cheek, always the first indicator of a simmering eruption, out of the corner of her left eye. Her mother had scurried to her side before her first words tumbled out, as if the speech was hers, too, and left with the same disruptive commitment. Alison trailed after her, leaving her own mother, Mrs. Pew, whose eyes were still fixated on the floor as if she couldn't stand to look at Kitty's things. Though she was blameless,

Elise wondered how the old lady felt being the heiress of the biggest tobacco company in the world, at the funeral of someone who had died from cancer after years of smoking. Elise knew such things bothered Rebecca, who, like her grandmother, had never smoked—anything.

Elise scanned the room for someone to take the floor, avoiding her sisters and Rebecca, who would defend Sarah to keep the peace.

The voice of her savior came from beyond the crowd. Dr. David King, Kitty's beau, came from the sitting room across the hall, where Kitty's jewels had been partitioned off until the auction began. A fit senior man, his olive-toned skin had retained most of its elasticity, and except for his entirely gray, but full, head of hair and beard, he could have passed for a man in his sixties.

Elise stepped away from the fireplace and went to paw the guest book on the entry table. The night's event was part memorial, part auction, and anyone who wanted to speak could, but from the lengthy passages on the pages, it seemed that most wanted to write. She didn't see the point—who were these messages for, exactly?

Hearing someone behind her requesting to sign the book, Elise stepped aside. "Sure." Her stomach flipped like a cliché when she saw it was Jasper Franklin, the photographer she'd requested for her *Vogue* cover story. "What are you doing here?"

"Hello to you too."

She resisted a smile at what felt like flirtatious scolding. She reached to hug him, and he kissed her jawline near her ear. He smelled like cologne and mint. Jasper was the type of man who anyone who could see would say was handsome. Intrigued first by his talent and further by his Google summary, Elise had formed an attraction to the thirty-something Black photographer even before they met.

Credited for resurrecting coffee-table books as an art form, Jasper's photographs won awards and were commissioned for ads and displayed on billboards and on the sides of buildings. His prints depicting college life, first

love, growing pains, Black masculinity, and substance abuse sold for upward
of five figures apiece.

Elise had learned of him a year ago, but they had only officially met
that March in New York, in the rooftop restaurant of her parents' apartment
building. He was out celebrating his current show's sold-out success; Elise
was escaping the drama of her viral post. They had shared a bottle of wine
and even took a snowy 4:00 am stroll. Elise would have let him kiss her had
he not offended her.

She rushed her words, remembering what was weird about the moment.
"Did *Vogue* send you?"

"I'm here for personal reasons."

Elise looked doubtful. "None of which have to do with me?"

"You were a side benefit." He grinned in a mischievous way that said he
wouldn't elaborate.

"How's that?"

"Six degrees of separation."

She smirked. "Six exactly?"

"Don't you like the mystery?"

She shook her head. "I do not."

"I'm here for my grandfather. He wouldn't have missed this, but he died
two years ago."

"Oh, he was invited?"

"Guess Kitty didn't know he died."

"Who's your grandfather?"

"He was a photographer for the *Los Angeles Times*," Jasper said.

"So he's why you started shooting."

He nodded. "He gave me my first camera. Taught me everything he knew."

"Was he Black?"

Jasper chuckled as if he was used to the question. "Yes. A trailblazer."

"How did he get started in photography?"

"He had a mentor."

"Who?"

Jasper winked. "Guess you'll have to read my next book."

"Ah! Good for you; you figured it out." The night they met, he had been at a creative standstill.

"It all fell in my lap."

"I bet your family is proud."

His fingers went to his chin. "They're supportive but worried about its reception."

"Why? Sounds uplifting."

"Quite a bit of our family business is involved. My grandfather has an extraordinary tale."

"I bet. Send me a copy."

"How's a preview?" he said. "We can have dinner at my place when you get in Thursday."

"I don't get in till late."

"You should still come by." His eyes settled on her, making her think things she shouldn't be thinking at a memorial. She pulled open the front door, needing some air.

He stayed on her heels. "This is Kitty's house?"

They sat on a bench just inside the first entrance to the jungle.

"It is," Elise said.

He gestured around them. "It's beautiful."

"Yes, many memories."

"I'm sorry for your loss."

"Thanks . . . though I probably shouldn't have been so candid."

"It was honest."

Elise changed the subject. "So, who else did your grandfather photograph? I'm sure he had more interesting subjects and events to cover than Kitty."

Jasper raised a brow. "There was no one more interesting to him than Kitty. He kept every photo he ever took of her."

"Are you trying to tell me your grandfather and Kitty had an affair?"

"No, they didn't even know each other then."

"I'm confused."

"The times. Him being Black and her being White—unless she introduced herself, he wouldn't have."

"But I thought you said Kitty invited him here?"

"They met years later."

Elise thought about the RSVP list. "What's his name?" Hearing more guests flooding into the yard, she peered through the trees, halfway wondering if Aaron had arrived yet. "Are you bidding tonight?"

"Yes, one of my grandfather's photographs is being auctioned."

"Which one?"

"Kitty's at a pool, looking to the side at something off camera."

Elise knew the one. It had been taken at Kitty and Nathan's old house in the Hollywood Hills. "I hope you'll buy more than just one photograph. The night is for charity."

"I told you, I'm here for personal reasons. That photograph completes my grandfather's collection."

"Which you need for your book."

"Yes."

"Well, being that my sisters and I are the heirs of her estate, you'll have to get permission before publishing any photographs of her."

"Not exactly true. But I do owe you the courtesy of a first look, which is why I'd like to make you dinner on Thursday."

"I deserve more than a courtesy," Elise said. "And that photo of Kitty—how did your grandfather take it? It was a private moment at her home."

"I told you he was the original paparazzo."

"He stalked her?"

"You're going to make me talk about this right now, aren't you?"

"No, that's your style." He pretended to look hurt by her reference to the sour way they'd parted seven months ago. Her need to remind him of it was evidence that she had missed him, though she hardly knew him.

"I'm sorry about all that," he said. "I was rudely opinionated for having just met you."

"And wrong. People certainly think I'm Black now."

Jasper had challenged her post, insinuating she knew nothing about the Black experience. "I didn't say people didn't think you were *Black*, I said no one cares what color you are. You're above race."

"You're *still* wrong, is what I'm saying." What made her angriest was that she never got to start fresh, to filter the story. She liked Jasper but hated how his assumptions put her in a position to prove that she wasn't what people said she was. It was a handicap.

"I'll take that. I apologize."

He'd apologized that night, too, so she wasn't convinced he meant it. She got angry remembering. *You've been treated like a princess your whole life; when have you ever really experienced racism?*

"Still think people would trade their problems for mine?"

Jasper's head cocked to one side. "Hell nah. Not after this Kitty news."

"Okay. I'll accept your apology then."

Guests started migrating back toward the house. She stood, receiving the signal. "You came into town just for this?"

"My flight leaves at eight in the morning."

"Stay for our Halloween party," Elise suggested.

He held Kitty's door open for her. Giovanni was standing in the hallway, directing guests back into the living room. She waited for Elise and Jasper to approach. "Mom's ready."

Elise nodded. "I'll be right there."

Giovanni waited for an introduction, whirling the extra cherries in her old-fashioned around with the stirrer.

"Jasper Franklin, my *Vogue* photog. Jasper, this is my middle sister, Giovanni."

They cringed at the sound of a bell.

"Mommie dearest calls," Elise joked before touching her cheek to

Jasper's. "See you later." She and Giovanni walked off together into the front room.

"You invited a guest." Giovanni called her a hypocrite for complaining about their mother's additions.

"I didn't."

"Small world."

"Itty-bitty."

"Need me to occupy Aaron?"

"Is he here?" Elise waved her sister off. "What? Gio, Jasper didn't come here for me."

They slipped into place for photos before their father commanded the attention of the room to outline the auction process.

Elise hadn't told a soul about the night she and Jasper met but thought of it every day since. The time with him had changed her. It was a welcome, intense attraction, one that rendered her mute for a few moments every time they locked eyes.

Now it signaled danger.

She wanted to believe that he had come that night, in part, to show her that he too had been thinking about their mishandled moment. But something about his presence bothered her. It felt like an unavoidable iceberg, not a life raft.

Jasper hated Los Angeles, and his complaints went beyond the common gripes about traffic, pollution, and superficialities. He hated its essence: its country-town zoning, the lack of four seasons, the health obsession, and the elementary nightlife hours. He wouldn't have made the trip for just any old picture his grandfather took, considering he had probably taken hundreds of thousands. That picture was paramount, Elise knew, though she couldn't remember where it had hung in Kitty's house. To find out why he was really there, she would have to cross the line on all fronts, sooner than planned.

She dreaded going there: opening the Pandora's box hidden in her car trunk could obliterate any possibility of their happy ending. She and Jasper would be an unfortunate casualty of the whole mess, a relationship ended before it started. She wished that he was, in fact, disconnected from Kitty in all the ways it mattered but knew better, especially after he dropped almost nine thousand dollars for the side profile of Kitty at the pool at her old house in the Hollywood Hills and then left—without it—during the next bid. Unsure whether he had accepted her party invitation or not, she pretended to get a call and left, hoping to catch him before he boarded the Sprinter van.

Her questions were urgent, but she couldn't go to him. Jasper's popularity had grown immensely in the last year, and though Andy could make it happen, the paparazzi were probably keeping tabs on Jasper's whereabouts too.

By the time she got to the end of Kitty's driveway, there wasn't a person in sight—except Aaron, who emerged from the shadows of Kitty's trees as if he'd been hiding.

"You're just getting here?" she asked.

"I just left set." He scratched his beard. "Who was that?"

"My *Vogue* photographer."

"You gave them access?"

"He was invited personally."

"By you?"

Elise looked at him sideways. "Are you jealous?"

"You were sprinting after him, damned near."

"He left his auction item."

"So?"

"So . . . he may be trying to extort us." It was her fear, but she only said it to Aaron because she knew he wouldn't take her seriously.

Sure enough, he waved her along. "Come on; I need a drink."

He reached out his hand, and she took it to put the room at ease, knowing his absence from her side had been noticed and interpreted. Sarah, standing with her friends across the room, looked relieved to see him, as if his whereabouts had also made her most-asked-questions list that evening. Giovanni made a beeline over with a drink for him, but Noele and their dad, engaged in conversation, only waved.

His grip was flaccid, did nothing to secure her, but the display worked as it always did. People rushed him to say hello, ignoring her until they wanted a photograph. Aaron was super personable and remembered tidbits about people Elise couldn't care less about. He always had a ready anecdote for whatever question he was asked; Elise listened as he made up a story to Maude and Lucy to illustrate how lovely Kitty was.

He lied so easily. Kitty hadn't been her lovely self to him. And Aaron knew that.

Kitty had never liked Aaron. *He won't be able to accept coming second.* Elise had ignored her then because Aaron was the sweetest guy she'd ever dated: hand-holding, flower-bringing, date-planning. Suddenly she had the perfect someone to attend events with, someone who liked doing all the talking. She upped his stature, and he made her more approachable, more down-to-earth. Elise had come to find out too late that they only shone in public.

She wished he would stop pretending and admit that it wasn't just her media tornado that had changed things between them. Even on the rare nights they were home together, Elise slept in their bed and he on the couch. Normally he opted for a hotel suite close to the Manhattan Beach studio, too tired to ride home in his chauffeured car. After one too many nights of that, Andy told her about Maya.

Only Andy knew Elise knew. He drove her to see for herself that first time, and every time since. Most people would shy away from knowing how their significant other was with another, but Elise couldn't look away. Aaron couldn't keep his hands off Maya or go more than a few days without seeing her. Elise was jealous—not of Maya, but certainly of their love. Well, maybe a little jealous of her too. There were memes about her ass, and her body did make any outfit. Elise had nothing against her; she was just insulted to come in second, as if brains and pedigree meant nothing. Aaron did things for

Maya he never did for her. Elise had played the eye candy on-screen for millions of dollars, now she was competing with the real-life version, who was sexier, more confident—but couldn't give him any of what Elise already had.

Watching them made her miss being loved. Loving someone. But calling off a wedding, when it was the only light news in her orbit, was unnecessary and would only bring more attention.

Also, Elise wasn't going to lose him to her in front of the entire world. They worked well together, and Aaron was such a good actor that when the lights and cameras turned on, he made her feel as though they even had chemistry. Those were the times she thought she could marry him and actually be happy.

That was before Kitty's passing. She didn't need a celebrity partner if she no longer cared about the institution. When the timing was right, Aaron would make the perfect diversion, and she had the photos to ensure it.

CHAPTER 16

Kitty

June 1955

The weekly wage of a telephone operator was three times more than Hazel made working sixty hours a week. Kitty was astonished she could get paid so much just to answer phones, but soon regretted not inquiring about the secretary positions during her interview with Ida.

Ida had broad shoulders and wore her hair parted and rolled at the nape of her neck. She used to be an operator and showed Kitty some switchboard shortcuts. What Ida didn't prepare her for was how disoriented the job would make her feel.

The telephone room was concrete, tile, steel, and hard plastic. It was cold, with harsh fluorescent light and no windows. Four rows of five telephone stations occupied most of the room. The operators did their best to bring personality to the space by decorating their stations; Emma's station had a bouquet of yellow fake flowers, a gold tube of lipstick, and a picture of the ocean on it.

Daphne led Kitty two rows behind it, to the fourth row. "Sit next to me." Her station was decorated with horses.

"Did you live on a farm?"

"God no, Meredith and I competed."

Kitty didn't know what that meant and was relieved when the phones started ringing, because she didn't want to hear any more about Daphne missing a horse. She talked about it like it was a pet. Kitty had never had a pet; most families she knew were too poor to feed an animal that couldn't help make them money.

"Telescope Studios, how may I direct your call? One moment, please."

Over and over and over. Every time Kitty thought she'd get a break, her phone would ring again. After an hour, her tongue grew sluggish, and her throat begged for water.

Emma kept looking back at her with a smirk. Unable to tell if she was being sympathetic or enjoying her struggle, Kitty pretended not to notice and worked harder. Her only reward was more calls to transfer.

They took lunch in thirty-minute shifts. Kitty ate an egg salad sandwich and an apple in fifteen, preferring to take the rest of her time in silence.

After work, everybody walked to Mitch's, where the subject of Kitty's dating came up again.

"We should bring her dancing," Judy said.

"Absolutely not." Emma shot Judy a look.

"Emma's right; they'd eat her up," Daphne said.

Kitty wondered who "they" were.

"It's not that—I don't want my little sister tagging along."

The table exchanged looks, surprised by her honesty with Kitty present.

"I'm not a good dancer, anyway," Kitty said.

"Me neither. I just go for the music," Meredith said. "I'll babysit her, Emma."

"I said no," Emma said.

The table quieted at the word of their queen.

After a moment, Meredith spoke. "So, how was your first day, Kitty?"

Kitty hesitated, feeling uncomfortable that she'd hated it so much.

They all nodded, reading her face. "This is why we say *we* have to be getting something out of it too."

"I had another date with Sam." When Judy started in on the details, Kitty started looking for their waitress. Her eyes passed over a Negro woman sitting in the corner near the door. Kitty watched her momentarily, wondering who she was, before their eyes met and the woman smiled. Kitty turned forward.

"How old are you, Kitty?" Meredith was asking.

"Almost eighteen."

"We're twenty-three, and I've never been in love. Daphne has."

"Shattered my heart," Daphne said.

Not knowing how to measure her feelings against the maturity of experience of the studio operators, she told them she loved Richard.

"If you did, you would have stayed," Emma said, flicking her cigarette butt into the ashtray.

"That's not true."

"No? Go back."

Kitty knew Emma was in character, but something about the way she said it rubbed her the wrong way.

"Do you miss him?" Daphne asked, misreading the emotion that crossed Kitty's face.

"I still think about him sometimes."

"You don't talk to him anymore?"

"We write"—the truth came out easier than a lie—"from time to time."

Kitty hadn't seen any harm in mailing Richard the letter she had already written. She told herself she wouldn't write again, but then he responded quickly, with confessions. Taking over his father's business hadn't been a choice: a teacher at the White high school had failed him to prevent his enrollment into the pre-med program at Central. He was miserable working with his father, and her return was all he was looking forward to. Kitty didn't have the heart to tell him she wasn't coming.

The girls giggled. "Kitty has a beau."

"No, no, no," Kitty said. "We're just friends."

Later, when Kitty and the others exited, she saw that the Negro woman in the corner was accompanied by a White man. Amazed that everyone filed out without a glance in their direction, Kitty stared. The woman stared back, as if asking this time, *Do I know you?* Kitty rushed to catch up with the others. They walked several blocks back to the lot, and when no one made mention of the Negro who had been in their space, Kitty fell in love with Los Angeles.

"I thought you broke things off with Richard." Emma started the car and shut off the blaring radio.

"I did."

"So why did you tell them you two still write each other?"

"It sounded more romantic. I wanted to have something to share."

"Well, congratulations," she said. "Now they're going to ask you about him, and it's going to keep coming up. I don't know how many times I have to tell you not to mix the truth with a lie."

"You've never said that before."

Kitty wasn't sure if Emma was jealous because of the others' interest in her or because she knew she was lying about still writing to Richard.

"Haven't you heard the stories about what happens to people caught passing?"

"I know what the risks are."

"Then why do you keep doing dumb things?" Emma said.

They rode home in silence and didn't speak for the rest of the night. Emma did a crossword puzzle, and Kitty read in her room. The next morning, Emma was up early and humming to the radio. She acted as though nothing had happened and even split her favorite chocolate-filled doughnut with Kitty in the cafeteria.

Kitty quickly became bored with the other operators. By the end of the second week, she was escaping during lunch for a walk alone around the lot.

Emma had promised her a tour, but they were always running late, and Emma was never willing to miss breakfast. "There's not much to see anyway." All film production was on hiatus, and only a couple of television shows were still in production.

Kitty didn't care; she was simply curious to see how the sets differed from their projections. She followed the directional signs affixed to the top corner of the lot's tan buildings to the soundstages. The entrance to stage C was the only door open.

Kitty entered the dark building to find herself in a maze of thick, black velvet curtains hanging from the warehouse-style ceiling. Hearing voices, she followed the path to the back of a crowd of about fifteen men. Peeking between their bodies, Kitty saw two women dressed in pants and button-up shirts performing a scene about who was cooking Thanksgiving dinner, on a stage outfitted as a dining room. The male crowd roared with laughter as the two began arguing. She was impressed. Neither woman was dressed in a corset or a frilly dress, yet they commanded the men's attention with everyday housewife banter. Normally, women were the voluptuous sidekick or the youngish love interest, not the center of a scene.

After another five minutes, the actresses called for a break. Kitty retreated, breaking into a run once she exited the stage, unsure of how long she'd been gone.

No one noticed her return. They were all clustered around Lois's station, eavesdropping.

"If we don't resume filming before December, there's no way we'll be considered for the Oscars," a woman's voice said. "And I don't have anything else on deck."

"He won't make any decisions until September," a male voice responded.

"You have to talk to him."

"Cora, we all have an investment in this. He won't listen." The man sounded tired.

"We have to make him."

On the walk to Mitch's, Emma explained that the woman on the call was Cora Rivers, the studio's biggest actress. "She's also Abner Tate's mistress. Starred in the studio's last four films. She was talking to Charles Mints, the director of her latest film, *The Misfits*. Abner wrote it for her. Everyone says the script is the ramblings of a crazy man; that, coupled with the expensive budget, proves that Abner has lost his mind."

Nathan didn't officially start for another two months but had put all production on hold until he could evaluate each project one by one. People were none too pleased about his decisions thus far. "*The Misfits* had already started filming when Nathan shut it down."

They slid into the same end booth at Mitch's, and the same waitress asked if everyone was having their usual. Kitty was the only one who ordered food with her vodka soda.

"We knew about Nathan's succession weeks before the announcement," Emma said. Whether it was a matter of hiring, firing, or a nasty habit, the phone operators knew all the secrets on the lot. Emma furthered her education with the daily trade papers and predicted firings. "The secretaries will be the first to go. They're so old, they'll never be able to keep up."

"And we'll replace them," Judy said, high-fiving Emma.

"I thought you didn't care about advancing at work?" Kitty asked.

Emma winked at her. "I do if it means marrying the new owner of Telescope Studios."

"You know him?" Kitty was shocked to have missed that detail.

"She's never even met him," Daphne said.

"She's obsessed," Meredith said.

"I'm obsessed about what his taking over means for us. He's really smart," Emma said.

Meredith rolled her eyes. "And rich, and tall, and—"

"And yes, very handsome," Emma said. "So what?" Everyone laughed, and Emma pretended to pout. "I figure I have as good a chance of meeting him as anyone working here. Anyway, you'll all thank me soon." Emma raised her glass for a toast. "New jobs by the fall!"

Kitty followed suit, wishing she'd had more time with Lillian before meeting Emma, who, she'd discovered, had ugly things in her. She'd accused Kitty of being ungrateful for wanting a secretary job when, really, she was being selfish.

On the Fourth of July, they woke early, packed a lunch, and drove almost an hour up the Pacific Coast Highway to the beach at Malibu. Kitty was surprised to see only White people on the sand.

"I thought there was no segregation here?"

"They lied," Emma said, gesturing for her help with the blanket. "It's not the law, but they don't hide their feelings. The pools, beaches—except for the sliver in Santa Monica—Negroes aren't welcome."

"Yet they swim in fish pee," Kitty said.

Emma stuck an umbrella in the sand and squatted to twirl it deeper. "And White kids pee in pools just like Negro ones, yet they're accepted everywhere."

Kitty ran down to the water. The sound of the waves crashing onto the sand sounded like her mother's tambourine. She couldn't escape the missing. At home, everyone would be going to the church soon. There was always a bake sale, and everyone sat out on their blankets to eat until the fireworks started. The fireworks were lit on the White high school's football field but could be seen from the rooftops of Cottonwood.

The ocean was ice cold, so she stayed ankle deep, liking the sinking sensation created by the water's retreat. She stared out, wondering if it looked different from the murky Atlantic, which her mother said had a graveyard of African bones at its bottom.

Hearing Emma calling her, she ran up the beach. She'd been in the sun too long. She collapsed on the blanket under the umbrella, which Emma refused to leave.

"Browning first and reddening second is a dead giveaway," Emma reminded her. In addition to the seven rules, she had a list of other things that could reveal Negro-ness: preferring spicy foods, not knowing the names of the most popular restaurants in town, using grease in your hair, and having interest in the Negro condition. Especially that.

It was why Emma kept her issues of *Jet* magazine hidden behind the books on her shelf. Kitty had called her out one morning when she tried to conceal it in front of the morning's paper.

Isn't that risky?

White people read Jet. *It's how they know what's going on with us.*

Then why do you keep them hidden? No one comes here.

I hide them from you.

You don't have to pretend you don't miss it.

I like to be informed, Kitty. That's not the same as nostalgia.

The national papers glossed over the brutality, while the Negro media highlighted the racial tension that was getting worse all over the country. It made Kitty worry about her momma. The South was beyond flagrant, and though Negroes weren't photographed hanging from trees in LA, economic prosperity, the benefit of the doubt, and common decency weren't things Negroes could rely on anywhere in America.

Emma promised they would get word if something happened to their mothers, but Kitty wasn't convinced. "What if no one's around who knows to tell us, or how to find us?"

"I'll be around, and we'll know."

Emma turned on the radio she had brought to distract Kitty from her envy of everyone else's freedom under the sun. She stood to shake her hips to the music. "Get up and dance with me."

"No thanks."

Emma smiled at a man running toward them after a football.

He whistled. "Nice moves!"

Emma collapsed next to Kitty. "Everything will be easier once you settle into life with a man," she said.

"Is that what you tell yourself?"

"It's true."

"I'm not interested in dating right now." Kitty was on guard; how could she fall in love? There was never a moment when she wasn't wide-eyed, looking down to make sure she didn't trip. Fairy tales never featured Colored girls.

"The girls have offered to set you up, and you should let them. It's borderline rude not to."

"What if he can tell I'm Negro?"

Emma sat upright. "That's your problem?"

Kitty had stopped Richard every time his mouth slipped under her collar, barely able to resist exploring the throbbing throughout her lower half when his lips moved to her neck.

"Seriously?"

"Yes. I didn't want to get pregnant."

"There are other things to do without you getting pregnant."

"Like what?"

What if her body looked different from what a White woman's was supposed to look like? Despite their stark differences in skin tone, both her and her mother's nipples were brown.

"You look White, and that's all that matters. Only carelessness and self-doubt can give you away. Do you still have feelings for that boy down south?"

"No."

"Are you still writing him letters?"

"No."

Another lie. She'd been writing to Richard all summer. Worse, she'd given him their home address to hide it from Emma, who had dominion over the post office box. The more she wrote Richard, the guiltier she felt about it. She knew she wasn't going back, and writing him was like a security blanket that kept her tied to Mary. Richard pressed for her return date in every letter, so they could marry before the semester started. His most recent had the question underlined in all caps. She'd been carrying her reply around in her purse for a week already, unable to mail it:

I'M NEVER COMING BACK. I CAN'T MARRY YOU. I'M SO SORRY. PLEASE DON'T EVER CONTACT ME AGAIN.

"Then why?" Emma pressed. "Do you still want to be an actress?"

"I never said I wanted to act." Kitty hadn't pondered that pursuit since leaving Winston but was still sneaking away at lunch a couple times a week to watch rehearsals.

Emma frowned. "You didn't have to. You used to recite lines from the movie in the theater and force me to trade stories with you."

"I thought you liked it!"

"Not as much as you, and it was your idea."

"Why do you work at a film studio if you hate it so much?" Kitty asked.

"It just happened that way."

"But you used to love going to the movies."

"I went 'cause you wanted to."

That wasn't Kitty's recollection.

"Who did you tell your stories to after me?" Emma wanted to know.

"I wrote them down, told them to myself."

"You'll be sorry having your head in the clouds when I get married and leave you."

"You're not even seeing anyone." Since Kitty had been there, Emma had spent every weekend up all hours of the night, drinking alone.

Emma threw a grape at her face. "I will be soon."

When it got cold, they wrapped up in blankets, watching others soak up the sun and play with their children in the waves. Sadness came to Kitty again as a little girl squealed, running from the waves, and crashed into her mother's arms.

Emma pointed to the Negro beach in Santa Monica on their way home. "It's aptly named the Inkwell." Every inch of the forty-yard stretch of sand was covered by a blanket or a brownish body. They'd enjoyed dozens of feet of space from others in Malibu. "I come early to avoid the traffic. There used to be another beach farther south, called Manhattan Beach, but they took it. So now everyone comes here." Emma tapped the steering wheel, anxious for the light to turn.

The ocean air blew the smell of barbeque to the street. Women stood in clusters, talking, as kids played close by. Their skin glistened in the sunlight. Around them, the men were arranging umbrellas and blankets on the sand. Music was playing from several radios, and boys were throwing footballs around.

"Don't you miss it?"

"What?"

"That." Kitty nodded toward the beach. "Them." Crossing over was easier when she never had to see her own kind. Then she could pretend that they didn't exist, that she wasn't missing anything. When she thought about it, Kitty hadn't had contact with another Negro person since the train station. Neighborhoods were segregated and far apart, and the lower-wage and hourly jobs around town that would have gone to Negroes (for a lesser wage in the South, of course) went to the rising Irish and Italian immigrant populations. Kitty's world had become White, save for the occasional passerby.

"No." Emma sped off as the light turned green. "There was nothing about being Negro that was good for me."

It would have been easy to assume Emma was ashamed of her race, but Kitty knew it was the circumstances of being Negro that had inflicted the harm. Emma chain-smoked every day to ease her nerves until her nonnegotiable six o'clock drink. Tobacco and gin, like the snuff tobacco Hazel packed in her lip, were her pacifiers. And marrying well was an obsession because she believed that by being some rich man's wife, she'd no longer be her father's illegitimate child.

Kitty didn't hold the hatred toward her past that Emma did. She missed it. Deep inside, Kitty knew her mother would never write back, but it gave her comfort to picture her reading the letters she sent. She wrote her every week, sometimes twice. And each week, Emma emerged from the post office empty-handed.

To feel close to her, Kitty cooked, remembering her moving about their small kitchen. After she fried some chicken for dinner later that week, Emma came in, yelling and slamming the windows Kitty had opened to let out the smoke.

"You can smell it halfway down the street. The whole neighborhood is going to know that Kitty Karr fries chicken." Her hands went to her hips as she waited for an apology.

Kitty dismissed her worry. "So?"

"How many White women do you know who fry chicken?" she said.

Kitty laughed. "Every single one who has a maid."

Emma exhaled her exasperation. "You don't get it."

"I'll say our maid taught me if that makes you feel better."

"I don't think people are going to suspect us just because you can fry chicken, Kitty," she said. "I think people are going to start dropping by, inviting themselves in, being nosey about who we are, wanting to get to know us."

"So, it smells good, is what you're saying?" Kitty poked a breast with the point of a knife as it sizzled in the cast-iron pan.

"I'm serious."

"You're being ridiculous," Kitty said.

Emma threw her hands up. "Don't blame me when the whole neighborhood starts ringing our bell."

"Fine. When I have a taste for it, I'll just buy it."

Emma shook a finger at her. "Stay away from the Negro side of town, Kitty."

"Is that what this is about?" Kitty asked. She honestly hadn't had the inclination. The influx of Negroes from southern states made her worry a tiny bit. What if someone recognized her? More people knew her than she knew. Sometimes she passed other Negroes on the street and accidentally made eye contact, as she had with the woman in Mitch's, forgetting that she wasn't supposed to. The funny thing is that, like that woman, they didn't look away like *they* were supposed to. Kitty was always first to break the gaze, and it made her wonder for blocks afterward if they knew she was one of them.

"You seem nostalgic. It's dangerous."

"Because I'm frying chicken?"

Emma touched her shoulder. "I know you're homesick. But you've got to get over it. Pretty soon, you'll start doing things and going places you shouldn't. Missing things it doesn't do you any good to miss."

Kitty pulled her hand away. She would always yearn for home, but that wasn't the only reason she was frying chicken. Emma didn't cook much, and when she did, the entire meal came from a can or a box. Kitty was used to more greens and beans, and her stomach had begun to turn on her.

Emma opened the refrigerator.

"You're not going to eat?"

Emma scoffed as if Kitty had said the most absurd thing. "Of course I am. Just need some hot sauce."

That night, they dined on hot, crispy chicken, and Kitty drank as many gin and tonics as Emma served. Emma put on Ray Charles and turned up the record player, dancing and twirling around the room, high on liquor. Emma could really dance; she was almost in a trance as she shimmied and shook her body to the melody.

"Can I go dancing with you all the next time?"

"Never." Emma was serious but still playful. She pulled Kitty to her feet and took her by the waist. "I'll teach you to dance though." Kitty started laughing as Emma spun her around like a spinning top. It wasn't long until the gin started sloshing around, and they both spent the night on the floor of the bathroom.

"This is why you can't come dancing with us," Emma explained.

"It was all the spinning."

"What do you think goes on at those dance halls? People are nearly flying across the room."

Kitty couldn't picture it.

"It's something to see, that's for sure."

Kitty wished she'd stopped talking about it if she wasn't invited.

On Sunday, Emma commandeered the leftovers and made a sandwich with the last chicken breast. She pulled it out on the beach with some mustard and hot sauce, making Kitty chase her down for a bite.

In these early days, Kitty would sometimes forget that she really wasn't White. She felt calmer, invincible even. People saw her and acknowledged her in a way they hadn't when she was Negro. Beauty had been a liability in the Negro world, but in the White one, it was a valuable commodity. It made her popular. She was no longer splintered but someone else entirely. Soon, she'd forget who Mary Magdalene was and relinquish her preferences. Whiteness had always been a tool, and it became a ladder she vowed to keep climbing when, one early September day, Emma handed her the latest issue of *Jet*. Inside, the picture of the bloated, mutilated body of a Colored boy named Emmett Till made her lose her oatmeal in the kitchen sink.

Word spread quickly at breakfast about the gruesome photos tacked to the message board. Trays of uneaten food went in the trash.

"He should have known better."

"He was from Chicago. Mississippi is like a whole other country."

"*I* wouldn't know how to act down there."

Daphne was the last at their table to brave the sight. She'd heard about the murder from a cab driver the other day.

Only with the table empty did Kitty ask, "Did you put those photos on the message board?"

Emma dug into her grapefruit with a soup spoon. "Emmett Till is national news, Kitty. It should have been in their paper."

For weeks after, Kitty woke to find Emma asleep at the foot of her bed.

CHAPTER 17

Kitty

September 1955

As Emma had predicted, a chain of firings was Nathan's first order of business. Executives were shuffled, and half the secretaries were gone by his second week. The operators awaited an announcement about interviews, but all that followed was a memo encouraging everyone to take more of an active role in the creative process by attending tapings and castings, reading scripts, and submitting feedback. Nathan envisioned the new Telescope as an incubator of ideas and wanted input from everyone, including the staff. He resumed production on all five of the studio's television shows but kept all films under evaluation.

Kitty spent her workdays waiting for an opportunity to go to the stages. No one, not even Emma, said anything about her disappearances, so she kept doing it and watched all kinds of rehearsals from the shadows, observing and taking it all in as if the process was the movie itself. She never got bored, no matter how many times they had to start a scene over.

Hearing Cora Rivers was taping a guest spot on the cop show *Windfall*, Kitty opted out of Mitch's one Friday night, curious to see what a movie star looked like in the flesh.

Emma was first to exit the telephone room that evening; the others followed like ducks. "You know you don't get paid to stay."

Kitty pushed in her station chair. "I don't mind." Kitty needed a greater distraction than Mitch's. She was still reeling from the news of the acquittal of Emmett Till's murderers that day. Nothing swayed the conscience of the all-White male jury, who took less than an hour to decide.

"I don't work even a moment for free." With a huff, Emma led the line out the door.

Others must have felt similarly, or were uninterested, because Kitty was the only staff member in the designated spot on the side of the stage. She was watching the assistant director, a short, balding man named Johnny Wish, make last-minute adjustments to the camera blocking when a trail of smoke wafted into her nose. A petite, blond woman was standing too close behind her. Her proximity caused Kitty to stumble back over the cords coiled on the wing of the stage.

The woman reached to steady Kitty by the waist. "Sorry. I didn't mean to scare you." Her hand went to her chest. "Lucy Schmitt." She tugged on her earlobe, engulfed by a diamond earring. The pair matched the crispness of her white-collared button-up shirt and were the center of attention with her ear-length blond hair tucked back. She wore no makeup, not even lipstick, and had the smoothest skin.

"Kitty Karr."

Still standing too close, Lucy put the cigarette to her mouth and spoke out of one side. "Want one?" She coughed a little, trying to exhale and speak at the same time.

Kitty hesitated. "I don't want to miss anything."

"Trust me, it won't begin for another thirty. I do the makeup for the show."

"Do you?" Kitty regretted questioning her but was surprised to meet a woman on set doing something other than acting.

Lucy didn't seem offended. "Let's have a smoke outside." Kitty followed her through the curtains and out of a side door to the alley between stages A and B. Kitty shivered, wishing she'd brought her jacket from the phone room. She hated how cold it got at night in Los Angeles; even in the dead of July you needed a sweater once the sun set. In Winston, jacket weather didn't start until late September.

"What do you do here?" Lucy leaned against the brick stage.

"Telephone operator."

"Isn't it terrible?" Lucy tilted her head back to a ninety-degree angle and blew out a long stream of smoke. Kitty would later learn that Lucy loved to look at the stars because they reminded her to keep her mind on God.

Unguarded, Kitty said, "I hate it."

"But at least you're on the lot." She handed Kitty a Lakes original.

"And it does pay well," Kitty said.

Lucy flicked her cigarette ash. "A lot of things pay well; doesn't mean you want to do them. You'll survive the phone room. It's where everyone starts."

"You too?"

"No. I came in with Cora. Cora Rivers." Lucy paused for an acknowledgment and then said, "The actress?"

Kitty rushed her exhale to answer. "Yes."

"Cora had an audition, I did her hair and makeup, and ta-da!"

While Cora floated from studio to studio for background and chorus gigs, Lucy built her career offstage. She was responsible for bringing to life some of the studio's most iconic characters; she was as much of an institution at Telescope as any of the men.

"Did you always want to work in the movies?" Kitty asked.

Lucy touched the top of her hair, disrupting her middle part. "Yes, but I was going to be a hairdresser."

"How long have you been working here?"

"Ten years—since I was about your age."

"How old do you think I am?" Kitty wanted to approximate Lucy's age.

"Barely twenty."

"I just turned eighteen on the nineteenth," Kitty said.

"Well, happy birthday."

"Thank you." Kitty hadn't told anyone about her birthday, because it coincided with the first day of the Emmett Till murder trial. It was easier for the day to pass without a fuss. Besides, there was no cake, no tradition. She wondered if her grandmother had known not to bake one that year.

"Why aren't you doing hair here?"

Lucy fingered the egg-sized ruby-and-yellow-gold brooch on the lapel of her shirt. Distracted by the sparkling of her earrings in the stage lights, Kitty hadn't noticed it before.

"Ever had something bad happen, and suddenly you hate something you used to love?" Lucy asked.

Kitty fumbled one of her earrings, thinking about Cottonwood. "Yes."

"It's like that with me and doing hair. What I liked was helping people feel their best, and being a makeup artist fulfills that need. I can make anyone look like anything. What do you want to be?" Lucy tried to guess, rocking back on the heels of her brown two-inch suede pumps. "An actress?" She smiled as if she knew she was right. "Of course, you'd be perfect."

Kitty was beginning to think acting was her destiny, the way people kept pegging her for it. "It seems near impossible." Casting was the busiest department; half of the studio's daily calls were about auditions that resulted in long lines of hopefuls spilling out of the studio gates. Emma and the other operators boasted that they were better catches, having worked before they got married and choosing to rest their laurels on more than their looks. Kitty's interest in acting would ostracize her, despite their equally measured husband quests.

"By standing in the casting line, yes; by working here, no." Lucy rocked on her heels again.

"I don't know how long I can keep answering phones."

"Not long at all if you keep coming to set. You'll meet directors and casting directors."

"How long have you been working on *Windfall*?"

"A month. We were in the middle of filming *The Misfits* when everything was put on hiatus."

"At least television is going again."

That meant nothing to Lucy. "Telescope is a film studio, and we're not making films. *The Misfits* was a shoo-in for the Oscars. The longer things are on hold, the worse morale will get. And Nathan Tate doesn't have to worry about having an income. It's elitist."

"Do you think there will be more layoffs?"

"The whole studio could be shut down if our new boss isn't careful." Lucy tossed her cigarette to the ground and opened the studio door. "Shall we?"

———————

Cora got laughs as a ditzy housewife hiding a dead body in her basement. Lucy kept whispering to Kitty about how gifted Cora was. Kitty had never cared for slapstick humor; she'd witnessed too much humiliation to find self-deprecation amusing.

Cora's black hair and blue eyes likened her to Snow White. Somehow Kitty had pictured her as a blonde.

Cora found Lucy on the side of the stage after the show. "How did I do?" She towered over Lucy (and Kitty) but deferred to Lucy as though she was a child.

"Great as usual." Lucy looked at Kitty. "You enjoyed it, didn't you?"

"Very much."

Cora looked at her but made no expression.

"This is Kitty Karr," Lucy said. "She's the only staff member who came tonight."

"Imagine that." Cora took Kitty's hand, still neglecting to introduce herself.

Kitty got the feeling she expected her to know her name. "Nice to meet you."

Cora dropped Kitty's hand and called over her shoulder to Lucy, "I'll be ready in a minute."

"Meet you at the car." Lucy turned to Kitty with an apologetic face. "She's under a lot of pressure right now."

"About *The Misfits*?"

"She's doing guest roles to keep her acting muscles strong." She whispered this time. "She's being dramatic, if you ask me; she doesn't really have to work."

"Her husband?" Kitty pretended not to know about Abner.

"Her father. She lives in a huge house in the hills above Sunset. Old money." Her eyes suggested ill-gotten gains. Kitty thought she was going to elaborate, but instead Lucy dismissed her. "It was so nice to meet you. Come back anytime. We're here rehearsing all week."

On her exit, Johnny stopped her. "Fill this out and bring it back."

"What is it?"

"We want your feedback on the performance. Thanks for coming."

"Why me?"

"Aren't you an employee?"

"Yes."

"Then your feedback is requested. Thank you for coming."

Walking home, Kitty saw Lucy leave the lot at the wheel of a dark-colored Mercedes. The windows were down, and she could see Cora in the passenger's seat, wearing a fluffy black fur. She heard their voices but couldn't make out their words over the music, a melody she couldn't name. Kitty wondered where they were going. It was the first time in a long time that she wished she'd been included.

———

Kitty returned her evaluation to the mailbox outside of stage C the following morning as the form instructed. Taking Lucy's invitation literally, she found her later that evening, mixing makeup backstage. Like Emma, Lucy was eager to make her over. "If you want people to take you seriously, you have to look like a woman, not a little girl."

"You sound like my sister."

"She's right." Lucy handed her a tube of lipstick. "Put some color on your lips."

"You don't wear makeup."

"I do." Lucy leaned into the mirror, examining herself. "The overhead stage lights are bad for your skin, so I try not to cover my face in foundation when I'm working."

"You don't need it."

"I don't wear it because I need it. I wear it because it helps me look my best. The better you look, the better you feel, the better you act."

Lucy taught her how to line her lips, curl her eyelashes, and blend foundation and blush, and supplied her with makeup for daytime and nighttime looks. "Don't leave the house without the bare minimum."

"Where are you going tonight?"

"A fundraiser," Lucy explained, leaning into the mirror.

"Your husband doesn't mind you working?"

"No, he's a liberal, thank God. What else would I do?"

Kitty liked her more, hearing that. She'd learned some White women felt "unfulfilled" under the expectation to stay home and rear children. In Kitty's mind it was a punishment Negro women could only dream about receiving.

"You don't have children?"

"No. It's not for me."

Kitty didn't understand. Babies weren't *for* people, they happened *to* people.

"I fell in love with the studio, found I couldn't give it up."

"How do you not get pregnant?" Kitty covered her mouth, realizing how forward she was being. "I'm so sorry."

Lucy smiled. "It's all right. Careful timing." She looked at Kitty in the mirror. "You've never been with a man?"

Kitty shook her head, embarrassed to be asked.

A knock came at the door, and Johnny, the assistant director, entered before he received permission. He was flustered and spoke with his hands. His shirt kept rising to show his pale, hairy stomach. "We have to film the rehearsal now. I need touch-ups on everyone."

Lucy tossed the eye shadow brush she'd been using onto her vanity table. "He's become such a pain in the ass. He acts like he must resurrect us from the dead."

"Please hurry," Johnny said, already exiting. "We're behind schedule, and the last thing we need is to go over budget."

Lucy rolled her eyes at Kitty. "He's the one upping costs." She locked her door behind them. "He could just come down here and watch it, but instead, the cameramen have to stay late to film it, which comes from the show's budget."

"Who is *he*?"

"Nathan."

"Where is he?"

"Around here somewhere." Lucy scoffed, but then her expression and voice softened. "I shouldn't be dismissive. He does have a lot to offer. He's very analytical. The problem is, it takes him forever to make a decision." After so many years at the studio, Kitty saw, Lucy knew the entire Tate family well.

After the rehearsal, Kitty received another evaluation form. She returned it during her lunch hour the next day, and that night, the director, Charles Mints, also the director of *The Misfits*, approached her.

"We got your notes." He fingered his sandy beard. "What do you think of this episode?"

"It's too sad, especially now."

He eyed Johnny and exhaled, relieved. "My sentiments exactly." It was understood that Kitty was referring to news of the death of James Dean, the hugely successful actor who had just died in a car crash. Hollywood and his fans were in shock. It wasn't the time for parallels on daytime television.

Charles pulled a script from his back pocket. "This is next week's episode. Let me know."

She returned her notes the next day, and Lucy traded her another episode, and then another, and pretty soon, Kitty had given feedback on the entire season of *Windfall*. Charles liked her "outsider" perspective and her ability to bring depth to the largely comedic show.

Mitch's became a welcomed afterthought. Kitty started writing again, waiting for Emma to get home in the evenings. Miffed by Kitty's disinterest in her established routine, Emma had begun to stay out later and later, seemingly in competition to prove who had the most interesting life. It was as if she wanted to make Kitty feel jealous enough to ask where she had been. What Kitty didn't know was that the other operators had become similarly irregular patrons of Mitch's, trading girls' nights for dates. Emma was the only one with nothing else to do.

Emma stomped in intoxicated one Friday night with news of Judy's engagement. Sam had proposed to the accompaniment of an orchestra on one of the sound stages.

"Everyone's invited for cake and champagne on Monday to celebrate." Emma fell into the chair across from the couch. "I can't get anyone to go out with me at all. It took Judy three months to get engaged. *Three months.*" She leaned forward to make the point. "When I first met Judy, she was still wearing her hair in two ponytails. I changed her hair, got her ready for the weigh-ins—I dieted with her for months—and now *she's* the one getting married. She's not even smart."

"She has a college degree."

"Only because her parents could afford to send her."

Tired of hearing her insults, Kitty asked Emma why she was friends with Judy.

"How can I ever really be friends with anyone except you?" Emma replied.

"That's a lonely life, Emma."

"Well, we can't have it all." She stretched her legs to rest her heels on the couch. "She asked me to be a bridesmaid." The wedding would be in London in May; Judy's fiancé was British on his mother's side and had royal ties. "His family lives in a castle. Judy showed me pictures."

"Maybe you'll meet someone. Someone royal."

Emma cut her eyes at Kitty as she prepared a drink.

"It happened to Judy, it can happen to you."

"She's White," Emma snapped.

"So are you."

CHAPTER 18

Kitty

October 1955

A month after Kitty became a regular on the *Windfall* set, another memo came from Nathan's office, announcing that the interview window for secretaries had closed. The operators were livid—no one knew interviews had even begun.

"See?" Emma couldn't wait to taunt Kitty. "You've been going to the stages, staying late, for nothing."

For answers, Kitty went to Lucy.

"I got you an interview to be Nathan's assistant."

"Is that different from a secretary?"

"Better."

"But the memo said interviews were closed."

"That's because he found what he was looking for."

"But how?"

Lucy wiggled a cigarette in the air as the signal for them to go outside. As they walked toward the stage door, she said, "He asked people to show up, and you did. They've been impressed with your feedback. Looks like you have a shot."

"What does being his assistant have to do with acting?"

"Access. Most people never even get to see him."

Kitty wanted to say yes, but it scared her. "My sister would kill for that job."

Lucy rolled her eyes. "Emma?"

"You know her?"

Lucy nodded. "Of course. She never told you about me?"

"No."

"I'm surprised. I got her a job here."

"As an operator?"

"Only after she had to stop working in casting, which is the first job I got her."

"She got fired?"

Lucy didn't hesitate to share as soon as they were alone outside. "When Emma first got to town, we introduced her—"

"Who is 'we'?" Kitty asked. Lucy often alluded to unnamed others in their conversations: *They* were going to dinner. *We* were invited to a play. Kitty sometimes felt as though Lucy wanted her to ask who these people were, but she didn't, assuming, anyway, that she was talking about either her husband or Cora. She only asked then knowing she had the right.

"My friends and I. Emma wants nothing to do with any of us now, even though we introduced her to the head of casting at Fox. Lincoln Harrison was smitten. You know, Emma is very smart, and because she didn't want to be an actress, it was the perfect match. Lincoln was used to dating women looking for an entry into the business. He took her on trips, treated her like a queen, and then proposed. Shortly after that, Emma met an actor. A handsome *Negro* actor." Lucy covered her mouth when referring to his race. "Lincoln caught wind of it and tried to ruin her life."

"She cheated?"

Lucy threw her hands in the air. "What does it matter? That's what everyone said."

This, Kitty saw, explained a lot.

"Ah, so she didn't tell you any of this either." Lucy shook her head as if to say it was a shame.

Knowing would have helped Kitty to exhibit more patience with Emma, but her secrecy wasn't surprising. She'd said it herself: no one wants to talk about the bad things. Maybe Emma had considered Kitty's arrival to be her new beginning.

"She was lucky not to be blackballed. I called in favors to get her the operator job. It's your decision, but being Nathan's assistant is your chance."

"She's going to be mad."

"She'll get over it. She doesn't want the job; she wants the man. And she'll come to that conclusion herself once she sees how much you have to work."

Lucy sure had an accurate pulse on Emma.

"Besides, she may not even be his type. Do you really want to give your opportunity to her? The interview's tomorrow," she said. "It'll be rude if you don't go."

Kitty nodded. "I'll be there."

"Good girl."

"How did you meet Emma?" Kitty asked.

"At a gala. It was like seeing a mouse in the corner, deciding when to dart out for the cheese."

"Cheese?"

"It's a saying."

"I know. But who was the cheese?"

"*She* was, that night. Anyway, it doesn't matter. I thought she was sweet. I have nothing against her; she's just—"

"Troubled." Kitty was relieved to say it, knowing Lucy would understand.

"A person has to be mad to do what we did. To continue to do it. Passing takes a sort of maddening bravery that most people don't have."

Kitty hadn't ever suspected. "*We?*" She studied Lucy's face in what

illumination the stars and the single light atop stage C provided. "I can usually tell . . ."

"It's the blond." Lucy parted her hair to show Kitty the dark roots sprouting from her pale scalp. She explained that she was Creole, from Baton
Rouge. "Negro and French. A little Portuguese." Lucy's great-grandparents
had been a quarter to a half Negro on both sides. Their mixing with other
Negroes in a beige-to-yellow range made generations of offspring with eight
variations of White and Negro traits. "They all consider themselves Colored
though. They come from slave blood, whether they look White or not."

That was how Kitty felt. Any feeling of superiority felt disrespectful to
her mother.

"Why didn't you tell me?" Kitty whispered, hearing footsteps on the path
between the stages.

"I wasn't hiding it from you. I thought you knew, that Emma told you."

"She never mentioned you. She doesn't know we're friends."

"Intentional?" Lucy wondered.

"Your name never came up. She never wants to hear about what I do
on set."

"And has no interest in learning." Lucy waved her hand in a dismissive
manner. "More reason we didn't become better friends. Working here is my
life, I'm not ashamed to say."

Kitty feared her relationship with Emma was also headed downhill. "We
used to be close." Or did they? Kitty didn't know anything about Emma, not
really. She never had. And Emma didn't know her. She couldn't owe anything to a stranger.

"People change; that's life. But being who we are changes you in ways you
can't imagine. Living as two souls within one body is not only exhausting but
mind-altering." Lucy lit her second cigarette. "She loves you though."

"How do you know?"

"She was always making plans for when Kitty came."

If their only allegiance was through the mothers they would never see again, Kitty thought, she was in trouble. "She told me I could go home if I wanted."

"You all are from North Carolina, right?"

"Yes, we lived about two or three hours apart."

Lucy looked puzzled.

"We're not really sisters, but we've known each other since we were children."

"Ah. Emma couldn't wait to tell me her father owned Holden's; I was wondering why you hadn't yet."

"*Holden's?*" When Emma said her father owned a store, Kitty couldn't have imagined she meant *the* luxury department store. It had been in jeopardy years ago but rebounded. Now Kitty understood how Emma's multi-unit home had been a gift.

"Don't be mad at her." Lucy looked up at the stars. "Sometimes it's easier to tell secrets to a stranger. Some never tell their story to anyone. It's safer that way, I guess. That's why I never push. The less people know, the less they can use."

Kitty wasn't worried about that. Being related to the Lakeses hadn't benefitted her; therefore, it couldn't benefit anyone else. "I'm thousands of miles from home, from anyone who knows me. Emma's my only family now."

"What about your mother?"

"She sent me—doesn't want me back."

"What a mother you had. This must be agony for her."

"For *her?*" Kitty choked without warning. "I hate her for this." In her last letter Kitty had told her so. Her mean streak surfaced as it had that day in Charlotte, pushing her mother for a response. So far, nothing.

Lucy embraced her. "Others look down on us for passing, but they don't know what we've had to go through, what it does to you."

Lucy didn't ask about her father, and Kitty was grateful for her restraint. She didn't think she could lie.

"There are too few of us as it is; we have to stick together. So, let's get you hired."

Lucy prepped her for her interview, explaining that first and foremost, Nathan needed her to think he was brilliant. "I feel bad for him, honestly—the son of a famous filmmaker, without any imagination whatsoever."

"Is it bias?"

"I wish." Lucy explained. "None of his films were accepted for viewing under his alias. Someone at his school leaked his attempts to the press, and Abner had to pay for entry, and decent reviews citing Nathan's capacity for growth, to save his reputation."

Nathan's door was open when Kitty arrived the next afternoon. "Thanks for coming, Miss Karr."

He pulled out one of the chairs in front of his desk for her. The sky view from his windows was serene, a far cry from the mess of papers, candy wrappers, and writing utensils on his desk. He had demanded his father's office, located at the end of a long, tiled hallway in the only two-story building on the lot. Abandoned nails were stuck in bare spots on the walls where art had hung.

"I'll get around to decorating when I get this place running again," he said, noticing her looking around. "Would you like a drink?"

"No, thank you."

He retrieved a glass from the windowsill, filled an inch high with brown liquid. He sat in its place and lit a cigarette. His lips were full and matched in thickness from top to bottom; he was every bit as good-looking as everyone said. He gestured the pack to her. She took one, needing something to do with her hands.

"Where are you from, Miss Karr?"

She fought to focus. "Boston."

"I went to college in New York but never made the trip to Boston." He spoke like it was the most absurd thing.

"I'm sure you were busy with your studies."

"I was. Everyone else was partying and chasing girls; I was making films." He opened a window. "Lucy Schmitt gave me your feedback on *Windfall*. Said you'd be perfect for what I'm trying to institute here." He finished his drink in one sip and started pacing the room. "You've been onstage most nights, yes?"

"I go after my day in the telephone room."

"That's a long day."

"I enjoy it."

"What about film interests you?"

"Everything. I grew up going to the movies and writing stories."

"Were your parents entertainers?"

"No, but we went to the movies a lot. My sister and I would make up our own stories."

"So you write?" He was surprised.

"Yes."

"What have you read on our roster?" He palmed a tall stack of scripts on his desk.

"All of this season of *Windfall*, *Last Loop*, *Around Town*, and *Misty Rain*."

"What are your thoughts on our material now?"

He stared as if he couldn't wait for her to speak, which made her nervous and caused her to blurt out the truth. "Predictable."

He groaned as though he knew it was true.

"But that's what viewers like." Kitty tried to soften her critique. "People go to the movies to escape, to make the world make sense."

He circled her chair and his desk as he relayed his own theory. "Our stories feel stale. My father is a great man, but Telescope is behind the curve. We have to grow, or the others are going to take us over. People will be kicking and screaming the whole way, but it will be better in the long run. There's a lot more everyone can be doing, even the secretaries, which is where you come in. Gone are the days when we can afford to have secretaries who just answer phones."

Kitty agreed. "We have operators for that."

He touched her shoulder as he passed, beginning his fifth loop. "Exactly. Secretaries need to be involved in the day-to-day operations of the studio. They need to be Janes-of-all-trades, capable of pitching in anywhere the studio needs them, whether that's reading scripts or taking dictation or being on the set. Higher level of skill. That's the reason for the change. *Everyone* has something to contribute." He sat down at his desk and took a deep breath. "And we need new voices. New writers."

Nathan griped for another twenty minutes about how the firings, of the older secretaries in particular, had caused an uproar in the press. Every article referenced Nathan's limited experience as the impetus for his lofty dreams. "They should be talking about *The Misfits*—which I was told, before I started, was a highly anticipated feature, but I got here and learned the script is shit. We have to make them care about our art again, Kitty. I want this studio to be the first one anyone ever thinks about when they think about film."

His optimism excited her. She'd never met someone so positive about the future. "I'm ready."

He reached to shake her hand but stopped short. "I need a right hand. Someone to accompany me to meetings, castings, and filmings. Keep me organized and informed of new material. You should be my eyes and ears. I'll throw at you as much as you can handle."

"Okay."

"You're hired." He went for her hand again, and warmth cascaded down her body as they shook. "Charles and Lucy think the world of you."

"Thank you, sir."

"Please, call me Nathan."

"Kitty, then."

She closed his door with a smile that spread from ear to ear. She tried to hide it before walking past the receptionist, but it grew until she was showing teeth and bidding the older lady au revoir.

Emma blocked Kitty's entry into their house. "How did you hear about the interviews?"

"There weren't interviews. I was offered an interview."

Emma let her inside and slammed the door. "So you've met Lucy Schmitt."

"Weeks ago."

"I told you to stay away from them."

"You never told me who they were. I met her on the *Windfall* set."

"If you didn't know Lucy was one of them, why didn't you tell me about the interviews?"

"Because I was told not to. 'Going to set and being more involved in the creative process' was a test for everyone."

Emma ignored that and put her hands on her hips. "What did Lucy tell you about me?"

"You haven't come up." Kitty was curious to hear Emma's side of things without influence.

"Don't you think it's strange she didn't tell you we knew each other?"

"We talk about film."

"I bet she told you she's Colored, though, didn't she?"

"Only the other day."

Emma chuckled before taking another sip of her drink. "She's incredible. You don't know what you've gotten yourself into."

"Then tell me," Kitty said, daring her. "Everything we do affects the other, remember?"

"This happened before you got here."

"Then why are you so mad we're friends?"

"A year ago, I was engaged to Lincoln Harrison—the head of casting at Fox. Lucy and Cora were jealous and went about ruining my life."

"Cora Rivers?"

"Yes, she's passing too." Emma grinned off Kitty's surprise. "Lucy didn't tell you *that* because she wants to befriend you first. Then she'll introduce you to Cora, who will set you up with a man so they can get close enough to him to use you both."

"Do you think that's why I got the interview with Nathan?"

"I'm sure. They put thoughts in Lincoln's head about me and a Negro actor, Jamie Harris, who Lucy said was her cousin. She wanted me to help get him in front of Lincoln. I was helping him prepare for the audition, so we were spending a lot of time together. He was funny and into the same books I was. Then Lincoln broke off the engagement, wouldn't talk to me. Just like that."

"Was there something going on between you and the actor?"

Emma looked crushed to be asked. "I wouldn't have jeopardized a life with Lincoln for anyone. I still love him."

Lincoln had later admitted he hadn't liked the way Emma entertained the Negro man's jokes. Although he knew their relationship was innocent, he couldn't shake the inevitable fact that would accompany his old age: his younger wife's sexual interest in younger men. He bought Emma the quadruplex on Orange Drive to apologize for his immaturity. But he never reinstated their engagement.

"So your father didn't buy this place? Lucy told me he owns Holden's."

"I haven't seen my father since I was sixteen. He doesn't know if I'm dead or alive, and I doubt he cares." It was one of the few moments of rare honesty Kitty had ever witnessed from Emma. When her sadness grew overwhelming, as it sometimes did, Emma became real, as if the pain stripped away her cover. "I didn't tell you because I didn't want to talk about Lucy and Cora."

"That's why you wouldn't take me on a tour."

"Yes, but she found you anyway. I thought she'd be off the lot with production shut down."

Kitty was happy to be found. She and Lucy had things in common that had nothing to do with being Negro—things that were far more important than being Negro, and that she didn't have in common with Emma. "She's working television."

"Be careful."

"She got me a job."

"She got me one, too, and later, she needed a favor. She'll need one from you someday. She and Cora are asking for trouble, the way they go back and forth over the color line."

"I bet if they helped you meet Nathan you wouldn't mind."

"Maybe, but I have you for that now."

CHAPTER 19

Kitty

Kitty arrived at the executive suite on her first day that next week to find a tower of scripts on her desk.

"We have to evaluate everything we have first," Nathan said, following her into her office. Kitty would be the gatekeeper determining what reached Nathan's desk for consideration. She couldn't believe her good fortune, landing a job in which her main task was to read.

"When you're finished, ask someone to bring up the next batch from the vault," he instructed.

When she made the request, she was told that Abner had deemed everything in the basement unsuitable for production.

"We'll be the ones to decide that," Nathan said. "I want to create my own legacy."

"That could take years." Kitty recited what Lucy had told her. "People will leave the studio if we don't turn a profit."

Nathan wasn't concerned. "I expect that. They don't trust me. My dad didn't keep his feelings about me to himself." Kitty felt a pang of softness toward him.

Nathan worked hard. He was manic with ideas from the moment he arrived to work, as if he'd been up all night, thinking and making lists. He started and ended his day on the other side of her desk. She appreciated him not summoning her in and out of his office; she was still learning to walk in her higher-heeled shoes. He was astonished by how fast Kitty read, and while script evaluation was an arduous task, she enjoyed his praise for pushing through. He read the ones she liked and came in each morning, before going to his own office, to discuss them. Reading and talking about stories reminded her of evenings with her mother, and soon she felt at home on the lot in his company. Richard had been smart—smarter than her in the practical subjects—but Nathan was a gifted conversationalist. He had big ideas, and she found herself hanging on to his every word, whether he was talking about Greek mythology or cowboys.

At the end of almost every day, he offered to pour her a drink, and each evening she declined, following Lucy's advice. *It's too soon for you to be so casual.* Kitty didn't know how to be casual with Nathan—she hid it well, but he made her nervous. She was always trying to impress him, to get him to look at her in the way he did when he read and loved one of the scripts she had recommended.

Her sanctuary was destroyed after only a couple of weeks, when Emma decided it was past time that she met Nathan Tate. She barged into Kitty's office after hours, dressed in sky-high heels, as if she was going to a party. Kitty and Nathan looked up from their script review.

Kitty noticed a twinge of disappointment cross Emma's face as she saw that Kitty's office was big enough for a sitting area. She walked right up to Nathan on the couch. "Mr. Tate, it is such a pleasure to meet you! I'm Emma, Kitty's sister."

Nathan rose to greet her. "Hello." He looked at Kitty. "I didn't know you had a sister."

Emma didn't break eye contact with Nathan. "I'm an operator here. I came to pick up my little sister." She reached to pat Kitty's head. "Ready, doll?"

Nathan turned to Kitty. "I'm sorry for keeping you late."

"We're going to dinner," Emma said. "I've barely seen her since she started this job."

"She's very dedicated."

"You both are. Would you like to join us? Have you eaten?"

Nathan started his exit. "No, no. I still have some work to do. It was very nice to meet you, though, Emma."

Emma touched his arm as he stepped around her. "Things have been running so smoothly since you started."

Nathan bent like a twig to her compliment. "Why, thank you."

"Will there be another round of secretary interviews?"

"For you, yes."

Emma beamed. Kitty knew he meant because she was Kitty's sister, but Emma had hearts in her eyes, as if he'd changed his mind about dinner.

"Come by tomorrow," he said. "Ask for Laura."

She grabbed his hand. "Thank you so much."

Outside, she winked at Kitty and slid inside her car, which was parked at the curb. Kitty rushed to open the passenger door as the engine started.

Emma slid over and slammed the door lock. "I have plans."

"Fine, but drive me home."

Emma scoffed. Her voice became muffled, but Kitty still heard her. "With your behavior, I think not."

"*My* behavior?" Kitty took a breath. She didn't pivot to look but assumed they were being watched as many of the office windows faced that side. "Emma, it's less than a minute's drive."

Emma waved as she pulled off. "Don't wait up!"

Kitty watched as Emma's car disappeared around the corner, fearing this was still only a preview of Emma's rotten core.

———

Emma replaced the first-floor receptionist. On her first day, Nathan gave her a script to read, something he'd done with all the new hires. Misreading it as an overture, Emma stopped him the next morning and, in the front lobby, presented him with a basket of muffins. He brought them to Kitty's office. "I'm more of a chocolate guy," he explained.

Kitty peeked underneath the red cloth. The blueberry muffins were arranged in a heart shape. "I'll put them in the break room." Kitty bit one and then took another for later, recognizing them to be from Canter's, the diner close to their house. The next day, Emma handed him an apple pie (again, Canter's); two days later, a cup of coffee; then a copy of William Faulkner's latest, with a note stuck in its pages suggesting they discuss it over drinks soon.

Nathan gave them all to Kitty. This chain of custody continued until Emma became upset that Nathan hadn't addressed, let alone returned, her advances.

Gossip started to circulate, and Kitty overheard it, straight from Emma's mouth.

She wants to be an actress.

Is she even talented?

He's found something he likes.

Must be nice having his attention.

That's the one thing Kitty will never give up—attention. Before she knows it she'll be too old to marry and too old to act.

Tears came before Kitty could return to her office.

As if he could sense something was wrong, Nathan appeared at her door. "Would you like a drink?"

She wiped her eyes. "Definitely not now." Already low, she didn't know what she might say with a loose tongue.

"A cigarette?" He came in and closed the door. He lit two before handing her one. "Want to talk about it?"

"It's just my sister. You're an only child; you wouldn't get it."

"Maybe not, but I can recognize jealousy a mile away."

Kitty smiled at his acknowledgment of her feelings. "She wanted this job."

Days later, Emma was transferred to the desk of a producer on the opposite end of the building. Emma boasted, calling the move a promotion, a view which Kitty publicly endorsed. Really, Kitty didn't want to fight. Talking against her to their colleagues—White people at that—was treacherous. Having accepted she could never trust Emma, that Emma would never wish her well, her sister's reassignment had in fact been at her own directive, a casual suggestion mentioned to Nathan that afternoon. He was bothered by Emma's attention and, though she didn't know it then, flattered by Kitty's care.

CHAPTER 20

Kitty

End of October, 1955

Lucy lived behind an iron gate in Beverly Hills. A few stars lived close by, but she never would say who. The two-story redbrick house had ten steps that led up to the front door and two large white plantation-style columns. Lucy hadn't just married into a political family; she'd married into a wealthy one.

Lucy opened the door. "My husband's grandmother left this house to him," she said, reading Kitty's expression. "And she was the poorest of his family members."

What Kitty had thought was the front door opened onto a patio with walls covered in ivy and vines with pink and purple flowers. Lucy gestured for her to take off her shoes. "So the maids don't have to clean the floors so often." Five or six pairs were already covered by a layer of flowers that had fallen from the dangling vines.

Lucy turned the brass doorknob to reveal a narrow hallway. "Laurie, Miss Karr has arrived!"

"I hope you're hungry," Lucy said.

She followed Lucy into a dining room, where two plates of roasted chicken, carrots, green beans, and biscuits sat waiting on a table for eight. The food smelled better than Kitty's cooking but not as good as her mother's.

"Surprise! It isn't much, but you should pat yourself on the back for getting that job."

"I should be thanking you," Kitty said.

"I only made the introduction. You're the reason you'll keep the job." Lucy sat at the head of the table, and Kitty sat at her right, with her back to the room's windows.

A reddish-skinned Negro woman entered with wine glasses.

"Eat with us." Lucy pointed to the seat across from Kitty.

The maid didn't reply but glanced at Kitty, then back at Lucy.

"It's fine," Lucy said, answering her silent question. "Kitty, this is my sister, Laurie."

"Oh." Kitty felt jarred. Their skin tones varied by twenty-five degrees, but if you really studied them—aside from Lucy's nose, which was wider—they looked alike. "Hello, Laurie."

Seeing her discomfort, both sisters laughed. Laurie's beauty mark, a perfect cocoa-brown circle underneath her right eye, moved as her face scrunched.

"If my sister has to work for someone, it might as well be me, right?" Lucy said.

"Does your husband know?"

"No. God, no."

Laurie left the room and returned with a plate. She sat next to Kitty. "And you're Emma Karr's sister, is that right?"

"Not by blood, but yes. Please, don't hold it against me."

Laurie looked at Lucy. "She's funny."

"I told you."

"Is it just the two of you?" Kitty asked.

"Yes. Laurie's eleven months older. We did everything together, until we couldn't, of course. She's always taken care of me—I was oily, red-faced, and fat as a kid. Got picked on all the time." Kitty couldn't imagine it. Even in her trousers and button-up, Lucy looked thin-boned: her thighs were the same circumference all the way up, and her arms were like twigs; Kitty imagined her midsection showed the outline of her ribs.

She took a longer sip of wine, nervous to ask the question on her mind. "Do you have other maids?"

"Just one other."

"My mother's a maid," Kitty said.

"Our father was a janitor," Lucy said. She stared at her. "Does it bother you that I have maids?"

"I'll never have one."

"But does it bother you?" Lucy pressed.

"It makes me think of her. I do better when I don't think about the past."

"Don't we all." Laurie pushed out her chair. "I have calls for Maude."

Lucy waved. "See you tomorrow."

Laurie waved at Kitty as she exited. "Nice to meet you." She was gone before Kitty could reply.

"She's always in a rush." Lucy twirled her fork in one hand like a baton and continued eating.

"What's it like having your sister working for you?"

"Like putting on a perpetual play, but I have to take care of her. This way I can see to it that she's paid a proper wage, isn't abused. I'm protecting her; God gave me a gift to do that."

"So you'll take the truth to your grave?"

"Yes."

"Does your other maid know you're passing?"

"No; too risky."

"Do you ever feel bad for lying?"

Lucy was happy to answer all of her questions. "No. My emotions are real. I love my husband. And what does it matter, really, me lying about being Colored? Who am I hurting? Stupid rules are made to be broken."

Kitty agreed. "I feel nothing, most often."

"That's because you had permission."

"What did you tell your husband about your family? Didn't he want to meet them?"

"Not after I told him that my mother is dead, and my father—who knows?—probably drank himself to death by now. He just assumed everyone was White."

"What if he finds out?"

"He won't."

"But *if*?"

Lucy shrugged. "I tell myself he's too committed to care. I've been a good wife, so unless he's just a bigot—which after careful observation over the last six years, I know he's not—he'll get over it. Maybe even understand." Lucy sliced a piece of chicken, commenting on how juicy it was.

It *was* good, Kitty thought, finally taking her first bite. The sauce was orange flavored, with just the right tinge of sweetness.

"How are you and Nathan getting along?" Lucy asked.

"Great. He's brilliant." Kitty felt herself blush.

"You know he's sweet on you."

"We work well together."

"It's only a matter of time before he smashes those lips onto yours."

"He does have nice lips."

"Ooooh, look at you, Kitty Karr. Falling in love with our boss."

"I barely know him."

"When is he going to green-light *The Misfits*?"

"He wants to focus on other projects."

"But we were a month into filming! The set is built; we have costumes and footage."

"He said the script is bad."

"It can be rewritten. Tell him Cora will quit if he doesn't resume production."

"Won't it ring truer if *she* tells him?"

"She doesn't really want to quit. You're our greatest chance of getting him to change his mind. You said it yourself—he asks your opinion on everything."

Aware of Lucy's manipulation, Kitty was nonetheless up for the challenge, seeing it might bring her closer to Nathan. "Why didn't you tell me about Cora?"

"About what?"

Kitty lowered her voice. "That she's Negro."

"It's not my business to tell."

"Does she set women up with men?"

"Yes, but not for pay, if that's your insinuation. Never for pay."

"Then for what?"

"Because it's smart. If you had a wealthy father, he would have promised you to someone suitable. Cora does the same thing. We have to look out for each other. We all could have stayed Negro to be poor."

Hearing another echo of Emma's philosophy, Kitty knew Emma had spent more time with Lucy and her friends than she admitted. But it was the first time that Kitty subscribed to the idea. Her newfound proximity to Nathan's wealth and power allowed her to imagine what it would be like should some of it rub off on her.

"Maybe I'll introduce you one day."

"To whom?"

"My friends," Lucy said.

Kitty didn't know what to say.

"She doesn't want you to associate with us, does she?"

"She told me to be careful."

"That's everyone's hope, but it isn't living. Do you feel unsafe with me?"

"No."

"Then you should meet them, make your own decisions. You didn't choose this life to then go and live someone else's."

"I didn't really choose it at all."

"You're still here, aren't you? That's a choice."

CHAPTER 21

Kitty

"Done. I want Cora off the payroll." Nathan dumped a layer of roast beef from his sandwich onto a spare napkin. "I was hoping that if I delayed production long enough, she'd quit, and everyone would just forget about that damned film. The script is shit. And so is she for what she's done to my family."

"But she's our biggest star, and it's our only slated feature." Kitty, she saw, had been tricked into an impossible situation, oblivious until now to how Nathan felt about his father's affair with Cora. "The media is expecting it. We can't afford bad press."

"I don't give a goddamn."

"Everything is ready to go. We can rewrite the script." Kitty used every angle Lucy had given her.

"I want her out of here."

"Why?" Kitty played dumb. "I thought all of her pictures have done well."

"It's no secret. She's my father's mistress—or was; he's not much good to anyone these days. First his mind went, and now his body is ridden with some disease the doctors can't diagnose." He poured drinks for them, ranting. "My father's always had an affinity for actresses, but Cora's had quite a hold on him. She came from nowhere. He bought her a house bigger than ours, while yelling at my mom about her spending habits. Of course, now that he's sick, it's my mother by his side."

"How did you know about the house?"

"He took me there a few times. All Cora wants is his money. She doesn't care about him. During one of his lucid moments, he asked to see her—crazy old man does love her—and she refused to come, to punish us for trying to untie her from his finances. She asked to speak to him just to say she wasn't coming and incite him to hysterics, I think. We had to call the doctor to sedate him."

"How long has Cora been in his life?"

"She says fifteen years, but it's hard to be sure. They were discreet."

"That's a long time."

"He's been married to my mother for forty." Nathan ran both of his hands through his hair. It was always the first indicator of his distress. "I know I shouldn't cancel production for personal reasons, but . . ."

She went to touch his arm but stopped herself. "I understand your feelings, but Cora's under contract."

"Which is why it has to be her decision."

"I think we should talk about her contract after the film."

"We'd have to find a writer willing to touch 'Abner Tate's masterpiece.' Someone we can also trust not to talk about the original."

"How about you?" Kitty suggested. "That way, if it gets out, it'll still be good for the papers."

"No one is supposed to know he's sick."

"Maybe it's time they did. It's nothing to be ashamed of."

Nathan looked as though he was considering it. "Listen, I'm not in a rush. This studio can survive on our television shows until next year."

"I don't think you have that sort of time."

"Or what? Mutiny?"

That was exactly what happened. No one on the lot, except the administration staff, got paid unless they were working on a project. Another month's indecision led to a petition for Nathan's removal, forcing him to green-light *The Misfits* and two other undecided films that would begin production in the first quarter of 1956. It was the first and last time Nathan went against Kitty's advice.

The weeks flew by, and they weren't any closer to finding new material to shoot in mere months. When Kitty stumbled upon some unfinished drafts about a young divorcée named Daisy Lawson, she went to Nathan's office. "She's the eternal optimist, still looking for love and getting into mischief."

"That's a new perspective." He leaned back in his chair to put his feet on the desk.

"I don't think housewives want to see family shows," Kitty said. "They're the ones home every day. There's nothing interesting about that." Kitty preferred romantic movies and musicals. Family shows reminded her of everything she missed, of the people she had never met who had occupied her rightful place.

"I agree. More women want careers and lives away from home these days. Is it for television?"

"Doesn't have to be. There are five short scripts. They could be lengthened into a movie," Kitty said.

"Let's try it. Can you have something in a week?"

"Oh . . . you want me to write it?"

"Do what you did with *Windfall*, but with scenes."

She knew what to do; she was just surprised he was asking her to do it.

Thinking he was reading her, he said, "Don't worry; we'll work on it together before anyone sees it." He propelled himself from his desk chair and poured a drink. "Do you want children?"

"That's an odd opener."

He apologized. "We were talking about the character, Daisy, and it made me wonder. If you're going to write, you have to think of these things, right? You have to have a connection to the material."

"Do you?" Emma had told her to delay answering that question for as long as possible. Some men found an aversion to motherhood unattractive, and to a few, it would pose a challenge. *You don't want them trying to get you pregnant.*

"Right now, the studio is my baby. I don't want to work here when I have kids—I know what that's like."

"My mother wasn't around a lot either. She worked at night."

"Doing what?"

She struggled to explain as they settled on either side of his desk. "Reading. Teaching reading."

"At night?"

Her mind raced for a plausible explanation. "Her students were factory workers."

"Immigrants?"

"Yes," Kitty said.

"That's noble. Your father didn't mind?"

Kitty shook her head no. "He wanted her to help people."

"My dad was charitable to everyone but me. This place might as well have been his son." His face froze as if he was picturing something. "My family is complicated. With my dad's illness, I'm learning just how much."

"I'm sorry."

"Thank you. It's never been a secret that he would have preferred someone else to take over, but my mother forbade it."

His mother's family's oil money, Nathan explained, had helped start the studio and kept it afloat over the last two years that Abner spent obsessing about *The Misfits*, to the detriment of the studio's bread-and-butter productions. Maybe Nathan would have been more suited to be an engineer or mathematician, but his mother had pushed her husband to cultivate their son's creative abilities. She held her ground, despite Abner's claims that their son had no talent for film beyond "his ability to spot a pretty woman."

Nathan had come to the lot every day after school but was never encouraged to make comments on set, let alone pick up a camera or write a script. He was a film lover but knew nothing about the mechanics of plot. According to his father, he couldn't even tell a good story about his own life. "Maybe I could have been a writer or a director had it been encouraged."

"It's not too late. You do own the place," Kitty reminded him. Kitty couldn't see how anyone—especially his father—could think so negatively of him.

Nathan shook his head. "I'm too old to be chasing childhood dreams. I can be just as brilliant at the head of the operation, pulling the strings and resurrecting Telescope. That's what pushes me these days: returning my family to glory."

"That'll make them proud."

He chuckled, but his reply wasn't funny. "I doubt they'd even notice." He reached for his cigarettes on his desk. "Shit, I'm just going on and on—you must think I'm a sap."

"No, I want to hear everything about you." She shifted her eyes away from his, embarrassed by her disclosure. "I should get back to reading." She stood.

He offered her two cigarettes. "For listening."

She waved them away. "I only really smoke with you." She walked down the hall to her office, dizzy with emotion.

Kitty had never met anyone whom she enjoyed talking to so much. It excited her to exhaustion. Every morning, she told herself she'd visit Lucy on the *Windfall* set, but every evening, she went home instead, favoring a bath. It was where she indulged in thoughts of Nathan, thoughts that had become too risqué to even write. Nathan's Whiteness complicated her feelings, and so she tried to suppress them, afraid of where they would lead. But something was pulling her to him, or back to him. It was as if she didn't have a choice. Sometimes, when they spoke, she got the feeling she'd known him her whole life, as if they'd had that same conversation before.

All of these things made Nathan the most interesting person she'd ever met. His equal adoration was addictive, and although she wasn't planning to act on her feelings, at last she mailed the goodbye letter to Richard.

She didn't open his letters anymore, knowing what they said. There was nothing he could say to change her mind; Richard and her life in Winston seemed so far away. Even her mother felt like a ghost, a memory she worked to conjure every night with pen and paper. Writing to Hazel had become her diary. She wrote in color, sparing no details, knowing there wasn't a thought or life event that would ever receive a reply.

CHAPTER 22

Kitty

November 1955

Lucy made a left leaving the lot instead of a right toward her house.

"Where are we going?" She'd invited Kitty over for dinner to celebrate the production news. Kitty assumed that meant Laurie was cooking.

"Blair House."

"What's that?"

"I want you to meet my friends."

"I don't know . . ." Continuing her relationship with Lucy was one thing; meeting the others was another. "Emma said it isn't safe."

"Do you feel unsafe with me?"

"No."

"Then trust me. Goodness, I've never met someone so reluctant to make friends." Kitty didn't have the heart to tell her that she'd gone years without having any.

They drove east toward downtown, then made a left onto a street in Hancock Park with brick houses with long driveways. Lucy pulled into the driveway of a gray one with a front lawn covered in a thicket of roses. She put her finger to her mouth to silence Kitty before they got out of the car in the backyard, where there was a large carport and an old shed. Both neighboring homes had lots of windows facing the property.

They entered through a long, narrow kitchen, too small for the house's size, with a gray-and-white checkered floor that matched the home's exterior. It was hot, as if the oven had been going, and the air smelled of cinnamon. In the center of the kitchen was a freestanding countertop with open shelving around the base, where multiple glass jars sat, filled with hard candies that likened the space to a candy shop. Dozens of champagne glasses sat on its top, along with dessert forks and plates with tiny rings of roses around the edges, similar to the ones Lucy had at her house. There was jazz playing—Miles Davis. Lucy motioned for her to follow her through a dark hallway, wallpapered with a rose vine design, toward the front of the house.

Standing in the front room, under a simple bronze-and-crystal chandelier, were two dozen Negro women, with skin colored near-White, light, yellow, medium beige, tawny, bronzy, brown-black, dark, and blue-black, and varying hair textures and features. The cluster represented the full color spectrum of the Negro race, Americans comprised of varying degrees of African and European blood.

The room fell quiet. Someone turned off Miles on the record player in the corner. It was clear they'd been expected.

Cora blossomed from the interior of the group like a budding flower. Although she was dressed down, in a drab black service-looking dress, and had her hair pulled back, she shone with genuine glee. She slipped her arm around Kitty's waist, an intimate gesture that was off-putting to Kitty, who remembered a frigid first introduction. "So glad you could make it. Welcome." She let Cora shift her body closer to the group. "Everyone, this is Kitty Karr, Nathan Tate's assistant at Telescope and Emma Karr's younger sister."

Murmurs accompanied this news. Kitty couldn't discern the exact words, but she presumed some of the others had grievances with Emma. "She arrived in June," Cora said.

"I met her at Lucy's." Laurie, Lucy's sister, came down the front staircase to the left of the living room where they were. Her hair hung long down, and bushy, as though she'd taken a brush to her curls. She waved at Kitty. "Nice to see you again."

The whispers ceased; it seemed Laurie had validated Kitty's presence.

"We're going to talk to Kitty," Cora said to Laurie. "Start without us."

Following Lucy back to the kitchen, Kitty heard Laurie ask for "the ledger."

"What is this place?"

"It's a boardinghouse for women who are passing," Lucy answered. "Makes it easier for them to transition. Gets them a job, helps them get on their feet."

"And it's our meeting place," Cora said. "It's easy for people to believe that the darker among us work here, so it's safe. It's been in the network for years now."

"Network?"

"Of Negro women. We belong to an underground resistance that spans the United States."

Kitty's eyes grew in size. It was a far cry from what Emma had thought they were up to, but perhaps more dangerous.

"There aren't any records of its inception, for obvious reasons, but semblances of this network began during slavery, when the one-drop rule classified anyone having one drop of Negro blood as Negro, and thus a slave. So Massa's babies, no matter how White they came out looking, became property," Cora said. "As more and more slaves became parented by their owners, the Negro race came to span the entire color spectrum, like the women here. Among the runaways were some of the fairest, who slipped through the cracks without detection, taking those who were darker with them. Passing women and men assisted runaways, then Union soldiers, by smuggling notes, goods, and guns to the North. They became abolitionists, teachers, politicians, doctors, lawyers. They influenced elections and assisted families whose head of household had been jailed or lynched. The passing women married White men of esteem and Colored freemen and became educators, provided shelter. It was through this work that passing women made alliances with other Colored women who couldn't pass. The web grew as more and more Coloreds left the South. And here we are."

Kitty leaned against the kitchen counter, looking between Lucy and Cora as they volleyed explanations at her.

Just as the White wives of slave owners—who later became KKK members and sympathizers who then ran for public office; started businesses; became lawyers, judges, and landlords; and joined various ranks of law enforcement and the military—were unable (or unwilling) to stop their men from their unspeakable crimes and petty actions, passing women influenced their men to do good.

Kitty learned that it was under that spirit that Blair House operated: to champion the rights of Negro women, whose burdens were doubled, being Negro and female. Their needs were often overshadowed or ignored by everyone, even their men, who were depleted, depressed, and often dependent mentally, spiritually, and economically. The virulence against Negro men was pressing, and as their ability to support their families as head of the household was inhibited, it was Negro women who had to take up the slack and absorb the shock of the blows they faced.

In order to solicit and then funnel donations for causes in support of the advancement of the Negro race, Blair House became an orphanage, a foundation for blind children, an animal charity, and a summer camp for underprivileged children. The rich people in their orbit needed tax write-offs, so they never refused to donate and asked few questions.

The benefit of the doubt was one of the many privileges of Whiteness.

"There'll be twenty-four of us with you. Twelve passing, twelve not."

"How do you make alliances? Laurie's your sister, you can trust her—what about the other women?"

"Like attracts like. Somehow, we get lucky."

"Like how we found you."

"You didn't find me; Emma told you I was coming. You knew who I was."

"We didn't seek you out," Cora said. "You came to my taping that night, and Lucy decided to befriend you."

"You were the only one who came to set. I didn't know who you were until you introduced yourself," Lucy clarified.

"How did you two learn about this?" Kitty asked.

"My momma raised Laurie and I up in the same way," Lucy said, "because we look so different. Our momma could pass but only did it to feed us. She had a job downtown. My father was too dark. It would have been better had he been the one who could pass. He was jealous of her, and his beatings cost her her life. I did her hair for her funeral, watched them bury her, and never looked back."

"I'm sorry," Kitty said. Fathers had created problems for everyone she knew.

"He thought being White was better and married her wanting to fix himself. When that didn't work, he beat on her, and on Laurie, whom he hated for the same reasons he hated himself." Lucy popped a champagne bottle and started filling the glasses on the counter. It was clear she was done sharing.

"Lucy and Laurie recruited me," Cora said.

"Laurie is our president," Lucy said, taking a sip of champagne.

Cora refused a glass. Lucy didn't offer Kitty one. "The three of us built this together. And with Billie and Nina."

"How?"

"Discretion."

"Feminine charm."

"Shrewdness."

"No, I mean what do you *do*? What work?"

"Negro inclusion in the film industry," Cora said. That explained her dedication to Abner, someone decades her senior, all these years. "He was starting to come around to hiring a Negro actor. Most times, they just don't want to be the first one. Pushing the envelope of change is hard. There's a lot of money to be made in Hollywood if they'd just let us in."

"We need better movies and characters first." Kitty hated the exaggerated dialect assigned to Negro characters.

"They want us to stay right where we are—you know what happened to Dorothy Dandridge after her Oscar nomination for *Carmen Jones*?" Cora didn't wait for Kitty to answer. "They asked her to play a maid. She did a triple performance—acting, singing, and dancing—and they wanted her to play a bit part as a maid."

Lucy interjected. "There's money to be made outside of performing—as costumers, hairdressers, directors, writers. It's an industry most of us don't even know exists."

"It's the only way we'll ever have a true say." Cora covered Kitty's hand. "Help us make Telescope the greatest film studio there is," she said. "With you having Nathan's ear, we can get films made about the things we need to talk about."

"Was the plan always for me to work with Nathan? It seemed like he'd made up his mind about hiring me before I interviewed."

"I won't deny it—your looks got you noticed, but you deserve that job," Lucy said. "He gave everyone a chance to show up. You did."

"Abner was a meticulous craftsman," Cora said. "I'm not sure Nathan has the magic touch. He'll need some help."

Familiar with that rhetoric, Kitty defended him. "He can do it, he just needs time."

Cora was impatient. "Time is what I don't have."

Lucy translated. "Cora wants to win an Oscar."

"*The Misfits* was a shoo-in, but with Abner sick, I'm not sure we can garner the same interest."

"What's the point if no one knows you're Colored?" Kitty asked.

"She'll reveal it one day, in some dramatic fashion," Lucy explained.

"Imagine their faces when they learn the truth." Cora chuckled as she pulled the collar of her blouse closed. "Sometimes the thought alone is enough to get me through the day."

Lucy shook her head at Kitty. "She's sinister; don't pay her any mind. This isn't about revenge or outsmarting anyone, it's about helping to make things right."

"That's why passing is nothing to be ashamed of. People been doing it since the beginning of time to survive, and not just us Negroes," Lucy continued. "Some Jews passed for gentile in the war if they could. It's survival." She paused. "As long as you're not passing because you think being White is better."

"I never wanted to pass in the first place. I had a fiancé, I had a life planned," Kitty said.

"Good, because *that* kind gives *our* kind a bad name. Some pass trying to love themselves better. That's not our kind. And sometimes it's hard to tell which a person is. We've determined which you are and we want you to join us."

"Yes."

Her answer came quicker than they expected. Cora's face turned grave. "It can be dangerous."

"I understand."

"If you get caught, or something happens, we can't help you. That jeopardizes us all."

"I understand."

"You'll be under a lot of scrutiny, and more often than not, things won't go our way," Lucy said.

"Do you want me to say no?" Kitty asked.

"I want to be clear. This is for life. You can't un-know what you learned today. You'll wonder who's who everywhere you go." She raised a brow at this part.

Cora patted Kitty's hand to draw her attention from Lucy. "We've had more disappointments than triumphs. The Emmett Till trial was heartbreaking. We had two jurors in the pool, but neither was picked for the jury."

"We're lucky it even went to trial," Lucy reminded her. "When you do get a win, there's no better feeling. Last year, I got Jack to donate the proceeds from the sale of his parents' house in Maine to the NAACP. Took me four years, but I did it."

"One day one of us will be in a position to really change things," Cora said.

"Last I checked, White women don't have that kind of power," Kitty argued.

"They do—by controlling the right White man."

"So you use marriage as a tool. That's why you match couples."

"Yes."

Kitty looked at Lucy. "Does my sister know about all of this?"

"Ahh, Emma." Cora shook her head.

"No. We determined she wasn't suitable," Lucy said.

"We were looking for a sixth in our unit, but—"

"Your what?"

"We operate in groups of six. Twelve passing, with you now, and twelve not. A unit is six."

"Why me?"

"You feel guilty being able to pass. Emma doesn't want to look back."

Yet another accurate assessment. Was Emma really that transparent? "Is that why you sabotaged her engagement?"

Lucy sighed. "Yes. Emma didn't know what to do with Lincoln and, as a casting director, he was too important to lose as an asset."

"But how would she have made him an asset?"

"Married him for his capacity to donate, for one. Gotten Jamie an audition. Anything but what she did. I mean, damn—I didn't think I had to tell her everything. He was in awe of her, and she ruined it."

Cora tried to soften Lucy's words. "It wasn't personal; our work always comes first. We knew we couldn't trust her to do anything serious."

"She has her own priorities." Kitty considered Emma to be a liability too.

"And you—well, not just anyone could have landed in such a position at Telescope so quickly," Lucy explained.

With Abner retired, it was now Kitty, not Cora, closest to the person who could advance the agenda.

"Lucy says you have his ear. He talks to you about scripts, staffing."

"Yes." Kitty was a little disappointed to know her conversations with Lucy hadn't been private and was happy she hadn't disclosed more. Who knew how they'd want to capitalize on that?

"Well, you just keep doing whatever it is you're doing," Cora said. "Nathan doesn't have the same ego as his father, and I believe we can get more done."

Folding chairs had been arranged around the living room. Kitty tiptoed through the center, behind Cora and Lucy, to sit on the stairs. She peered through the railing, listening to Laurie at the podium, centered in the cedar-trimmed doorway.

"They're planning a boycott of the city buses in Montgomery, Alabama. Before the end of the year." Negroes there would walk to work, refusing to pay the same amount of money as White passengers only to face humiliation and relegation to the back of the bus.

"Those White folks won't know what hit them."

"Wives will just fire their maids. How will they eat?"

"They'll have the same problem with every maid in town."

"Can you imagine those women doing their own dishes?"

The room erupted with laughter.

"Caring for their own children?"

"Picking up after their own husbands!"

Cora yelled over them. "The longer it goes, the more shameful it'll look, and the more dangerous it will get. They'll get desperate once they realize they're going to lose. It won't be funny."

"People will have to walk in sun, rain, sleet, snow," Laurie said. "We have to support their efforts, no matter how long it takes."

"What about the people who can't walk long distances? Will there be carpools?"

"We need to raise money for gas and to buy cars." Laurie looked at the beige-colored woman sitting to the right of the podium, whom she called Nina. "So bigger donations now."

Nina McCullough was Blair House's best fundraiser and one of the prettiest women in the room. Married to a hotelier, she had someone to tend to her every whim. She sat next to Maude Reade, who was scouring the paper. "That poor boy's death may have done more for the cause than anything could have."

"They're going to do an interview," the Blair House secretary, Addie Banks, said. She sat slightly behind the circle, near the window, taking notes. Her skin gleamed in the light as though she'd just applied lotion. She wore her hair in thick French braids that accentuated the slant of her eyes and her high forehead.

"Why now?"

"To brag about how they got away with murder."

"Reporters should have worked harder for a confession." A woman named Liberty Stills flung away the side of the paper she had been sharing with Maude. Liberty sat taller than everyone in the room, and her feet were nearly twice the size of everyone's, Kitty noticed as she crossed her ankles.

"The acquittal opened people's eyes."

"*White* people's eyes," another, sweeter voice echoed from a woman who wore a perfectly coiffed wig. Cora identified her as Harriet Stafford.

Kitty was skeptical. White people existed on the periphery of their pain, never having to feel it in their hearts, in their bones. She surprised herself by saying so. "Everyone at Telescope thought there would be a conviction, but they never said anything about the acquittal. It was forgotten completely when James Dean died."

Cora whispered to Lucy, sitting a few stairs above her and Kitty, "She's quick."

"Told you," Kitty heard Lucy respond.

"If they ain't open already, I don't know what else can do it," said the petite woman next to Harriet. Her tangerine lipstick made her pale skin sallow.

"That's Billie. She's with us." Cora pointed.

Lucy hushed them as her sister took the floor again.

"Bring up the riots, the boycotts; talk about the protests and the dogs. The murders. Talk about the news. Keep it on people's minds," Laurie instructed. "In the grocery store line, at dinner"—she looked up at the stairs—"at the studio, don't let people just exist in their worlds. Make them aware."

"Isn't that impolite—or worse, couldn't it raise suspicion?" Kitty asked.

"You don't have to have a strong opinion to put it in someone's mind," Laurie said. She walked to the middle of the room to meet Kitty's eye. "You can't be afraid."

"I am." Edna, a straight-haired redhead, sat next to Addie by the window. "My husband's agitated by some of my conversation in social settings. I've made myself unpopular with some of the wives." The medium-brown-skinned woman on her opposite side took her hand. "I want to leave him," Edna said.

"And what are we going to do without the little bit of protection he provides?" This speaker had a round face colored like a black walnut. The room was split in reaction to her question.

"What Wilma means is, you can't," Laurie said. "As a police officer, he's too valuable."

"But we're starting to become unpopular anyway," Edna said.

"Guess you'll have to work harder to prove you're one of them," Wilma said.

"I'm unhappy!"

Wilma mocked her. "Poor princess. Who isn't?"

"I'm actually quite satisfied," Lilly Brown said, putting her hand to her chest. She hovered at the paper-bag line and wore too much makeup. At this comment, Kitty saw Harriet knock knees with the woman on her other side, who stifled a smirk.

"That's 'cause all you do is socialize with those other sadity Negroes," Wilma hissed.

"She ain't wrong," Liberty said, under her breath.

"Wilma, you're welcome anytime," Lilly said.

"They'd take one look at my black—"

Cora stood up. "Hey! Enough." Lips smacked, but everyone quieted.

"Edna, your leaving could cause problems for everyone," Laurie said. "Wilma's not wrong. You're going to have to work harder."

Emma's warnings flooded Kitty's mind as the room compiled suggestions for Edna to fix things. Everyone agreed. Edna would have to display some sort of cruelty or sanction it.

What Lucy and Cora were up to was indeed worse than Emma could have imagined.

After announcements, the oldest of the group, a preacher's wife named Bertha Mills, stood to lead them in prayer. She wore a long floral dress that covered everything but her hands, feet, and face. Her gray hair was pressed but fuzzy at the edges, as though she'd been sweating.

After a solid two minutes, Kitty's eyes, which never closed, met Laurie's across the circle. Laurie widened hers in exasperation before jostling Bertha's hand to finish.

"Desserts in the kitchen," Bertha said in a raspy voice.

Ending on a sweet note was symbolic, Lucy said, meant to remind them to be grateful for each other, Blair House, and the opportunity to help their people. These were blessings so many others didn't receive.

With champagne and coffee cake, Kitty settled alone in a chair in the corner. The others stood about the room in clusters of likeness that couldn't always be physically identified. They all looked so worldly; Kitty imagined all of them had careers, children, and husbands. She wasn't sure she fit in. Lucy kept eyeing Kitty to urge her to mingle, but Kitty ignored her, pretending to be consumed by her extra-large piece of coffee cake. She was beginning to feel as though she could be ejected from the circle as fast as she'd been included.

The women usually dispersed, one or two at a time, over the course of two hours, and the first that day was Billie. "Wish me luck; I have an audition."

Wilma started again. "I don't understand all of this performing." She had burn scars on her hands and arms. "Any one of us could win an Oscar for the roles we play every day."

"Wilma, we've talked about this," Lucy said, in a parent's tone. "It's about access, and the images people see of us around the world."

Wilma took a step toward Lucy, as though she was squaring off for a fight. "But it's not images of us—it's images of them that they don't know are us." Others started to notice the exchange.

Lucy didn't move. "And you find no satisfaction in that?"

"Don't matter unless people know, Lucy-Goosey."

Lucy pointed at her. "Don't call me that."

"I'm playing. It rhymes."

Lucy's cheeks blazed. "If you have a problem with our initiatives, bring it to a vote."

"No, I get it. We're in LA."

"Correct."

Wilma left next, causing a flood of departures among the most pigmented. No one was rude or hasty, but leaving then was taking an apparent side. With only those who hovered twenty degrees above and below the color line left, Kitty was reminded of the tension that had defined her life. She hadn't left Cottonwood and come all the way to Los Angeles to fight among her own kind.

When Nina went out the back, Lucy called Kitty to the front door, where she and another woman were putting on their coats.

"Kitty, this is Mamie. She runs a nightclub, a grocery store, and a thrift store over on the Colored side of town."

Kitty was confused; this woman was as fair as she. Mamie seemed to understand. "I pass only occasionally."

"Jack's parents are hosting Christmas in Washington this year," Lucy said to Mamie, before turning to explain to Kitty. "Jack is thinking about running for office. Senators on both sides of his family, so he's practically a shoo-in."

Lucy's parents-in-law were hosting a donor event before Christmas to explore their son's political future, she told the women, and Lucy needed new clothes.

"Would you leave Telescope?" Kitty asked.

Lucy tied her black scarf around her head in the hallway mirror. "If being a senator's wife was more beneficial."

"Cora's going?" Mamie made an O of her mouth to apply a frosty-pink lipstick.

Lucy opened the door for Mamie. "She wouldn't miss it."

"Good for her." Mamie wiggled her brows before opening the front door and walking off down the wide, paved street.

After shutting the door, Lucy turned to Kitty. "I don't have to explain why dating in the political sector is important, do I?"

Kitty shook her head, and Lucy linked arms with her. "Let's go shopping. His family has to see me as a political asset—maybe even a future First Lady." She winked.

Back in the car, Kitty got a better view of the house. Rose and ivy vines climbed the walls, highlighting the ten drawn window shades. "Isn't it suspicious with the house all closed up like that?"

"It's not always like that. And typically, as long as you're quiet, people in this neighborhood mind their business." Hancock Park was an exclusive, old-money neighborhood in Los Angeles. "The house was donated to us."

"By whom?"

"Anonymous."

To Kitty, the lush green lawns and the thick Georgian columns made it look as if it had been plucked from a White neighborhood in Winston.

"It's gorgeous, isn't it?" Lucy said, noticing Kitty's wonder. "Mine and Laurie's childhood home was one room."

Lucy now lived in a house far grander, but Kitty appreciated she hadn't forgotten where she came from. "My momma and I slept in the same bed," Kitty said.

Lucy started out of the driveway and then hit the brakes as a black Buick lurched from its parked position at the curb. The Negro man at the wheel waved in apology, distracted by kisses from his passenger. When he made a U-turn in the middle of the street, Kitty saw Nina McCullough nestled underneath his arm before they passed in opposite directions. "Was that Nina?"

Lucy handed her cigarette to Kitty to light. "If anyone or anything made your sister uncomfortable around us, it was Nina. But that's only because Emma didn't understand." Lucy tapped the steering wheel as she drove. "Love is rare for women like us. So if you find it, grab it. But you must know, sometimes we're mistresses first—sometimes forever—and usually second or even third wives."

"That's a sin." Kitty wasn't religious, but she did believe in the basics; marriage-only consummation had been the easiest one. Seeing what her mother had gone through raising her, being unmarried with a child wasn't a road she planned to travel, or even parallel. Lying, stealing, and killing— most folks, if they were being honest, could see just cause for all three.

"For us, it's a haven. As a mistress, you get all a man's affections and none of his expectations. You never have to worry about him wanting a baby. You eat at the best restaurants, get gifts of jewelry and fine clothes. You're taken care of, but you don't always become a wife."

"Is that how you met Jack?"

"No. I've been lucky. Happened to me just like it does in the movies. Twice. People say love like that doesn't really exist, but they couldn't write about it if it didn't. Losing it is agony. That's why I understand Nina."

"Your first love was Negro?"

Lucy held up her fingers. "And my second and third. Have you ever been in love?"

"I'm not sure." Despite her sadness over how things ended with Richard, her feelings for him weren't enough to return to what could have been. Still, she worried about him and hoped that he didn't hate her. Thinking he did hurt her more than losing what they'd called love.

"What about Nathan?" Lucy gave her a curious look when they stopped at a light.

"I'm not sure."

Lucy adjusted the rearview mirror. "Marry one day, but only if it's right. After all, you can be married and completely disregarded by your husband. Then it's all work and no reward. Security is important. But men will be there, trust me—and for you, especially."

"Maybe we should all marry so we don't die alone," Kitty said, thinking of her mother, who probably would. A lump rose in her throat. Hazel never talked about having romantic interests. She was Lefred and Adelaide's willing third wheel, but she was thirty-five, and it saddened Kitty to think that would be the end of her story.

"Marriage doesn't ensure that. The only surety is money. It's just as easy to fall in love with a rich man as it is a poor one." Again, Lucy sounded like Emma. "Marriage is a good thing, but there's a lot of responsibility in it too." She rolled her eyes. "More for women."

"Now." Lucy's voice lowered. Kitty had noticed they all whispered when speaking about Blair House; soon she would adopt the same practice, able to conduct an entire conversation at a barely audible pitch. "That was Thomas you saw Nina with. Her first husband was also Negro. He was the love of her life; that's why she vacillates over the color line the way she does. They knew each other as kids. He was a cook and got hired at a hotel downtown. They promised to promote him, but instead, they stole all his recipes and let him go. He started drinking, disappearing for weeks. To leave, she passed, hoping he'd never find her. Two years later, she met Titan."

"Is it a coincidence she married a hotelier?" Kitty asked.

"Nothing we do is by coincidence." Lucy pushed the gas pedal, flying through a light just as it turned red.

Holden's, just down the road from Blair House in Beverly Hills, was three stories high, with gold-trimmed windows and doorframes. When they pulled up to the curb, two Negro men in black tuxedos and red bow ties approached either side of the car. Kitty went for the door handle, but Lucy stopped her. "Let them."

"Good evening, ma'am." The man, who was balding, kept his eyes to the ground.

"Thank you, sir," Kitty said.

He looked at her, startled she'd spoken.

Coming around the car to take her arm, Lucy joked, "Why don't you kiss him on the cheek too?"

Kitty hushed her. "I was being polite."

"You don't thank people for doing their jobs, Kitty."

The store's golden double doors floated open thanks to a second pair of older Negro men. This time, Lucy greeted them both. "Mr. Banks. Mr. Stills." Neither acknowledged her nor flinched at her greeting. Their faces remained blank, trained not to betray them. "Addie's and Liberty's husbands," Lucy said as they continued toward the women's department. "Liberty's husband is writing a piece, and Mr. Banks offered to let him shadow him."

"Liberty's husband is a writer?"

"A prolific writer. He writes speeches for the movement."

"You didn't know the men at the car?"

"No. Unless I say so, we don't, and you should act regular. Don't be too nice." She sifted through a rack. "Does Emma have a charge account here?"

"No," Kitty said, "because her sister does."

"What does that matter?"

"Emma took her real name. We both took her sisters' real names."

Lucy didn't look happy to hear this but, seeing the clerk coming, held an emerald-green dress up to her rail-thin frame. "This would be perfect for Christmas. My in-laws do a big party every year, with tree trimming, carols, a petting zoo, and fireworks. Quintessential Christmas."

"It's beautiful. Is that your right size?" The salesclerk smiled as though she knew Lucy. Lucy stared at her. The clerk stammered a bit before adding, "Mrs. Schmitt?"

Lucy spoke then, still a little unfriendly. "It is, but I need one in her size too." Lucy gestured to Kitty's yellow dress. Borrowed from Emma, it was a little big. "We're shopping for her. She needs a signature look," she said.

The salesclerk pulled out a measuring tape and secured it first around Kitty's hips and then her bust. She scurried off as though Lucy's instructions were clear.

"The way you dress is a message to the world. You're about to have a whole new life, and it's time to *say*"—Lucy shimmed her shoulders—"*something*. You'll come everywhere with us, and you'll need to be dressed."

"Where?"

"Ballrooms for parties and fundraisers, dinners at private homes and clubs, the opera, plays—everywhere," Lucy said, sifting through the dress rack.

"But Nathan expects me in the office until evening."

"We rarely go before nine." Lucy handed her a red ball gown with a full skirt. "You'll want to always look your best. No one's going to be persuaded to do something by someone who doesn't look like they belong."

The salesclerk returned with an armful of clothes. Lucy picked about fifteen pieces for Kitty to try on: separates and matching sets in neutral and bright colors, and more evening gowns.

In the dressing room, Kitty admired herself in outfit after outfit, feeling more like the version of "Kitty" she imagined. Every skirt, dress, and jacket was made with the finest fabric and looked just right on her frame.

"I can't afford any of this." Kitty touched the red skirt. "This alone is two weeks of my pay." She had opened a savings account with the money her mother gave her, but she didn't want to touch it.

Lucy took everything to the cashier. "Telescope has an account for costuming."

Their purchases left them with little sitting room in her car. Lucy tried to wrangle the ruffles and netting of several dresses behind the seats. "I think I got carried away." Once she'd secured one side, the other would pop up. They howled at the ridiculousness of it until they were red in the face and gasping for air, their joy painful now. Kitty rode home smoking a cigarette and feeling as though life couldn't get any better than it was right then.

But it did.

When she got home, she found Emma in a good mood. Every light was on, Little Richard was playing, and she was cooking. She spun around, pointing a metal soup spoon like a weapon when Kitty tried to sneak past the kitchen.

"What's all that?" Emma pointed to the dress bags Kitty was struggling to hold. A dollop of tomato sauce dripped from the spoon onto the floor.

"Clothes from Wardrobe." Kitty had made sure the scripted Holden's name was hidden before she came in.

"That's a lot of things."

Kitty nodded at the stove. "Nice of you to cook."

Emma pouted her lips. "It's not for you per se. It's for dinner tomorrow night. You're my tester."

"Who's it for?"

"Rick."

"Who?" Kitty was thrilled to hear a man's name besides Nathan's come out of her sister's mouth. "Let me hang these things. I'll be right back."

Rick Denman, Kitty learned, was a friend of Judy's fiancé. He was an executive at a manufacturing company, and they'd been out, almost every evening, for the past month.

"Why didn't you tell me?"

"'Cause I always talk about things too soon, and they never work out." In the same breath, she grasped both of Kitty's hands. "But I think he's going to propose." He had invited her to his family's house in Minnesota for Christmas.

"That's wonderful!"

"I don't know if I should go. He has four sisters. His wife died five years ago, but she was close with all of them." Emma feared her ability to win over so many people. Lincoln's parents had been alive but barely coherent, a state Emma preferred; they wouldn't have known had he gotten married, had a child or, quite frankly, died. These were safer familial circumstances. "You know how nosey women can be."

"Go." The proposal was Emma's greatest chance for happiness before Judy's wedding, paramount for Kitty's peace.

"You really think so?"

"Yes. You're in here cooking for him, and you don't cook for yourself."

Emma dropped the spoon against the side of the pot. "Is it too much?"

"No. You like him." Kitty found it sweet.

"I've never been happier."

Remembering Lucy's words about her duty as a sister, Kitty put on an apron. "Might as well make him dessert too."

CHAPTER 23

Kitty

November 1955

"She sings here twice a month," Lucy said of Billie, who was onstage two nights later at Reed's Nightclub. She was backed by a Negro band, but aside from them and the servers, everyone, including the dance line, was White. Kitty recognized the saxophonist as the man who had been with Nina in the car.

Kitty's unit, plus Mamie—who had decided to pass that night to scope out musicians—were at a table in the back.

"Some are Cuban," Cora said, of the dancers. "Half the time you can't tell the difference until they speak." Cora gestured to a table near the stage, where Billie's husband sat. At thirty-five years old, he was already a judge. "He's her biggest fan. Goes to every show. Sweet—but also how she got three children."

"I thought having children wasn't a good idea?" Kitty asked.

"Billie got lucky. Both her parents are half-White, so far it worked out— which, you know, is rare. All three of them are White as snow. She'll never tell them," Cora said.

"Never?"

"It's a personal choice."

"Is singing her work?"

"It's just a hobby. She's working to get more libraries built around the city," Cora said.

"How?" Kitty remembered going to the library for story hour sometimes in Charlotte. She liked going until she learned she couldn't borrow a book, because she couldn't use her real name on the library card.

"By steering her husband's passion for advocacy away from animals and toward the Colored folks down the street."

"He wasn't suspicious?"

"If he wasn't a good person, he might have been."

"But he is," Nina said. "Talked about the Emmett Till trial nonstop to anyone who would listen—wanted those boys to be found guilty."

Kitty was introduced when Billie brought her husband over after her blues set. "Kitty's in development at Telescope."

He and Nathan, it emerged, had gone to the same university. "Tell him hello for me. Bastard sure got lucky."

"Don't you all . . ." Cora sniped under her breath as he and Billie kissed goodbye. She slid into the chair next to Lucy. "He starts a trial tomorrow."

Maude put out her cigarette. "Can we go now? I'm hungry." She looked down at her uneaten plate of smothered chicken.

Kitty had never heard sweeter words. Her baked chicken was under-cooked, and so was the lemon cake she'd ordered instead.

"Oh, sorry, I forgot to tell you." Billie looked around the table. "They brought in a new kitchen staff. Complaints about how many Blacks were on payroll."

Maude's hand popped in the air. A very young, blond waitress came over. "The chicken was disappointing tonight."

"This too," Cora said, pushing her meat loaf to the center of the table. Nina followed with her Cobb salad, as did Mamie.

"Can you send over the manager?"

Billie gave a sympathetic look to the girl, who looked ready to cry. "Let me get some help."

The help was Liberty and Lilly.

"Guess you all heard," Liberty said, slowly reaching for the first discarded plate. Her lips barely moved. "They had them prep for the weekend and then let them go this morning."

Kitty continued eating around the raw bits of her cake.

"Tell them to call Jimmy at the hotel; we'll hire them," Nina said.

"Will do," Liberty said.

"Still want the manager?" Lilly said.

"Several calls over the next week or so would be better," Lucy said.

Liberty's tone dropped to address Kitty. "Kitty, give me your plate."

Kitty sighed and let her fork drop. It seemed no one ate in Los Angeles.

As the slice passed by, Nina put her cigarette out in it. "I'm ready too."

"All right; see y'all in a bit," Liberty said. She and Lilly led the line as those passing let their voices carry over the music about how disappointing their meal was.

At the door, Nina and Mamie decided to take a cab.

"Be careful," Cora said, as the others piled into her Rolls Royce, chauffeured by the Tates' longtime driver, Percy Mitchell, who was also a friend of Blair House.

Almost an hour later, they arrived at an older but stately house with a porch and baskets of lilac flowers hanging from the windows.

"Where are we now?" Kitty asked.

"Mamie's Place. Everyone is a friend here."

Something savory Kitty couldn't name engulfed her nose as the tempo of the music coming from inside pulsed through her body. The door opened, and a rush of heat hit her face as they all piled in, squeezing through the tiny spaces between dancing bodies and out of the back door to where tables sat in the open yard.

Kitty took a deep breath of air and the cigarette Maude handed her. She and Kitty had bonded earlier after learning they were each the lightest in their family. Maude's family tree was a stump beyond her great-grandparents, but none of them were White.

"My father is White," Kitty said, feeling defensive at the way Maude said it.

Maude seemed surprised. "You're directly mulatto?"

"That means half and half?"

"Sorta, yes—who can keep up?"

A familiar group waved them over. Nina was already there and had changed from her dress into trousers and a button-up shirt.

"Nina, did you tell—" Cora started.

"Please, not tonight," Laurie said, with a drag of her cigarette. She brushed some of her hair back, but it rose again, still untied and bushy. "I'm in a good mood, and"—she nodded toward the house—"Charles is here." Laurie's longtime beau didn't know anything of her involvement with Blair House, atypical for the non-passing women there. Many of their husbands helped the mission, or were involved in their own efforts, but Charles thought Negroes should stop pushing for inclusion. He wanted to leave the country and be done with it.

"Tell people our hotels are hiring," Nina said. "That's the point."

"Have you confirmed that?" Laurie said.

"Don't worry."

"I'll put it in the newsletter." Sammie, short for Samantha, drummed her plum-painted fingers on the table. She had just married an officer in the NAACP. She had a slender face, perfect for her short, coiled halo of brown hair.

"She's a typist for the organization," Edna, seated next to Sammie, said to Kitty from across the table.

"Mostly I get coffee and file their memos after the fact." Sammie shrugged. "But at least I'm in the room."

"And it's an important one to be in," Laurie said.

"Are you two sisters?" Kitty pointed between Sammie and Edna. Their skin tones varied by five shades, and their features didn't match, but that meant nothing.

"Cousins," Edna said.

"He could have not wanted you to work at all," Lilly interjected. Being able to provide for a wife and three children was her husband's biggest source of pride. Lilly, only ever having wanted one child, was overwhelmed with three. Kitty would later hear from Harriet, who tutored some of the Blair House kids on the weekend, that Lilly was often hours late to pick hers up. Harriet was a teacher's assistant at an exclusive all-White preschool. The all-White aspect was an expectation, but not a rule, that Harriet was working to dismantle.

"Your husband's a doctor; you more than make do," Sammie said.

"We have a lot of responsibilities too—his mother just moved in."

"If William was the only one working, we might not eat," Sammie pointed out.

There was a strained laugh, acknowledging not only the difference in pay between White and Negro men but the economic challenges of activism. Like the NAACP, Blair House collected money for others, but it wasn't a regular income. Those with access to disposable funds, like Nina, subsidized the needs of those in Blair House who were relegated to a lower class. This wasn't always just about color; the ones among them who married uneducated White men, like Edna, struggled too. Later that night, Kitty would watch Edna waving from the bus stop as Sammie drove off in her husband's Buick.

"That's why I plan to be rich. Can't depend on any man." Wilma taught high school chemistry and mixed hair potions in her kitchen in her spare time. Last summer, she had suffered second-degree burns while experimenting with hair-straightening formulas.

"Not everyone is fortunate enough to be as educated as you," Lucy said.

Wilma ignored Lucy and spoke to the table. "Hair like ours, you can't even take a hot bath without it curling up at the edges."

"So?" Laurie fluffed her own.

"So, nothing. I'll be rich." Wilma didn't perm her own hair but wore wigs because she didn't want to have to do her hair five days a week.

"If y'all stop covering it and straightening it, maybe it'll grow," Laurie said.

No one wanted to hear this.

"Not everyone wants to run around like who it did and why," Lucy said. She wasn't only referring to Laurie's hair but her whole look; she was pretty but made no effort to accentuate anything. She reminded Kitty of Hazel.

Mamie appeared. "Wilma, you can use the bathroom in the back," she said, as if she'd heard the conversation.

"See?" Wilma said. "I have a clientele."

"It's a party, and y'all are doing perms?" Laurie said.

"And I'm first," Mamie said, running her hands through her short hair. Some looked surprised. "What? Plenty of fair Negroes like me have hair that curls up like a slinky at the slightest sweat." She and Lilly followed at Wilma's heels, the first two in a quickly growing line. Kitty would later learn that they and others were members of some elite Negro social clubs that Laurie and Liberty outwardly blasted for fragmenting the race.

Liberty arrived then, just as the table was clearing. Maude scooted over so she could fit between herself and Lucy. She looked like a Black Olive Oyl.

"Liberty writes a national column," Lucy said to Kitty.

"Oh, you and your husband are both writers?"

Lucy explained. "We went to Holden's."

"Yes; my column runs in a few Negro papers," Liberty clarified.

"She's also writing a book." Maude sounded proud. At this, Liberty smiled broadly.

"About all this?"

"I don't know what it is yet."

"Is Liberty your real name?" It sounded like a writer's name.

"It is—my mother had a wicked sense of humor." She was, she explained, named after her great-grandmother, who died a slave in Tennessee. "She lived to be a hundred and three. And she was tall and big like me." She opened her palm to show how large her hands were. Kitty had baby hands next to hers.

"I've been helping Liberty uncover her family history," Maude said.

"How?"

"I have access to the records." Maude worked as a secretary for the *Los Angeles Times*.

"I'd like to help," Kitty said, realizing a slight interest in her family tree.

Lucy shook her head. "The studio will keep you plenty busy."

———————

The women of Blair House represented every social class, allowing access to information from top to bottom. Because the network was so uniquely orchestrated, inclusion only came if there was a need to fill. Kitty had gotten lucky.

Of those who were passing, some had matched with well-to-do men, with generational wealth many times over, and were in positions to influence some of the most powerful men in the country who just happened to be their husbands, fiancés, and boyfriends. Regardless of social status, all the women were opinionated, cunning, and well read. They met every week to trade information, organize, and fellowship.

Kitty would have to memorize every lie, and would soon be able to identify them by the stories they told about their past lives: deceased parents, adoption, rich Northerners, poor Midwesterners. In one way or another, they had all been on the run. They didn't get along with family, had big dreams, or faced violence at home that pushed them to roam. They said whatever was needed to elicit enough sympathy to make the past an impolite subject.

"Why?" Kitty sat in the kitchen of Blair House the next Saturday night for more instruction.

"We all must know the same information about everyone. That's safest," Cora said.

"Especially because we have so many alliances across the color line," Laurie said, chopping onions for soup.

"Different levels of access. Different treatment by men. There are places I can go, things I can say that Laurie can't. And in the same way, there are places she's allowed that I'm not. Laurie's skin makes her invisible. If I were to interrupt my husband's whiskey and cigars, the room would fall silent and remain that way, making it nearly impossible for me to hear anything. Meanwhile, Laurie has free access. They hear everything in service. Oh—you know." Lucy looked at Kitty and then at the room to explain. "Kitty's momma is a maid."

Kitty's twinge of embarrassment was soothed by Lucy's explanation of the role's power. By Lucy's logic, it was the Negro servers at the White men's clubs who had the best access. "Or the janitors."

"You'd be surprised to know what people throw away," Cora jumped in. "Every office, even the Oval Office," she winked, "needs someone to empty the trash."

Thus, the women in service at Blair House, just as in Cottonwood, knew everything about the White folks of Los Angeles. They passed information to everyone else for purposes of leverage and planning. Their word was the last, a directive that came from Laurie—only they could abort a plan, in mid-execution if need be.

Second in line were the writers, Liberty and Maude, and then those with access to politicians and heads of industry. Those passing focused on collecting money and running their mouths about the things that mattered.

Some, like Kitty, had longer-term goals.

"Wilma will start her hair care line soon, and we'll back that."

"She can hire Colored chemists," Kitty said, understanding.

"Well, yes, but to run a company, Wilma needs more than just scientists. She's insufferable, but she could potentially create thousands of jobs for Colored people one day."

"Is that where some of the donation money goes?"

"To her, but also to Addie and Olivia, who are starting a maid service."

"We help Mamie and her husband—they want to open a new place."

"How much does Blair House make?" When Cora called it a network, Kitty realized, she wasn't exaggerating.

"In due time," Lucy said, looking at her gold watch. "We have to go get dressed. Oh, I forgot—there's a little complication. Kitty tells me Emma took her real sisters' names for their own."

Laurie understood the gravity of the statement but shook her head. "The Karr family doesn't ring a bell."

"They own Holden's," Kitty explained.

Laurie looked between her sister and Cora. "Y'all didn't tell me that."

Cora had the simplest answer. "Guess we'll have to make sure the coincidence is on their part."

"What does that mean?"

"That when people meet the other Kitty Karr, they'll think of you, instead of the other way around."

Lucy's voice rose. "Well, in the meantime, I brought it up to say we need to check guest lists a little more closely."

"I'll mention it," Laurie said.

They arrived to the home of the banker Addie worked for, to celebrate the engagement of his daughter. Most of the guests had been invited that night just for cocktails and "canapés," Lucy told Kitty to say. They were included in a smaller group invited for dinner because Cora, through Abner, had known the bride since she was a young girl. The manor's corridor had two sets of stairs that led up to an open-air courtyard. Liberty, Bertha, and Lilly were serving that night. The banker had also bought dozens of Bertha's dinner rolls and her rum cakes. She moved slowly with a tray of cheese puffs, as if her feet hurt.

Addie met them in the red-bricked open space with a tray of champagne. "May I show you to your seats?" She looked through their group at no one in particular.

They followed, greeting a few people who said hello. Thanks to their husbands, Lucy, Billie, and Nina were well-known socialites. Maude was the newer, brainy beauty and, as the movie star, Cora was adored. Kitty was easily accepted as a part of the crowd.

Addie's pace increased down a hallway of closed-doored rooms.

A set of double doors opened to reveal a banquet hall and a long wooden table. Kitty found her seat between Lucy and a car manufacturer named Henry Polk, a jolly man who always wore a plaid tie. Knowing the Montgomery bus boycott would need cars, Kitty watched the women at work.

"How's the car business, Henry?" Lucy asked. She took a bite of steak.

He groaned. "A little stagnant, to tell you the truth."

"Really?" Lucy looked so innocent.

His wife joined in. "I told Henry he has to do something."

"People have more money than ever to spend."

"Negroes love your cars, Henry." Cora, overhearing, made a joke.

"Part of my problem," he said.

"Why do you care what color your customer is? It's only more money for you," Billie said, lighting a cigarette.

Henry coughed and reached for the whiskey he'd brought from the cocktail party. "Volume. More Whites than Coloreds can afford a car."

The future bride spoke up. "Coloreds seem to have more money than we do these days—"

The men squelched her exaggeration.

"They'll never catch up," Cora said. "But Jane makes a good point. They have more money to spend than ever, graduating from secondary schools and working in trades now."

"Still, being first pick to the Coloreds doesn't scream 'high class,'" Henry grumbled.

"Neither does being a sponsor of the KKK," Cora said.

Henry turned beet red as the table began to laugh. "It's not the Klan."

"May as well be," said a dark-haired, blue-eyed man who spoke with a Spanish accent. Had he not spoken, Kitty would have assumed he was White. Seated next to the host, he fumbled with his orange-and-yellow paisley tie. "No one belongs to the group but men like you."

An older man with a gray moustache leaned in. "If you learned English, we might consider you."

"You'll let me join now because I'm rich enough." The man pointed his finger. "Richer than you."

Another white-haired man spoke up. "Money talks, señor."

"Then why can't the Negroes join?" Maude said. "If they have money, their interests align with yours."

Kitty heard a few men snicker, and a White woman with a bird comb in her hair spoke up. "Class has always been the real factor. You don't want to join the Klan because of"—she lowered her voice—"the rednecks."

"Hey! That's my family you're talking about!" This was a joke that made the table laugh.

"Mrs. Abraham isn't wrong. Educated Negroes have more in common with you than the Irish." Cora smirked.

One man yelled, "There's nothing I got in common with a—"

"Kellen!" Billie said. Later Kitty would learn he was her brother-in-law.

"Some here don't seem to be able to control their tempers." Kellen's wife patted her brow.

"And at an engagement party, no less. How uncouth!" Nina said.

"I do agree," the host said. He nodded back at his waitstaff lining the wall. "Maybe an apology?"

"Please," Lucy said. "I don't want my food spit in tonight."

The man stared at her, and Lucy stared right back, until his wife patted his arm. Kitty was sure he was going to storm out when he stood, but instead, he bowed halfheartedly to the people behind him. "Apologies."

Kitty sensed the faint satisfaction of the line.

Back at Blair House, they laughed about this scene, while Laurie recorded the donations everyone collected that week.

"Once the boycott starts," Cora said to Kitty, "we'll suggest he give a few free cars to the cause—could result in Negro customer loyalty later."

"If he doesn't agree, we'll start opposing boycotts among the Whites and Coloreds, and he'll be forced to," Maude said. She and Liberty would disseminate the information.

Laurie joined their circle with a leather notebook and pen.

"And then we can quietly accept his donation," Lucy said.

"We wouldn't want the crackers to get word and burn the cars."

"People aren't all bad; sometimes they just need to be pushed to do the right thing."

"But he wouldn't be doing it because it's the right thing," Kitty said. "He'll be doing it to save his profits."

"People's souls are their business," Lucy said.

Inside Blair House, they fortified one another's. Aside from their duties to the group, they convened to celebrate and enjoy one another. If Kitty had time, there was always something happening at Blair House. But she didn't.

With Emma occupied by new love, Kitty was out with her unit four or five nights a week. She worked all day and then went home for a quick bite before Nina's or Cora's chauffeured car arrived. They were invited to everything happening that mattered—dinners and parties at fancy private residences and clubs, the theater, the fair, movie premieres, Disneyland. Kitty never spent any of her own money and never knew who was paying the tab. As food, liquor, cigarettes, transportation, and the events all happened without her assistance, she came to understand this was the way it was. Dressed to be noticed, these women used every event as an opportunity to solicit money, influence opinion, and gather information from the exclusive sect of White, rich families able to shape America to suit their interests.

If the men themselves didn't have a hand in the mechanics of government, they advised or had the ear of those who did. Their surnames were those of American royalty, titans in every industry. They were dignitaries, oil mavens, manufacturers, bankers, engineers, and creatives; famous faces, musicians, writers, actors. Many were obscure, but all were influential and either came from money or were "self-made," as Nina liked to say.

"Whatever *that* means, already being White." Cora argued with her every time she classified a White man this way. Her resentment was not unfamiliar to Kitty.

"Some are born into wealth; others have obtained it themselves."

"How hard is it to make money when the world bends to your whims?" Cora, everyone said, had been unusually bitter these days, though things in her orbit were moving again. She was dating an esteemed gentleman whom she and Lucy were tight-lipped about.

"Says the actress," Maude joked.

"It's not even close," Cora resigned.

"It's all relative; everyone has their cross to bear," Kitty said, knowing how precarious Cora's situation really was.

From a fly-on-the-wall vantage point, Kitty learned how the network worked. Someone from or a friend of Blair House was working everywhere they went. Their presence made her feel safe, should things take a turn, but unable to perform.

Instead, she eavesdropped on the men who talked over and around the women about the news, politics, rumors from the South, books, religion, and the arts. They were deep thinkers, and like Blair House—although for different motives—wanted an end to segregationist policies that were disrupting their profits. These men were the ones who could be influenced, if not by conscience, then by dollars and cents. And it was their women who were ready to give to everything—not out of goodwill but because charity was tied to social status and tax breaks.

At a fundraiser for a hospital, Kitty finally decided to say something. She sat with Edna and Mamie, passing again that night to solicit funds for her business, two smartly dressed businessmen, and Nina, who had come alone.

"We can open the doors, but how much 'equality' can we guarantee, since we all have different abilities?"

"I'd say hurdles," Kitty said. "Hurdles that have impeded abilities."

"Yeah, has to be hard to be somewhere you're not wanted."

"I don't see why they want to." The two tall businessmen seemed nice at first. Kitty had thought they were brothers, until one sipped the drink of the other.

"They want to improve their lives."

"Then they should work harder."

"What do you think they're doing?" Kitty said.

"Honestly? A lot of complaining, not enough doing."

"And what are *you* doing?"

He lit a Lakes. "I'm not sure equality makes sense."

Kitty pushed her chair away from the table. It was infuriating to her how he didn't believe in equal rights for Negroes but had to hide his relationship with his "business" partner. The cockiness of it—as if no one knew. She headed for the bar, all the quicker for seeing Edna's red mane in line.

"I'm so mad I could spit!" she whispered.

The woman, not Edna, turned with a knowing look. "First time with this crowd?"

"Oh! I'm so sorry, I thought you were someone else."

"Don't apologize." She ordered a gimlet and looked at Kitty. "What would you like?"

"I'll try a gimlet." Kitty touched the woman's shoulder. "Thank you." They looked to be about the same age.

"You're welcome. I'm Claire."

"Kitty."

"I'll need two or three to get me through the night. What happened to you?"

Kitty was honest but unsure of how to elaborate if pushed. "Just ignorance."

"Welcome to America, honey." She chuckled as if to show that Kitty should too. "I find myself so bored at these things."

It wasn't Kitty's exact feeling but it was close. They sat in chairs just outside the hall's doors. They could hear the music. "The party's started." They looked as the doors opened and a thin, barefoot man grasping two bottles of champagne appeared.

"There's my party animal," Claire said. He bent to kiss her. "I was looking for you."

"Meet Kitty . . ."

He kissed Kitty's hand.

"Karr," she said.

"Love you. I'm going back in."

Claire shook her head. "We never leave until the cleanup." Her husband, Winston, was a photographer. Claire had kick-started his career among this set, having known most of them before marrying. "I've attended a lifetime's worth of events like this. We're talking in baby gowns and slippers."

These hints of wealth used to make Kitty uncomfortable, but now they piqued her interest. *How rich?* "Are you on the fundraising committee with Nina McCullough?"

"Yes, we're donors."

"Oh, you're a philanthropist."

"I'd like to think so. I never feel like I'm doing enough."

"I know"—Kitty tried to pitch—"I work with an orphanage; I wish I could adopt them all."

Claire smiled and rose from her seat. "Well, you enjoy your night."

"You too . . ." Kitty watched her go, unsure of what had spoiled things. Not in the mood for dancing, she went outside for a cigarette, where she caught sight of Nina getting into a car with another Colored man. Kitty couldn't tell who it was.

Liberty saw it too. After seeing Kitty talking so long to Claire, she had followed her. They avoided eye contact, wary of strangers, but Kitty heard her whisper, as she held the door, "Don't tell."

Kitty didn't have to be reminded. She already knew the pattern. Whenever her husband traveled (which was often), Nina arrived at events in a cab instead of her chauffeured car. Now Kitty understood it was so her house staff couldn't track her comings and goings. Those were the nights she spent with one of her Negro men—the saxophonist wasn't the only one. In the coming weeks, Nina would disappear with a bartender, or an usher, or one of the few Colored patrons present, sometimes leaving the others to get home alone. One night at Mamie's Place, she disappeared with Dr. Mills, just missing colliding with his wife on the way out.

Everyone looked the other way. Their personal lives were to remain private, and for good reason. *If we're ever caught, our stories about one another have to be the same,* Lucy had told her. *It's better to be labeled a "nigger lover" than be found out to be Negro.*

Kitty was scolded about her behavior at the banquet.

"You're there to talk and learn what they may have to offer us."

"We have bills to pay—it takes money to run a business, even if that business is helping people."

Kitty, fearing repercussions, tried to do as she was told, but it was difficult. Deep down, she didn't want these people's help. It was always the same, and it was tiring.

The rioting and boycotts are proof—the country's Negro problem has become a headache.

They considered themselves to be liberals and called Southern Whites' behavior "despicable," "shocking," and "hard to stomach." They argued with the few bigots who showed up from time to time, yet, more than once, even they made nigger jokes while red-faced and pissy with liquor.

The others always confronted bad behavior with a gentle authority, speaking to the men as if they were children. *Such talk around women—my goodness!*

Most disturbing was that the bad behavior was merely for sport. It didn't mean they supported the government's blatant disregard of "the Negro situation." A lot of them had even donated to the NAACP. *I just want this business settled, so we can all move on.*

"Donate to the campaign of someone who wants things to change," Lucy said at a judge's retirement party. "Like Jack." She pointed to him in the other room.

"Takes more than one politician, Mrs. Schmitt."

"I don't see what the big deal is—they'd only have to mingle in public. Negroes are always going to live together, because they can't afford our neighborhoods."

"Even if they can, they aren't welcome. Coloreds wanted to move into our neighborhood, so we collected money and bought the house ourselves."

Kitty doubted her ability to be polite, so she stayed quiet, a rare instance in which Emma's advice prevailed. Their laughs lingered, sending her home to chain-smoke—her vice to Emma's gin.

Her only solace was knowing that sometimes, the servers had spit in the drinks these men reached for, men who never once said thank you or looked them in the face. When the libations were unsanitary, trays were carried on the left, so those who knew would wait for the next round. Being White, Kitty saw how easy it was to ignore Negroes—even when they were standing in front of you. Society demanded their invisibility, and as such, the servers might as well have been the air. That was why these subtle changes in behavior were never noticed.

Some Whites did feel they were good people, and paid their Negro maids, nannies, butlers, and drivers well to prove it. "Top dollar! For the holidays, they get their choice of meat—ham, a roast, turkey. Hell, I'll buy 'em chicken or pig feet if they want!" Wives wrapped their children's toys, abandoned from the year before, for their staff to give to theirs.

These were callous attempts at goodness thrown out with defiance, daring someone to be ungrateful. At times like this, Kitty thought about the Lakeses and what little she and her mother had been given and how much they were owed. The Lakeses kept the same employees for years, but without raises—only perks, like the ones the men Kitty was now in the company of bragged about.

Few of these men were brilliant, but they were all self-absorbed, plotting the next mountain to climb, oblivious to the luxury they had of being White and male. Kitty wondered if her father was like these men. Some of them were judges and lawyers like him. And rich like him. They likely knew her father or her grandfather, some maybe even personally. The whole world smoked Lakes.

She told herself that keeping her secret gave her power—over everyone—but really, she had no choice. As on that day in Charlotte when she'd assumed her half sister's name, she never knew when or if someone would know her family better than she did. Worse than that, she could be in the same room with her father or another Lakes and not know it. Emma's threat was worse, because she could be recognized.

Kitty's truth would make her more valuable at Blair House. But she was too chicken to unearth her roots, let alone attempt to reap the benefits of her lineage. Her great-grandfather's face was etched into her memory, from her momma's snuff tobacco can, but her father she had never seen. She avoided his face even when it was in the paper. Even now.

Who she did look for in these places, but never saw, was Nathan. Most nights she left him at the studio, working, but still she wished him everywhere. "These men are his father's associates," Lucy explained. Nathan hadn't yet earned his own invitation into the club.

Nina pointed out the eligible men to Kitty, who found she preferred

Nathan over all of them. Theoretically, they had little in common, but their experience of disregard was most significant: being ignored, excluded, forgotten. Abner wouldn't mean to let it, but nature would soon have its way with his mind and erode tunnels through his memory, erasing Nathan altogether. Hazel, on the other hand, had extracted Kitty so efficiently from her life, sometimes she wondered whether she'd ever been seen.

CHAPTER 24

Kitty

Late December, 1955

Before the studio closed for the holiday season, Nathan gave Kitty his rewrite of *The Misfits* to read. Between that and working the phones when the Montgomery bus boycott began, she had sufficient distraction from Christmas, though it was forced upon every inanimate object in town. Light poles, benches, and tree trunks were wrapped in tinsel, Christmas trees were displayed in every store window, and lights were up in every tree. Kitty found herself scowling at the happy families dining and shopping. Emma hadn't wanted to get a tree—she'd be with Rick's family until just after the new year—and so the Christmas spirit passed over the Karr household.

Kitty didn't know different anyway. Hazel hated Christmas. In their home, there was never a tree or Santa or even Jesus, though she was a believer. She worked on Christmas Eve and Christmas Day, so they went shopping in Charlotte the day after, when things went on sale. Kitty used to resent it. Now she would give anything to do nothing on Christmas with her mother.

"Lots of guilty givers during this season," Billie said. Their unit was boxing donations for Montgomery. Days had already been spent at Blair House writing letters, making press calls, and canvassing White neighborhoods for donations.

Lucy cut some tape. "I hear Nathan stayed in town for the holiday. That should cheer you up." Lucy, having noticed Kitty's melancholy, had begun calling her Scrooge.

"I haven't heard from him."

"He's probably working." Lucy winked. "I'm starting to think the two of you may be made for each other."

"Maybe," Kitty said. To both her horror and amazement, Kitty had missed Nathan since the studio had been closed for the holidays.

"Finally! She admits it!!" Lucy started cheering and hit her shoulder. "Don't do anything I wouldn't."

"Not a chance." Kitty blushed, remembering Lucy's admission of having sex with her husband a few times on the lot.

———————

After the last of the boxes had been mailed, Kitty went to the studio for a few days in a row, looking for Nathan. Drawn to the stages as always, she began rewriting the script by reciting each character's lines aloud on one of the sets. Acting the different parts became her freedom from the confines of the other versions of herself she'd created. She enjoyed these predetermined destinies.

Living in La-La Land was how she forgot it was Christmas Day until a man wished her a merry one as she came up the sidewalk to her house. She almost screamed but heard something familiar about his voice.

"Mary, it's me." Richard opened his arms, expecting a hug, only to be pushed farther onto the porch, behind the hanging ivy.

"Did anyone see you?"

"No."

"Are you sure?" Kitty shut the front door behind them harder than she intended. "How long were you waiting?"

"An hour, I guess."

When he turned on the table lamp, she raced to close the blinds. "What are you doing here?"

Richard looked wounded. "It's Christmas. And I've missed you." His white-collared shirt and brown pants looked dusty and wrinkled, as though he'd walked from wherever he came from.

"Didn't you get my letter?" Kitty asked. "I'm not coming back."

"You don't have to. I've moved here. And I wanted to tell you—I owe you an apology for lying about not getting into Central."

"You don't. I understand why you did."

"I couldn't tell you, not when you had all these dreams about moving and me going to medical school. I couldn't stay in Winston anymore, especially after getting your last letter." He reached for her hand to pull her to sit on the couch with him. She resisted. "It took me some time to get things together to leave, but I'm here."

Kitty's stomach dropped with dread. "You really moved here?"

"I rented a room. Now I can find a job and enroll in school. Mary, I'm going to be a doctor. Soon, I can take care of you the way I promised to."

"It's not about that, Richard."

"It is for me. I can't lose you." His voice quivered as he pulled her hand again to sit.

She shook him off. "Richard, I'm not going back."

He threw his hands around. "I said I've moved here."

"No—I'm not going back to being Colored. My name is Kitty now. Kitty Lane Karr. I have a job, a life. I'm happy."

"But you told me you'd marry me."

It had been agony to mail him her regrets; she couldn't look at him now.

"Is there someone else?"

"No." She saw he didn't believe her. But it was true, although her desire for Nathan far surpassed anything she'd ever felt for Richard.

"What's so great about being White?"

"I'm an assistant at one of the biggest film studios in the world."

He smirked. "You mean a secretary."

"An assistant to the head of the studio."

"That's a fancy word for 'secretary.' You don't need a college degree to do that."

"And yet, it pays more than being a Negro school teacher."

"Once I'm a doctor, you'll see. I can make you happy." But Kitty knew better. The nasty reality was that Kitty could take better care of herself being a White woman than Richard could as her Negro husband.

He stood to kiss her. Letting him would have been the kind thing to do, but she turned her head. "I won't marry you. And I never want to see you again."

Her rejection made him mean. "You broke your mother's heart, running out the way you did."

Her instincts were to defend herself. *My momma broke mine.* She wanted to tell him Hazel had sent her, but she knew her mother didn't want all of Cottonwood in her business. As with everything in her life at this point, the fewer people who knew the details, the better. "Now, please go," she said. His eyes started to cloud over, dimming the last of his light, so she gave it one last push. "Please, Richard—leave me alone."

His pride sent him out of the door.

Kitty watched him from behind the blinds. He didn't stand as straight as he had only months ago. He pushed his large hands into his pockets, kept his head down. Maybe he'd been that way all along and she hadn't noticed, not having someone to compare him to. And just to think: in another life, he would have already been her husband.

She would, in the years to come, think of Richard, then brush the memory off as soon as it came. Breaking his heart would be her one regret; hers ached every time he came to mind. It would be decades before the pain stopped, before she told herself: they'd been too young to marry, and it wouldn't have worked anyway. And then the only lie: her passing had had nothing to do with it.

———————

Emma's ring caught the sunlight coming through the living-room window; it cast a blue-hued sparkle against the wall every time she moved her hand. She detailed Rick's New Year's Eve proposal from Kitty's bed. "We went outside to set off fireworks. He dropped down on one knee and asked me to be his wife." With his whole family there, Emma finally received the acceptance she'd been craving.

"We'll marry in a few weeks." She had to be married before Judy's wedding so she could apply for her passport under her married name, Emma Denman, instead of her sister's true name.

There was always something to consider. Kitty was grateful for Emma, who reminded her of such things. The Lakes name carried similar weight.

"Did you write to your momma?" Kitty asked.

Emma's face dropped. "Why do you have to bring that up?"

"Don't you think she'd like to know?" Kitty hoped Emma's marriage would bring news about her own mother.

"Why? She can't be here, and the last thing I need is you reminding me." Emma stormed out and slammed Kitty's door and then, a second later, her own.

For all the lectures Emma gave about letting go of the past, she was the one who couldn't. She was battling regret—something no one could fix, especially when she denied its existence.

———————

Kitty entered an engagement of her own with Nathan after he read her version of *The Misfits*. She'd combined characters, deleted entire scenes, and changed the ending. He was offended; maybe a sentence from his draft had made it through intact. "All you had to do was read it."

There was no point in lying. "You can get better."

He flipped to a page. "How is it that you can just do this?"

"I think in pictures."

"Did you even read my dad's version?"

"No." That was a lie. Abner's version was the ramblings of a man with a failing memory, but the bones were there. Nathan had boiled them until the marrow dissipated and they were whistle clean and ashy.

"You should read some of his old scripts; he really used to be good."

So should you.

He put his hand on the script. "I'll show it to Charles. Get his opinion."

The next time she saw her script, it had a cover page listing Nathan Tate as its author. For a week, he kept forgetting to give her a copy or tell her the rehearsal times. Finally, Kitty got the rehearsal schedule from Lucy and showed up. When the script landed in her hands, he froze like an animal caught speaking by a human. He avoided her on set and left early. The next morning, there was a check on her desk for an exorbitant amount of money. It gave her some satisfaction, but she couldn't ignore the reality of his first inclination. She pulled Lucy and Cora aside after a Blair House meeting.

"You're lucky he paid you." Cora looked at Lucy, surprised by Kitty's naivety. "You should forgive him."

"He wasn't going to. He was hoping I'd never know. I don't know if I can work for someone like that."

"Your name will never go on the script, Kitty," Laurie said. Kitty turned around. Laurie always appeared out of nowhere, as if she'd been listening around every corner, and carried an all-knowing, omnipresent air. "They won't let you be Telescope's creative successor—not in name anyway." Kitty had forgotten her Whiteness couldn't save her from the plans, wants, and needs of her greater male counterpart.

"What if he accepts my resignation?"

Cora and Laurie spoke in unison. "He won't."

"Kitty, he *needs* you." Lucy touched her arm. "He took credit for your script, and now he'll have to produce another of the same caliber. He'll beg you to stay, and the longer he begs, the more grateful he'll be when you forgive him."

"But I'm angry; I can't believe he did that." Kitty held out her plate for a slice of lemon meringue pie.

Lucy shrugged. "Get even."

Cora explained what she meant. "If you marry him, it'll all benefit you in the end."

Kitty deposited his check and put her original copy of the script in a safety-deposit box. The next morning, she handed Nathan her resignation letter. He was near to tears having to address it.

"I knew it was wrong, and my way of apologizing was to do what I should have done in the beginning."

"Pay me?"

"Yes. Was it not enough?"

"I don't know the rate for stolen work."

This he didn't apologize for. "My father's script couldn't have been rewritten by 'Kitty Karr'—"

"But it was."

"You said yourself it would be good for the studio if I were to write something."

"But you didn't."

"I did, and you trashed it."

Because it was terrible.

"Regardless, no version would have passed the board's approval with your name—or any woman's name—on it."

"I see." Kitty started toward his office door.

"Wait—you can't blame me for that. It's just the way things are."

"You own the studio. Who else shall I blame?" She went for the door handle.

"Kitty, I'm not the only decision maker." Over her head, he pressed the door shut. "What can I do? What do you want?"

"Nothing. Nathan, I thought you were someone else, and now I see you're just as greedy and unfair as the rest of the world."

He stepped around her to block her exit. "Listen, I can't lose you."

"There are other smart women on the lot. Every one of them wants this job."

"And I want you." It sounded like he wasn't talking about the job anymore. He looked desperate for her to stay. "Kitty, please forgive me. I have so much to prove here, and your script was so good, and it seemed so easy . . . until I saw how I hurt you."

It wasn't an absolution of his character flaw, but she believed he was sorry—wanted him to be, anyway. "I'll stay, but only if you keep paying me. Above my weekly pay."

He held his hand out for a shake.

"And I want to write under my own fake name."

"We can't be a team anymore?"

Kitty winced at the whine in his voice. It wasn't enough to be the head of the studio, without any prior experience—now, he wanted to take the credit for writing features too? She cursed herself for having suggested it in the first place.

"People are expecting a follow-up from me now."

Confirmation of Lucy's hypothesis gave Kitty confidence, and she pushed to change his mind. "Tell them it was a one-time gesture, to pay homage to your father, and your focus is at the executive level. No one will question that."

He whined again. "I've promised one."

"That was a mistake, seeing as you can't write."

His mouth gaped open for a split second, astonished by her insult, before he composed himself with a deep breath. "I can see you're still angry with me."

"No, but it won't help to lie to you. You can learn, though. I've never had lessons."

"And I will—but first, just help me write one more feature?"

Kitty held out her hand again, agreeing. "And a monthly expense budget."

Nathan laughed. "For what, exactly?"

Kitty didn't return his smile. "I've been meeting a lot of people. It would be nice to be able to host them and see what ideas they have for Telescope."

"Where are you meeting these people?"

"Lucy Schmitt has been showing me around." Kitty evaded a direct answer.

"I see." He went to his window. "Be careful out there, Miss Karr." Noticing his formality in addressing her, she wondered if he was cross. "Everyone will want to share their brilliant ideas with you."

"You can trust my measure of quality."

He studied her for a moment. "That's good to know."

His gaze caused Kitty's breath to quicken and a familiar throbbing in her heart—and then under her skirt.

"Stay and have a drink with me," he said.

"Not tonight." Kitty wanted to but, enjoying the brief redistribution of power, waved goodbye.

Nina's city beautification fundraiser was the first event of the new year. The cocktail party and art auction were in full swing when they arrived; cigarette smoke loomed over everyone's heads like a rain cloud. The room had no windows, so it was the type of environment in which you had to join in on the smoking or risk suffocation. Kitty, deciding to join in, navigated around the perimeter of the room to the bar. Just ahead of her in line was a woman she recognized as Claire, holding the tips of her middle and pointer fingers against her nose to block the smoke. Kitty stepped ahead of her to put her cigarette out in the ashtray. "Gimlet time again?"

"Oh, hi!" She was perkier, maybe drunk.

"Having fun?"

"I had better company tonight." She pointed into the crowd on the dance floor. "Brought some of my clients."

"I thought you were a donor."

"That's not what I *do*. I give the models career advice."

"Like a manager?"

Claire nodded, clearly surprised Kitty knew. "What do you do?"

"I'm the assistant to the owner of Telescope." It did sound impressive.

Claire's eyes lit up. "How wonderful." Suddenly, Claire became the most talkative person Kitty had ever seen. She had question after question about her job, its function, working with Nathan . . . Kitty couldn't sufficiently answer before she had something else to say. Kitty bulged her eyes at Lucy, begging for rescue.

"Conversation must be riveting—neither of you has touched your drink." Lucy started to the bar.

Claire followed, introducing herself. The cycle repeated after she learned that Lucy also worked at Telescope.

"Are you interested in working at the studio?" Lucy finally was able to ask.

"Not per se . . ." Claire stopped, seeing someone behind them. "I'm sorry, my husband is calling me." She gave a regretful smile and a hug to each.

"Thank God," Lucy said.

Again, Kitty watched her go. She could only take short steps in her long tan dress; her legs were bound by the fit.

"Is she Negro?" Lucy asked.

Kitty couldn't tell. "I don't think so."

"Be careful with her."

Kitty was puzzled. "Why?"

"What do you know about her?"

Kitty recited the facts as she would at a meeting. "She's a donor. Manages models. Her husband is a photographer. She's old money, probably. Why?"

"She peppered us with questions so she didn't have to talk about herself."

Maybe Lucy was right, but Kitty didn't care. Her chatter was a reprieve from the work.

It was instantly clear how essential the Negro dollar was to the continued financial viability of the bus company in Montgomery. Many employees had already lost their jobs; the buses used less gas, needed less maintenance, and sat idle. Meanwhile, Negroes were still going to work somehow, some way—with their heads held high, sometimes walking tens of miles a day. This realization caused panic, and an increase in the death threats and violence against Negroes all over the South.

"Many of them don't even ride the damned bus!"

"Their Whiteness blinds them, makes them stupid," Kitty said, calling on her momma's words.

Blair House was funneling monies for protection—the young Dr. King remained a proponent of nonviolence even after his house was bombed—but everyone was waiting for a slaughter.

They were split in their belief about whether things would ever change. The only good was that the boycott became national news, and many Whites they encountered would now donate outright.

"Why don't we solicit monies from Negroes?" Kitty asked. She had long wondered this but felt too new until now to question things.

"We give dues."

"I mean from others, who aren't a part of the house."

This caused a stir. "They ain't got no money to give!"

"We should be soliciting to give a monthly stipend to them."

"The government has done that for White people," Liberty said.

"Maybe they'll do it for us," Kitty said.

The room laughed for the first time in weeks.

CHAPTER 25

Kitty

Spring 1956

Emma's need for a short engagement coincided with Rick's dread of another formal wedding, so they married at the courthouse in April, with Kitty as their only witness. Kitty struggled with losing Emma to marriage. It had become such a belabored point, she had never considered what it would be like for her when it finally happened. The nights Emma slept over at Rick's had been like a short vacation, but when Emma officially moved into her husband's home in Pasadena, Kitty began to think differently about her own prospects of marriage.

She had Blair House, but had never lived alone before and missed Emma's sometimey company. Thinking they could have a better relationship now that Emma had married her heart's desire, Kitty called a few times. Her maid answered every time, claiming she was unavailable, and Emma never called back.

Kitty soothed her loneliness with work. The promise to green-light two additional film productions kept Nathan and Kitty working late into the evening. It was on such an occasion that she heard Nathan screaming in his office. She listened outside the cracked door.

"I want Cora Rivers off every single one of his bank accounts! How could you not have alerted me to this? I gave her a reasonable amount of time. No wonder she accepted my offer so graciously—she thought we'd never find out!"

Apparently, Cora was suing the Tate family for alimony while bleeding Abner's accounts dry. Aside from the goals for Blair House, Kitty learned that Cora now needed her acting pay to live; the Tate family had sold her house off Sunset (the one Lucy said Cora's father had bought her). No one at Blair House knew, because Cora had been using Abner's funds to keep up appearances—her Rolls Royce and Percy came to mind.

Knowing it was her duty to help, Kitty came in. Even seeing it was her, he waved her away, pointing to the phone.

She entered anyway as he finally slammed the phone down. "We're going to have to delay filming. We need another lead for Cora for *The Misfits*."

Kitty began to panic. "Nathan! We can't! We start in a week."

"Cora's been stealing money from my father. I want her gone. Immediately."

"Stealing? How so?"

"Taking money from his accounts to pay her bills. I only found out because the payment for her monthlong stay at the Beverly Hills Hotel wouldn't go through."

Kitty softened her normal tone. "How else is she supposed to live? She hasn't done a film in years; wasn't your father taking care of her? Helping ease things financially?"

"We've done enough for her financially. She can get another job."

"She has one. She's the star of your picture."

"I want her gone."

"At least settle her contract."

Nathan looked at Kitty as if she'd suggested he pay her from his salary. "I think she's gotten more than she deserves. I may file a case against her."

"You're angry at your father, not Cora."

"Well, I can't take it out on him; he wouldn't notice."

"So you want to air out all the details of your father's personal life? What would your mother say?"

Nathan began to pace with plans. "We'll start casting this week. We don't have to get too far off schedule." He pointed at her as if he'd just had the best idea. "Why don't you stand in for rehearsals?"

"No, no, no . . ."

"Just until we find someone."

It was tempting. Kitty had enjoyed playing on set over the break but didn't know if she had any actual talent.

"Just see how it goes. We can always hire someone else."

"We *will* hire someone else."

"Okay, but for now, you know the lines, the motivations—rehearsals need to begin."

"I would say yes—"

"But?"

"You'll be accused of firing Cora for someone younger. That won't be good for me. I've had enough problems as your assistant."

"What do you suggest?"

"Pay out her contract and let her live in one of the houses owned by the studio."

"So, continue to support her?"

"At least for a while." Kitty had a feeling Cora wouldn't need it for long. She hadn't gotten many details about her and Lucy's D.C. trip, but Cora had been wearing a thick diamond bracelet and necklace upon her return.

Nathan puffed his cheeks. "Fine, if Cora agrees to say she quit."

"Where is she now?" Kitty asked.

"Packing up her hotel suite."

"Send a car for her. I'll go unlock one of the bungalows."

———————

The house—a modest three-bedroom, two-bathroom—was two streets down from Kitty's.

"Thank you for what you did. And for your discretion," Cora said, pouring tea.

"It's no problem."

"I'll tell them soon," Cora said, referring to the others at Blair House. "For the longest time, Abner denied that his memory was going, and I did too. He had such a brilliant mind, and sometimes he was agitated and forgot things—even back when we first met. And he was in his thirties then. Now he's useless, and I'm without a job or my home. I thought that, at the very least, the house I've been living in for twenty years was mine and I could sell it."

In the end, Abner had neglected to make provisions for her in the circumstance of his demise, after promising time and time again that he would. While the Beverly Hills Hotel was luxurious, moving into a hotel had meant Cora had to give away or sell most of her belongings.

"He was the first man I'd ever been with. Met him a week after I got to town. I was seventeen years old and, you know, it was like having a rich daddy." It was the closest to a confession about her past Cora would ever give. "I would tell you to be careful, but you're in a better position at Telescope than I ever was. Abner was a control freak; you have creative influence. Life says it's your turn." Cora agreed to quit, and for Kitty to stand in.

Kitty found solace on the stage when she was alone but confessed her worry about her ability to perform on command.

"You're perfect—you wrote the script."

Kitty admitted her hesitancy.

Cora didn't want to hear it. "You have to try."

"What will you do?"

"I'm not sure yet."

"I'm sorry about all of this."

"Don't be. I stumbled upon acting. I went on chorus-line auditions to be a dancer. Then I met Abner, and the rest is history."

She would announce her father's death days later at Blair House, saying she had to move because her stepmother, knowing she was Negro, sold the house to spite her. No one questioned the plausibility of the story. Kitty would keep Cora's secret, even from Lucy, understanding the shame of being unaccounted for.

Nathan summoned Kitty after watching tapes from the first week of rehearsals of *The Misfits*.

"Take the role. Charles says you're a natural."

"He hardly said anything to me on set."

"You didn't need much direction." He pointed to the small television. "See for yourself. Your performance helped everyone else."

Kitty had noticed this. By the third run-through, they'd stopped fumbling with their scripts. "It's beginner's luck."

He insisted. "Please. It's fate."

"I've had one week of rehearsals."

Nathan tapped her nose with his finger. "You'll be fine. You have my support—everyone's support."

It had been decided. Nathan took Kitty's face in his hands. "You, my dear, are going to make us all a ton of money." He kissed her forehead. "I want to tell everyone how brilliant you are, but I think we'll let your beauty and talent speak for themselves now. I don't want anyone trying to steal you."

Coined "the princess of Telescope," Kitty Karr needed an origin story. Nathan crafted a bigger story than Kitty's original cover but, ironically, one a tad closer to the truth: he declared her the heir to a cotton fortune who had fled her privileged Southern life for Los Angeles to be a star.

CHAPTER 26

Kitty

Summer 1956

Sometime after the Fourth of July, a series of hang-ups went around town, calling for an urgent meeting at Blair House. It was two in the morning before everyone arrived.

Nina was missing. Two nights before, she and Maude had gone to the Santa Monica pier for ice cream when a Negro man, claiming to be Nina's husband, dragged her down the pier and out of sight.

"She was terrified, and I pushed her away." Maude started sobbing, and Lucy embraced her.

No one called the police, because Nina's Whiteness vanished the second the Negro man called her his wife. She was forgotten as soon as she disappeared, thanks to Maude, who distracted the crowd with her tears over her friend's betrayal.

Only a few acted shocked that something like this could happen to Nina.

"This isn't your fault," Lucy said, still consoling Maude. "That man *was* Nina's husband. Upon her decision to pass, one day Nina said she was going to the store and just never came back. He'll never get over her."

"Question is, how did he find her?" Cora asked. She had looked angry, not sad, when she arrived.

"LA is big, but it's small. Especially among Colored folk."

"Especially when people talk . . ." Liberty let her voice trail off, which naturally incited questions.

"Someone told him where he could find Nina?"

Liberty continued her insinuation. "Who told someone, who told some-one."

Eyes exchanged glances, processing the breach in loyalty and security.

"Where is he now?"

"Gone."

"She'll be back."

Maude cried out again. "It's been two days!"

Laurie shook her head with regret. "We told Nina to move, but she'd already fallen in love with Titan and refused." Laurie began to pace the room. "We need a new story. Cora and Billie, you all were on a boat down there. Say Nina was . . . with some man. The boat docked, and you assumed she had already gotten off. Let them think she drowned."

The room agreed.

"You're going to tell the police she was having an affair?" Kitty asked.

Laurie looked at Edna as if to instruct. "We must. It doesn't matter what really happened; it only matters what people believe. Finding out what really happened to Nina could lead to them finding out about us." Any story was better so long as it ended with Nina still being White.

"What about her husband?"

"It'll embarrass him, make him less likely to push for an investigation," Cora said, explaining the fragility of the male ego.

Laurie flung her fingers in the air. "The sun is rising. Go home."

Days later, Nina was found tangled in a fishing net near the pier. Cora and Billie were quoted in the paper as planned. Maude was erased from the night altogether. The word of two prominent White women erased the memory of the angry Negro man in the minds of the people on the pier that night; he became the nameless White man Nina's husband thought she was having an affair with. Not too long after that, as predicted, Nina's death was ruled an accident, and the case was closed. There wasn't a funeral, and her husband remarried within a year.

Nina's death jolted Kitty back to the reality of the danger she could face. The women convened at Blair House to refuel the emotional depletion they shared; it was one of the few times their pain wasn't categorized by skin shade. Everyone realized how vulnerable they were, how insignificant they could become. How beauty sometimes led to tragedy. Some had been jealous of Nina's glamorous life, but they felt bad about their envy now. The need to possess, to own her, was the masculine greed that had killed her.

Eventually, the leak was discovered: it was proven that Wilma was the one who knew Nina's ex-husband, and she was removed from their ranks. Kitty used work as an excuse to disassociate. Like the deaths of Joshua Hunt and Emmett Till, Nina's murder haunted her. She sought refuge with Nathan, whose calm nature settled her. She felt most safe with him, inside the confines of the lot's walls and story lines, among the things she could control.

———————

Kitty fell asleep watching the latest edit of *The Misfits* in one of the screening rooms. There had been ten or more such sessions—Nathan insisted on seeing every cut before and after everyone else's notes. It was Kitty's job to be there every time. Having loved it *five* cuts ago, she drifted off five minutes in.

When she woke, startled by her dream or the silence, Nathan was smiling at her. "You look like a baby when you sleep."

She hid her face. "Why were you watching me?"

"It's what I look forward to every day."

Kitty sat up straight and clenched the sides of her chair as he walked up to her and bent to kiss her. Her eyes closed involuntarily as their mouths moved, synchronized as though their tongues had their own secret language. She never wanted to stop kissing him and would have fought against it if forced. Nathan exposed her need to connect, to touch and find an emotional dwelling in another. It felt dangerous that first time. She pulled away, panicking, but he pulled her back, and she let him, surrendering, sinking, being swallowed whole by what felt natural. He sank on the floor in front of her, unbuttoning her shirt with one hand and the top of her skirt with the other. He had an urgency for her body, and she mimicked his motions, feeling the same. She vacillated about whether to stop him every time his hands or tongue went somewhere new but then pulled him in, binding them together.

They became a couple without any formal discussion, though there were valid reasons to end their romance before it started. Kitty didn't trust her ability to keep her secrets from him, and Nathan was embarrassed he'd fallen for the ingénue. Wanting her was typical—but their attraction had originated from their conversation, from imaginations that seemed to have been born from the same place. For nine months they had worked side by side, knowing their commitment to the studio was more important than their feelings. Now their love bolstered their creativity, blending their relationship and work into one.

When they weren't at the studio, they escaped to remote beach spots or to his house in the hills. Most nights they would share a roof, whether at his place or hers on Orange Drive, each dependent on the other for sleep. He proposed marriage within a few months, which she eloquently delayed, but did not refuse, with reminders about their continued focus on the studio.

CHAPTER 27

Kitty

October 1956

The premiere of *The Misfits* was bigger than anyone expected. The crowd of reporters and photographers made Kitty feel as though she were hovering outside her body in a space where it was both loud and quiet, light and dark. Everyone was yelling, but she could hear each voice clearly, as if the reverberations were being transmitted through individual funnels into her ear.

When it was time to enter the theater, Nathan held her back, clasping her elbow with his fingertips. "It's bad luck to watch your film at the premiere." He put his tuxedo jacket around her shoulders.

"You made that up. You're worried they won't like it."

"I'm serious, it's bad luck. Don't you worry. Your beautiful face is going to be wildly famous. You'll see." After a year of working together, and months as a couple, Nathan was the only person who could calm her, the only person she wanted to. Their relationship was a mutual stroking of their egos, the shining twinkle, a gold glittering reflection of the other. Time had stopped the first time their lips touched, and every time since.

A flash of light ruined it in the present.

Kitty's eyes opened in time to see a lone photographer duck into the shadow of the theater awning, less than twenty feet away.

Nathan barked into the darkness. "Credentials, please! Where do you work?"

A butterscotch-colored Negro boy, skinny and no more than sixteen, emerged into the light.

"What's your name, son?"

"Michael Walker, sir."

"Michael, do you know who I am?"

"No, sir."

Nathan gestured to Kitty. "Do you know who she is?"

"Miss Kitty Karr. I couldn't get close enough to take a picture earlier."

"Because you don't have credentials?"

The boy smiled. "Yes. I'm working on putting a portfolio together. I apologize, sir. I was just trying to capture the moment."

"What if I gave you an exclusive with Miss Karr here?"

He looked down at his camera, dangling from his neck. "I have that already."

The boy's boldness would have angered a lesser man, but Kitty could tell Nathan was impressed by his confidence.

"That photo," said Nathan, lowering his voice, "could make things very difficult."

"Are you married?"

Nathan laughed aloud. "No, but she's going to be a big star. No one will think I deserve her."

"Because you're her boss?"

"So, you *do* know who I am." Nathan turned to Kitty. "Smart kid." He produced his wallet. "I'll pay you for that film."

"Those were the last shots on the roll."

Nathan lowered his chin to meet the boy's eyes, judging his sincerity. "Come by the studio next week." Nathan handed him some cash. "I'll give you more when you bring the photos. Get yourself something to eat and get home. Don't you have school tomorrow?"

The boy didn't answer; he was busy counting the bills. It was about fifty dollars.

"Come by next week," Nathan said. "Remember, I'll give you more—and an assignment."

Grinning, the boy went to shake his hand. "Thank you, sir."

Nathan handed him a business card. "Early next week. And not a word of this to anyone—do you understand? Or the deal is off."

The boy waved and trotted off into the night.

"That was nice of you," Kitty said, taking Nathan's arm to his limo.

"People just want a chance. I'm willing to help anyone bold enough to go after what they want. He's out on a school night, snapping photos with an old camera from the pawnshop—he's obviously interested in photography. We'll see if he's any good."

"I love you."

He pulled her to him by the waist. "Baby, I've loved you since the moment I saw you."

Kitty awoke the next morning in Nathan's bed to reviews that would solidify her star status. Critics praised her rare balance of comedic and dramatic talent, and for months after the premiere, fans lined the sidewalk of the studio for the chance at a sighting of Kitty Karr. Her image was plastered all over town and in papers all over the country; she imagined her mother had clipped out a picture. Photographers stalked her every time she left the lot. As solace for the loss of her privacy, now she got the best of everything for free: food, clothes, purses, art, and beauty treatments.

Her movie posters lingered into her second LA holiday season. After a few days of enjoying her face being bigger than Santa's, she was painted over. The city was ready for the next thing.

CHAPTER 28

Kitty

Winter 1956

Emma's maid called a week before Christmas to invite Kitty over for the weekend. Kitty accepted without hesitation, though the two hadn't spoken since the spring. Kitty sent an invitation to the premiere, but when Emma never called to say she couldn't make it, or sent flowers in regret or even a note of congratulations, Kitty suspected that her silence, along with quitting her job, was an attempt to sever ties. Or she'd grown envious, like others at the studio—except Lucy—who never spoke to her anymore.

The invitation felt like an olive branch. Perhaps Emma had been adjusting to marriage. Kitty had been busy, too, and decided to forgive Emma, rationalizing that she hadn't reached out either.

Emma's Pasadena home had a large yard and a redbrick pathway that led to the front door, where a large brass lion's head was mounted. An older Negro maid opened the door. "Good day, Miss Karr."

Kitty picked up her bag before the woman could. "Good day. I'll take this to my room, if you'll show me."

The house was old but palatial. The hardwood floors creaked with every step but gleamed, as did every wooden surface, including the backs of the dining-room chairs. Floral wallpaper, even on the ceilings, made the rooms feel small but pretty, with bouquets of fresh flowers decorating the tops of most surfaces.

The maid had to put both feet on a step before ascending to the next. Kitty wondered how she managed the household chores. "Is it just you?"

"Mostly."

"Where's Mr. Denman this weekend?"

"Out of town." She was tight-lipped and kept checking the doorknobs in the hallway. The fifth one opened, revealing a montage to yellow tulips.

The maid transported a vase of yellow roses from the dresser to the night-stand in front of the window. "Brought these in from the garden."

"Very pretty; thank you."

"You hungry?"

"Yes, ma'am," Kitty said.

"Abigail, Miss Kitty."

Kitty felt uncomfortable telling the older woman not to call her "Miss."

"I'll let Mrs. Denman know you're here," Abigail said. Out of the window, Kitty saw Emma reading in a lounge chair by the expansive but shallow pool.

"That won't be necessary," Kitty said, watching Emma reach for the glass by her chair and take a long sip. "I'll join her shortly."

———————

Hearing the kitchen door creak to open and slam shut, Emma yelled over her shoulder for another drink.

"It's me," Kitty said.

Emma's face was flushed and slick. "What are you doing here?"

"You invited me for the weekend."

She looked puzzled for a second and then said, "I guess Rick thought I could use some company. He's gone until Monday."

Kitty gestured to the *Jet* magazine in her hands.

"These are Abigail's," Emma protested. "She leaves them all over the house. Even Rick picks them up sometimes." Emma reached for the silver cigarette case on the grass, revealing an alarming view of her bony back. Emma's appetite had never been robust but her body now looked as though she had eliminated solids.

"How have you been?" Kitty asked.

Emma fumbled to light the cigarette dangling from her lips. "Bored." She seemed irritated she had to say it, as if Kitty should have known.

She changed the conversation, holding it captive to the perils of making the house a home. She wanted the remodel to move faster, complaining about how much she had to do to make Rick's Pasadena mansion feel as if it was half hers. "That nasty floral wallpaper, the old furniture—everything was decorated by his late wife. I hate living inside her fantasy."

"The wallpaper *is* overwhelming," Kitty said, with little patience for her mood. Emma had everything she wanted, including a nonjudgmental live-in maid who kept her drinks coming. She seemed committed to her own doom.

Emma might have been truly bothered by his ex-wife's presence but her tone, laced in pretension, made Kitty roll her eyes with both irritation and amusement. Anyone who even remotely knew Emma knew that her only goal in life was to be a wife. To keep peace, though, Kitty extended the sympathy she was after: "You poor thing."

"They were only married for five years. She's *dead*, and still, her presence is like a stain." Emma threw the ice from her cup onto the cement and yelled toward the house again. "Abigail! Another drink, please!"

"How about eating?"

"Abigail!" Emma yelled louder this time.

Hearing the kitchen door creak open, Kitty watched Abigail struggle over. She tried to hurry, but her shoes kept slipping off her heels.

"Sorry, ma'am; the radio was on. What can I get you?"

Emma glared over her shades. "Did you invite Kitty here?"

"By request of Mr. Denman; yes, ma'am."

"Why didn't you tell me?"

"I thought he did, ma'am."

Emma rolled her eyes to say she thought she was lying. "Can we get ham sandwiches, deviled eggs, and two drinks—the vodka with lemonade? Do we have any made?"

"Yes, ma'am."

"Would you bring two waters, too, please, Abigail?" Kitty asked.

As soon as Abigail was out of earshot, Kitty scolded Emma. "She's too old to be running back and forth serving you."

Emma sighed in justification. "Abigail's been taking care of Rick since he was a little boy. She lives here, and he pays her very well. He paid for both of her children to go to college."

"Your doing?"

"No, that was all before he met me. Her children are grown. He's a good person, Kitty, and he loves her."

"I never said Rick was bad."

"Considering the crowd you've cozied to, I didn't think he was good enough." Emma blew smoke into her face as she handed her the cigarette case. "Lucy and Cora had a lot to do with you acting now, I'm sure."

"No, it fell into my lap. The whole thing. It was impossible to refuse."

"Reviews say the film is good. Congratulations."

"Thank you."

"Everyone wants to know who Kitty Karr is now. Your face is everywhere."

"I can't believe it myself sometimes."

"Well, I don't want people knowing me. I don't want to be photographed or interviewed. No one should know you have a sister."

"That's why you didn't come to the premiere?"

"I have family who would love nothing more than to recognize me in some newspaper and ruin my whole life."

Kitty realized how self-centered she'd been to forget that. "But you could have at least called me."

"I'm sorry."

"You can't cut me out of your life. How would I hear if something happened to my momma?"

Emma groaned. "Would it even matter at this point?"

"Of course it would matter!"

"You wouldn't go back."

"I would so!"

"You would not, you liar!" She spoke in a whisper, hearing the kitchen door open again. "You could never return to that miserable place without yearning for here."

Emma reached for her plate and, after two bites of the ham sandwich, abandoned it for another cigarette.

"Are you going to finish eating?" Kitty asked. "These hot peppers on here are good."

"I wasn't really hungry to begin with."

Watching Emma drain her second vodka lemonade in an hour, Kitty began to consider that she'd been summoned. "Why don't you come back to the studio?"

"Rick said he's not doing his job as a man if I'm letting others pay me for my time. Funny thing is, I would be perfectly happy with two or three kids to care for. But that won't ever happen, so what's left for me?"

"How about college?"

Emma sounded impatient. "I don't have records as Emma Karr."

"That's right. Come work with us, then."

"Kitty, I just said—"

"No, charity work. He can't say no to that." Kitty didn't have permission to tell Emma about Blair House, but she did then, in short summary, omitting key details and without calling it by name. She thought Emma might be receptive, being that she was so unhappy.

She was wrong. Emma was horrified. "*That's* what you've been doing? And I thought the acting was insane. You're crazier than I thought!"

"I'm like any other White woman trying to do some good."

"White women have their own fights; our struggle doesn't affect them." Emma pointed toward the house. "Her lot in life allows me to sit out here and complain about my own."

"That's why I do it."

"You're playing with fire."

"I'm not protesting or writing or giving speeches! I just get people to give, and I'm doing what I can to nudge Nathan at the studio. The easiest thing would be to convince Rick to donate."

"I can't jeopardize my marriage."

"You wouldn't be."

"I would be asking him to write a check to the NAACP!"

"Doesn't he give you an allowance? Give some of that." Kitty realized she was giving away too much information.

Emma crossed her arms. "Can I be honest without you getting upset?"

Kitty waited, knowing that precursor was simply a forewarning that the conversation would indeed incite the very emotion named.

"I don't see how you could jeopardize your whole life—and mine—for people you don't even know."

"I know my momma. I can't sit back and do nothing when people are dying, Emma."

Tears came to Emma's eyes. "Goddamn it," she said, wiping them. "I can barely get out of the bed in the fucking morning, and here you go coming to make me feel worse."

"It makes me feel better doing something to help."

Emma chuckled. "You all think things will magically improve once we get some laws passed. Maybe a few of us will live in neighborhoods like this one and drive expensive cars, and we'll pat ourselves on the back, ignoring the fact that—as a whole—we're still way behind and we'll always be." Emma squinted. "I want equality as much as you, but I'm not willing to jeopardize the comfort *I* worked for, for people who've never done anything for me. And you're stupid to want to."

"We have an obligation. Things won't be better for any of us until they're better for all of us."

"They're already better for me. I grew up locked in the attic, and now, I'm the lady of a house twice as big as the one I grew up in."

"You were *locked* in the attic? You never told me."

"No one wants to talk about the bad things, Kitty. There's nothing I would do to jeopardize what I've built, and if you continue down this path, you'll become nothing but a memory to me." With that, Emma collected her drink and cigarettes and tossed the magazine onto Kitty's lap. "I'm going to take a nap."

————————

Emma was still in her room at dinnertime. The door was locked, and knocks were met with silence. Kitty was going to go home until Abigail offered to feed her. "There's cornbread, butter beans, and okra in here already made—I can fry some fish. It'll only take a second."

"Yes, please." Kitty followed her into the kitchen like a dutiful child. Watching her shake salt and pepper on the catfish, Kitty remembered how Hazel only salted the beaten egg; all the other seasonings went into the flour. *Fish is salty already; you only need a pinch.* Sure enough, Abigail's fried fish would taste slightly salty.

"Emma told me you've worked for Mr. Denman for many years," Kitty said.

"Yes, ma'am."

"Please, it's Kitty."

Abigail looked at her. "Mrs. Denman prefers the formalities."

"She's asleep."

Abigail smiled. "I'm glad you came. She gets lonely."

"She didn't seem happy to see me. Any idea why I'm here?"

"I told you, she gets lonely—real lonely."

"Are she and Rick having problems?"

"Miss Kitty, I cook and clean. That's all."

Kitty let her lie, knowing for certain now it was her, and not Rick, who had invited her that weekend. Kitty could see Abigail wasn't yet ready to trust her.

———————————

Abigail was already making breakfast when Kitty woke up the next morning. When Emma still hadn't surfaced at almost noon, Kitty inquired.

"She stays up late." Abigail began clearing the plates from the table, running from the conversation.

"She doesn't eat well either." Kitty pointed to the rows of spices and flours collected like souvenirs on the shelves. "I know you miss cooking."

Abigail produced a single key from a drawer next to the stove and unlocked one of the doors in the kitchen that Kitty had assumed was another pantry. There was a staircase behind the door.

"She told me not to bring you up here," Abigail said.

"I'll take the blame."

She gestured for Kitty to follow her. When she opened the door at the top, stale, sour air hit Kitty's nose. The shades were drawn but, in the darkness, Kitty saw Emma lying facedown and sideways on her bed, snoring. Clothes, dishes, makeup, and books littered the floor and furniture.

"She stays up all night, drinking and pacing. I pick her up off the floor drunk. She slept on the bathroom floor last night. I found her naked, sound asleep. She'd taken all her clothes off and run a bath. I covered her with a towel and left her there." Abigail whispered to explain, "Last time I tried to help her into bed, she tried to hit me."

Kitty laughed at the look on Abigail's face. Emma could rile a person.

"Does Rick know?"

"No. She doesn't drink as much when he's here, but she's still up all night, pacing. He comes down sometimes, and they fight. He sleeps on the third floor; it's been that way for a while now. He used to fawn over her—always wanted her to join him on his trips," she explained. "Now he barely speaks two words to her at meals. Still, they sit at the table, silent."

"Is he seeing someone else?"

Abigail began to stutter. "Now, Miss Kitty, please—"

"You called me. Might as well tell me everything I need to know. I know you know what's going on."

"I can't—"

Kitty touched Abigail's shoulder. "You can trust me." This was an emergency, she felt; anything could have slipped during one of Emma's binges.

A look of recognition appeared in Abigail's eyes, and in a split second, Kitty knew she'd given them away. "My God."

Kitty didn't confirm, but she also didn't correct or clarify the woman's realization. "I have to protect her. You understand that, don't you?"

Abigail looked at Emma, whose arms were hanging, deathlike, off the bed. "I don't want any trouble."

"We're at your mercy."

The floodgates opened. "I've seen gifts tucked in his suitcase, gifts he doesn't give to her."

"Do they fight about it?"

"She pretends not to know, but they fight about her drinking."

"I thought you said he didn't know about the drinking."

"He doesn't know how bad it is."

To distract herself from further worry, Kitty started tidying. Abigail followed suit with the glasses, plates, and other trash covering the floor. Side by side, they cleaned, forging an alliance against whatever was trying to take Emma down. Careful not to crash glasses or make unnecessary noise, they moved slowly, working in quadrants around the room. Their care was in vain, Kitty finally decided; a band could have marched through the house and Emma wouldn't have stirred.

It was after four in the afternoon before she did. Groggy and rubbing her eyes, she propped herself up on her elbows. "You're not supposed to be in here." Her head dropped to the pillow as if she couldn't bear to hold it upright.

"You're a drunk."

Emma slid off the bed and walked to the bathroom, pausing every three steps as if she was going to be sick. When she made it to the toilet, Kitty came to the doorway.

"Can I have some privacy?" Emma asked, reaching to close the door on Kitty with her foot.

Kitty slammed it open. "Did Rick find out about you? Does he suspect anything?"

"No!"

"Are you sure? Who knows what you might have spilled while drunk."

"He doesn't know!" She put her head in her hands. "He wants a baby. Before he left for this trip, he told me that if I won't agree to have at least one, he'll divorce me."

"What about a diaphragm?"

"That's what started all of this. He found it and threw it away. My doctor is one of his scotch-and-cigars buddies, so I can't get another one without him knowing. Meanwhile, Rick's been directing Abigail to fatten me up so I can get pregnant, and I just refuse to eat and make up reasons not to share a bed."

"But you're not pregnant?"

She flushed and turned on the sink. "No, but I have to fix it so I can't *get* pregnant. I can't refuse to sleep with my husband forever." She looked at Kitty. "I need you to ask where I should go. I can't be seen or heard inquiring about such things." She sank to the floor and started crying, wailing in a way that made Kitty want to plug her ears. The emotion made Emma sick, and she started throwing up and dry heaving. Finally, she crawled away from the toilet to lie on the bathtub rug. Kitty sat on the floor and pulled her head into her lap.

"Do you ever imagine what your life would be like if you didn't pass?"

It was the last question Kitty had expected Emma to ask. "Not anymore."

"Of course not," Emma said. "You created a life for yourself. All I did was find myself in someone else's."

"But you have everything you wanted."

"Nothing to call my own. I'm a fixture, like the furniture. Everything is his."

"Rick loves you." Kitty could tell by the way he had tried so hard to give Emma everything she asked for.

"He's wonderful—he is. But he's not enough. I didn't know how much I wanted a baby until he did." Her eyes glazed over. "Maybe there was a baby meant for me . . . who passes on God's gift like that?" Her wanting, Kitty saw, made her question everything. "Dreams of babies keep me up at night. The drinking puts me to sleep." She emitted a small, sad laugh. "I was so busy managing you, I didn't manage myself. You've pushed for everything you want and look at you now. Perhaps I should have pushed a little harder too." She buried her face in her hands. "I can't pretend anymore. I'm miserable in this so-called charmed life."

———————

Lucy volunteered to take Emma to the man, located two hours outside of Los Angeles, who took care of such things. Rick was traveling again, and Emma would stay with Kitty on Orange Drive until she recovered. Kitty felt they could trust Abigail to care for her, but Emma argued her loyalty was to Rick.

Emma returned with intense abdominal cramping. It took both Lucy and Kitty to get her into the house.

Bloody sheets, a stained mattress, and hours spent sitting on the bathroom floor while Emma soothed her cramps in a hot bath were moments Kitty wouldn't soon forget. If she never married, she thought, she would never be forced into a position where she had to remove her own womb.

Rick was heartbroken to hear of Emma's "miscarriage." She was too weak to leave Orange Drive, and the blood-stained mattress served as proof. Kitty settled on the couch in the living room while he paced, and Emma slept.

"I don't know what to do." He was fumbling to undo his tie, having come straight from work.

"Activity would do her some good."

"I try to take her out, but I've been really busy with work."

"She's bored, and because of it she's started mixing cocktails."

Rick was willing to do anything to make her happy. "What about a trip to Europe, or Boston? She might like a visit home." He didn't say it, but Kitty knew he was hoping that if he could fix her, they could try to get pregnant again.

"No, not Boston. What if she went back to work?"

He frowned. "She was paid so little—I'm not sure it's worth having to get another car so she can get there."

Kitty remembered how much her operator salary had seemed to her then.

"I'd rather she develop a hobby," Rick ventured.

"Piano?"

"Then I'd have to buy her one." Rick bit his lip.

Kitty wondered why that was a problem; they had plenty of space.

"And . . . it would take a while for her to get good."

Hearing Emma call for him, he rushed down the hallway. They left shortly after, with Emma wrapped in a blanket in his arms as though she was a baby.

Before she knew it, Emma found herself on their neighborhood beautification committee, visiting an elderly woman at a nursing home, and volunteering at the library three times a week. Emma called every week with feigned apathy—she wanted Kitty to know how cared for she was, how lucky. She was trying to turn her husband's affection into yet another competition between her and Kitty, who was genuinely happy for her, knowing she needed him and that feeling of superiority to validate her life.

The library was the only thing that stuck. She was hired in a part-time capacity sorting the racks. Nonetheless, witnessing a vast improvement in Emma's self-esteem, Kitty recruited her formally into Blair House. This time, Emma began donating monies from her own paycheck and advocating for diverse hires in the public library system. She started a reading group to teach literacy skills to Colored women.

Emma never relinquished her gin, but it became less of a crutch and more of a pacifier again. Rick was happy to have his wife back, and Kitty was proud she'd become a more productive citizen. Neither made a fuss about her one or two nightly drinks.

CHAPTER 29

Kitty

January 1960

Kitty's fame was a personal accomplishment, but it hadn't done much for Blair House. There were twenty projects in preproduction at Telescope, and none of them had a Colored face in it. Kitty's second film, like every Telescope film, featured an all-American White cast pondering their existence in an idyllic, recycled story line. Ticket sales were good; Nathan had no reason to make a change.

No one knew the extent to which Kitty's rewriting and tweaking had gone. She'd doctored hundreds of projects at Telescope, though most would never see the light of day. Some aired, infused with her catty wit, but the two feature-length scripts that had gained Nathan's respect were hers entirely. Still, her work was nothing without his name.

For Blair House, she had become a largely unavailable hassle. Special arrangements had to be made and planned days in advance in order for her to visit Hancock Park—for anything. The only benefit was a wider pool to plumb for donations.

Firmly cemented as a force in her own right, Kitty had expanded her circle. She and her unit frequented the homes and shows of muralists, photographers, singers, musicians, writers, and designers who couldn't stop talking about politics, and the protests, and the violence. There was always a donation box circulating for something (along with a joint) as they listened to music, drank, and debated life until the sun came up. In these colorful spaces, Kitty felt free, able to escape her narrow black-white view. The feeling inspired her.

At first, she was enamored by the youngish rainbow tribe.

"Any encroachment on a person's quality of life is wrong." Tim built movie sets. His family was from Los Angeles before it was settled; he was half Tongva Indian, and all his arguments centered around religion.

Jim Crow qualified; however, he said, the problems of Negroes seemed far away from Hollywood.

"Not true. The clubs barely want brunettes, let alone Negroes." Marie was Cuban. She and three others were recording an album and fighting their label to pay for a Spanish-language version.

"Dancing in a club is hardly the marker of the advancement of a race."

"My wife meant, their daily lives are affected—the simple shit we do every day." Bradley was a photographer who, before Marie and her group showed up, had come a few times with a young model.

"People just want to live in peace."

"Wouldn't that be a utopia." Elaine was an East Coast Ivy Leaguer from a professorial family.

"Yes, you Americans are too cynical." Leon was an older Italian director who smoked cigars, indoors, no matter where he was. He complained about immigration and how hard it had been for his aged mother to move to California.

One evening, they were at a book reading at Manuel's house. Manuel was a muralist and the older brother of Julián, the Spanish novelist Kitty wanted to recruit as a writer at Telescope. Kitty was talking to him about this when three Colored entertainers walked in. She didn't recognize them. Maude's eyes said they weren't friends of Blair House.

The room swirled with champagne and questions. The performers were relieved to be accepted, and the others were relieved to be trusted.

Kitty waited for the political talk to commence. Sit-ins would begin in North Carolina soon, to begin the process of desegregation in restaurants all over the South. It was all the group had talked about for weeks.

Kitty had even admitted a tiny bit of her Southern roots. *I was accepted to college down there.* Richard and her other classmates briefly came to mind.

I'm so glad you didn't go, Elaine had said.

Only in private did Emma sneer that her father's stores would eventually be affected. Holden's was branded by a different name in the South, and each one had a lunch counter.

After an hour of casting talk that evening, Kitty realized that politics was being avoided with the inclusion of those Colored guests. The servers noticed too. Kitty watched the performers and the servers avoid each other, separated by class.

The knowing of the interworking of the room made Kitty miss Blair House. Even though she was with her unit, she felt stifled in public. There was always a writer around, ready to report her doings and sayings in the gossip columns. Maude combatted a lot of it in her own column, newly published in the *Times*, but Kitty was tired of having her picture in the paper. Even when she wasn't trying, there she was.

For this reason, Kitty had started talking around Negro issues, like the creatives. They talked about the rise in student activism and the parallel anti-apartheid movement in South Africa instead of segregation in the South.

"You're living in La-La Land, right along with Nathan." Cora hoisted herself onto the wooden kitchen counter in Blair House. She worried that Kitty had grown lazy loving Nathan and had forgotten the real reason she was with him. It wasn't entirely untrue. Kitty and Nathan worked hard but took many breaks, sometimes to make love or to clear their heads in Malibu, Kitty's favorite place.

"But I don't have anything to pitch."

"How can that be?"

"Write something they have to hire a Negro actor for," Cora said.

"*Imitation of Life* may win an award this year," Lucy said.

"Not Best Picture."

"But it's the right time to push."

"I have been!"

Lucy's and Cora's eyes rolled. They didn't understand how hard it was to write in a Negro character of substance in a Telescope script. Most of the story lines would seem unrealistic, or would be altered altogether by having a Negro in a role other than that of a maid or driver. They also didn't understand how little control she truly had. "I want to do more acting, but Nathan, I think, has a problem with me getting so much attention."

"No man wants his woman to be a pin-up girl."

———

Later that week, Kitty pushed for a scene to be added to a film called *Highway*. The lead actor, a hitchhiker, would take a ride from a Negro man, and they'd be pulled over by the police and experience the difference in their treatment.

"No one would believe they'd be stopped twice."

"They would with a Negro in the car. That's the point."

"Honestly, beautiful"—Nathan, brushing his teeth, spit into the sink, then turned to her for a kiss—"I want to stay as far away from reality as possible."

Kitty followed him into their bedroom. "The Negro problem is our problem. We can't ignore what's happening around the country—in our own city! Art is supposed to speak about the times, to *mean* something."

"We could face a boycott over that."

"Sidney Poitier was just nominated for an Oscar!"

"And he didn't win."

"So? He's working; there are plenty of Negro actors who are working. No one is getting boycotted."

"You don't know how many sales those studios have lost because of it, do you? I assure you, if those films were popular, it wouldn't be so hard to get one made." He pulled on his pajama pants and began looking for his shirt.

"It's only hard because of people like you, who can't see the future."

"I want to make money, not get involved in politics. People go to the movies to relax and have fun. It's a family activity. I don't want them leaving my movies frowning."

"How are we supposed to advance as a society if we don't talk about it?"

"It's not your concern. You're an actress; don't make more of yourself than is necessary."

"Last I checked, I've always been more than an actress. Especially to you." She threw his nightshirt to him from the laundry basket of clothes he hadn't put away, which was a quiet protest of her insistence that he *not* employ a maid.

"Yes, darling, but whether you write the script or not, I have no interest in producing a movie with Negro actors talking about Negro issues. Southerners are my best moviegoers." He kissed her cheek, pulled back the bedcovers, and patted her side of the bed, inviting her in. "What happened to the Daisy Lawson character? Write that for yourself."

Kitty's heart sank at this suggested compromise, knowing his mind was already made up. Telling the story of a divorced White woman was, to him, progressive.

"Or write yourself a love story. Get more women into the theater."

"*Imitation of Life* did well."

"Entertaining but unrealistic."

Kitty touched her lips like the secret was going to spurt through her lips and land all over his face. Sitting there in the bed in his blue silk pajamas and combed-over hair, he looked and sounded like a boy, naive about his luck.

"Besides," he continued, "no one would need to pretend to be White in New York. They say Harlem is full of opportunity."

Kitty sauntered back to the bathroom as he went on.

"Don't forget our job is to make people feel good," he yelled. "Not guilty about the things they can't control."

Kitty yelled back, "But they *can* control it! That's the point."

"Control that mess happening in the South? Hell no, they can't. Not even the government knows what to do."

Kitty brushed her teeth, thinking only of the way he called the degradation of the American Negro "a problem," as though it was something they brought upon themselves. She stood before the mirror and for the first time understood why some of the women at Blair House had, like Nina, floated back over the color line, carrying on emotional, sometimes sexual relationships with the Negro men they met through the resistance. Kitty never did, knowing the grass wasn't greener.

"Fine," she said, spitting in the sink. "I'll find myself the role of a lifetime." Kitty might not have been able to control Nathan as Blair House hoped, but adopting Cora's dream of winning an Oscar was second best.

"You do that, dear."

So, Kitty started going out again, not just to work for Blair House but also for fun. She met some of the Telescope dancers at a club. Planning to use them for inspiration, she left with new friends. There were lunches with voice-over artists who also could draw. A couple of actresses met her for lunch. She had macaroons and tea with a group of poets from London. She played tennis with a French museum curator who gave her an open invitation to Paris. There was an Indian man she didn't speak to but who, recognizing her, gave her a gold necklace. She was photographed so often without Nathan—and most noticeably with these male creatives of color—that people began to talk. These rumors reached Nathan and created questions in his mind about whether Kitty was his.

He was sitting in the dark when she came over after dinner with a Spanish director, who had written a film about the first conquistadors in America.

She curled up on his lap to tell him about it. "He's a genius; you have to meet him. I have a copy of the script for you to read."

"Out until all hours of the night with a man you refer to as a 'genius.'" Nathan shifted his body, causing her to fall on the cushion next to him. He put the bottom of his cold, wet glass on her bare thigh. "Why won't you marry me?"

Kitty sighed. Being that he was a film executive, Kitty thought he would have appreciated her lack of interest in common milestones. "You know I'm focused on my career."

"You can do whatever you want after the baby."

"You've never mentioned wanting a family."

He shrugged. "Did I need to? It's the natural progression of things. I was waiting to meet the right woman, I did, and eventually I want a child. Maybe two or three."

"Two or three?"

Now the palm of his right hand came down on her leg. It stung. "I want a son—or a daughter, someone to pass all of this on to."

"I can't get pregnant right now. What about Daisy Lawson?"

"It can wait."

Kitty threw out more reasons—a fear of childbirth, no maternal instincts—and he dismissed every one. "We'll get you help. Anything you need."

Kitty, distressed to learn her career ambitions wouldn't protect her from what was expected, started sleeping at her own home. She also increased her savings deposits and hid some cash in the attic of the house on Orange Drive. She had no plans to leave but, if necessary, could be ready in less than an hour.

Lucy thought all of it was tied to the rumors about her exploits in a mixed crowd. "Marry him," she advised.

———————

Kitty, sobering to the reality that her lifestyle was in danger, did as she was told. They married in a private ceremony at the Beverly Hills Hotel, with only Nathan's family in attendance. Kitty sent clippings from the *Los Angeles Times* to her mother. Maude told her Nathan distributed their wedding photos. "Consider yourself lucky to have a man so proud to be a husband."

She did, but she also felt guilty, especially after Nathan gifted her his mother's favorite six-carat emerald and gold necklace. The woman had a collection fit for a fourteenth-century queen. Kitty touched her earlobes, admiring the way the gold balls from her mother matched the deep brilliance of the twenty-four-karat gold in the necklace. She had always thought the dark hue was a sign of age and perhaps poor care, when maybe it was indicative of quality. Noticing, Nathan handed her a small black box. "I thought you could use another pair of earrings."

She moved her head when he reached for her lobes. "Thank you, but I like these."

He pointed to the box. "Aren't you going to at least look at them? They match the necklace."

She shook her head. "But these were my mother's, and I—"

Nathan bent to kiss her neck. "Don't worry; they won't go missing." He went for her ears again, and she swatted his hand. He frowned, offended now. "You wear those plain old balls all the time."

The characterization stung, and she wished she could defend their worth. Trading up felt disloyal, but she let him replace the earrings with the new jeweled clusters, as if she needed another reminder that the past was truly gone.

CHAPTER 30

Kitty

January 1964

Years passed without further talk of a baby. After three films, four years of matrimony, and nine years together, Kitty and Nathan were partners in life and business. Their intellectual and creative interests were their sustaining strength, and when one grew bored, it was the world's admiration of the other that brought them back.

Riding home after a friend's play one night, he couldn't keep his hands off her. She'd received a standing ovation once the theater crowd learned she was in the audience, and Nathan had beamed at her side, marveling at all the people staring at his wife. Once they were inside their house, he unzipped the back of her sequined dress even before they made it upstairs.

Having sex with him was something Kitty always enjoyed. She never told him how much, and never initiated it, but also never turned him away—never. From some of the stories she'd heard, she gathered that she only knew great sex. Nathan seemed to be in awe of her when they made love, touching her as if it was the only task that mattered. He ran his hands through her hair, grabbing her head as he kissed her. His assertiveness was part of their dance, but that night, after a third time reaching for her diaphragm, she had to use her entire body to resist him.

"Just be here with me." He pinned her arms above her head against the bed. Normally, he cared if sex was good for her, but that night he acted as if her body was only there for his pleasure. The nightmare only got worse when he released himself inside of her. In that moment, Kitty hated him. He already owned her career, and that night, he showed her he thought he owned her too. After it was over, he crawled over her onto his side of the bed and went to sleep.

Kitty wiped herself clean with a hot washcloth. She ran a bath, already sore between her legs, and sat there until it turned cold, unsure of what had just happened.

In the morning, he kissed her forehead just as normal. She flinched, but he didn't seem to notice. He wanted sex again that evening, and his tenderness made her question what she remembered happening. Still, it hurt. She took another bath until the stinging stopped. She gave him the benefit of the doubt after talking to Lucy, who said that sometimes "they just need to do it like that."

Weeks later, in February, nausea sent her running to the bathroom before daybreak. She knew instantly that she was pregnant. Their family doctor confirmed it with a jovial smile. "Maybe two months, very early." His right hand went to his balding head, and he bowed almost, as if to say that being a father was the single most important job of his life. Kitty vomited all over his white coat.

Kitty started packing as soon as she got home, knowing her husband's desire for a baby was stronger than his interest in her happiness.

She put her bags in the trunk of the old dark-blue Mercedes she used for errands. She had only the essentials: the leather pouch her mother sent her off with, her writing notebook, some cash, and photographs. For clothes she packed only the items Nathan wouldn't notice were gone: the pairs of underwear reserved for her monthly, the trousers and shirts he hated, and her mother's earrings.

She called Nathan at his office to report an Emma emergency. "I'll probably have to stay a night or two." By the time he called to check, she'd be in Kansas, almost home.

She never made it more than a mile. She never backed out of the driveway. Leaving her husband, giving up her career, it was too hasty a decision to make in an afternoon. She loved her husband and her life. And if the baby were born passable, she would have thrown away her mother's sacrifice for nothing. Besides, she wasn't due for another seven or eight months. Anything could happen before then. It could even slip away, as Lucy said all of hers had. Deciding to ignore any circumstance or outcome not in her favor, she reasoned that her cover was her good luck charm. Kitty Karr had given her a reality comprised of many people's fantasies. With this thought came the delusion that everything was going to be fine.

After seeing what Emma had gone through to heal, convincing Kitty to get the operation was futile. Lucy returned with a potion from the old doctor who had done Emma's operation. "It'll be like having a bad monthly."

Kitty wouldn't drink it. Emma tried again, then Laurie, Maude, Billie and, finally, Cora. Kitty refused each time, and when morning sickness hit her badly one morning, she told Nathan and made her decision final. Her Blackness slid off easily, like a coat, but she couldn't spare another slice, handle another loss, especially between mother and child. A part of her wanted to be able to send her momma a picture of her baby.

"Take this time off," Nathan suggested. "We should keep your pregnancy private."

"You think I'm going to look that bad?" Relieved, she played along.

"No, darling, but real life distracts from the fantasy. You're a movie star. The world shouldn't see you looking normal, and pregnancy is as normal as you can get." Always thinking about how to leverage the press, he imagined her at his side in filmable condition, holding their baby, when he announced her new film.

Her days became occupied with the remodeling of their third floor, currently their attic, into a nursery. Weekends were spent combing through design books. Kitty's job was to identify the pages she liked in the stacks of magazines.

Nathan held up a card of yellow paint swatches. "Which?"

Kitty picked the one closest to her skin tone. "Pale Butter works for a girl or boy."

Nathan wanted to name the baby after his father's parents: Solomon for a boy, or Sarah for a girl. A pro at feigning it, Kitty worked to match his excitement about their growing family, but when she was alone, she resented him for her being pregnant in the first place.

A nagging discomfort in her lower back came during her fourth month. The doctor said the baby was growing and pushing on a nerve, but Kitty convinced herself that the pain foreshadowed the suffering ahead. The baby's color was going to give her away, and her bodily discomfort served as a constant reminder. Unable to get comfortable, she couldn't sleep for longer than a few hours anymore. She became delirious and short-tempered, and Nathan's efforts to care for her were met with contempt and verbal assaults. Helpless and dismayed by her moods, Nathan insisted on hiring help.

Kitty couldn't stand the thought, especially being in pain as she was. She didn't trust her ability to conceal her parts in such close quarters. Despite Kitty's protests, Nathan hired a midwife to live in until the baby came.

Lucy told her to thank her lucky stars. "She's your last chance for an ally."

CHAPTER 31

Elise

Sunday night, October 29, 2017

After the auction, guests were ushered out with cookies for their rides home and the inner circle moved to the kitchen for more drinks. Elise used the transition to disappear into the jungle, across the dirt path, and through the hedges to her parents' house. She predicted it would be hours before anyone went looking for her, especially since Aaron had also left. He couldn't wait to leave and Elise couldn't wait to see him go.

The backyard motion lights came on every twenty feet as she rounded down the driveway to their ten-car covered parking lot. She pulled a brown banker box from underneath the beach blanket she always kept in the trunk of her forest-green Land Rover. Though the contents were heavy, she walked fast, more concerned about being seen.

Truthfully, Elise had thought Kitty's recorded instruction about the organization of her belongings was as ridiculous as her mother said. Kitty had nailed down every detail: where her houseplants should go, how to wrap her furs, the exact mothballs to purchase before storing her sweaters. Her gowns had gone into different piles based on when and where they were worn.

Elise had started two days after Kitty's passing and, five days later, hours before her sisters' arrival, she had finished the last recording and realized that Kitty hadn't made any mention of the Louis Vuitton trunk. Impossible to miss, it took up a lot of the bedroom floor space.

Elise unlatched it to find underneath the stale linen, arranged in careful order, the things that changed everything.

1. A handwritten letter:

Dearest Elise,

I chose you to handle my affairs because I knew you'd follow my directions. Your mother would have hired people, and your sisters—well, who knows when they might have gotten around to it.

Life is about timing; you know that much by now. Years ago, I told your mother what I'm about to write. You all may end up hating me, as she did, but I stand by my decisions and I don't regret them one bit. I lost some things but I gained a lot too. That's how everyone's life goes.

Your grandma Nellie begged me to tell you girls when you were younger. Maybe she was right, but I was unable to see what good it would do. All I knew was I couldn't count on my daughter to do it.

It took me years to summon the courage to tell your mother, and when I did, it came out all wrong, at the wrong time. She missed the most important parts, the parts that might have stopped her from hating me.

Elise, my name is Mary Magdalene Ledbetter and I am your grandmother. Born in North Carolina to a Black mother, I came to Los Angeles when I was eighteen years old and became a White woman named Kitty Lane Karr. When I gave birth to your mother, it became clear that I couldn't raise her as my own without jeopardizing not only the life I had built but the lives of others I knew. My fame had become bigger than my White identity at that point. I owe your grandmother Nellie my whole life for agreeing to raise your mother. She gave me the best of both

worlds—freedom and family. Knowing your mother, you, and your
sisters has been the greatest pleasure of my life.

In my memoirs is everything I never got the chance to tell your
mother. It'll all make sense after you read.

All my love,

Kitty

2.   Scores of eight-by-ten-inch envelopes dated from 1963 to 1969,
     containing paparazzi-like photographs of Kitty.

3.   The two black Moleskine notebooks Kitty started writing in
     the year she was diagnosed with cancer.

4.   Two fading, frayed-edged photographs, both of the same Black
     woman holding two different White children. Names were written
     on the backs of both: *Mary, age 4, Shirley Claire, age 2.*

5.   A pair of gold ball earrings.

It made sense then why Kitty, a recluse, wanted her home established as a
historic landmark, her things auctioned, and her papers and photos digitized.
She knew her worth would escalate after the news and wanted her family to
benefit. Perhaps she wanted the truth to be easy to spread.

Twenty-four hours ago, the truth, in short letter form, was enough to
reckon with. To learn that Kitty purposely lied made Elise feel as if she'd
been talking to a stranger all along, and she decided everything in the box,
including the memoir Kitty wrote between the two Moleskines, could remain
unread for a little while longer. Elise had tossed everything back into the box
and locked it in her Rover.

The confession clarified their family dynamics—Kitty's hovering over their lives, her sisterlike relationship with Nellie, and their mother's consistent emotional distance from Kitty—but exposed layers of pain that further complicated the present.

After years of speculation and resentment, there was an explanation for Sarah's emotional limitations, but Elise didn't understand. She had had both Kitty and Nellie in her life. Why had she chosen to conceal it?

Her mother's appearance in the labyrinth hours later had solidified her decision not to tell anyone about Kitty for now, understanding and seeing that her mother's world was crashing down too. Somehow, she knew then that Kitty's secret wasn't hers to keep, and she stayed awake meandering through a million emotions.

Dawn had brought anxiety about the studio meeting, her sisters' arrival, and not a single wink of sleep.

Jasper's appearance that night in such a private setting forced her to put the pieces together.

She finished reading Kitty's Moleskines as the snow-white light of the fall morning came through her bumblebee stained-glass window, shell-shocked to learn how Whiteness had altered the lives of two generations of her family. Learning those origins were from the bloodline of a rape sickened her. Rape of African slaves and their descendants, she knew, was a common practice, a constant threat by which Whites established dominance, indulged fetishes, and bred more slaves to increase their wealth. It was routine, a part of the system—something that had happened long ago, to people that she didn't know, as in a movie. Now, meeting Hazel through Kitty's words, she could see her great-grandmother's angular-shaped face in her own, her eyes in her own. She could feel her energy and Kitty's. It hit her, then, that what her mother feared was the story of her own creation.

Elise heard her mother in the kitchen—already prepping for her party, no doubt—and went down to help, deciding, still, to keep Kitty's secret until it could no longer be contained. Jasper would be the measure of that.

But it was her father who turned from the counter. "Hey, good-looking."

"Morning. Where's Mom?"

"Asleep." He turned on the coffee grinder and pushed up his robe sleeves. "Want breakfast? Julia put some lox in there for today."

"Sure."

He hummed to the refrigerator, shuffling his feet to the beat in his head. "Good work night?" Elise asked.

He raised a brow. "Not that type of work."

"*Dad!* Gross."

He chuckled, handing her a cutting board and two bagels. "How's your guy?"

Elise pulled a knife from the magnetic board next to the stove. "Fine."

He unsealed the lox pack and forked it onto a platter. "And there are the other two. Want breakfast?"

Giovanni, dressed in sweats, an old Care Bears T-shirt, and tennis shoes, stopped short. She, too, had clearly expected a hectic prep morning. "Where's Mom?"

"Asleep still," their father said. Both of her sisters looked relieved. Noele was still in her pajamas and moved robotically to the dishes cabinet, as if she was sleepwalking.

"First time she's slept through the night in weeks."

Elise wondered how he knew that. He was always in his studio at that hour, which was why Elise had felt the need to watch her, to make sure she always came back inside. Last night was the only time that week she'd forgotten to check.

When Sarah had yet to stir at the noon hour, Elise slipped out of the kitchen while her father and sisters loaded the dishwasher.

Understanding all her mother had been holding, Elise felt guilty for her eulogy. When her mother answered her knock with a weak voice, she felt even worse. "Mom . . ." She opened one side of the double door.

Sarah, peeking over her fluffy duvet to see it was her, told her to shut the door. "Elise, I don't have the energy to fight."

"I wasn't—I'm sorry for what I said."

Sarah turned on her side.

"Mom, we should talk."

"I need to rest before tonight."

Hurt, Elise retracted her overture. "God forbid the party doesn't go on." Elise closed the door harder than necessary, to elicit a reaction, but there was nothing.

CHAPTER 32

Kitty

Summer 1964

Nellie Shore arrived to the Tates' home without a smile or much to say. Her mouth and jaw turned downward in a frown, but there was kindness behind her almost-black eyes. Nellie's skin matched the depth of her eyes and was a stark contrast against the bright patterned dresses she favored, which covered her extremities down to her ankles and wrists. She was a young woman but dressed like Bertha, who was twice her age.

"You're five, maybe six months along," Nellie said, examining her. They were indeed growth pains and there was, she reported, "nothing to do but wait."

The baby would take after Nathan. He was six feet tall and had eight inches on his wife. "The baby's uncomfortable too. You'll both get adjusted again soon," Nellie reassured her.

Kitty appreciated Nellie's care but resented her presence. She needed space and privacy to plan should the baby's birth give her away. All day and night, Nellie sat in the corner of Kitty's room, reading, save for trips to the kitchen for her meals. Kitty couldn't be rude; Nellie helped her to the bathroom and ran her baths at the perfect temperature, with herbs and oils. It was the only thing that soothed her physical discomfort and mental anguish.

The middle of the night was always the hardest. About three weeks after Nellie arrived, Kitty had a nightmare. She started panicking and crying about how she had never wanted to be pregnant in the first place. Nellie hushed her.

"You're going to wake your husband." Nellie ushered her into the bathroom and shut the door; the moon provided their only light. "This baby is coming whether you like it or not." She stripped her from her sweaty nightgown. "You best make peace with that. Children know when they aren't wanted, and you'll have hell to pay in its upbringing."

Kitty whined. "This pain is only the beginning of my punishment."

Nellie ran water for a bath. The additives smelled minty. "What do you have against this baby?"

"I'm not supposed to be a mother."

"You don't mean that."

Kitty challenged her. "How do you know?"

Nellie pulled a pipe from a pocket in her dress and put it on the sink. "I've seen it all. Don't worry. I'll get you through this and deliver the baby when it's time, Mrs. Tate."

"Please," Kitty groaned, "call me Kitty. Aren't we peers?"

Nellie gave her a blank look.

"I'll be twenty-eight in September," Kitty said. "How old are you?"

"Thirty-three," Nellie said, crumbling between her fingers a marijuana bud, which she packed into the pipe. She lit the pipe before handing it to Kitty. "Inhale."

Kitty did so a few times before the fire died. A floating sensation in her head and body allowed her to relax back into the tub. Water covered her legs and half of her swelled middle. "What if something goes wrong?"

Nellie sat on the closed lid of the commode. "It won't. I've been doing this since I was a child. I started assisting my aunt when I was nine. I was born with the gift, and I have twenty-one years of experience." Nellie performed "essential medicine," like the old man Emma had seen, and her services were reserved for and passed along to those in need of assistance with the most delicate conditions. She couldn't work in a Colored hospital because she didn't have formal training.

"How many babies have you delivered?"

"Yours will make fifty-three."

———

Kitty's body did stretch, leaving purplish-bluish marks on her stomach and hips that she would lament for years. The discomfort left remnants of its fury in her temperament; she was sullen and yelled at Nathan, who kept bringing her scripts and samples for the nursery. It felt cruel to have to prepare for a life she wasn't sure would still be hers. She still didn't have a plan.

Nellie snatched the covers off her legs one afternoon. "We're going on a walk."

"I can't." Being on her feet for too long made her hip bones ache.

"There's a wheelchair waiting for you downstairs."

It was hot outside. Kitty put her hand to her forehead to shield herself from the sun. Nellie plopped a hat on her head.

"Why won't you settle on the design for the baby's room?" Nellie asked.

"He told you to talk to me?"

"No, but I see how hurt he is when you refuse to look through those pictures with him. He's been asking my opinion on the furniture and whatnot."

"You can tell him. I don't care."

"If you're not careful, he'll transfer his affections to the baby, and you'll never get him back."

"Is this a warning from experience?" Kitty knew nothing about Nellie's personal life. She never talked about her husband or anyone else and never went home, even on the weekends, when she could have.

"We don't have children."

Kitty was surprised, her being a midwife. "But you're so maternal. Didn't you want them?"

"I never considered it. I knew I couldn't have babies since I was a young girl." Nellie explained that she had never started menstruating. Her aunt said she was born without ovaries.

Kitty reached over her shoulder to touch Nellie's hand. "I'm sorry for all my talk about not wanting this baby."

"No bother. I'm the oldest in a family of ten; having children wasn't something I felt I'd be missing out on. I'm warning you 'cause I've seen this time and time again. Having a baby can be difficult on your marriage."

"Do you normally live in until the baby is born?"

"It's easier that way."

Kitty turned to look back at Nellie. "For who?"

"Ha!" Nellie laughed, surprised by Kitty's forwardness, and then resigned herself to honesty. "My husband hasn't worked since we moved here. I let him face his frustrations in peace."

Kitty had heard this before. She wanted to ask whether his frustration had caused a temper problem, a drinking problem, a woman problem, or all three. "What type of work does he do?"

"Farmer, by trade, but he'll take anything at this point." His agricultural skills were easily transferable, but those jobs weren't open to Negroes.

"Did you come here to farm?"

"Long story."

"I don't have anything to do but listen," Kitty said.

Nellie's husband had owned their land in Georgia; he was one of the few Negroes who did, and came from a long line of planters. That land had been passed down three generations, an inheritance from his White great-great-grandfather, Frederick Shore, to his mulatto son, who earned enough building iron gates to buy his freedom.

"His father didn't set him free?"

"He was too valuable. His ironwork is all over Georgia."

"What a legacy."

"A lot of trouble, is what it is. They were after that land for decades, and they finally got it. We arrived here with nothing but the clothes on our backs. They heard people were meeting on our farm and burnt our house down. If our neighbor's daughter hadn't overheard their plans, I wouldn't be here today. We hid in the back of a milk truck. The driver was a childhood friend of Clifford's. White man. He hid us at the risk of his life and his family's. His wife drove us to Kansas in the trunk of her car, with their three children in the back seat. We took the train west from there."

"What were the meetings about?"

"Unionizing."

"Is that why he can't find a job here?"

"No. He's never worked in service before, and those are most of the jobs available."

"The studio's always looking for janitors. I'll let Nathan know."

"Clifford has too much pride."

"Let him get hungry enough."

"That's how it goes in my mind too." It had been five years, she said, and his anger cut so deep it was a wonder he was still breathing.

Kitty convinced Nathan to give Nellie a raise. Whether Kitty's baby was born looking Negro, White, or something in between, it would have to pass through Nellie's hands. Nellie would only help her, if it came to that, if she genuinely liked Kitty—loved her, really. Kitty knew it wouldn't be easy. Around White folks, Nellie, like every Negro, wore another face, and Kitty understood that she would never reveal her real self unless Kitty did first.

Kitty almost did when Sidney Poitier finally won his Oscar. Nellie, Kitty, and Nathan were all watching the ceremony together in the living room. When Nathan hugged them both, Kitty felt annoyed. Was he cheering so as to not offend Nellie, or was his enthusiasm genuine? Kitty wasn't sure.

She kept her eyes fixed on the television but contemplated stealing a look at Nellie. She wanted to share the joy exploding in her body. If she did it, right then, Kitty knew Nellie would hear her without words. But Nellie wouldn't look away from the TV, even after the commercials. Kitty understood she had also felt Nathan's veiled apathy.

CHAPTER 33

Kitty

Fall 1964

Kitty first saw Sarah in a dream. She was three or four years old, with Hazel's rich coloring and two thick, dark-brown ponytails braided down her back. Sarah was on her tiptoes, reaching for a cake in the middle of the table. Decorated with sprinkles and a ton of candles, it looked like one of Mrs. Nora's. As the child's little fingers clawed into the icing, Hazel appeared at the head of the table. "Who said that belongs to you?"

There had been hints of Hazel before in Kitty's dreams, but she had never appeared in full form. Kitty reached for her, but the movement propelled her awake.

She went downstairs to Nellie's room, off the kitchen. Nathan had offered her a room on the second floor, to be closer to Kitty, but they both refused. Kitty wanted to maintain privacy, and Nellie wanted the service quarters so she could smoke on the back patio before bed.

Nellie opened the door fast. Her hands cupped Kitty's belly. "Is it time?"

"I'm fine." Kitty pushed her way in and shut the door. "There's something you should know about me."

"I know you're Colored," Nellie said. "You told me outright during one of your fits. Remember that night I gave you my pipe? That's why. I worried you'd say it to your husband, so I started watching you like a hawk."

"Why didn't you say something?"

"I knew you had to tell me eventually. I can see the panic in your eyes when you talk about the baby. It's like you're not sure if it's yours or not."

Kitty's hands went to her stomach. That was exactly the way she felt.

"You've made yourself sick worrying that the baby won't look White. I see ones like you all the time. Most times they don't even know they're Colored."

"She won't be able to pass. That's what I came to tell you."

"She?"

"I had a dream. I saw her." Seeing Nellie stiffen, her anxiety began to rise.

"Do your dreams come true?"

"I don't know; it's the first one I've had like it. It was so real. I saw my momma and the baby, except she was a child. I need your help. I have to find a couple to adopt her. I'll pay for everything—"

"Won't your husband notice the money gone?"

"I have savings." Kitty hadn't spent a dime of her own money in years; Nathan was generous and gave Kitty full access to his accounts even before they married. "The baby deserves to benefit from her parentage, but I don't want to see her. No one can know I'm her mother."

"What are you going to tell Mr. Nathan?"

Kitty hung her head. "That she died."

Nellie sat on her bed. "What about telling him the truth? He seems reasonable."

Kitty wasn't so sure. "He'll never understand me having lied to him since the day we met." Thinking of Emma, Lucy, and the others, Kitty added, "It's not just about me." Kitty began to cry, and Nellie grabbed her hands to bear some of her pain.

"As Negro women"—Nellie emphasized the plural—"we make hard decisions." She held Kitty's hands tighter and began to pray aloud.

Kitty's eyes fell to the ground, but she couldn't close them. She said grace over meals and quick thank-yous when something went her way but never at length. She wanted to feel the passion that made Nellie's brow furrow and the cadence of her speech change, but Kitty had stopped knowing what to say to God years ago. She felt ashamed to try now that she needed help. She also wasn't sure it would do any good: although she and Hazel went to church, instead of scripture, it had been their favorite poem they recited before bed each night, like a prayer.

Nellie waited for an opportunity to induce Kitty and, in the meantime, went to Blair House, disguised as an adoption agency. Maude dressed as a White nun to meet with her. Just in case, they had to find a couple who understood they had only a fifty-fifty chance of gaining a child. Paramount was that the parents' identities stay concealed from all parties.

Call it luck, or destiny: Nathan announced a trip to the desert to check on a production two weeks before the baby was due. He would only be about three hours away.

Nellie made Kitty a tea to help start labor as soon as he left. They hadn't yet found a home for the baby, but his short absence made the delivery imperative. Labor lasted nineteen hours. Kitty, already proven to have no capacity for pain, developed a rash on her arms and chest that made her skin look like raw meat. Finally, the baby—a girl—took her first breath in Nellie's arms.

Nellie handed her to Kitty, who pulled the blanket away from her body to examine her. She did, in fact, have Hazel's cocoa tone, as in the dream. Her lashes were so long they rested on her cheekbones. "She's beautiful. Her name is Sarah." She had a circular birthmark in the middle of her chest that contained smaller, freckled shades of brown like God had been using her chest like a palette.

"His mother's name, right?" Nellie said.

"Right, so it can't be changed." Kitty traced the baby's tiny ear. "Don't worry, I'm always going to take care of you." The baby wrinkled her nose, as if she didn't appreciate the interruption from her dreams. When Kitty kissed the top of her head, she began to faintly snore. She looked, though, like no one Kitty knew. For a second it made her feel better about what she had to do.

"Will you take her?" Kitty asked.

"I'll wake you when it's time to feed her."

"Thank you." Nellie put Sarah down in the basket she'd set up. "I know," Kitty continued, "we've been talking about finding someone—but I'd prefer you over anyone."

Nellie stared at Kitty as though she didn't understand what she'd said.

"It's the same deal. I'll provide for her and I don't want to see her. There's no reason for us to be in contact after you leave."

Considering it, Nellie said, "Maybe she'll be good for us"—referring, Kitty understood, to the state of her marriage.

"Will he be good to my child?"

Nellie looked offended. "He's a good man, Kitty."

"But does he want a child?"

"He doesn't know what he wants, but it'll be hard for him to be miserable with a beautiful baby smiling at him."

"What will you tell people?"

Nellie paused. "That she's my sister's child, who died."

"Is that true?"

"No, but we're not close. She'll never visit."

The baby whimpered, and Nellie jumped up to get her. She cuddled Sarah at her neck. Unable to witness her easy assumption of the role of mother, Kitty reached for the water on her nightstand, trying to ignore the pain, the flood of aching despair brought on by a loss that hadn't even occurred yet.

Kitty spent the next two days with Sarah in the nursery. Nathan, who had always thought the baby would be a girl, had already mounted yellow block letters with her name on the wall.

"Oh, Nellie." Kitty got tears in her eyes when she saw it. "Can her middle name be Hazel?" Kitty asked. "It's my mother's name."

"How sweet. Is she still alive?"

"Lives in North Carolina."

"Maybe we'll go there one day. I'd be honored to meet your mother."

Kitty didn't have the energy to even pretend like it was possible. Her fame prevented her ability to blend in, even if she were brave enough to go back.

Kitty indulged Sarah's every whim and murmur, fed her as soon as she wanted to eat, and watched her sleep. It was cute the way she wiggled her mouth and nose like a little piglet. Her eyes finally opened, and while she hadn't inherited the blue-gray halo, she fixated on Kitty as though she was trying to commit her face to memory.

The easy words of the poem her mother used to recite to her also quieted Sarah. Pleased to have remembered it, she felt as though her mother was right there. As Sarah dreamed, Kitty told her the things she would probably never get the chance to say again. It took all night to explain why.

Clifford came first thing in the morning. Kitty gave Sarah to Nellie the first time she reached for her. Then she shut herself inside the nursery, leaving Nellie to let herself out. She locked it when Nathan came home after receiving the urgent message from Nellie at his hotel. He banged on the door, begging her to let him in, worried about what her grief could push her to do. She slid her fingers underneath the door to comfort him. Letting him console her for this was too much to take.

Nathan refused details of the baby's death, even when Nellie called to offer them. He didn't want to see the body or have a funeral. He had the nursery furniture covered and the door and windows locked. The house sold that way years later.

Kitty's unit came by with condolences from Blair House but controlled the conversation, committed to, it seemed, a set of previously agreed-upon topics to ensure no lulls and, thus, no opportunities for the truth. Kitty was relieved not to be asked; she didn't want to tell any more lies. They may have had their suspicions, but as always, it was safer they didn't know.

She didn't make plans to see them soon or suggest it. Sarah had changed her willingness to take risks; she had to be around to provide for her. Regardless of what happened to Kitty, they all could see the change. Lucy encouraged her to focus on her marriage and get back to work. Kitty never went to the mansion again but would become one of Blair House's most lavish donors.

The Tate house, once full of conversation, fell silent. The holidays passed, and even after the New Year, Kitty wasn't inspired to write. She feared her gift to craft fairy tales was gone. She stayed up late into the night, trying to force words onto paper, which only resulted in chain-smoking and thoughts of Sarah. When she closed her eyes, she could hear the echoes of her shrill cry. The pain was suffocating, and without Nellie, Kitty learned the comforts of gin, and drowned in the missing of her baby. Nathan didn't stop her; he too, had become heavy-handed with his pour.

Kitty had misjudged things. It didn't matter that Sarah wasn't really dead. She would never be her daughter, and that felt like a death in itself.

Emma called every day. Sometimes Kitty answered the phone, sometimes she didn't. With Nathan only plugged into work and her Blair House duties nonexistent, she knew that anything anyone wanted could wait. Then one night, Nathan was working late, or maybe fell asleep on his office couch, which happened often (even during the day when he started reading scripts), and she called Emma. It was 11:02. Emma only had to hear her voice and, by 11:29, was ringing her doorbell.

CHAPTER 34

Kitty

January 1965

"How is Mr. Tate handling it?" Nellie set her glass of water down on Kitty's coffee table.

"He's been sleeping in his study again." Kitty looked down at Sarah with a smile. She responded with a spit bubble, eyes still locked on Kitty. It was as if, after four months, she recognized her. She was a fat baby, with legs and arms composed of rolls, and dimples piercing her cheeks and thighs. "Nothing's changed about his life. I can't sleep, and he's maintained his usual ten-hour workdays." Her lull in work and sequestration indoors was ripping their relationship apart at the seams. Nathan loved his "Kitty Karr star." And because her celebrity persona was the furthest layer from the self she'd revealed to him, she felt like a puppet. Kitty knew it was up to her to fix it.

"Where is he now?"

"He stays overnight with his mother once a week." Nathan's father had an around-the-clock nurse, but his mother needed emotional support. They were very close, and Kitty, always maintaining distance from his family for obvious reasons, encouraged their quality time.

Kitty, plagued by Sarah's phantom cries, had called Nellie in the middle of the night. Whispering into the phone, huddled in the corner of the kitchen, with the sink water running, Kitty had begged Nellie to bring Sarah for a visit. Nellie heard the panic in her voice and worried that Kitty was being cavalier in her invitation. Kitty assured her that home was the last thing on her husband's mind.

"He spends as much time away from the house as possible to lure me out. He wants me to get back to work."

"That's smart," Nellie agreed.

"I do miss my career, but I couldn't care less about acting again if she's not in my life," Kitty explained.

Nellie's eyes darted from Sarah up to Kitty as if she wanted to snatch her.

Kitty readjusted Sarah to kiss her cheek. "I'd like to see her, sometimes." She cleared her throat. "I need to see her . . . I know I said I didn't want to, but it's been harder than I imagined. Nothing else will change, but please let me be there in some way to see her grow up." Kitty was nervous for her answer, unsure if she could accept a no.

"I already told you I didn't like the idea of you not being in her life." Nellie put her hand over her heart. "I didn't like the idea of you not being in *my* life." Suddenly at peace, Nellie closed her eyes and nestled into the sofa.

"Are you okay?" Kitty had been so consumed with Sarah she hadn't looked Nellie squarely in the face.

"I'm exhausted. Sarah has me up every three hours or so."

"Where's Clifford?"

Nellie smacked her teeth. "On a farm, tending to horses. Haven't really seen him with the extra shifts."

"Do you need more money?"

Nellie flicked a hand. "You're doing too much already."

"Not if Clifford's working and leaving you without help." She thought about the puttering pickup truck he'd dropped Nellie off in. Kitty had worried it would leave an oil stain in the driveway she'd have to explain.

"He's saving up to leave us," Nellie said of Clifford.

"Can't you try to make it work?" Kitty wanted her daughter to have a chance at everything she didn't, the first being a father.

"How, if he's never around?"

"Have you tried?" Kitty gestured to Nellie's body, covered per usual in a floor-length shift. "You could show some skin. I bet you sleep in a long-sleeved nightgown, too, don't you?"

"When it's cold!" Nellie waved her off, but Kitty could tell she was embarrassed by the subject. "What's wrong with him has nothing to do with me." Turning serious, she balanced her elbows on her knees. "I don't want Sarah to ever know that you're her mother. We'll tell her we're friends. Best friends."

"But she'll learn soon enough that that's not how the world works," Kitty said. "And she deserves to know where she came from."

"Did it help you?"

Kitty paused. Learning who her father was hadn't done her much good. "Maybe when she's an adult, the world will have changed. We can tell her then."

Nellie shook her head. It was her bottom line. "I couldn't bear for her to grow up, learn you're her mother, and wish you had been the one to raise her."

"Babies are closest to whoever raised them. They don't know the difference."

"Don't they?" Nellie pointed at Sarah, now asleep on Kitty's lap. "That baby doesn't cry with you. When she's with me, I can't get a moment's peace. Tell me she doesn't know who her mother is."

It was their first disagreement about Sarah's rearing and a sprinkling of what would follow. Kitty agreed to Nellie's terms, knowing anything could happen between "then and never."

In the meantime, their arrangement gave Kitty the best of both worlds—the highlights of motherhood without the daily slog of mothering. Feeling optimistic again with her child in reach, Kitty went back to the lot, only to face rumors about what had happened to her baby.

Kitty went to Nathan for answers. "I thought no one knew I was pregnant."

He looked more unnerved than usual. "I didn't think so either."

"Then I think we should tell the truth and be done with it."

The pair let the news pass quietly at the studio, with assistance from Lucy. From there it circulated as a whisper among intimate groups and eventually became an unspoken, known public fact.

Kitty explained her reasoning to Nellie. "If someone suspects anything or, God forbid, I'm found out, no one will ever have a reason to go looking for her."

As the word circulated among the circles of the who's who, Kitty received condolences and an invitation for tea from Claire Pew, the talkative photographer's wife, whom Kitty hadn't seen in years.

CHAPTER 35

Kitty

February 1965

Pulling into Claire's circular driveway, Kitty was impressed to see a sapphire-blue Rolls Royce in the garage. Kitty had been pleased but surprised to hear from Claire and accepted her invitation out of curiosity. Her new money didn't touch Claire's wealth, but her fame made them equals.

"Kitty Karr! Lovely to see you." Claire brushed one of her curls out of her face before moving aside to let Kitty enter. In her parlor were ham sandwiches, strawberries, and lemonade.

"Yes, thank you for inviting me."

Claire handed her a plate and said, in a somber tone, "How are you doing?"

"I have my days."

Claire sat down, stirring the Earl Grey tea she'd prepared with milk and a cube of sugar. "Our son was almost six months old when he died."

"I'm so sorry." Kitty produced a cigarette from her bag.

Claire rushed to light it. "I'm so sorry for *you*."

"Thank you."

"The doctor said these things happen—it was no one's fault. I came in one morning because he hadn't stirred yet. He was cold. Must have died in the middle of the night." Claire was reliving her pain in an effort, Kitty suspected, to make her talk about her own, but all it did was make her regret coming.

"My grandmother died a few months later, and I spent three months in a mental institution," Claire said. "All of my friends are afraid of me now."

Her honesty was shocking, but Kitty sympathized. "No one calls me anymore, but it's probably for the best."

"Pain like ours makes people uncomfortable. I had no one to talk to about it. It drove me insane."

Claire's ability to display the bad parts of her life made Kitty jealous, but it did help to know she wasn't the only one who had fallen to such depths. Things were better now, being able to see Sarah, but she knew the grief of which Claire spoke.

"I keep wondering if there was something different I should have done."

Claire reached across the table to cover Kitty's hand. "There wasn't."

Kitty greedily accepted Claire's comfort.

"You know, there are plenty of women who would benefit from you telling your story."

"Maybe I'll write about it."

Claire's head went to one side. "You write?"

Kitty rushed to downplay her admission. "I dabble."

"Like, what kind of writing?"

"I doctor scenes."

"Well, you should write a whole something. It would open up a new market for you."

Kitty looked at her curiously. "Thanks for the career advice."

Claire explained. "I used to run public relations for my family's company, but I've always wanted to work in film." Claire talked fast, as though she was afraid Kitty would be angry.

"I could let Nathan know," Kitty said, understanding now why she'd been invited.

Claire clasped her hands together. "Would you?"

"Sure, but—are you going to try for another baby?"

"Absolutely. I was born to be a mother."

"Then maybe you should wait to start a new career."

Claire waved a hand. "I can work while pregnant."

"I couldn't imagine filming pregnant."

"Are you going to try again?"

"Never," Kitty said. If she ever got pregnant again, she would drink whatever potion was supplied.

"You may feel different in a few years. I was the same."

Race aside, Kitty wasn't sure. She loved holding and kissing Sarah, but she wasn't envious of Nellie's work as a mother. And that was putting it nicely.

Claire seemed to think she could do it all—and maybe she could, Kitty considered, but Kitty had no aspirations to try.

"I can't just party with my husband for the rest of my life."

Kitty smiled; she intended to.

"Would you like to stay for dinner?" Claire asked. "Winston, my husband, is working late. I made lasagna."

"You cook?" Claire looked like the type who grew up having the basics done for her. Kitty had first picked up a knife when she was seven.

"I have a short list of specialties."

"I hope lasagna is one of them." Kitty didn't know what lasagna was and was sure she'd mispronounced it.

Claire bumped Kitty's shoulder with her hip before pulling her from the chair. "Come see."

Kitty was pleased by the kitchen's savory aroma; it was complex and heightened by the warmth of the oven.

"Did you always like to cook?" Kitty asked.

"Yes, it runs in my blood. My grandmother was a baker." She stirred the sauce before lighting the pilot. "Half an hour. Wine?" Anticipating a yes, she handed Kitty a glass.

Kitty swirled her glass as Claire did before taking a sip.

Claire pulled a pan from an overhead cabinet, setting it and some oil on the table in front of Kitty. "I normally drink white wine because I eat so much cheese and it goes better. That and grapes is a standard meal for me."

"My stomach doesn't like too much cheese."

"You haven't had the right cheese. My grandparents had cows, and their cheese was so fresh and creamy, I could have eaten pounds of it if they'd let me." Claire pulled open her refrigerator. "There's a Cornish hen and potatoes from the other night if you're starving."

"It's fine. I'm not too hungry, I was more enjoying your company."

Claire directed Kitty to lay the strips of pasta in a pan. "Did you always want to be an actress?"

"Yes. I'd only admit that now that it's happened, but yes."

Claire handed her a tool with a silver wheel on its end to cut the dough she'd rolled out between them. "We need another layer of noodles. Wide strips." She held her palms apart to show her. "Although"—Claire was in the middle of a thought—"it seems like a lot of pressure."

"People expect me to be everything no one else is, including my husband."

"He *is* a movie guy, Kitty."

"Yeah, but . . ." Kitty let herself trail off. She was talking too much.

"Rough patch?" Claire nodded knowingly before Kitty could answer. "It's natural, with all that you two have been through."

"Or maybe I'm just not bright and shiny anymore."

"Imagine how it is for the rest of us, who aren't as genetically blessed." Tomato sauce splattered on top of the noodles. "Winston works for *Playboy* now."

"How's that?"

Claire collected her thoughts as she reached for a wet noodle. "I know you make a living off your looks—"

"And talent."

"Yes, and *talent*, and I do not want to offend you, but I wonder if, as women, we're on the verge of liberation or merely building a jail we're willing to live in."

"Concerning the nudity?"

"Well, yes, but *everything*. Our own lives."

"I think it's both." For Kitty it was more of the latter, though, and Claire agreed.

"In my jail, we have rules. He knows I won't stand for cheating," Claire continued. "So as long as he's sleeping with me, I don't worry about it. My father had a mistress throughout most of my parents' marriage, and they slept in separate bedrooms."

"Did your mother know?"

Claire gestured a slap in the air. "She hit me once when I tried to address it."

"There must have been something between them to make her stay."

"Money. Her duty. Who knows? He's a pig. Countless accusations. You can't imagine."

"Accusations of what?"

Claire wouldn't answer but raised her brows like Kitty should know. "My family paid off some women—the ones they knew of, anyway. That's why he never learned his lesson. And he's a judge, so they just sweep it under the rug." Lost in thought, Claire came to with a panicked look. "Please don't tell anyone I said that."

"I wouldn't. My father wasn't a great person either. He never had anything to do with my mother and me."

"Trust me, mine has yours beat. I didn't know it, though, until I was much older. I'm thankful for that." Claire slid the lasagna into the oven and grabbed the wine. "Fifteen minutes more. Let's sit in the other room."

Walking down the hallway, Kitty discovered she was a little drunk. Her pace slowed as she looked at the photographs covering the walls. She became fixated on one of a little girl, likely Claire, sitting atop a black horse. Her legs hung halfway down the horse's belly, as did her fire-engine-red hair. At least twenty other kids stood around the horse; behind them were decorations in the trees and a table piled high with gifts.

Claire came to her side. "My fifth birthday party." If that was the definition of a birthday party, Kitty had never had one.

Claire pointed to a series of Christmas photos. In each was a massive lighted tree and presents that covered the ground and came to the very edge of the picture frame. "We had Christmas every year at my grandmother's house in North Carolina."

"What part?" Kitty was starting to feel like she didn't care if Claire was White or not; maybe they could be friends.

"Do you know it?"

"Parts."

"The land has been in my family for five generations."

"Cotton?" Kitty asked.

Claire sighed. "Such a Northerner's question. Mostly tobacco. It's a miracle some of the properties are still standing. My grandparents have a beautiful house there. It sits on a hill, back from the street—it's hard to miss. I planned to get some renovations done when my grandmother died, but I was outvoted. I don't know what condition it's in now. There's a creek behind the house; we used to climb down the hill to play there. Amazing we never got bitten by a snake."

"You sound adventurous. I wouldn't dare—"

"I was raised with my boy cousins; I had no choice." Claire pointed to a small, oval-shaped silver frame a few feet away. "This is my grandmother. Pretty, huh? My grandfather didn't deserve her."

The woman had a heart-shaped face and thick eyebrows that framed her almond-shaped eyes. She was striking.

Kitty scanned the wall. "Do you have a picture of him?"

"Hell no." Claire, it seemed, held a collective disdain for the males in her family. "Let's not ruin the mood."

On the wall near the front door was another of Claire's birthday photos.

CRYSTAL SMITH PAUL

This time, she was standing in a chair, about to blow out the candles on a massive cake in the center of the table.

"You had a birthday party every year?"

"My parents never missed a chance to have a party." Claire pointed to the wall. "That wasn't my real birthday though. *Life* magazine interviewed my grandmother, and that photo was taken for the magazine." Claire's grandmother stood next to her, dressed as though she was going to a ball. "I thought the cake was for me."

"Did she let you have any, at least?"

"As much as I wanted."

Kitty looked closer, unsure of what she thought she saw. At the far left of the frame was half of a face, half of a body, standing against the wall. It was a familiar half: the roundness of the face, the straight nose, the dried-tobacco-leaf tone. It was her mother, she thought. It was Hazel. Claire was a member of the Lakes family.

Claire was her sister.

Kitty studied Claire's face, suddenly hating it, unable to recognize even a hint of familiarity in her features. She was trained to notice these things but had somehow missed every clue. It was also her own grandmother who was interviewed in *Life*, as the founder of BabyCakes.

"Who is this?" Kitty pointed, needing final confirmation. Her palms went to her chest, as if her heart needed comfort for what was coming.

Claire looked over her shoulder. "My grandmother's maid. She cared for me when I was there every summer. She took care of my grandparents until they died. Missing her funeral is the one thing I regret about not having been home. My family's insane; I couldn't go back."

Kitty felt a knot in her stomach. "Whose funeral?"

"The maid. Hazel was her name. Breast cancer, five or six years ago now. I regret not being there. I dropped so many things when Adam died. . . . She meant a lot to me; I was devastated."

Kitty's heartbeat sounded in her ears, blood rushed to her head, and her

veins pulsed, causing her head to pound, matching its cadence. She touched
the wall to steady herself.

"Are you all right?"

Kitty jerked the front door open. Claire started patting her back and,
as it always did when she was emotionally distraught, Kitty's vomit sprayed
Claire's porch steps and bushes. "I guess I gave you too much wine on an
empty stomach." She tried to help her inside, but Kitty pushed her away,
unable to ask not to be touched.

"I feel so bad! Please, what can I do?" Claire started panicking.

"It's fine. I'm fine." She started walking toward her car.

"Wait—your purse!" Claire went inside to retrieve it.

Kitty didn't wait. She slid into her Mercedes and, with a hand smear of
vomit on the steering wheel, drove straight to Emma's.

CHAPTER 36

Kitty

Every light in Emma's house was on. A line of cars was in her driveway. Expecting the door to be open, Kitty walked in. Emma rose from the head of the dining-room table. "Kitty! We weren't expecting you."

Abigail looked up from serving the first helpings of greens. "Did I miss your call, Mrs. Tate?"

Kitty pointed at Emma. "I need to talk to you."

Emma glanced at her husband, who stood too. "Kitty, is everything all right?"

"No, no it's not, but I need to talk to my sister alone. Please." She looked around the table. She didn't recognize anyone, and they were all looking at her as if she didn't belong.

Emma hurried down the hall and led Kitty outside to the pool.

"You said we'd know if something happened."

Emma didn't have to ask what she meant. "You couldn't have gone back."

"I would have found a way."

"And I couldn't take that risk," Emma hissed.

"But I didn't get to say goodbye! I didn't get to be there for her."

Emma wouldn't back down. "No one gets to say goodbye!"

"I don't care what you and your mother do. You should have told me mine was sick."

"She didn't want you to know. She didn't want you to come back, Kitty."

Kitty knew Emma was telling the truth but hated to admit it. Tasting the sour sweet of vomit still on her tongue, she reached to turn on the hose. "Still, it was none of your fucking business to decide for me."

"I was following your mother's wishes." Emma stepped back so her mint-green dress and matching shoes wouldn't get wet from the splash on the concrete. "Honestly, I almost wanted to tell you. But I was afraid you couldn't handle it."

"*Me?* You're the one that crumbles every time the past comes back to you." Kitty wanted to hurt her now.

"I haven't made any mistakes as grave as yours."

Kitty turned the hose on her, covering part of the hole with her thumb so it sprayed directly into her face.

"Kitty, stop!" Emma tried to fight the water with her palms. Abigail came to the kitchen window and quickly left. Maybe she didn't want to get involved, or maybe she knew Emma deserved it. Kitty forced her thumb into the hose harder, until Emma screamed. "Stop! Listen to me. There's more."

Kitty removed her thumb.

"I have some things for you. Come by in the morning."

Kitty pointed at the back door. "No, now."

"They're at the bank."

Kitty raised the hose as a threat. "You swear?"

"Yes."

"Meet me there at nine." Their bank was closer to Kitty's house, some distance from Pasadena.

Emma started toward her door but stopped short. "How did you find out?"

"None of your fucking business." Meeting Claire was a coincidence that would only make Emma paranoid. "You weren't ever going to tell me, were you?"

"No."

Kitty drove home with tears in her eyes, grateful her mother had lived long enough to know she became a star, like the women in the picture shows they used to go see in Charlotte.

She parked down the street from her house for almost an hour before going inside. It was after ten, and Nathan would no doubt rush to greet her with inquiries about where'd she'd been. Her face was puffy, and she didn't trust herself not to tell him the truth should he ask her what was wrong.

"I assume you've seen all of this already." They sat outside the bank in Kitty's car.

To that, Emma confessed. "I've known who you are since we were little girls. My momma told me."

"Two of a kind. Borne of wealthy fathers with money we'll never see."

"I liked knowing we were sort of the same."

"You never said."

"I was ashamed then, just like you."

The first item was her birth certificate. The line for the father's name was blank, but a W had been written under "Race." The next document was a note dated July 10, 1937. Written on a notecard with N. M. LAKES embossed top center, was the record of a remittance of five thousand dollars to Hazel Ledbetter.

There, in black and white, Kitty learned how her entire life had been sponsored by guilt.

The other items were photos so old that lines of color were missing through the center. In the first, Hazel held the hand of a pudgy young Claire Pew. On the back was written *Shirley Claire, age 7.*

"This is my sister. We have the same father." Kitty wondered if Claire knew about the money.

"You knew her?"

Kitty shook her head. "My mother used to take care of her."

Emma, in a rare urge to touch, hugged her. Kitty stayed close despite her still-fresh disgust over Emma's yearslong silence.

The other picture was of Hazel holding Kitty as a toddler. Taken in front of their house in Winston, it was the only photo Kitty had of her mother, and the youngest image of herself. Kitty shook her head at Emma. "I don't know how to forgive you."

"You have to. I'm the only one who really knows you."

Kitty tried to pull away, but Emma wouldn't let her go. Having someone who knew Mary bore little importance to her now. Her mother's death was the last of Mary—she had no place in Kitty's future.

Emma wouldn't take any blame. "Keeping secrets doesn't make you weak. Knowing everything doesn't do anyone any good."

But the secrets made Kitty want to write. She went home imagining, as she used to, what it would have been like to grow up in that mansion with the red door. Manic to write the story she didn't yet know the ending to, she took catnaps and didn't answer the phone. She survived on popcorn and listened to Miles Davis.

Thrilled she was working, Nathan didn't ask what she was writing. He would soon regret his inattention.

After months of writing, Kitty had copies of *Down South* delivered to the producers, directors, and artists around town whose opinions could influence the popularity of an unsold project.

Sent out under the pen name Hanes Austen, it began like a fairy tale, a picturesque ode to the Old South written from the perspective of a housewife that turned into a devastating, highly critical manifesto about greed, destruction, and perversion. Knowing Nathan would reject the script's racial content outright if he knew she had written it, she intended to sway him with others' praise of the work.

The script came up at a dinner party for the birthday of the wife of a Telescope investor. A few wealthy businessmen present (all of whom were pro-integration, as a means to widen profits) were surprised it had gained popularity so quickly and were planning to bid.

"The Old South will be the topic of the year—and very marketable based on the current climate." Harry was a banker who smoked cigars in between bites of food; Blair House had leaned on him often for support over the years, for access to his political connections. His brother, Jett, who sat next to him devouring a steak, had already bid. He argued that whether you liked the film or not, or believed its assertions or not, it was compelling, essential cinema. Rumor had it their youngest brother had participated in the Freedom Rides.

"And it has a strong female character, which will appeal to all women," Harry said. "Kitty, have you thought about playing the lead?"

Kitty smiled internally to maintain a straight face.

"No, she hasn't, because no one will go see it!" Nathan raised his glass for another pour of whiskey. "As soon as word spreads about how depressing it is, it'll lose popularity. Films are supposed to suspend reality, not be a two-hour newsreel."

"Have you read it?"

"Don't need to."

"You *must*. This writer, Hanes Austen, is going places."

"Our studio has done—is doing—well with our brand of comedy, and I don't intend on rocking the boat."

"You don't want to be the only studio making nothing but fluff. Conversation is what makes change."

"I'm not here to change the world. I'm here to entertain, and I'm telling you, it won't make any money."

As expected, Nathan caved to pressure after several directors at Telescope got ahold of the script. In the end, Telescope outbid every other studio for the script. When it was time for everyone to meet the brilliant writer, Kitty confessed.

Nathan was horrified—and intrigued—by the places her mind went. "Where did you learn enough about that stuff to write about it?"

"I made it up."

"You don't write like that for me."

"You would have rejected it. Well, you *did*, until—"

He cut her off to avoid being reminded. "What do we do now?" The studio was already receiving hate mail from the announcement of the film, and Nathan didn't want those attacks turning to his wife. So, he told everyone Hanes was British and his visa had been rejected—implying that the government was seeking to avoid the controversy—which only heightened everyone's interest in the film. "They can't limit our free speech!"

Down South became Telescope's first priority, and *Daisy Lawson* was postponed, as Kitty had wanted from the beginning. Gloating that Nathan couldn't take writing credit, Kitty reminded him he would have to direct.

"Anyone else would expect to have at least one conversation with the writer." She had, of course, planned it all this way. Creating Hanes gave her power, because he mattered to the people pulling the strings.

Hanes Austen went on to have an illustrious career at Telescope. He never set foot on the lot, but his rudeness (or quirkiness, depending on who you talked to) was excused because rumor said he was a descendant of the famous novelist, Jane.

CHAPTER 37

Kitty

Winter 1966

Telescope had invited press for a private screening of *Down South*, and Claire rang the Tates' doorbell early the Saturday morning after.

"I need to see your husband."

Seeing Claire's anxious demeanor, Kitty was relieved that Nathan had already left that morning for the studio. "He's not here." Kitty knew but asked anyway, "What's wrong?"

"The film is oddly close to my family history. I need to know who the hell the writer is." She'd attended the event with her husband.

"It's a composite of Southern planter families."

"A judge in Virginia with a hefty inheritance from a tobacco family— what other family would it be?"

"The story takes place before the Civil War."

"Why are you defending this?" Claire began to yell. "In addition to the story line, every other second someone's putting a Lakes to their lips."

"You're overreacting."

"I am not. I'm going to sue Telescope—bankrupt it. I only came by first out of respect for you."

"Please, don't do that." Kitty knew she sounded desperate; the panic was sure to give her away.

Sure enough Claire paused, squinting in the sunlight. "Do you know the writer, Kitty?"

"It's not about you."

Understanding, Claire took a step back from the door. "Do you hate me or something? You used my family for your script?"

"It's not my script."

Claire was not convinced. "Kitty, you wrote the truth in fiction, things that won't be hard to connect to me. I thought we were friends. I talked to you about losing my child, about my family—more than I ever have with anyone—and you use it for your own gain?" She was stuck between disbelief and anger. "I will sue the studio to kill this picture. You won't get away with this." Claire rushed from the porch but then pivoted on her camel-hair heels hearing Kitty call after her.

"Hazel Ledbetter was my mother. She was raped in your grandmother's house when she was sixteen." Recognition fired in Claire's eyes, so she continued. "The Lakes manor is in Winston-Salem. It has a red front door; people say Nora Lakes painted it that color so her husband would know which home was his. My father's name is Theodore Tucker Lakes; they used to call him Teddy. He was a redhead when he was younger—red-red, like you. All of his brothers were. I threw up that day at your house because I saw my mother in that photo on your wall. The BabyCakes photo from the magazine."

Claire didn't speak for a long while—long enough for Kitty to fear she'd gotten it wrong.

"I can't believe it's really you," she finally said. She whispered, as though they weren't alone. "My grandmother told me about you before she died. When she got sick, she sent for me. I went down there, and she told me what my father did to your mother, what he's done to others. It rotted her insides that she couldn't support you in the way she wanted to."

"She told you that?"

Claire reached for Kitty's hands. "She loved you."

"She didn't even know me." Kitty had never been convinced Mrs. Nora knew her name. Her birthday cakes, punctured in excess with candles, had always been nameless. "Did she know I passed?"

"Now I know she suspected it. She used to tell me you were 'in the wind.' Your mother wouldn't talk about you at all. She didn't trust my family, and she was right not to." Claire put her hand on Kitty's shoulder.

Substitute the details, and America was full of such centuries-old secrets, about so-called "illegitimate" heirs to a fortune. Swept under the rug and exposed only by an overserved, bitter relative or by deathbed whispers, as in the case of Nora Lakes. Knowing Emma and others at Blair House, Kitty knew how common her narrative was, how many of these skeletons were entombed.

Kitty invited her inside to show her the photos from Emma's security box.

"I told you I used to stay with my grandparents during the summer, and I remember playing with another little girl. I used to ask your mother about that little girl, if *she* had a little girl, but she never would answer me."

Kitty didn't remember ever visiting the Lakes manor, let alone meeting Claire.

"Who else could it have been?"

"I wasn't allowed at your grandparents' house, Claire."

Claire let this sink in. "And yet your mother was still so good to them. She died before my—our—grandmother. No one knew she was sick, and she was taking care of my grandparents." Claire looked like she might cry. "Oh, I loved your mother."

"But not enough to go to her funeral," Kitty scolded.

Claire shook her head. "No one was talking to me at the time. I didn't know she was sick until after she died."

"I didn't either."

"When's the last time you spoke to her?"

"The day I left Winston. June twenty-second, nineteen fifty-five."

Claire's mouth fell open. "So I'm how you learned."

"She wanted it that way. She didn't want me to know she was sick."

"I suppose it's only right that your sister be the one to tell you," Claire said.

Unsure if she wanted an answer, Kitty stammered over her next question. "Does our father know?"

"About everything?"

"Any part."

"I honestly don't know. I haven't spoken to him in more than ten years."

Now Kitty whispered. "Did he . . . hurt you?"

"Never, but he showed me no affection at all. I went off to college and learned more about his reputation than I could handle, and we haven't spoken since. Not directly, anyway."

"Is he still in Virginia?"

"Charlottesville. He and my mother have a home there."

"I don't want them to know you found me."

"It wouldn't matter," Claire said. "They'd never admit they know about you. So release the film. Dare them to reveal themselves. They haven't got the courage."

It seemed that their grandmother, Nora Lakes, had had the courage. She sounded nothing like the woman Kitty knew through her mother's eyes. "She used to give me a birthday cake every year. Three tiers, iced by hand, just like the one in the *Life* photograph."

Claire looked away. "She never baked for us."

"It was guilt."

"That too."

"What was she like?"

"Very proper. Well read and bred. She grew up in New York. She used to put me to sleep with stories about her life."

Kitty imagined sharing a bed with Claire, listening to their grandmother's voice.

"You were close to her."

"Very. She was a storyteller, like you, and kept a diary every single day of her life. I have the volumes of her diaries in my attic. You're welcome to read them. She had a fascinating life."

"Was her family well-off too?"

"No. She grew up poor, and then poorer after her parents died."

"How?"

"They were murdered. Her father was a bootlegger. She and her sister were waitressing when she met our grandfather. He called her the 'city mouse' he took in."

"How sweet."

Claire nodded at Kitty's sarcasm. "My grandmother started with nothing—yet she died wielding the power at the head of a distinguished American family. What she lacked in pedigree she made up for in beauty and intelligence." Claire smiled. "You certainly take after her."

"Do I?"

"You have her eyes," Claire said.

"Whose?"

"Grandmother Nora."

Kitty shook her head. "I have my mother's eyes."

"Grandmother Nora had gray eyes just like yours."

"My eyes aren't gray. They're grayish-blue."

"That's pretty specific."

"I told you, I have my mother's eyes. I grew up looking at them."

"I thought your mother had dark eyes."

"No."

Claire didn't seem convinced, which made Kitty angry. "Her eyes weren't something about her you'd miss! You say you loved her, but you can't remember how unique her eyes were. Did you ever even look her in the face? *Really* look at her?"

Claire embraced her. "I was a child then too. I'm sorry for everything that's happened to you, but it's over now."

Kitty's splintered selves converged, and the flood of emotion she was trying to prevent crashed into her center. "I miss my momma."

Claire held her up against the heavy current that made her crumble to the floor.

For many reasons, they would never call each other sister, nor would they ever speak again—even after the birth of Claire's second child, a daughter she named Alison.

Claire called a few times, but after Kitty's hanging up in her ear, she stopped. At every one of her child's milestones, Kitty got a letter from Claire, saying how nice it would be for Alison to grow up knowing her aunt. Kitty never answered.

Nathan, suddenly interested in civil rights when it came to publicizing *Down South*, made sure the studio secured radio interviews, editorials, and speaking engagements at the top liberal colleges and some Ivy League universities. Kitty noticed his agitation while discussing the press tour over dinner at their favorite seafood restaurant in Malibu. "Is everything all right?"

He took a sip of his water. "I don't know how you'd feel about this, but I think we need a balanced view of the film. From Whites and Blacks."

"What did you have in mind, darling?" Kitty loved how Nathan's worldview had expanded during the filming of *Down South*. In preparation for his directorial debut, he spent many hours in the library reading books about the Civil War, slavery, and politics. When he came home one night with Frederick Douglass's autobiography, Kitty fell more in love with him.

"You—*we*—should visit some Negro colleges." He gave her a pleading look.

Kitty dipped a mussel in butter. "As long as we skip the Carolinas."

Nathan scoffed. "Right."

Down South was boycotted by Whites in the Carolinas, where Lakes tobacco was still produced. Blair House saw to it that Blacks responded with a boycott of Lakes cigarettes, which Kitty had purposely smoked in the film. It was a peculiar satisfaction, shared with the others of Blair House, though Kitty's feelings were far more sinister.

While it had been a good idea in theory, her visits to some of the prominent Negro colleges—Spelman, Morehouse, Hampton, Howard—caused protests and hot and cold reads from both White and Negro media on their appropriateness. Nathan said the controversy only made their film—and Telescope—that much more popular. He came home a month later with proof: Kitty had been nominated for an Oscar.

Kitty and Nathan arrived on the red carpet ten minutes before the theater doors closed. They had originally planned for press, but Kitty had been shaky since the morning. Nathan patted her knee as the limo made a final right turn. "Do you want some champagne? You have like two minutes."

Kitty shook her head.

"Nervous is good. That way, whether you win or lose, you're just grateful to be here."

"You're right." But Kitty wasn't nervous; she was sad. Happy to be there, but sad nonetheless. She kissed him quickly before the driver opened her door.

Photographers rushed them, but Nathan made a path through to the only reporter to whom he had promised an interview.

"Kitty, such a performance—your nomination was well deserved." A mic and camera went to her face.

"That feels amazing to hear; thank you. We worked hard to make the story come to life."

"You did—and you dressed to win tonight, I see. Who are you wearing?"

"A hand-sewn Joyce Martin." Joyce Martin was a highly sought-after dressmaker who also happened to be a member of Blair House. As she was already a solid fixture in fashion, Joyce's gowns cost several thousands of dollars and were commissioned years in advance. She only made six customs a year but had never been worn to the Oscars. If Kitty won, wearing a Joyce Martin would be making history twice.

"Oh, my. And you, Mr. Tate—"

Nathan happily took the spotlight as Kitty's gaze drifted into the camera lens. The reflection of her own eyes—an indigo blue that night—pulled her imagination through a dark hole to the other side of the camera, where her mother sat watching her live on television. She was at the Lakeses' (Hazel had never had a television), dressed in her church clothes for the special night with Mrs. Nora and Mr. Lakes, whom she'd wheeled in to join her. A physical flutter started at her breastbone, a painful wishing that her mother was still alive, just so the possibility could exist.

Winning the Oscar for Best Actress that night was the sweetest vindication of her existence, a twisted parody. The industry's acclaim was the glaze; its sweetness, bitter.

At the after-party, the women of Blair House gloated, silently passing their pride through their eyes. Some were guests, and others were staff. They hadn't operated in units around Kitty in years, but her victory was the best reason to do so. Kitty Karr was in fact the first Colored actress to win an Oscar in a lead role, and nobody would ever know it.

CHAPTER 38

Kitty

Summer 1968

The Tate household was humming along. Kitty and Nathan were back in a creative groove, having started work on a film about a set of math-prodigy twins. Heavy into directing, Nathan was happy in his creative niche. He was spending the summer doing casting calls in middle America, and she was working with the writer to button up the script. This arrangement allowed for lots of time spent with Sarah.

Sarah was flourishing in school at the elite Center for Early Education and visited Kitty's home at least once a week to swim, read books, and run around the yard. Nellie used the time to complain about Clifford, who didn't approve of the way she was raising Sarah.

"He thinks I'm spoiling her, treating her like she's White. Says she's going to have quite a fall ahead."

First he was going to leave, and then she was, and after four years they were still together because Nellie, like Kitty, so desperately wanted Sarah to be raised with two parents. Kitty was over those fantasies and felt Sarah had enough love without him.

"Why don't you move into one of the duplexes on Orange Drive?"

"*Can* we?"

"Emma would allow it."

"And what happens when the neighbors see it's just me and my little Colored daughter living there?"

"We can turn it into one house. Build a private entrance for you to drive into. People won't ever see you."

"What a solution," Nellie said.

Kitty didn't understand her sarcasm.

"When she starts school, she'll have to catch the bus from the other side of town so no one will know that she lives next door to them. She won't be able to play with the other kids in the neighborhood."

"She has her school friends."

"I don't want to be beholden to you," Nellie said. "I have a career that can support us. I don't want to rely on you for the rest of my life."

"But that was our agreement."

"So you can see her whenever you want. I can't continue bringing her here multiple times a week. This"—Nellie flung her hand around Kitty's large utility kitchen—"isn't our real life."

"You sound like Clifford."

"He's partially right."

"You're being stubborn. The house is paid for; it's in a good school district. This is about her, not us."

"*I'm* thinking of her. *You're* thinking of you."

Kitty sprung from her chair, desperate over her lack of control. "She deserves everything I didn't have." She started pacing the kitchen, putting away the peanut butter, jam, and knives they'd used to make lunch. "I worked too hard to have her growing up feeling like she's less of a human than anybody else. She's royalty, goddamn it."

After over a decade in Los Angeles, Kitty was one of the biggest actresses in Hollywood; she couldn't go anywhere without the accompaniment of a herd of photographers. She and Nathan had moved to a fortress of a home with high shrubbery, security guards, and a gate. It was in that sprawling, state-of-the-art kitchen where they now sat.

"No," Nellie said softly. "*You're* royalty. Sarah is not."

Kitty returned to the table. Even as her mouth opened to speak, she hesitated. "My father is heir to the Lakes Tobacco Corporation. I have more money than I could ever spend, and I won't have her thinking she's less than anyone else. She will have the very best of life. I don't care what I—we—have to do."

"We'll tell her when the time is right," Nellie said.

"When she's old enough."

"When it's necessary."

"We'll know."

"We'll decide."

They went back and forth as they always did—as they always would—about Sarah.

"Together," Nellie said.

Kitty warned her. "Things happen before you're ready—most times, before you know they're happening."

That was the story of Kitty's life, anyway.

CHAPTER 39

Kitty

December 1968

The morning before Christmas Eve was interrupted by a knock. Kitty opened the door to find two White men in cheap black suits. "Good day, Mrs. Tate," the blond-haired one said.

"Can I help you? Who are you? How did you get up here?"

He opened his suit jacket to show an FBI badge. Feeling her heart flutter, Kitty stepped out onto the porch and closed the door behind her. "How can I help you?"

He pulled a file from his briefcase and handed it to the older man, who was smoothing his mustache with his thumb and pointer finger. He had a salesman's grin.

Nathan opened the door behind them. "What's this about?"

"We just have a few questions for you and your wife, Mr. Tate."

"Do we need a lawyer?"

The two agents looked at each other. The older man spoke. "We believe you and your wife may have been victims of fraud. Do you know Cora Rivers?"

"Of course."

"You know her to be the operator of a charity called the Blair House?"

"The Cora I know worked for me as a film actress," Nathan said.

Kitty braced herself for questions about the house in Hancock Park and just how many members of Los Angeles's society women were pretending to be White. Her whole life flashed before her eyes as she envisioned herself and her friends being arrested.

"We'd like to talk to you about some financial matters. May we come inside?"

Nathan ushered them into the living room. Kitty started to the kitchen, but the blond-haired agent stopped her. "We'd like to speak to both of you, ma'am."

Kitty sat down, trying to hide her need to clutch the arm of the couch.

"Do you handle most of the charitable contributions your household makes, Mrs. Tate?"

"Yes."

He placed a copy of a cancelled check on the glass coffee table. "Is this your signature?"

"Yes."

He handed her another check, and another. The checks, written to Blair House and its other fake entities, dated as far back as 1955; there was a thirteen-year-long paper trail showing her support for every Negro cause since the Montgomery Bus Boycott in December 1955: the integration of schools in Little Rock, Arkansas; the sit-ins and Freedom Riders; plus ongoing support for the Democratic Party and Medgar and Martin and even funds for the arrangements for Dr. King's funeral that April. She eyed Nathan as he shuffled through the stack of cancelled checks, trying to read him.

For the next hour, the agents sought answers about these charities and about Cora, who they believed was—along with others they wouldn't name (or didn't know)—responsible for the reallocation of funds from these shell charities to the civil rights movement and, most troubling to them, the Black Panther Party.

Some of the Blair House women had long thought those donations could bring trouble, but they had continued, passionate about the struggle for Black liberation. Sure enough, it was Blair House's association with the Panthers—the target of the Bureau's larger investigation—that landed them under surveillance and, subsequently, categorized as a national threat.

At last, Nathan seemed to lose his patience. "Pardon me; I'm confused. Why are you here again? I thought you said a crime had been committed," he said.

"Yes, sir. These are dangerous people. Cora Rivers—on her own, or under instruction—has been defrauding dozens of rich families for years."

Nathan shook his head. "She's cunning, yes, but Cora poses no harm."

"Sir, Ms. Rivers had an extramarital affair with your father, is that right?"

Nathan went stone-faced. "How do you know that?"

"We're the FBI, Mr. Tate. We try to do our homework. Is that information correct?"

"Yes."

"And she left your father after his illness, did she not?"

"Yes, but in her defense, he didn't know her, or any of us, most of the time by that point."

"Yet she continued to be supported by your family."

"She had access to his accounts. They'd been together for a long time."

"And you, sir, don't think that classifies her as dangerous? Someone draining the bank accounts of a sick man?"

"Cora was abiding by an agreement made with my father that we weren't privy to."

Kitty watched Nathan spin the details of the past.

"I can't see Cora working for people like that," he went on. "She's married to a senator."

"A senator?"

"Yes, or a former senator. I'm not sure. She lives in Chicago now, I think."

The agents eyed each other. At last, the older one spoke. "Are we talking about the same person?"

"Are we?"

"Cora Rivers isn't Black?"

Disgust settled on Nathan's face. "Telescope has never hired a Black leading lady."

The agents' eyes landed on Kitty. "Have you seen Cora, the actress, recently?"

"Not in years."

The older agent slid a card across the coffee table as if he hadn't heard her. "If you do, call me first."

Nathan let them out, and Kitty braced for tense words upon his return, but he sped past her, saying he had calls to make.

Kitty couldn't discern anything from his tone, but then he didn't come to bed that night. Around midnight, Kitty found him in his study. He was in the dark at his desk and spoke as soon as she walked in, as if he'd been waiting. "You never wondered, in all these years, what Cora was doing with the money?"

Kitty was careful; she knew he knew something she didn't. "I thought I knew. I trusted her when she said it was going to help single mothers get on their feet."

"How many families?" He slurred the last word.

"I don't know."

"Did you ever meet them?"

"Yes."

"Did you ever go to the place?"

"Which place?"

"Blair House!" he yelled.

"Yes."

"When?"

"Years ago."

"Seems like you would have been more involved, seeing as you've donated nearly half a million dollars."

Kitty blinked, hearing the dollar figure. "Excuse me?"

"I looked through the bank accounts. That's what I was doing all day. I called the bank and found other checks that they didn't. You wrote a hundred or more checks to all these different charities. You know more than you told those agents. Where did that money go?"

Too many places to tell. "To the families at Blair House."

Months ago, Nathan had cautioned her about her spending. His mother had died, and in settling her estate, he had wanted to stop using checks—said it had something to do with taxes. It was the first time he'd ever mentioned Kitty's spending, and she worried her higher monthly withdrawals had been noticed. Sarah's school tuition had increased with her matriculation into kindergarten, and with the country rioting all summer following Dr. King's murder, she'd spent more than usual. She'd studied him carefully for days, looking for any change in behavior or indication that he knew more than he should. Only when she woke to an envelope full of spending money on her vanity table did she relax, realizing he didn't care how she spent money, he just wanted it to be impossible to trace. *Tell me before you run out.*

He didn't have that cavalier attitude now. He swiped a pile of papers, writing pads, folders, and scripts onto the floor. "You're lying to me! They know it, and they'll be back with more questions."

Kitty was unsure of how to untangle herself. He knew more; she could feel it. Still in a rage, he yanked a row on his bookshelf to reveal a safe. Inside was a stack of thirty or more oversized brown envelopes. He flung some at her. "Every time you see her, I do too."

Kitty's hands were shaking as she opened the first envelope. Inside were pictures of Sarah and Nellie's visit just three days ago, to exchange Christmas presents. In the second were pictures of her swimming with a fat-legged, toddler-aged Sarah in their pool.

"You took away my choice to be a father. You took away my chance to be in her life."

"I did it to protect her."

"I'm your husband. I would have protected you both. It's my job."

"How long have you known?"

"For some time."

She wanted to relish in the memories the photos conjured (she didn't have any photos of Sarah, for obvious reasons) but was bothered by his deception. "You had me followed?"

"At first for security, but then I found out she was alive, and I wanted to see her all the time."

At Nathan's request, her whole life had been documented. Spying first became a practice of his to build a case against Cora in the matter of his father's funds. Meeting the Negro boy outside the premiere of *The Misfits* had only fueled it. Nathan hired him to follow and photograph Telescope's stars, pictures which he then sold to the media to increase his actors' exposure. The young man's photos were never credited, but Nathan paid him well, far above what any White newspaper photographer would make. Later, his photos were used in Maude's celebrity column at the *Los Angeles Times*.

Photos of Kitty sold well, and soon Nathan wanted the young photographer to follow her exclusively. It was lucrative, but also, Nathan had always been obsessed with Kitty. To Nathan, she was even more beautiful when she didn't know she was being admired. He hid it from her well, having the luxury of Michael's lens. What Kitty didn't know was that the safe had a drop bottom where even more photos of her were stored.

"Why didn't you say anything?" Kitty said. She wasn't sure if she was terrified or delighted by his restraint. His deception served only himself. "I had to ensure her safety. It had nothing to do with you, Nathan. I lost her too. She doesn't know I'm her mother."

"You made the decision to take her from me. From both of us."

"How was I to know that you'd accept her, that you'd accept me?"

He turned as red as a beet. "Because I fucking *love you*, that's why! I lied to the FBI for you. I won't let this ruin everything we've built. I can fix this, but you *must* stop what you've been doing."

"Nathan—"

He held his hand up. "You have responsibilities as an employee of Tele-scope, as a wife, as a *mother*—none of these roles support your participation in politics. You're not to spend another dime helping any of these pointless crusades."

"We're talking about people's lives!"

"What about *our* lives? I've given you everything, made you a star."

"*I* made me a star. And you, too, since we're being honest."

Nathan moved swiftly in her direction. She flinched. She didn't expect to be hit, but his anger was startling; she'd never seen him so enraged. "I own the sky in which you shine, and you're going to do what I say."

"I make my own money. Support for the cause is needed now more than ever." While Kitty had no intention of crossing back over the color line, the reality that she could be pushed suddenly didn't seem as scary as it once had.

"If you continue this, they're going to find out about you. About Cora. About *all* of you. And I won't be able to protect you. They want to end the Black Panther Party—cut off its finances, jail every member."

"They don't suspect me. I can continue supporting the cause."

"Our daughter should be enough of a cause for you. We could both end up in jail. Then what?"

"You're not going to jail, Nathan."

"*You* could—and what would I do without you?" His voice cracked and got higher on the end, as it did when he was choking back emotion. She reached for him, hating to see him in pain, but he stepped back before she could touch him.

"I'll do what I can to fuel the phantom Negro Cora Rivers theory, but you have to listen to me." He was still exasperated. "They don't know about those other checks yet, and we have to appease them so they stop digging. They follow the money, and you've left quite a footprint. Any legal issues and we could lose everything. We have to protect our daughter and her inheritance. *Everything* is at stake. I need you to listen to me. For once."

"I'll do what's best for my family. That's what I've always done."

"That's what you think you've accomplished here? We never would have been in this mess had you not lied about the simplest of things."

"People are dying—have died—all over the country for the simplest of things. For the right to be, to exist!"

"And *they* aren't *you*."

Now Kitty was the one who yelled. "They *are* me! You'll never understand what it's like. You just see a pretty face, your Kitty Karr star—you don't know the truth about me, where I come from. You don't know how it feels to be ashamed of who you are, to hide parts of yourself, to carry hate for people who say they love you."

"Do you hate me?"

Tears sprang in his eyes when she shrugged. He was the only one who had ever been free: a White, rich man, he owned everything, just as he'd said. He could go anywhere without restrictions.

He was quiet for a long while and then went to her, pulling her close. "Perhaps pretending not to know was easier for me too."

Relieved that he didn't ask anything more, she gave in to his pleas, which were later reinforced by what she learned from the others at Blair House.

The two agents had knocked on Kitty's door at roughly the same time as two others arrived at Lucy's. She and Laurie had been making a fruit cake.

Lucy was high on their list because a few of the charity accounts were in her name. Once she proved the account signatures weren't hers and that she hadn't seen Cora in years, they ended the interview.

No one at Blair House had. Cora had changed her name twice by then, married a senator, and moved to D.C.—not Chicago—three years before the FBI showed up.

The signatures on the account and deposit slips belonged to Laurie, whom neither agent had acknowledged. She listened for a while, as an invisible party, and then slipped away to put everyone on notice before they'd even left.

Word circulated of their theory in the following week.

"Maude said they're on the hunt for a Negro girl, so . . . I'm worried," Lucy said.

Kitty didn't say what or who had given them that idea. When some Panthers, only a long drive away from LA, were killed, Liberty, Addie, Lilly, and Sammie left Los Angeles as if they were fleeing a lynch mob. Eighteen hours later, the house they were hiding in was raided, and they were all charged with crimes against the United States.

At least they didn't shoot them.

Might as well. They're going to jail for life.

That's not dead.

Might as well be.

CHAPTER 40

Elise

Tuesday evening, October 31, 2017

Elise sat on the Perch with a bottle of champagne and small bites from the caterers, attempting to rally for the occasion. Though it was arguably dangerous, the invincibility of youth had always pulled Elise and her sisters there to greedily observe the happenings of their parents' parties long after they were sent to bed.

Sarah had promised to dial down the extravagance, but Elise saw no evidence of that. Their backyard looked like a carnival. It was only the best for the family's closest hundred, which included living legends, sparkers of cultural phenomena, budding icons, and reserved masters with extreme intelligence and talent from every discipline and creative arena, from all over the world. The epic fete would go until dawn and boasted a candy treasure hunt, a haunted maze, costume awards, a movie, and a full dinner as standards.

There was already a line around the main tent where, inside, guests could pet lion cubs, exotic birds, and monkeys. Giant edible gummy bears, lollipops, and chocolate bunnies and bears were strung up in the hedges of the labyrinth, likening it to a scene from *Willy Wonka and the Chocolate Factory*. In the center of the maze, Sarah's bench had been replaced with a giant jack-in-the-box candy dispenser. You could only keep what you caught, but the supply was endless.

The Ferris wheel was well oiled and spinning without a hitch, happy to be on display. Its beauty would grace social media all night as the preferred backdrop for everyone's photos. Elise wondered if the white spoke lights could be seen down the hill that cloudless night, or if they blended in with the stars, seemingly unmoving, an unknown celestial gem.

"Everything looks great." Giovanni crawled through the window, interrupting her thoughts. She secured her flat-ironed hair into a low bun as the wind started blowing it across her face.

"It always does."

"She went for the gusto." Noele straddled the windowsill, gesturing for Elise to open the champagne. She passed a glass to Giovanni to hold for the pour.

"Sounds like you're happy she did."

"I'm excited about my costume." As a kid, Noele would sometimes appear at breakfast dressed as Santa Claus in the middle of July. That year, she and Giovanni coordinated: Giovanni would be Neve Campbell in *The Craft*, and Noele was a black bird with a ten-foot wingspan. She'd had the wings made with real ravens' feathers.

Noele eyed Elise's sweats. "You don't look close to ready."

Two weeks ago, Elise had planned to be a lion. Her curly-coily hair displayed the reddish hue that 23andMe attributed to distant Irish blood and was a perfect dupe for a mane. Everyone expected her to win the costume contest for the fifth year running.

Elise didn't answer her sister as the extended, party version of their mother's laugh rose to their ears. She was in the center of a crowd, gesturing to her face paint, explaining, Elise figured, how many hours it had taken to create her unicorn costume. Her horn, secured to the top of her head, was twelve inches long and covered in silver glitter. She wore a tight silver sequined floor-length gown to match.

She was in full celebrity mode, touching the hand or arm of each person she spoke to, giving them a split second of intense attention. She had a way of making everyone feel as though they were the most important, interesting person in the world. Some said she stared, but if you knew her, you understood her interest was a compliment—most people she looked right through.

"We should finish getting dressed." Giovanni adjusted the straps of her black bodysuit. "She's making her way down for the cake." Giovanni looked at Elise and spoke with obvious insistence. "You'll be down once Aaron arrives?"

"He's here already." She didn't point him out, but Aaron had come as Count Dracula, with Maya dressed as Cookie Monster. Both were expertly disguised, but had given sneak peeks of their costumes on Instagram.

"Is Jasper coming?" Giovanni asked with a sly look.

"I hope so. We have a lot to talk about."

"I bet."

"The shoot is Friday."

Noele had seen him but hadn't met him. "He's fine."

"That he is," Elise said.

"He flew cross-country to talk about the shoot you're not even shooting here. He likes you. And you like him too."

She did, but didn't know what to think of him now. "He came for the photo of Kitty by the pool," Elise explained, "not for me. I was a 'side benefit.'"

"Who invited him?" Noele asked.

"His grandfather worked at Telescope."

"That's random."

"Yes, it is." She tried to keep a neutral face.

"Must be fate," Giovanni said.

"I thought you liked Aaron," Elise said.

"*I* do, but I'm not sure you do . . ." Giovanni looked at Noele for backup.

"Stop being stubborn and come to the party."

"I'm in mourning." Elise would rather plunge off the Perch than be subjected to a barrage of inquiries.

"Mom is going to be pissed. People will talk."

"They're already talking. She doesn't care."

"What do we say?" Noele asked. "When people inquire about your absence?"

"Jewish people sit shiva for at least seven days. Sometimes a month."

"We aren't Jewish."

"We don't know who or what we are. Theoretically." By any chance set of circumstances, Kitty's story could have been lost forever. Despite their positioning in life now, they were descendants of American slaves, and their ancestors' records were hard to find and vaguely recorded, the oral histories long gone.

"Clearly you need to have some fun." Giovanni didn't know how foreign a concept "fun" sounded to Elise at the moment. The last time she'd had it was seven months ago, with Jasper. Her sisters left her then, to head down for the grand entrance in which she was supposed to partake.

Sarah floated down to the second level, where a Lucite stage covered their pool. Her hair had a few extensions that hung almost to her waist and blew in the wind, upping the drama of her costume. Sarah's hair had always been long; she never got anything more than a trim because hair, as in most Black families, was a beauty mark. When Sarah wore hers back, her almond-shaped eyes made her look somewhat Asian, causing inquiries about her ethnicity. *It says "Negro" on my birth certificate,* she'd reply. The inquirer's discomfort with her use of the word ensured the line always got a laugh.

Alison was behind her, dressed as a sexy lion tamer (to complement Elise's planned costume), with fishnet stockings and long, fake red nails. James ascended the stage behind them. "Welcome, everyone!" He strutted on stage in his black tux, winking and pointing into the crowd at, Elise knew, no one in particular. He couldn't see past the glare of the spotlight; his eyesight was failing, which he used as an excuse to smoke more weed. He was the only one who could get away with not wearing a costume; anyone else who arrived in plain clothes or dressed off-theme was turned away. The tux was a private protest of the event itself but, ever loyal to Sarah, publicly said he was the ringmaster.

"How is everyone doing?" he said. "It's been a rough year, I know, but we're still here." He always gave a speech at parties, as if people needed a reminder of who their hosts were. Like her mother, he was his most pleasant self in celebrity.

He pulled his wife close and began to sing "Happy Birthday" in her ear. Sarah closed her eyes, nestling her face against his. To the world that would see the pictures later, they looked in love, suggesting that their rumored troubles were over.

The crowd joined in as waiters carried a three-tiered lemon cake with lemon cream cheese frosting, as it was every year, to the stage. Elise's sisters trailed them like a parade.

Sarah blew out what appeared to be a hundred candles, to the crowd's uproar. To avoid conversations about age, the cakes were always exorbitantly lit but never had numbers.

Elise took a picture and captioned it HBD MOM on Instagram, to document her presence. Framed through the leaves, her mother looked angelic with her hands clasped at her chin. The post got more than a million likes in a minute. A refresh of her feed showed Aaron's repost of her post as a story. He was still on his phone at the edge of the dance floor, presumably texting Maya, who was at the bar. Elise had seen them separate just before the cake. He still hadn't texted *her*.

The traditional birthday song morphed into Stevie Wonder's version, and the whole backyard started clapping and singing along as if they were at a concert. Elise scanned the crowd for the real singers, waiting for them to take over, craving peer attention.

Billie stood out under the pole light on the left side of the stage, with her round face painted bronze like a penny. She was the circus admittance token. When Elise was growing up, Billie was always the first one at the piano, ready for a duet of one of her hit songs with the singer who'd recorded it. She had a great voice too. Billie wasn't clapping or singing that night. Her beady eyes were on Sarah as she twirled about.

Elise wondered what secrets Kitty had left her friends with. Her scan for Lucy and Maude was soon interrupted by a text from Jasper: I'M HERE. WHERE ARE YOU?

She texted back without a second's delay: MEET ME ON THE PATIO.

Elise hoisted herself through the window and ran to her closet, where she threw on a black dress and wrangled her unstyled coils back into a bun. To avoid being recognized, she put on the peacock-feathered masquerade mask tacked to her bulletin board that she'd worn some years before.

Expecting her to approach from the party, Jasper stood with his back to the patio doors. Prince was blaring, and she was able to get right up next to him before he noticed. He wore a werewolf mask.

"A mythical choice."

"Your mom is a unicorn, so I'm on theme. You, however—" He gestured to her mask and plain dress.

"Come on." They went down the stairs, past the bar stand and clusters of the animal kingdom.

"Is your boyfriend—excuse me, fiancé—here?" Jasper asked.

"He's not either."

"But is he here?"

"He was earlier, with his girlfriend."

"You know *Vogue* is pulling wedding dresses for your cover."

She stopped walking. "Is that what you flew for five hours to tell me?"

"You know why I'm here." Jasper pulled the back of her dress as they approached the border of their yard. "Where are we going?"

She gently pushed a cluster of vines aside to reveal the third opening through the hedges. "To get your photograph."

He didn't let go even after they'd turned onto Kitty's dirt path, lit every six feet or so by a staked bulb.

"Your mother looks like a fairy tonight. A unicorn fairy."

Elise chuckled. "That's Tinker Bell, always sparkling and floating about."

Jasper questioned her sarcasm. "Sore subject?"

"I don't think we should be partying, is all."

"I can see that."

"But no one can tell my mother anything."

"Well, she is Sarah St. John."

Elise smiled. "I'm aware."

"Are you close?"

"Close enough, but we were raised by our grandma." Stern and chocolate-skinned, Nellie had tempered the decadence of their environment with the heavy hand of Black Southern rearing. "My parents worked a lot."

"Your dad's mom?"

"My mother's. She kept our heads screwed on straight."

Nellie gave them chores, forbidding the house staff to do anything for them but cook. Straight As were expected, and they were kept busy with extracurricular activities, as if it were possible to skip over the part where they realized their hierarchal position in the world. Nellie raised her granddaughters sensibly—fairy tales weren't real, and neither was Santa Claus or the Tooth Fairy.

Elise mimicked her voice. "*You may be fortunate, but you're still Black.*" Now Elise revered her as a saint for stepping in the way she did. While limiting, her rigidity was her way of loving, of protecting the girls from any confusion or wishful thinking about their classification in the world. She did her best to save their mother.

Jasper sounded surprised. "Sounds like my grandma."

"Yeah, Kitty was a nice break."

Nellie had reared them with good manners and sensibilities, but Kitty sprinkled their lives with magic. She let them eat ice cream for dinner, baked them elaborate, tiered cakes for their birthdays, and bought them too many presents to count. Now Elise mimicked Kitty. "*The world could use more little spoiled Negro girls.*"

"She said 'Negro'?"

"She didn't mean anything by it; it's just the word she was used to using."

"I guess she did live through a lot of history."

"Existed right in the center of it." Elise kicked a rock. "Until cancer took her too."

"Too?"

"My mom's mom died of cancer when I was twelve."

Jasper paused and then, "I'm sorry to bring up bad memories."

She opened Kitty's front door, where his photograph sat against the wall.

"That's what nine thousand dollars gets me? A spot on the floor?"

"You left your nine thousand dollars here."

She gave him a look. "Tell me about the photo, Jasper."

"Nathan and Kitty." He showed her a black-and-white photograph on his phone of a couple kissing in a parking lot. He gestured for her to swipe. "My grandfather took these, and in exchange for them, Nathan offered my grandfather a job taking photographs of Telescope stars that he would then sell to the papers. When he discovered Kitty was Black, he had to decide whether to tell Nathan or not."

He paused as if he'd been practicing for her reaction. She ignored his cliff-hanger and kept scrolling as directed. All the photos were shot in the long-lens style, like the ones inside the dated envelopes Kitty left, but these were ones she'd never seen before.

One was of a very pregnant Kitty, being pushed in a wheelchair around the neighborhood by her grandma Nellie. The two shot through a window in Kitty's old house showed her cooing over an infant. Finally, there was one of Nellie and a baby, wrapped in a blanket, leaving Kitty's with a tall Black man; Elise recognized him as her grandma Nellie's estranged husband. Her mother hadn't seen him since she was in the second grade.

Elise pretended to be unimpressed. "What do these prove?" The photos were in black and white, so Kitty's true color was invisible, as it was in real life, and the baby was mostly covered by cotton. Kitty could have been giving her child up to an adoption agency.

"In isolation, nothing. However"—he pointed to the ground—"this color photograph is the other half of a photo I have that shows your mother at age two or three with Kitty. It was the photograph my grandfather showed to Nathan as proof that your mother was his child. Nathan cut it in half, not knowing my grandfather had a second copy." Elise's pulse thudded in her ears and chest, panicked by this complication. "My book is about my grandfather, but it's about you and your family too. He kept copies of everything."

"Pictures never tell the whole story."

"My grandfather's do. He followed Kitty all the time and saw it all with his own eyes, took photographs of every moment. He kept her secret for four years, knowing what telling could mean for her life. But then he had to consider what it would mean for him if Nathan found out he knew and didn't tell him. He had to think of his family and his livelihood."

"And what about me and mine? I can't let you tell this story. I'll understand if you want to pull out of *Vogue*."

"Elise, you've misunderstood. This isn't just Kitty's story. It's my grandfather's too. I have a legal right to it. My grandfather owned his photographs, and I own his estate."

"All your pictures show is my grandma Nellie bringing her baby, my mother, to meet her best friend. That's all."

"You know I can disprove that. I'm offering you the chance to tell Kitty's side of it. If not, it'll be told through my grandfather's lens, which—I'll be honest—doesn't paint the most favorable picture."

"And why is that? Because he never got his chance with her?"

"He wasn't ever convinced Kitty was sorry for what she'd done."

"Sorry for what? She didn't have a choice."

"We always have a choice; we only say we don't to soothe our conscience from what we're capable of."

"You don't understand what she did. What it means. She didn't purposely hurt people."

"You've never considered how Kitty's decision hurt you? How it hurt your mother?"

"It's all I've been able to think about. She left everything for me to find after she died."

Jasper's eyes crossed and skittered around. "Wait—you *just* found out? Why won't you talk about it?"

"Have you ever stopped to consider that perhaps Kitty doesn't want her story told?"

"Then why would she leave it to you like she did?"

"She wanted us to know our history."

"Then you owe it to her to tell her truth."

"It's still the truth if no one knows."

He tucked the photograph under his arm. "Except in my truth, it looks like she took the easy way out by passing."

She choked on his simple but common opinion, hacking as though she was going to regurgitate a hair ball. Alarmed, Jasper hit the center of her back with his palm. "Bitter pill?"

She pushed his arm as he went to do it again.

"You know this is what your grandmother wanted."

"What? To have her story distorted? To be judged by people who don't know what she went through? She hurt so much, and she triumphed anyway. I can't let you destroy her legacy."

"Then help me tell her story." He moved to the door. "I'll see you Thursday."

"Wait."

He looked back.

"Who else knows about this?"

"My family."

"Not your publisher?"

"I wanted to talk to you first."

"So, you did want my permission."

"No, I want your help. Your support."

Elise felt even more conflicted. Why had Kitty kept this secret for so long? It couldn't just be because she was really Black. Even twenty years ago, Kitty's story might have been celebrated. In the fifties, the sixties, and even the seventies, Elise understood her choices, but after leaving the business, there was no life-or-death reason for Kitty to continue the façade. Unless there was.

CHAPTER 41

Elise

Wednesday early morning, November 1, 2017

Sarah was eating alone at the kitchen island, still in her costume. Though it was after three, she was unruffled; even her lipstick had crisp lines and was still a rich burgundy. She reminded Elise of Kitty then, even though they didn't really look alike. They had the same oval face and slightly-larger-than-normal ears, but there was no glaring marker of their relation. Vanity was their genetic link.

She didn't look up as Elise sat down. Sarah never ate while hosting, preferring to reminisce about the night over a meal. She normally would have asked Elise if she was hungry, inviting her to recap the night, but she was still angry. Elise could see her cheek twitching between bites of pulled chicken and hummus from her saucer-sized plate.

"You weren't going to ever tell us, were you?"

Sarah remained silent so long Elise repeated herself.

"Do your sisters know?" Sarah said.

Elise shook her head.

"She put it on all those recordings she left?"

Elise hesitated; she didn't trust her mother to know all the details just yet. "Something like that."

"She would drop this bombshell and leave the questions for me to answer."

"You could have just told us a long time ago."

"It caused me a lot of pain finding out Kitty was my mother. Seeing how close all of you were to her, I knew how it would make you feel." Sarah dropped her head between her palms. "I miss her so much, but her death— God, strike me down for feeling this way—it relieved me from the heaviness I've felt my whole life."

Tears streaked down her bronzed cheeks. She seemed embarrassed to cry but wasn't in control of it anymore.

In a gesture that surprised them both, Elise got up to hug her.

"How did you find out?"

"She came to the hospital when you were born, broke down crying, and just blurted it. Your grandma Nellie was furious. They started arguing, and Kitty left. Your grandma tried to tell me everything she knew but having just had you, I didn't want to hear it. I couldn't empathize with Kitty's decision to give me up."

Elise challenged this. "But you didn't really want kids." Her mother's admission on a public stage had felt like betrayal, because they would have drowned in the cocoon of extremity had it not been for their grandma Nellie and Kitty who, like a fairy godmother, took the reins after Nellie's death.

"I wasn't *itching* for motherhood but, Elise, when you came into this world, you were *mine*."

"You were seldom around."

Both Nellie and Kitty had begged Sarah to work less, but neither challenged her or forced her to listen. They just continued picking up the slack with her children. Sarah ate dinner at home maybe twice a month but always returned with gifts. After a long absence, she'd pick them up early from school for a trip to Disneyland, or surprise their class with an ice cream truck. One time they went on a hot-air balloon ride. She was the perfect mother in these moments—attentive, generous, and gregarious—but they didn't happen often and after Grandma Nellie died, never. There was cruelty in her rejection. Sarah didn't suffer her ambivalence about mother-hood in silence.

"I could have done things differently, but I think you can now understand how demanding acting can be. I was booked for *years*, Elise. But coming home to you and your sisters was always my greatest joy." She paused before a bit of comedic relief. "Cut me some slack. Fuck—I labored for what felt like days to have you naturally, only to find out I couldn't."

Elise scrunched her face, knowing the rest. Sarah's hip bones never adjusted for delivery; she'd had an emergency C-section and then two more, and had the keloid scars to prove it.

"So, to go through hell for none of the joy? I couldn't understand it. I don't see how she couldn't have kept me."

"What did Grandma Nellie say?" Elise sat down next to her.

"She left it alone. She understood my anger and respected my decision when I refused to see Kitty, or let her see you, until your first birthday party. She only saw you then because she crashed your party, knowing I wouldn't make a scene."

Picturing it, Elise emitted a sad giggle.

"She started showing up more to see Nellie. We just tried to be as polite to each other as possible."

"You never talked about it again?"

Sarah looked regretful. "She tried several times, but I didn't see the point. I tried to repair our relationship when my mother died, but Kitty wouldn't leave it alone."

Elise remembered her mother and Kitty going shopping and out to lunch in the months after Grandma Nellie died. These outings quickly drew paparazzi attention, and their sitcom, cancelled in 1979, was put back in syndication. Soon after, Sarah started another film and detached again.

"I thought we could have a relationship, but being around her always ended up making me angry."

"You never suspected it until she told you?"

Sarah chuckled. "I've asked myself that many times."

Elise *had* suspected something. She could never name it—and never would have guessed the truth—but had always sensed there was something more behind Nellie and Kitty's bickering. Sometimes it was over *Jeopardy!* or a board game, but the underlying quarrel always centered on their dueling philosophies about raising the girls. They argued about everything: how they liked their oatmeal prepared, what their favorite books and colors were, how they liked to wear their hair. It made Elise—who, as the oldest, was the only one with an accurate pulse on her sisters' picky and abrupt changes in preference and interest—nervous. There were many times she wanted to correct one or both of them, only to sit back, feeling their argument wasn't about the thing they said it was.

The polarities, Sarah admitted, had inflicted an undercurrent of sadness that left her confused about her place in the world. "I had the mother who raised me and the one who gave me this incredible life that everyone dreams of. One was White and the other was Black. My Black mother was comfortable thanks to my rich White mother. When my mother died, I felt disloyal for loving Kitty so much. I wanted Kitty's attention and to please her in a way I never felt the need to do with my own mother."

"She was a star. You looked up to her."

"I've often felt she gave me this life as an apology," Sarah said. "As if fame and wealth would surpass any possible longing for what I missed."

"Did it?" Elise said.

"Until I found out she was my mother." Her tone changed. "I should be grateful. There are millions of talented Black women. Kitty gave me my start, and the sad truth is she only had the opportunity—to make things better for her kin—because she pretended to be White. So I kept Kitty's secrets, because of what was at stake. Our livelihoods, and thus our lives, were on the line."

Elise nodded, understanding the dilemma. Sarah pushed her plate to the side and began to swivel James's gold wedding ring, which was on her left thumb. He always gave it to her before departing for the studio, to avoid the risk of scratching it and his equipment. When her hand began to shake, Elise reached for her.

"Mom, we don't have to talk about this anymore. But I do have to tell you something," she started, but Sarah stopped her.

"Let me finish. The night she died, I got this urge to go see her. I laid next to her and held her hand." Sarah wiped her eyes. "About an hour or so later, she stopped breathing. I could feel the air leave the room." Sarah teared again. "I should have come earlier. You were right."

"I was so angry at you. I thought you missed it."

"You're always so angry at me. But don't you remember? I woke you."

Elise's grief had made her forget.

"Mom, we're going to have to tell people about Kitty."

Sarah shook her head so hard, the horn, secured with dozens of bobby pins, finally shifted. "The safest thing is leaving her White."

"'Safest'? She didn't commit a crime."

"It could be argued that what Kitty did was fraud, and if that happens, your inheritance could be in jeopardy."

"No one would dare make that case and open the studio up to that kind of scrutiny. They'd all look like racists. Can you imagine? The boycotts, the hashtags?"

"Elise, there are some things that are just best left unsaid, unspoken. The more things change, the more they stay the same. People don't like to be reminded of their shame. You'll be at the center of a controversy you can't stop."

"It wouldn't be a controversy—"

"You see how they've been acting now! We can talk about her being my mother and your grandmother, but not that she was Black."

Elise was puzzled. "How do we get around that?"

"We'll say Kitty had an affair, and I'm the product of it. She gave me up for adoption, told everyone I was dead. But she can't be Black."

"So tarnishing her reputation is better?"

"Kitty wanted to be White. Die White."

"She told you that?"

"Well, she didn't give up her Whiteness for me."

"She had to protect herself then—her money, her name."

"And so do you. It isn't worth gambling your Oscar over. You see Kitty didn't."

"I don't care about winning."

"You don't mean that."

Elise confessed that the only reason she had even entertained lobbying to win a nomination was to honor Kitty. "She thought *Drag On* was my best performance yet. She's no longer here to say congratulations if I do win, so who cares?"

Her mother looked pained to hear it. "I do. Your father and I do."

"But it wasn't acting Kitty cared about. She only cared because of who she really was and what it meant. What it would mean, right now, for people to know the truth. It wasn't about winning."

"What makes you think Kitty wanted her legacy reduced to a stereotype? She'll be painted as the tragic mulatto. I'll be the poor little rich girl with adoption issues, and you, my dear, will be given no credit at all for who you are and what you've become. They'll say you don't deserve it, I don't deserve it, and Kitty didn't deserve it because she lied, ignoring the fact—which is what they won't want to hear—that she was forced to. Kitty isn't special. Hers is just one American story; there are countless others just like it."

"That's what's important."

"They won't understand."

"We should try. She wanted us to."

"She's dead. She doesn't have a say."

Elise crossed her arms. "I don't think she wanted *you* to have a say. But it's not up to either one of us anymore. That's what I came to tell you." Elise came to her point, knowing Sarah would be upset she hadn't led with it.

"My *Vogue* photographer knows about Kitty—it's the subject of his next book."

Sarah tapped her taupe nails on the counter. "What does he think he knows?"

"That Kitty was Black, and you are her daughter."

"There's no way he can prove that. There's a record of my death; it's been documented in interviews."

Sarah's cheek twitched as Elise relayed what Jasper had told her. "Jasper's grandfather saw it."

"He's dead." Sarah waved her hand. "I think you can handle Jasper."

"Mom, it's his story too."

"Give him another story, Elise. There are many sides to the truth."

"But what if Kitty wanted people to know she was Black?"

"She would have told them herself. She wouldn't have left it up to you, my dear."

"But she kind of did. Kitty would have explicitly requested our silence had she wanted it. She waited to tell when she would have no control over the outcome. Why?"

"Because she was dramatic."

"I thought you weren't mad at her anymore?"

"I'm not mad at Kitty." Sarah clenched her teeth. "I'm mad that she had no choice but to do what she did. I'm mad that her having no choice impacted me in the ways it has. Unleashing this story exposes the White roots that burrow, snake, and choke. I don't want to be choked. Not a word to anyone."

Elise left the room to avoid the fight scene she knew all too well, the one that would end with Sarah crying about how her children loved Kitty (and Nellie) more than her. Elise couldn't speak for her sisters but, in that moment, she might have asked her mother to consider how she could possibly feel otherwise.

CHAPTER 42

Kitty

Spring 1969

The new normal in the Tate house made Sarah a topic of daily conversation. Nathan loved looking at her pictures, imagining the moments they never had as a family. Some of the secrets were gone, but the truth had been romanticized and glossed over with the threat of the law. They both wanted to live as close to the fantasy as their imaginations would allow.

Nathan was always looking for parts of himself in Sarah. So Kitty indulged him in details about their daughter's personality, the funny things she did and said that couldn't be ascertained from a photo, like how she hated foods with a skin. "Apples?"

"Nellie has to peel them."

She liked to swim, and at four and a half was reading at a second-grade level. Nathan bought her boxes of books, which Kitty rationed to Nellie over several months. "She doesn't want her spoiled."

"I've been thinking," he said one night as he pulled back the bedcovers for her to climb in. "How about we reformat Daisy Lawson for television?"

Kitty groaned. "Television is brutal . . . I'd rather just write it." Kitty dotted on her eye cream.

"Remember, Daisy develops a close friendship with her neighbor, the nurse, and her daughter. If we cast Sarah as the neighbor's daughter, would you do it?"

"An *interracial* show?"

"We could keep her close."

Kitty touched his cheek. "Close to *you*, you mean."

"I grew up on the lot. It only seems fair that my daughter should too. Maybe she has her mother's talent."

"Don't call me that." Kitty shrugged. "We can always get her acting lessons."

"Talk to Nellie about it."

"I will." Kitty opened her face cream jar.

"She can never know we're her parents," Nathan said.

Kitty looked over at him. "When she's old enough, Nellie and I decided we'd tell her."

"No. No one can know. What if it gets out? We have a business—*you* are a business—and I'm not sure how the FBI or the world will adjust to finding out the truth about you."

"The FBI—they aren't concerned anymore. Besides, telling our daughter is different than telling the world."

"Kitty, have you ever considered how she'll feel, learning we let the world think she was dead because she was too dark?"

His rationale hit her like a dart. She panicked, reevaluating her original assumption that she'd be able to explain, and Sarah would someday understand, as she had come to understand her own mother's reasons. It was love, but Nathan's perspective made it ugly. "We don't have to make those decisions for quite some time," Kitty said. "She wouldn't understand now."

"She'll never understand," Nathan said. "That's the thing about lies; you have to keep them alive."

———————————

Kitty and Nathan's largest conspiracy, beyond the resurrection of Telescope or dodging the FBI, was the crafting of their daughter's future. Kitty's loyalty shifted at last from her race and, for the first time, rested solely with Nathan. His knowledge of Sarah was their secret, one she would keep from everyone—especially Nellie, who she feared would feel threatened by it.

Nellie agreed to allow Sarah to join *The Daisy Lawson Show* but maintained control over Sarah's school schedule. As the show's writer and star, Kitty gave herself a lot of camera time with Sarah, so she could help her with her acting. Sarah often found her way to Kitty's dressing room or onto her lap during rehearsals, and Kitty indulged in her affections in those moments, but off set she was physically distant, out of respect for Nellie. Kitty deferred to Nellie in all decisions unless it affected the show and, later, Sarah's career.

The demands of the show had ended their private home visits, but quietly, and in plain sight, Kitty and Nellie coparented. Nellie controlled the day-to-day, while Kitty told Nathan which strings to pull, aiming to secure Sarah a career.

The Daisy Lawson Show became a hit, and the cast and crew became a family. Lucy was the makeup artist, and Nellie was there every day as Sarah's chaperone. Nathan rarely came to set, inciting rumors that he didn't expect or want the show to last because of its interracial nature. They let people think what they wanted. Anything was better than the truth.

Kitty knew he stayed away because of Sarah, fearing that if he got too close, he'd be unable to resist smothering her with a thousand kisses.

Instead, he watched her from the hidden observation room built into the ceiling of the filming stage. At the request of Abner Tate, one of these rooms had been constructed into every sound stage on the lot. Hailed as a genius, Abner Tate had been a controlling lunatic who spied on his employees from a bird's-eye view. It was how he knew the rumors before they started, how he kept the upper hand.

Engaging in such spying was also the best advice Nathan had ever received from his father. Nathan spent his first weeks at Telescope out of sight, giving orders by phone, watching the daily happenings go on without him, moving like a sleuth in the shadows. It was from one of these observation rooms, above stage C, that Nathan had first spotted Kitty. She was the reason he'd issued the memo encouraging staff members to attend tapings. He knew she would come. He wanted a wife. Her talent was the wild card that made it all seem meant to be.

CHAPTER 43

Elise

Wednesday morning, November 1, 2017

Minutes before the teams coming to clear out Kitty's house were expected, the doorbell rang. Elise opened the door to find two men, one Asian and one White, dressed in suits. "Can I help you?"

They each produced a badge. "FBI agents Miller and Kim. Is there somewhere we can talk?"

Elise closed the door a bit so her voice wouldn't carry to her sisters, eating bagels in the living room. "Actually, no. We're in the middle of a move."

"When would be a good time?"

"What do you want?" Elise asked.

"We have a few questions for you."

"Contact my publicist," Elise said. "I'll be traveling for most of the month."

"Would you be willing to answer some questions now, so we can get out of your hair?"

"Not without my lawyer."

The agents looked at each other and then at her. "You are not in trouble, Ms. St. John."

"Then who is?"

"We just have some questions. Can we please come in?"

"I told you, we're in the middle of a move."

"Who is 'we'? Is someone else inside?"

"I'm expecting movers. What are your questions?"

"Did Mrs. Tate inform you of her intentions to gift you and your sisters her estate?"

"No."

"Any idea why she would leave that kind of money to you and your sisters?"

She's our grandma. "We were very close. She lived here, next door to us, for thirty years." Elise looked to the right at her house.

"Has anyone else asked you about the inheritance or contacted you about it?"

"Just her lawyer, and the media, of course. And now you."

"Is Mrs. Tate's lawyer also your lawyer?"

"No. Why?"

"Mrs. Tate had some unsavory associates in her past, and with her passing we wanted to make sure all dealings related to Mrs. Tate's estate, and your inheritance, happened without duress."

"How does her gifting her estate to my sisters and I seem like coercion?"

Like everyone's, the agents' interest was piqued by race. Elise doubted the validity of their inheritance would be under question had they been White.

"You think she was going to give it away to charity, but we coerced her?" Elise was getting mad. "There's nothing I can buy now that I couldn't before."

"That's exactly our point. Why give the money to you?"

Elise ignored the question, as it had already been asked and answered. "Who were these 'unsavory' associates? Kitty has had the same friends for decades. Maybe they know? Have you talked to anyone else?"

"I'm sorry, all of that is also classified. Do you know of a charity called Blair House?"

"I don't." Elise was doing her best not to fidget, feeling anxiety from her sisters, who had tiptoed near the door to listen.

"Do you support any charities?"

"Here and there."

"Did Kitty talk to you about her political views?"

"No." The extent of Kitty's political and social commentary had been the Obama T-shirt she wore while filling out her vote-by-mail ballot.

"Do you run your own social media accounts?"

"Yes."

"You're, what—the fifth-most-followed account on Instagram?"

"For now."

"Do you use your profile for promotion?"

"Yes."

"Of what?"

"My work."

"Did you post this picture of you and Hillary Clinton, Bernie Sanders, and Barack Obama?"

"Yes. President Obama, yes."

"Did you also post this picture of Colin Kaepernick?"

"Yes."

"What about these videos?"

"Yes."

"Were all these posts considered work promotion?"

Elise closed the door another inch. "Gentlemen, the movers will be here soon, and I can't have TMZ hearing about us being questioned by the FBI. Please contact my publicist, Rebecca Owens, and I'll find time to meet with you with my lawyer present."

As she shut the door, the older of the two tried again. "What are you going to do with the money?"

She put her head through the crack. "Give it away." She closed the door, resting her forehead against it to steady her breathing. She didn't realize until then how nervous she had been.

"What the fuck is going on?" A thousand crinkles lined Giovanni's forehead. Noele was holding her arm as if they were ten and twelve again. "Do you know why they were here?" Giovanni scanned her face for the answer.

Elise got a sickening feeling. "I'm not entirely sure."

"You're lying." She always knew. Giovanni pushed past her and headed home.

Noele, slipping back into the role of the baby, ran the opposite way, to find their father, Elise knew. It was only then that Elise looked up and over the hedges at her mother, who had been watching from a second-floor window the entire time.

"What did they want?" Sarah demanded as Elise walked into the kitchen, already having heard bits from Giovanni. Her voice held an urgency for truth, but it was clear that her stance on Kitty's secrets had not changed.

"They asked about a charity called Blair House," Elise finally said.

Sarah hadn't heard of it either.

"They said Kitty had some 'unsavory associates,' wanted to know if we've been contacted by anyone."

"Have they talked to anyone else?" Sarah asked.

"They wouldn't say."

"I'll see if anyone else had some unexpected guests." Sarah billowed out of the kitchen.

"Start with Kitty's guest list," Elise called after her. She turned to her sisters and father, who wanted answers about their cryptic exchange.

"What's going on?" Giovanni said.

"I told you to talk to Mom," Elise opened the side door. "The movers are here."

CHAPTER 44

Elise

Thursday evening in New York, November 2, 2017

Jasper's apartment was in an unassuming four-story brick building just over the Brooklyn Bridge, in Dumbo. He had the entire tenth floor but tempered her expectations: "I'm still renovating." It was an old warehouse with high ceilings, brick walls, and cement floors covered every five feet or so with earth-toned area rugs.

Photographs decorated every inch of the walls, as it was once at Kitty's house. In the center was the original heater from when the space was used for textile manufacturing. A projector sat on a dining table that had benches instead of chairs. Jasper gestured for her to sit on his worn leather couch, covered in blankets to disguise holes. He went into the kitchen, and she opened his first book, *Daze: An Undergraduate Account of Life,* from his coffee table. She flipped through, stopping at the intimate photographs, a few of the same girls.

He handed her a glass of wine and sat next to her with a remote control.

"All your old girlfriends?"

"A few. All lasted just long enough for me to finish their series. I become consumed by my subjects," he said. "It's the only way to do them justice, but I admit I may go overboard."

"Is that a warning?"

He fumbled with the remote. "I want to apologize. I didn't mean to come off as a bully."

"A bully and a stalker."

"I'm sorry. I was intense, but I think it means something, us meeting the way we did."

"It's serendipitous."

"Just wait. May I present *Chain Links* now?"

It took twenty minutes to go through the slides that told the story of how a poor Black boy, from a small town in Florida, became the keeper of one of America's oldest, most common liaisons, so common it lurked within many a family tree. The story wove the web among Jasper's grandfather, Telescope, and the St. Johns. It told of two men's obsession with Kitty, and how his grandfather's quest to protect her secret jeopardized his marriage. The show ended with a photo of Kitty and Jasper's grandmother, on the night Kitty came to explain the photos her husband had of her. It was a powerful picture, full of juxtapositions among race, class, and societal taboos, reconciling under one roof.

"I love it." Elise was impressed by Jasper's storytelling. She momentarily forgot about Kitty's side of it and found herself feeling bad for the position it put his grandfather in.

"I have your permission?"

"The FBI came to see us yesterday."

Jasper stiffened. "You should have led with that. What did they want? Do they know about Kitty?"

"No, but I'm thinking that's pertinent information."

Jasper started to pace. "This story has legs . . . Every time I think I've gotten to the bottom of it, another surprise appears."

"If your grandfather was following Kitty, some of his photos could be evidence."

"Of what?"

Elise shrugged. "They had questions about a charity. Did he ever say anything about Kitty's social life?"

"Not specifically, but she was out all the time. She was a movie star."

"I need to see everything." Having just categorized Kitty's photos, Elise thought she might recognize the younger versions of her friends and associates.

"They're in storage."

"After the shoot tomorrow, then." Taking this as her opportunity to leave, she stood. "Thanks for the wine."

"You can't go now! I have so many questions."

She gave him a regretful look. "I'm shooting the cover of *Vogue* tomorrow, and it's already midnight."

He laughed, embarrassed. "Good excuse."

She held out her arms for a hug, and he wrapped his around her waist, pulling her close until her head had no option but to tilt upward at him.

"Tomorrow, I'll show you whatever it is you want to see."

"Thank you for waiting to do anything with your book."

"I wasn't ever just going to release it without telling you. You know that, right?"

"I know."

"Now I want to trash the whole thing."

She pointed at him. "Don't do that. But I get it."

His chestnut brown eyes settled on her. It would have taken just one kiss for her to end up in his bed. Tempted by the undertow, she lingered, relishing in how her body felt against his, how good it felt to be close. But before she liked it too much and stayed, she patted his back. "Unhand me," she said and, smiling, pulled open his door.

As planned, Elise told *Vogue* anecdotes about her family's neighborly relationship with Kitty. She applauded her strides for women and race relations and gave them the exclusive story about Hanes Austen, the reputed writer of *Down South*. The writer was satisfied, and their conversation flowed into chatter about *Drag On* and Kitty's opinion about it being her best yet.

"How special, if you were to win the Oscar!"

Hearing the interviewer say it, it rang true in a way Elise hadn't wanted to admit. Winning would keep her in the news cycle, but so would the charitable donation of Kitty's estate. She was damned if she did, damned if she didn't.

"I don't want to jinx it. Kitty's validation of my talent was enough."

"How do you plan to carry on her legacy?"

Elise appreciated the classy reference to her inheritance. "Help people."

Jasper shot her in a rented downtown penthouse, in the bright natural light of the snowy November morning, with slicked-back hair and an even, dewy, bare face to show her eyes. That was key. The magazine insisted on a white dress, which Elise spun into an angel reference instead of a bride. Looking into Jasper's lens made her want to perform for him. She wanted to impress him and found strength, under his gaze, against the strangers occupying the space. Underneath their professional demeanor were opinions about her life; she could see both wonder and contempt in their eyes. She realized then it was their judgment that kept her controlled: either quiet, to avoid mention, or anxious about the coming commentary. Apathy was a defense mechanism. She caught herself about to allow what strangers might say to change her feelings about the family legacy she was on the verge of sealing. It may have been all ego, but it was then that Elise decided that she *did* care. She cared very much about winning and obtaining her status as a serious actress.

Feeling claustrophobic under the spotlight, she tore the netted neck of her dress down over her shoulders, apologizing in mid-rip to the horrified stylist and promising that she'd cover the cost. She hated turtlenecks and said she preferred the simple, A-line spaghetti-strap dress that hung on the rack. She kicked off the pink kitten heels and asked for a wipe to remove the red lipstick. Already feeling more like herself, she began her own dance with Jasper as she moved about the apartment, ignoring the ten other people there. However things turned out, she was shooting the cover of *Vogue*—something Kitty had never done—and she was going to do them both proud.

———————————

"Great job today." Jasper opened his door before she knocked. "Want a preview?"

"I wait until they pick, so I'm not disappointed if I liked another one better." She followed him to his kitchen, where he handed her a bowl of pesto pasta.

"Smart." He pointed to the black metal table against the wall, where a few boxes sat. "That's everything." He was confused about what his grandfather's photos could possibly reveal.

"I don't think Kitty was the only one passing in her circle," Elise explained.

"Others at Telescope?"

"All over, maybe. I need your help fact-checking." She sat on a countertop stool. Jasper opened his refrigerator and produced Parmesan cheese.

"Do we *need* to go digging?"

"You did!"

"That was before . . . honestly, I don't want my name anywhere near any of this anymore. The FBI doesn't just show up to fish for information." He sprinkled cheese into two bowls in front of her.

"That's why I need to know everything," Elise said. "I need to know what to protect."

"This is what I meant by your privilege." He rounded the corner and handed her a bowl. "The FBI comes, and I lose interest; the FBI comes, and *you* want to dive in."

"You don't think it means something, her leaving all this in my lap?"

"I've said so, but at this point, I think you should let it go." Jasper twirled linguine on his fork and held it over to her. "Eat, woman."

Elise did as she was told. He gave her a second bite from his bowl before feeding himself.

As she suspected, there was a pattern in the photos: the same group of women, this one house. Even Rebecca's grandmother made an appearance in a few shots at the Gramling Hotel. Mrs. Pew was easily recognizable. As the founder of the publicity firm Rebecca and her mother now ran, a picture of her in her early thirties had hung in the office entryway for decades.

"How's your mom taking things?"

"She's fine."

"Hopefully this can improve things between you two."

Elise looked at him squarely. "Things are fine with us."

"I'm not trying to pry. I want to get to know you, personally."

"Me being slightly paranoid about your intentions is common sense—"

"Even now? I told you, forget that book."

"Did you know about Kitty in March when we met?"

Jasper nodded. "So meeting you felt like a sign."

"Or slightly opportunistic?"

"Not after Kitty's invitation came for my grandfather. I owed it to you to tell you what I knew. And besides, it's my family history too."

Elise's breath quickened as he clasped his hands on either side of her waist. "You know it's not like that." He sat her in the windowsill, fitting his hips between her legs. His lips were smooth and full. His tongue reached for hers, and their mouths moved in perfect syncopation. Their bodies clung together, mirroring the other's movements and placements on their faces, necks, and backs. Time was suspended, and life couldn't have gotten better than it was right then until he tried to take off her shirt. Beyond the cold windowpane on her back, there was the problem that his uncovered windows faced the other side of his building.

Sensing her discomfort, he pulled away to look at her. "I'm sorry. Too fast?"

"Just not right here," she said.

Without another word, he lifted her from the sill and carried her through his apartment and into the darkness of his bedroom.

Falling onto the bed, she wrapped her legs tighter around his waist, allowing their natural rhythm to resume until they were naked. The motion of their bodies rooted her to the moment, and she couldn't think, only do. The street traffic noise, only six stories below Jasper's apartment, faded, as did any doubt, worry, or care about the future.

She awoke first. They were naked, limbs tangled. The sky was cloudless. She took it as a sign of good fortune and went back to sleep. Three hours later, their legs were still intertwined, and hers ached. She slithered from underneath him to find her phone screen full with missed messages. Her mother must have told her sisters about Kitty. She climbed back into bed and kissed Jasper's back. His skin felt cool. She lay there for half the morning, enjoying the peace away from everything having to do with Kitty Karr.

When she got hungry, Jasper suggested they go to the restaurant on her rooftop where they first met.

She kissed him in appreciation of his sentimentality. "I need to be on a plane shortly."

"Is everything okay? I thought you—we—had the weekend."

"Me, too, but apparently my sisters and I weren't the only people the FBI visited. It's best I—"

Jasper held up a hand. "Say no more." He reached for his phone. "Then I'll order breakfast while you get dressed."

She slipped on her sweatshirt. "Really, I need the air."

Elise wanted to be alone so the paparazzi, who she knew had followed her to Jasper's the night before, could get another picture. They tried to be stealthy, but Elise saw them, as always. If it were the two of them, the cameras would blow their cover, greedy for comment. It would cause a commotion on the street, and the story, thanks to some random iPhone user, would be online before they could get back indoors. This way, the paparazzi could suspect all they wanted, but they would wait to build a case for more money. It gave her a day or two, and timing was everything.

She returned to Jasper's building less than twenty minutes later with two coffees and two pastry bags. Pretending to not know one was being watched felt like work: maintaining her angles, ignoring the cameras, and avoiding eye contact with "the extras"—New Yorkers and some likely tourists—who might later relay their sighting of her on the street.

CHAPTER 45

Elise

Saturday evening in Los Angeles, November 4, 2017
The FBI had visited Lucy, Maude, and Billie before Kitty's memorial. They decided not to say anything about *anything* until Sarah's courtesy call, but then came in person to deliver a cascade of information that Elise flew home to hear before her press tour in London.

"We siphoned donations from rich people to send to the movement," Lucy said.

"What movement?" Noele asked.

"The Civil Rights Movement, honey," Maude whispered, gesturing for her to listen.

"Some of us were considered victims," Lucy continued, "but we would have been suspects and perhaps convicts had the FBI known we were Black."

"Some of our colleagues were charged with crimes against the United States," Maude said.

The women believed time had made them safe and were secure in the thought that no one had ever spoken of Blair House, uttered the names of the women they met, or even looked in its direction if they happened to pass by it since. Prosecution had been a real threat, and what had happened to some was never forgotten. Still, they continued to operate—quieter, safer—until most of the group's members were unknown legacy leftovers.

"So, if people were to find out Kitty was Black—" Sarah asked. It was a clear and annoying attempt to emphasize her stance, having heard tidbits already on Wednesday when she made calls.

"It could turn a lot of us into suspects."

"It could threaten all our identities."

"But it could also keep us safe." Lucy pulled an oversized leather ringed notebook from her purse. She opened it on the table, and everyone gathered around to see. "This is the ledger. Everyone and everything connected to Blair House is recorded here. Real names, fake names, addresses, donation amounts."

It was the missing link between Kitty's stories and the details about the work they'd been conducting.

"No one can prove that all these people listed in here weren't involved."

"Because year after year, they donated."

Elise thumbed through the ledger, which showed a year-by-year balance of all the donations Blair House received.

"They got massive tax write-offs for charity donations and profited," Noele said.

Lucy nodded. "And our accounting records could make the argument that the 'fraud' was a ring."

The names and donation amounts were blueprints of family trees—the full lineage, not the skeleton in the family Bible or listed on a census form. This ledger indicated rights to wealth and property, all over the country, that had been long denied: Kitty's lineage to a tobacco fortune; Emma's to one made in clothing. Lucy and Laurie were descendants of the biggest landowner in Louisiana. Billie's White relatives, on both sides, had been poor, but they got money from the government and began manufacturing their own cooking oil.

Noele's eyes got big. "Rich people donate to these fake charities to write off millions in donations on their taxes."

"They didn't know we were funneling money to the movement, but they were happy to look the other way in terms of legitimacy. Most of them would do anything to keep their families in the dark."

"No one is going to want the FBI to start digging into their taxes or family secrets," Giovanni said.

"They could donate," Elise proposed.

"The first ask would be to find out if there's an active investigation," Lucy corrected her.

Noele's eyes stretched. "That would be extortion . . . on our part."

"How?" Giovanni said.

Noele started talking with her hands. "Forcing people to give money to us or inquire with the Justice Department in exchange for our silence about their family secrets is *definitely* extortion."

"We'd be accusing them of fraud," Elise said.

"Motive to commit extortion."

Lucy ignored their back-and-forth. "Some of these last names would make our involvement, and any interest in our true identities, a mere footnote."

"At this point, no one can out us but ourselves," Billie summarized patting her forehead.

"I think the families would very much care, finding out their wife, mother, or grandmother wasn't who they thought she was."

"That's why I said that some families will go to great lengths to keep their secrets," Lucy said. "There are many of us who passed for White, all across the country. And we know many names."

"Like Cora?"

"Yes, but she made sure it would be very hard to find her unless you have this ledger."

"You were supposed to burn it," Maude said.

"Laurie and I thought long and hard about it. But ultimately, it was her decision. It's all her handwriting, except for a few entries." Lucy pointed. "Like Cora's last entry."

Cora Rivers disappeared from LA at the end of 1965, with a new name and a marriage on the horizon. She told her political king her real name was Janie Crawford and that Cora Rivers had been her stage name. All of these details, including his name, were listed.

"Janie Crawford is the heroine in Zora Neale Hurston's book, *Their Eyes Were Watching God*," Lucy said.

"I know; it's my favorite," Noele said. "Seems a little risky, no?"

"Or cheeky," Giovanni smirked.

"That's Cora. We didn't know until she updated her record in the ledger."

"I don't think it's risky—how many Black people, let alone White people, even know of the book?"

"Funny," Maude said with a smile, "that's what she said."

"And apparently she was right," Lucy said. Her fiancé easily accepted the lie, eager for her acting days to be behind them. "She changed her name again when they married."

Cora stayed away from the camera during her husband's presidential run; the possibility of her being recognized as a former actress, his advisors said, would threaten his reputation as a serious politician. He lost, but they remained in Washington, D.C., where he enjoyed a long career behind a desk in the White House, privy to the influence and respect their name afforded. Cora worked just across the street. They had two sons. Revealing her identity now, as with Kitty's, would be publicly disruptive. She was an icon in her own right, and still White. She looked different now—some plastic surgery and ninety-two years of age disguised her—but the truth was in ink, her handwriting in the ledger. She had been the center of the case, something that could be proven not just by the records but by Jasper's grandfather's photos.

Elise laid out the ones she had brought. They all saw themselves; many of the images matched moments Lucy and the others remembered.

"Did he know they were all passing?" Noele asked Elise.

"There's no record of that. Just Kitty."

"I guess what we're saying is, it's whatever you all want to do. Tell or don't tell. It's your decision to make," Maude said.

Elise closed the ledger and pushed it across the table to Lucy. "Let's pretend we never saw this."

"Thank you," Sarah said.

After the Golden Girls left, the sisters resettled in the South Wing's den with Kitty's box.

"We really need to donate everything. If something illegal did happen, if we're not in possession of the documents, I would think there's no crime?" Noele said. "I have to research that."

"I think we should give the money toward reparations."

"For slavery?" Giovanni's doubtful tone matched Noele's expression.

"And everything that's happened since."

"For Black people? You know that'll never happen."

"We don't need permission." Elise looked at her sisters. "We have the funds to start a trend. We could get others to contribute."

Noele started to speak, but Elise stopped her.

"Noele, relax. We're not going to threaten anyone. We can privately share their history with them and ask. If they say no, they say no."

"We have to show how interconnected the American social fabric really is," Giovanni said. "Show them how it affects them to get them to care. That's always been the missing piece. We're the other side of the family."

"What time period are the reparations for? Is it enough? How Black do people have to be?"

"The rule is one drop."

"Well, then there's a whole lot of Black White people."

"What about the homeless? How do we make it equal?"

The who, what, when questions continued. Elise held up her hands. "I don't have all the answers."

"You better . . ." Giovanni said.

"She's right. This is crazy—"

"Not just crazy, it's stupid." Sarah walked into the den. "The FBI will be back; it will fuel their suspicions."

"But we didn't do anything."

"At the height of the FBI's power," Sarah began, "J. Edgar Hoover said that the biggest threat to national security was Black unity. They killed a sympathetic president, Martin, and Malcolm; dismantled the Black Panthers, labeled them as enemies of the United States; and then flooded our communities with drugs and guns and sent in more police for more arrests to fill up prisons. And that's just in my lifetime. So, if money is power, giving people this money makes them a threat." Sarah spoke like she knew from experience.

"We don't have to say what it's for, or even list our names," Noele said.

"True," Giovanni said.

"But Kitty wanted to die a legend. And she deserves that. She pulled off one of the greatest tricks in history, and saying it, however dangerous, not only honors her, it honors the struggle and makes it damned hard to ignore."

"It's still the truth if people don't know," Sarah said. "Wanting people to know is your ego."

"The story isn't about Kitty being Black, it's about what being White got her." Elise painted a scene. "And about all she lost."

"She's right, Sarah." James appeared in the doorway.

"What?" She looked at her husband in complete disbelief. "We didn't raise her to be a crusader—"

"Hear me out." James sat on the couch. "I'm the one who told Kitty to do it this way."

"What?"

He reached for Sarah's hand. "You weren't talking to her, so she talked to me." Aside from the nurses, James had been Kitty's only other regular visitor. She had stopped letting her doctor beau visit when she became bedridden.

He looked at Elise. "I knew you'd understand what you were called to do." They shared a beat before he continued. "But I didn't account for all this other business, and I agree with your mother." At this, Sarah softened and sat next to James.

"Donate the money—but quietly, anonymously."

"Does it matter then?"

"Will the impact be the same? Probably."

Elise didn't want to hear this. What else was she going to use her platform for? She wanted to quit anyway, after the Oscars. She felt obligated to speak, pushed to because she hadn't before.

Elise had lost her voice just before she turned six. She and her father were on their way to the airport to visit his family in North Carolina. Raised in the segregated South, he hadn't gone to school with White people until Juilliard. Terrified of his children growing inflated with the air he had breathed into their celebrity bubble, they went back to North Carolina every year. That year her mother was pregnant with Noele and filming a movie, and Giovanni, the perpetual whiner, wasn't invited.

Elise was riding high in one of the rear jump seats of her dad's Porsche, where there was just enough room for her and her *Beauty and the Beast* backpack, looking at the sky through the sunroof, enjoying the force of the wind as her curly ponytail whipped across her face. She was excited for the trip; she loved how hot it stayed at night, catching lightning bugs, and playing with her cousins in the sprinklers. She loved the food and the choir at her grandmother's church. Their voices made her feel something in her body, like the voice of Smokey Robinson, who was playing on the radio. Her father sang to her as he exited the 405 freeway. *I would do anything, I would go anywhere.*

Century Boulevard, the street that provided the most direct access to the airport, was blocked with police cars. Her father made a quick turn down a side street to avoid the holdup. He sped some; they were cutting it close for their first-class flight. Seconds later, two police cars were after them. Her father pulled over, and as he was reaching for his registration, four cops surrounded the car with their guns drawn. *Get your Black ass out of the car.* Already a successful producer but unidentifiable among the masses, James

St. John's name carried no weight with them; and he, as they reminded him, *was about to be a dead nigger, regardless.*

Her father didn't turn around to look at her but spoke in a voice she'd never heard him use before. *Stay in the car. No matter what happens to me.*

It was April 29, 1992, and the officers on trial for the videotaped beating of Rodney King had just been acquitted. Los Angeles, impacted by decades of racial tension and police brutality, swelled with anger. Pockets of the city had already started to explode, just as James and Elise were on their way to the airport.

James got out of the car slowly but was tackled. They pinned each of his limbs to the pavement, accusing him of having stolen the car. Elise curled into a ball and covered her eyes, terrified by the police officers barking bad words at her father. Seconds later, two of them came back to the car. Elise held her breath as the pair began rummaging through the car.

"Fuck."

Elise opened her eyes to see a White officer with squinty eyes staring over the seat at her. He groaned and hit the seat with a fist.

"Relax, man." This officer was White, too, but he smiled. "What's your name?"

Elise couldn't find her voice. The other grabbed her wrist, pulling her out of the back seat. Elise started yelling, and her father, who was facedown in the street with three officers kneeling on his back, told her to calm down. Elise started kicking, trying to get to him. The officer only held her tighter and tossed her like a ball into the back seat of a police car. The next thing she knew, she was sitting alone in a metal chair in a cold room, shivering without the jacket packed in her backpack. There was only one window, and the only thing she could see through the black wires running through it was a sea of uniformed White strangers. She knocked on the glass, but no one even looked at her. Hours passed. She didn't know where her daddy was. She knew her phone number, but no one would let her call her mommy. They just kept saying, *Someone's coming.* Her parents always said that if she got lost, she should look for someone in a uniform; clearly, these weren't the uniforms they meant. It was dark before someone came. *Dirty,* Elise remembered him saying as he shook his head at her, smelling the stench of her urine-stained jeans. After nine hours, Elise and James left the police station with their lawyer. When they finally reached home, Elise traced the cuff marks on his wrists with her fingertips. Elise's bright young mind exploded as she processed the concept of hypocrisy. She became slow to stand for the Pledge of Allegiance at school. The teacher sent her to time-out every day, and then Elise refused to come out of time-out, preferring to continue reading.

The St. Johns sued the LAPD. Her parents took her to her favorite Mexican restaurant to talk about her upcoming interview with the lawyer. They knew what had happened but not what the officer said or how he made her feel. Elise was out of diapers shortly after she started walking, at seventeen months, and was beyond embarrassed that she hadn't been able to hold it. She felt she had let the side down by giving in and relieving herself. Her parents said testifying was her choice, and so she refused to talk to anyone about that day. James's story couldn't be corroborated, and the case never went to trial.

Elise felt tears spring to her eyes. "I should have testified." James put his hand on her back.

"You never should have been in that position."

"But she was, and neither one of us could protect her," Sarah said, looking at Giovanni and Noele who had never heard this before.

Reality grounded the room. The business of righting wrongs sometimes ended in murder. It would have seemed overblown, conspiracy-driven even, had Charlottesville not been in recent memory.

Sarah had the last word. "Either give the money away or don't, but everything else—*everything*—is off-limits."

CHAPTER 46

Elise

Monday, November 6, 2017

"Look." Rebecca balanced Kitty's small brass mirror in her palm. She'd been looking for an icebreaker since they boarded the plane to London.

Elise recognized it immediately. "Oh, you got it!"

"Paid a lot for it."

"I took it for polishing, and look . . ." Rebecca turned it on its back to reveal the tiny initials MML engraved on its bottom. "After no one said anything at the memorial, I figured you didn't know, and I didn't have permission to tell you."

Elise hadn't been the only one who Kitty wrote a letter to. Mrs. Pew, Rebecca's grandmother, had received one tucked inside her memorial invitation. She'd been so shocked to hear from Kitty, she told Rebecca and Alison everything immediately.

"Talking about Kitty means we'll have to talk about my family too," Rebecca said. "Some of them are no better than the rapists and murderers in the news. If people go digging into Kitty's history, they'll find Teddy Lakes."

Elise understood her frustration.

"We don't even know that side of the family," Rebecca said. "It's not fair. My mom knew they were bad people and kept us away."

"Then say that. Publicly shame it."

"And then what?"

Elise couldn't answer—truthfully, she kept arriving at the same dead end.

"You have to let all this go," Rebecca pleaded.

Elise felt her eyes roll. "Sarah talked to you?"

"She did."

"I—we—decided to give the money to a few charities," Elise said.

"Good, because talk about reparations will cause issues. *Tons* of questions." Rebecca waited for her agreement. "Right?"

"Yep," Elise opened the plane window shade.

"And I won't be around to help."

"I know." In four days, she was off to Milan to meet Gabe.

"Moving to work, I think you should skip even mentioning Kitty on this press tour." Rebecca waited for Elise's agreement.

"What about the studio?"

"I pushed back. We did give *Vogue* an exclusive, so everything about Kitty is off-limits now."

"Probably best not to give the FBI any more information," Elise said resignedly.

"Correct." Rebecca's tone heightened like it did when she had an idea. "You could name a few charities you all will be donating to."

"We don't know."

"I'm reminding you of all the positives because we do have another issue: there are photos of you staying overnight at Jasper's."

"That took longer than expected."

Rebecca rolled her eyes. "Seriously? You couldn't have given me a heads-up?"

"I want to call off our wedding, and I knew how that would go, so . . ."

"Not in your favor. There's an interview with a waitress—she's been fired, of course, but she puts you there with Jasper in March."

Elise knew who it was. Poor thing had run into the corner of a table when Elise walked in that night.

"This is going to be terrible for you."

"Not really. The night I met Jasper was the night I found out Aaron was cheating on me with Maya."

Rebecca gasped. "Maya Langston?"

"Yeah, he's in love with her." Elise scrolled to the evidence on her phone and passed it across the aisle to Rebecca.

"So, *he* cheated on *you*."

"Yeah, but we can spin it as a mutual breakup and praise ourselves for our acting skills during a tumultuous time in our relationship. That way the film, and our *talent*, maintain center stage."

"Shit, you've gotten pretty good at spin."

Elise smiled at her. "I've learned from the very best."

"Only when it comes to you," Rebecca said with a laugh.

"Well, we've been the best team." Elise reached across the aisle for her hand.

"You started talking about quitting, and it occurred to me that I'm just floating. My life is contingent on yours."

"Rebecca, you don't have to *do* anything."

"I can hear the contempt in your voice."

"You can't help who you were born to. None of us can." Elise got an idea. "If you want to do something, you could donate money in Kitty's name."

"I will, but anonymously. Technically she's my great-aunt. How crazy is that?"

"Insane. Maybe you could convince the Lakes corporation to donate."

Rebecca scoffed. "They certainly have exposure." Elise could tell she didn't take the suggestion seriously.

"Others would follow suit if they did. Or if they had another reason to."

"A reason like what?"

"Kitty's story is just one of many."

Rebecca groaned. "I thought we were on the other side of this."

She picked up her phone to text Aaron's publicist. "I'll sync with Marcus about the talking points."

Elise gestured for her phone back. "No, I'll text Aaron myself. He doesn't know I know about Maya."

"No wonder you've been so cranky. All this stuff you've been holding in."

Elise shrugged. She was used to a heavy load. Rebecca didn't get it—never would—and it was okay. Hitting SEND on her text to Aaron cut some weight.

Later, after Aaron and Elise gave an exclusive of their breakup to British *Vogue*, Aaron moved on publicly with Maya the day he landed back in Los Angeles.

CHAPTER 47

Elise

Out of curiosity, the St. John sisters spent subsequent months trading researched information. Deciding the details of their donation took a back seat as they learned facts about their background from the Internet. Giovanni was back on set, and Noele was in New York, but they talked more than they had in years. It was fun, until it became clear how many innocent people, like their mother, could be hurt.

Only Jasper cared about how many could be helped. Her sisters had other passions and thought of it as a hobby. Her mother wouldn't talk about it, and Kitty's friends cut off all communication. Only Jasper could dream about it turning into something good. They brainstormed what an ideal reparations plan would look like and expanded the visual timeline his book had started.

With Jasper, over the course of weeks, Elise made a decision.

She persuaded Lucy, after showing up unannounced on her Beverly Hills doorstep, to give her the ledger. She would connect all the dots, look through census records, and scour the Web. Jasper's father was a professor of African American history at UNC Asheville and enlisted a few of his trusted graduate students to help under a nondisclosure agreement.

Then she'd mail letters, which would no doubt hit the desks of the upper echelon in America (and Europe too), requesting donations to the reparations fund. Researched information from their family trees would be included as incentive. It was merely a marketing push—a solid "why." By going ahead and starting a fund herself, Elise hoped others would contribute, which would help increase the pressure for reparations at the federal level.

In that first phase, reparations recipients would have to get a blood test to prove both African and European ancestry. Applicants would receive money to pay off student loans, start businesses, and buy houses. There would be money set aside for drug and alcohol abuse treatment, for lawyers.

Phase two would consider formerly incarcerated individuals and the homeless. Things would happen in short phases, but eventually, with government help, every affected American would receive financial assistance and concentrated resources.

Helping everyone would increase the country's wealth and finally create the utopia imagined long ago by rich, White men with the time to ponder the meaning of human existence from their porches or shady, grassy spots—time granted by their West African slaves and their offspring, who did all the work.

Like them, Elise had time to dream.

CHAPTER 48

Elise

March 2018

Elise froze when they called her name as the winner of the Oscar for Best Actress. Her father's assistance to stand just looked like a tender moment on camera. To Elise, it felt like he was pulling her into reality for the first time that day.

Elise had been on a red carpet many times before, but that evening had a lot riding on it. The part of her that didn't care about winning had been replaced with an intense longing. She planned for a memorable evening, but the day began chaotic, with her parents' house inhabited by twenty extra people. The St. Johns were all going to the ceremony and dressing at Sarah and James's. The comradery was meant to give Elise support, but she couldn't hear herself think. She put on her headphones to disassociate from the noise while she got a facial and her hair straightened.

Things almost went downhill when her gown was too loose in the bodice—seemingly a minor issue, but good luck finding an available seamstress to work on an eight-thousand-dollar gown hours before the Oscars.

Refusing to panic, though she was starting to sweat in her scalp and ruin her press, she stepped out of the dress and fetched the joint from the sill of the rose window. To the surprise of the room, after lighting it she offered it to no one, not even her sisters. She turned to the window, not-so-patiently waiting for a fix.

She was a little mad at herself. The gown had fit two weeks before, but she had allowed her mother's reminders that the night's photos would live in infamy to kick up her anxiety. Elise had shifted into high-gear prep: two workouts a day, a smoothie for breakfast, a salad for lunch, and soup for dinner. No bread, no snacks. Only still, room temperature water.

"Don't we have another option?" Elise would be disappointed not to wear it. The royal blue, black, and silver gown was a combination of her and Kitty's favorite colors. But it was also beaded and full-length, substantial on her frame, like a weighted blanket. Elise imagined it sliding off if it was not properly sized.

Her stylist held up a roll of double-stick tape. "I think it'll work unless you start to sweat."

Elise handed her joint to Giovanni's makeup artist and went back to the mirror. "I'm changing anyway for the after-party."

The tape was an ingenious idea and made the dress cling to her body as intended.

She had been the queen of the red carpet, even though the questions centered around Kitty, and Elise's anticipation of the night's tribute. Elise gave a version to about fifteen different outlets, smiling at all attempts to get her to mention Jasper. He, with a push from his publisher, had curated the night's video presentation. Elise and Jasper weren't public, but reporters were desperate to validate the rumors—all of the rumors—surrounding the St. Johns.

Her father escorted her up the stairs to the stage. Stepping in front of the mic, she was unsure of what she was going to say. A production assistant waved for her to go.

Her mother, sensing what she was about to do, gripped the armrests of her chair. When the PA cued her again, Elise quickly started speaking.

"None of us can help the circumstances of our birth. It's by mere chance I have the life I have, and it's all thanks to my grandmother, the late Mrs. Kitty Karr Tate."

As anticipated murmurs began in the crowd, the cameras circled the St. John family, seated in the first row. Sarah looked as though she wanted to die.

"Kitty grew up dreaming of being on-screen but felt, being Black, that those dreams were unrealistic. So, she left the segregated South and passed for White upon arriving to Hollywood in 1955. She knew it still wouldn't be easy, but she successfully removed the barrier of her race to give herself a fair chance." Elise spoke louder over the increasing noise in the room.

"And that's why my sisters and I will be donating her entire estate to a reparations fund. We must heal the original American sin that's been continually recycled in different forms, even today." Elise paused for a second to gauge the reaction, but there was only dead silence now. Unsure if this was indicative of real interest or shock—or both—she rushed to continue as the production assistant signaled for her to wrap it up. She figured she'd been granted some grace, considering the topic and the Academy's recent diversity issues.

"Slavery is only the beginning of our grievances. Reconstruction was thwarted; then came sharecropping, then Jim Crow, the civil rights movement—and even still, Black Americans can't live in certain areas, go to certain schools, get certain jobs, earn the same pay. And all the while, wealth has been building, growing for the people who have always had it. But we don't want revenge," Elise said. "We want what's owed."

Elise heard cheers, and some boos, as her stage went dark and the host rushed out onto the second stage with a half-done tie. Improvising, he loosened it more and swung it around his neck for a laugh. Uncomfortable silence followed and Elise hesitated at the microphone. She started to scold him but didn't want the gravity of her speech eclipsed by her reaction to the comedian's crude gesture. She exited behind the curtain as production assistants ran around the auditorium with the anxious encouragement of the audience.

Backstage, cameras and production crew trailed Elise to the loading dock, where Andy allowed only one photo with the trophy. Into the live-feed camera, she directed viewers to the website she had quietly created for information.

She walked out of the back door into another flare of camera flashes and yells. Knowing there was no escape, she stepped toward the chaos, into the light, ready to answer all of their questions. She had heard about all the risks, everyone's concerns. More rumors would circulate. There were probably tax implications she didn't even know of. The whole thing could come crashing down before one dime was ever given out. But Elise had decided weeks ago to let the chips fall where they may—to wing it. She figured the details would work themselves out. That was the American way.

Acknowledgments

I'm overwhelmed with gratitude for the support and love I've received around this book. It's been in me for as long as I can remember. To anyone who has ever uttered a word about it, thank you.

To my grandmothers, Mamie and Magdalene, and my great-grandmother Nellie, knowing you was an honor. I strive only to exceed your wildest dreams.

To my parents, your skills are top-notch. Thanks for instilling education and showing me what hard work, dedication, and sacrifice look like. I hope to return what you've poured into me, tenfold. Thank you for the freedom to be me.

To Christopher, the true witness of the crime. We've journeyed each stage of our individual creative passions together. Guess we're both rebels. Thank you for supporting "writer mode"—the good, glorious, bad, and the ugly—and for always being able to see beyond the fray to the big picture.

To Brian, always my voice of reason and the best big brother. To my nephew, Jason, and nieces, Emily and Millicent: always dream big.

To all twelve of my aunties, you've always been my inspiration. Thank you for the love, the lessons, your loyalty, and for giving up on me leaving the room.

To my larger extended family on all sides, thank you, I love you.

To Tracey Evans, Corinne Edelin, Belinda Daughrity, Raechal Shewfelt, Kamillah Clayton, Zach Ehren, Dee Horne, and my parents for ever reading a draft.

To Lauren Shands, Danielle Combes, Takkara Brunson, Emily and Maurice Rodgers, Kalia Booker, Love Muwwakkil, Jasmin Ratansi, and Natalia Sagar for the encouragement, forcing me to have fun, and never asking me why.

To my childhood friends and the Sessions for the storytelling.

To my Love of Learning family and my Spelman sisters for two of the best experiences of my life.

To Alka Sagar, Jill Feeney, Arin Scapa, Christina Soto, and the rest of my colleagues downtown, such a pleasure.

To Corey Mandell and Talton Wingate for helping me make sense of the pictures in my head.

To Catie Boerschlein, Kendall Hackett, Jessica Castro, and Matthew Schmidt, I've been lucky to share this journey with you.

To my agent, Latoya C. Smith, you've literally made my dream come true. Thank you for everything, every step of the way, and for loving this book.

To Retha Powers, my dream editor. Thank you for investing in these characters, this story, and my voice. I love writing even more thanks to you. Onwards! To Natalia Ruiz, Molly Lindley Pisani, and Molly Bloom for your insightful reads and comments. It was a delight to view it through your eyes.

To Amy Einhorn, Sarah Crichton, and everyone at Henry Holt, thank you for your vision, hard work, and love for this book.

About the Author

Crystal Smith Paul has led an eclectic career as a writer, editor, and paralegal for the United States Department of Justice. She attended Spelman College, UCLA's School of Theater, Film and Television, and received her master's in journalism from NYU. Her nonfiction writing has appeared in *Salon*, *Jezebel*, and *HuffPost*. She currently works in digital marketing for wellness and beauty brands, while spending her nights and weekends writing creatively and staying on top of pop culture.